Tell Me
Tease Me

One Night with Sole Regret Anthology
Volume 3

Olivia Cunning

CONTENTS

Tell Me   One Night with Sole Regret #6   1

Tease Me   One Night with Sole Regret #7   217

Other books by Olivia Cunning

Sinners on Tour Series

Backstage Pass
Rock Hard
Hot Ticket
Wicked Beat
Double Time
Sinners at the Altar
Coming Soon:
Sinners in Paradise

One Night with Sole Regret Series

Try Me, Tempt Me, Take Me
Share Me, Touch Me, Tie Me
Tell Me, Tease Me
Coming Soon:
Treat Me, Thrill Me

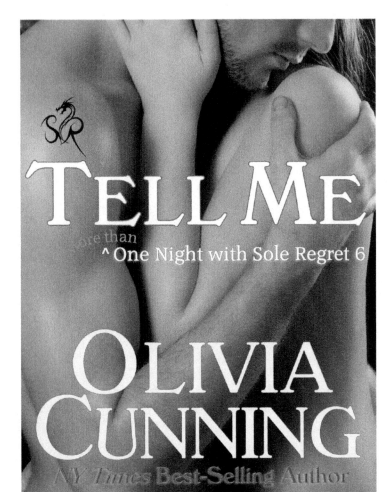

TELL ME

more than
^ One Night with Sole Regret 6

OLIVIA CUNNING

NY Times Best-Selling Author

Tell Me

One Night with Sole Regret #6

CHAPTER ONE

THIS IS BULLSHIT, Gabe thought.

Lounging in his favorite recliner, he crossed his legs at the ankle and took another draw off his Corona as he tried not to glare at the latest intruder on Sole Regret's tour bus. They had yet another woman touring with the band. As if it wasn't bad enough that the pregnant chick had decided to set up camp on the bus sofa, now Kellen was courting some red-headed ice queen who'd taken up permanent residence at his hip, and Shade's ex-sister-in-law turned fuck-buddy kept showing up at their gigs unannounced. He was sure that if Adam's woman didn't have to work and Owen's new flame wasn't pretending she was mad at him, they'd be on the bus too. And here Gabe was telling Melanie that she couldn't join them on the road. That the band had a rule about women on tour, and rightly so.

Well, screw that. If the rest of the guys were allowed a little female company to occupy them during the long, boring hours between concerts, then he sure as hell wasn't going to upset Melanie again by making her feel unwelcome. She was more than welcome as far as he was concerned. Assuming she even wanted to ride on the tour bus. Spending countless hours on the road with a bunch of guys wasn't exactly the perpetual party everyone thought it was.

Gabe set his beer aside and pulled his phone out of his

pocket. He dialed Melanie's number, his jaw set in a hard line. He wasn't going to consult the band on this. He didn't care if they thought he was pussy-whipped, or worse, in *love* with the sweet little accountant he'd met in Tulsa. He shouldn't have to take shit for inviting Melanie to the show that night. The guys hadn't bothered asking if their women could join the tour, so why should he be the only one following the rules?

"Hey, you," Melanie answered. Her soft voice made the back of his neck tingle with pleasure. "I was just thinking about you. I can't wait to see you tomorrow night. Did you make it to New Orleans?"

"We're on the road somewhere in southern Louisiana. We should be there in an hour or two. Are you at work?"

"Yeah, but I can take a little break," she said. "This spreadsheet can wait."

He was counting on that. "Can it wait until Monday?"

"Huh? Why?"

"I miss you." He glanced up to make sure the guys hadn't heard that because even though he was willing to go to bat for Melanie, he'd be much more comfortable if he kept his love life and his band mates as far apart as possible.

If any of the guys had heard what he'd just said to Melanie, no one said anything. Not even Owen, who lived for messing with people. It was weird that the guys had stopped going ballistic any time one of them showed the slightest weakness for a woman. Hell, Kellen was holding Dawn's hand in front of everyone and no one had said a thing about it. And Dawn was gazing into Kellen's eyes as if entranced and speaking to him in a soft, sensual tone. Or she was when she wasn't too busy laughing at Owen's stream of jokes. Now wasn't that just a homey trio?

Granted, Gabe was in a bad mood. Sexy conversations, video chats, and text messages from Melanie had him so horny he couldn't think straight. He hadn't seen her in five days and five long, lonely, cock-in-a-permanent-semi-rigid-state nights. The woman had him so worked up, he was surprised he hadn't done something truly embarrassing. Like fly to Wichita on one of Sole Regret's rare nights off just to see her.

"I miss you too," she said. "I stopped at a lingerie shop on the way home from work last night. I was going to keep it a secret and surprise you with my new garters and thong—"

"Don't!" he interrupted. "I can't take another set of blue balls, Mel."

"I could help you with those," she said in that voice he associated with sex, though they hadn't even had actual sex since she'd started using that sensual tone. Yeah, she had him all sorts of out of his head and into a mentality that focused solely on satiating his libido. With her. He hadn't even considered sating his lust with another woman, even though he was hornier than a herd of longhorn cattle.

"I'll head for the ladies room and put you on video chat," she said in a sultry voice. "I'll show you what you do to me and then you can show me what I do to you."

Hell yeah, he could.

"Just talking to you makes me wet," she continued.

Gabe sucked a tormented breath through his teeth. He could tell, by the low tone of her voice, that she was turned on. He was already familiar with that tone too. In fact, he heard it when he dreamed of her and then woke up so uncomfortably hard that he'd started habitually masturbating in the middle of the night. His cock was apparently trying to reclaim its misspent youth. He didn't know how Melanie did it—put him in a constant state of arousal—but he couldn't take it anymore. He needed her. Yesterday. Not to mention *now*. And tomorrow.

"Woman, you're going to be the death of me."

He already had a change of state going on in his pants. Just how hard could a cock get without any visual or physical stimulation? Pretty damned hard, apparently. She just had to use that voice on him and he was ready to roll. She couldn't possibly be as great as he remembered, could she? In his mind, he'd exalted her to goddess status. If he elevated her any higher, she'd have to orbit the moon just to return to Earth.

"I plan to make you a very happy man Saturday night," she said.

He had no doubt she would, but he wanted to be a very happy man now. And until she was pressed against him, staring up at him with those beguiling hazel eyes while he buried himself in the slick heat between her legs, he was marginally happy at best. "How about making me a very happy man in five hours?"

"More like five minutes. I'm in the ladies room now. Are you ready for me?"

He knew what that meant. No way was he going to watch her on video chat in front of the entire bus. He hopped out of his recliner, hurried to the bathroom, and jiggled the handle. Locked.

"Let me in," he insisted.

"Just a minute," a soft feminine voice said from inside. Lindsey was in the bathroom again? He knew she was six months pregnant, but did she really need to piss every twenty minutes?

"I've started wearing skirts to work every day," Melanie whispered from the phone he had pressed to his ear. "Do you know why?"

Yeah, he knew why, but he wanted to hear her say it. "Tell me."

"So it's easier to touch myself when I think of you. And I can't seem to stop thinking about you, Mr. Banner. Do you want me to take my panties off now?"

"Wait until I can watch you do it. I want to watch all of it."

"Where are you?"

"Waiting for the bathroom." He knocked on the door again, as if Lindsey would have forgotten he was out there in the twenty seconds between interruptions.

"Almost finished!" Lindsey called.

"Hurry."

"You should feel how hot and swollen my pussy is for you, Gabe," Melanie said in his ear. "Just hearing your voice does that to me."

He knew the feeling. God, she was driving him insane.

"Don't start without me," he said, rattling the bathroom door handle as if he was about to piss down his leg.

"Too late," Melanie said. "I've already started. I have to hurry or I'll be missed at my desk and someone might come looking for me. You wouldn't want me to get caught with my hand up my skirt, would you?"

Damn it. If Lindsey didn't hurry up, he was going to miss it. He knew Adam was napping in the bedroom at the back of the bus. He wondered how dead he'd be if he woke the guitarist and told him to get lost so he could watch Melanie touch herself and touch himself without a live audience.

"What are you doing?" he asked Melanie. "Tell me."

"I've got my skirt hiked up around my waist. I'm holding my pussy is in my hand while I wait. It aches for you, Gabe."

He knew what it was like to ache for someone. To ache for *her*. "Rub your clit through your panties, Mel. Make yourself wet for me while you wait."

"Yes, Gabe." She released a little moan. "That feels so good. Can I take my panties off now? They're getting soaked."

He stifled a groan of torment. "No, but slip your fingers beneath them and tell me what that sweet pussy of yours feels like."

"Hey, Gabe," Owen called from the common area. "Are you talking to your mom again?"

Gabe tensed and then cringed.

There were several boisterous laughs from the main cabin, but he refused to look that way. *Shit!* Were they listening? Could they hear all the dirty things he was saying to Melanie?

"It's slippery and swollen." Melanie obeyed his request. "Hot and smooth and *oh*! I need to come."

When the door before him unlatched, he yanked it open. Lindsey gasped, her eyes wide, and put a hand over her distended abdomen.

"Sorry it took so long," she said.

Not sorry enough to get the hell out of his way. He took her by the arm and turned, effectively ejecting her into the corridor and himself into the privacy of the bathroom.

"Okay," he said to Melanie as he locked the door behind him. "I'm alone now. Take off your panties for me. Show me what I want to see."

He pulled the phone away from his ear so he could watch as she switched to video chat. He caught a glimpse of her lovely flushed face before she set her phone on the bathroom counter. He loved how she wore her hair to work—her long brown curls all heaped on her head in a messy knot, with tendrils falling down around her heart-shaped face. His need to free those beautiful tresses and bury his hands in them was almost pathological. When she chatted with him on her laptop at home, she let her hair down for him, shook it out, ran her hands through the long, gorgeous mass of curls, but she wouldn't do that now. Not when she was at work. But she would do other things for him. Naughty things.

Melanie stepped back from the phone so that he could see her. Her tight, gray skirt was bunched up around her hips, and an illegally sexy pair of black lace panties hid her sex. Did all businesswomen wear that kind of underwear under their office attire? If so, he was going to start hanging around water coolers.

When she pushed her glasses up her nose and nibbled her lower lip, his cock jerked with excitement.

"Fuck me," he said under his breath.

He hadn't known she'd worn glasses the night they'd met, and if men didn't make passes at girls with glasses, then he had a gender identity crisis going on.

"I'll show you mine if you show me yours," she said with a naughty grin, her voice echoing slightly off the bathroom walls. Did her colleagues have any idea what kind of sexpot lurked behind her conservative facade? They'd better not. She was all his.

"Are you hard for me?" she asked. "Tell me, Gabe."

"I'm always hard for you, baby. I belong inside you. Balls-deep inside you."

"Show me."

He reached for his fly and tilted the phone down, watching his screen to make sure she had a good view as he unfastened the buttons of his jeans one by one. He slid a hand down into his underwear and freed his throbbing erection from its confines, shuddering in bliss as his hand skimmed his cock's sensitive surface.

"I swear it gets bigger every time I see it." Melanie's comment drifted up from the phone.

"It gets more desperate for you every time you see it." He drew his phone closer to his face so he could see what she was doing on her end more clearly. He needed a bigger screen, he decided. No. He needed her here. Live in the flesh.

"This is where I want it, Gabe," she said. He didn't catch much of what she was doing as she moved but after a moment of holding his breath in anticipation, he released it in an excited *whoosh* as her pussy was displayed on screen, her fingers spreading her lips so he could see her intimately. So intimately. Her finger probed her opening, and she said, "In here. I want you here. Your fingers, your tongue, your cock. Right here."

"Yes," he said breathlessly. "That's exactly where I want to be."

He imagined himself buried inside her as he began to stroke himself. His hand was a poor substitution for her soft, silky heat, but it would have to do. He could hear her timid moans as her fingers slipped in and out of her pussy. He knew she'd have been louder if she'd been at home. She really put on a show for him late at night when he was alone in his bunk and she was in her bedroom. The first time he'd talked her into having phone sex, she'd been a little hesitant, but now she completely got off on it. And it made him crazy for her. Fuck, everything the woman did made him crazy.

His ass clenching rhythmically, Gabe pumped his hips as he thrust into his hand. He could almost feel her body against his, her pussy gripping his cock as he imagined fucking her against the bathroom wall. On the screen, her fingers moved to her clit, and she was soon trying to stifle her cries of release as she came for him. He scowled when she dropped her phone with a loud clatter and he could see nothing but blackness and hear nothing but her faint ragged gasps for breath.

He paused, waiting for her to return to him. After a long moment, her face appeared on the screen. Her glasses had slipped down the bridge of her nose. Her eyes were glassy, her cheeks were flushed, and her lips looked swollen, as if begging for kisses. *His* kisses.

"Sorry," she said. "I don't know why doing this at work turns me on so much."

He grinned at her. "I do. You're naughty, Melanie Anderson."

She chuckled softly. "I was a good girl until I met you."

"And that's a bad thing?"

She shook her head, sending a few escaped curls dancing around her shoulders. "It's a very, very good thing. Now come for me, Gabriel Banner, before I have to go back to my desk and pretend I care about numbers when I'd rather be stuffed with your cock."

He smiled at her. "I love it when you talk dirty."

"Soon I'll be whispering those things into your ear. Soon I'll be able to feel you inside me again. Your hard body against mine. Your breath against my skin."

"Yes," he groaned. "God, baby, do you think about me as much as I think about you?"

"Do you think of me constantly?"

"Yeah," he admitted. "Every waking moment. Hell, you're even in my dreams."

"Then yes, I think about you just as much. I want to watch you come now, Gabe. Show me."

He grinned at his good fortune. He was one lucky son of a bitch for finding a woman like her. He loved turning her into a naughty girl. It had been a goal of his. And... mission accomplished.

Gabe set his phone on the counter so he could take his cock in both hands. Knowing she needed to get back to work, he tried to hurry for her. Because she was watching and making little noises of appreciation and offering soft words of encouragement, it didn't take him long to erupt. He caught his load in his hand, holding his palm at a distance so she could watch his fluids jet from his body. She'd told him that watching it come out made her cunny quake, and he was all about giving that sweet pussy an added thrill.

He took a moment to recover his breath and then lifted his phone from the counter, holding it between his jaw and shoulder as he washed his hands in the sink.

"I'm going to be inside you the next time I come, Mel," he said, drying his hands on a hand towel and then closing his fly.

"God, yes. I want that too. I don't know if I can wait until tomorrow night to see you again," she said.

"Good." He smiled crookedly. "Get on a plane and meet me in New Orleans tonight."

She paused for a long moment and he wondered if maybe she didn't want to see him as badly as she claimed. Maybe her insatiable need for him was all an act. Maybe reality would be a whole lot different from the games they played on screens.

"But you said you didn't want me at your shows," she said quietly.

He could tell by the tone of her voice that his words had hurt her.

God, I'm an ass.

"I'm a liar, Melanie. A cowardly fucking liar. I do want you at my show and I need you in my bed as soon as possible." He just hoped her needs matched his own.

CHAPTER TWO

MELANIE DASHED UP the two flights of stairs that led to her third floor apartment. She unlocked the door and was kicking off her shoes before she'd even closed the door behind her.

Her new roommate, Nikki, looked up from the screen of her laptop and smiled a warm greeting.

"You're home early. Did you get fired or something?"

Melanie shook her head and rushed toward her bedroom. Was she really going to drop everything just so she could see Gabe a day earlier than planned? Hell yeah, she was. Why was she even questioning herself? It wasn't as if she got much done other than thinking about him anyway. She had never been so consumed by a man. Never. And she hadn't even known Gabe long. How had he managed to work himself so deep under her skin so quickly? Damn, she had it bad for the guy. It should have served as a warning to slow down, but instead her need had her speeding up, wheels skidding as she drifted around corners and careened through barriers to chase him. Her emotional brakes were malfunctioning, but she had no desire to have them repaired.

Nikki appeared in Melanie's closet doorway as Melanie yanked a suitcase from the top shelf and was instantly buried in an avalanche of extra pillows and linens. She kicked them aside impatiently, not bothering to pick them up. Leaving a mess would have normally driven her nuts, but she was in a hurry.

"What's wrong?" Nikki asked. She backed up as Melanie barreled out of the small walk-in closet. It was more of a stand-in closet—not much room for walking. "Melanie?"

Melanie heard the panic in Nikki's voice, not that she was surprised. Nikki tended to overreact to everything.

"I have to hurry if I want to catch my flight," Melanie said.

"Oh God," Nikki said, and Melanie found herself and her

suitcase crushed in Nikki's embrace. "Who died? Was it your grandmother? Oh, Mel, you must be heartbroken. Go ahead and cry, honey. You'll feel better if you let it all out."

"No one died, hon," Melanie said. "I'm going to New Orleans."

"But I thought you were leaving for Austin to see Gabe tomorrow night."

"Plans changed. You can stop hugging me now. I'm in a rush."

Nikki released her, and Melanie tossed her suitcase on the blue coverlet at the foot of her bed. She unzipped the case before rushing to her dresser for underclothes. Thinking she had all night and tomorrow morning to pack, she hadn't planned what she was taking for her weekend with Gabe, so now she just started flinging various colors of panties and bras into her suitcase, hoping to sort it all out when she got there. Or maybe she wouldn't need underwear the entire weekend. She'd be okay with that too. She added her new lingerie, still in the bag, just in case.

"Did Gabe dump you?" Nikki asked. "I will skin that lanky drummer alive if he did. I can't believe he'd get your hopes up like that—make you think you meant more to him than a cheap one-night stand—and then at the last minute cancel on you."

Melanie shook her head at Nikki again, dragging summer clothes from a drawer. "Why do you always think the worst?" she asked, even though she knew why Nikki expected The Worst. The Worst had been following Nikki around all her life and she had a hard time functioning when it wasn't kicking down her door. "I'm going to see Gabe in New Orleans. He has a show tonight, and he invited me to come. I just hope I can get there in time. The flight I'm on will be cutting it close."

Nikki squealed and grabbed Melanie in another crushing bear hug, but this time she jumped up and down as if they were on some *Let's Get Laid* game show and Melanie had won the grand prize. She couldn't deny that Gabe was a fabulous showcase.

"I knew he liked you." Nikki squealed. "I just knew it. I'll go get my bag."

Nikki released her and was dashing off into the small, windowless office she was using to store her personal belongings while she stayed on Melanie's couch. Temporarily.

What? Wait. Oh no. No no no.

Melanie dropped her armload of clothes into her suitcase and hurried to stop her friend from packing.

"Nikki, you can't come with me."

The delighted smile slid from Nikki's face. Her bottom lip quivered, and Mel's damnable soft heart twisted in her chest. "I'm sorry, hon. We'll do something fun together next week. I promise."

"But... Just before you came home, Shade called and said I should come with you to the concert. He wants to see me again."

Melanie was floored. Despite his torrid one-night fling with Nikki, Shade—the lead singer of Gabe's band—hadn't called her roommate all week. That had resulted in Nikki's need to consume copious amounts of chocolate ice cream and cry herself to sleep in Melanie's bed for three nights. She had just progressed to sleeping on the sofa a few nights ago when she'd finally accepted the inevitable. At least Melanie had thought Nikki was over the guy.

So why would Shade call out of the blue and get Nikki's hopes up again?

He wouldn't.

"Nikki, stop making shit up. The thing with Shade isn't going to happen."

"If he sees me again, then he'll have to admit there was something special between us."

She'd started saying things like that as soon as she'd moved into Melanie's apartment. Initially, Nikki had been fine with the casual sex with Shade thing—even bragged about it—until Gabe had proven so attentive to Melanie, and then suddenly Nikki had decided she was actually in love with Shade and that he'd used her for sex. Nikki was positively heartbroken over the entire ordeal and needed constant coddling and a perpetual sympathetic ear. The way Nikki's emotions did 180 degree reversals in a matter of minutes always sent Melanie's head spinning. But she'd known Nikki for a long time, and she was used to her friend making up problems when life took a break from kicking her for real.

"Nikki…"

"Please take me with you, Mel. Please. Please!" She clasped her hands in front of her chest and shook them for emphasis. "I promise I'll never ask you for anything ever again."

Melanie had heard that before. "I'm sorry, hon. Maybe next time. I only have one ticket." She checked the time on her cellphone and cringed. "And I need to hurry or it's not going to matter, because I'm going to miss my flight." And if she missed her first flight, that would set off a chain reaction of fail. She had to switch planes in Houston. Ironic because Gabe had been in Houston only two nights ago. She'd have loved to have seen him then as well. That night and every night. But it just wasn't possible. Curse her responsibilities for destroying her opportunity at perpetual bliss.

"I can't believe you don't care about my happiness," Nikki said.

Oh for fuck's sake, Nikki. "But I do care. That's why you're never seeing Shade Silverton again."

"Then why do you get to see Force?" Nikki crossed her arms over her chest and scowled.

"Because he asked me to come and I like him, so I'm going. You can sleep in my bed while I'm gone. I know my sofa is hard on your back." An excuse she'd given Melanie when she'd crawled into bed with her the night before. The woman was a complete bed hog. Melanie had given up fighting for covers sometime around three a.m.

"You're sure I can't come?"

If Nikki's lip pouted any further from her face, it was liable to fall off.

"I'm sure."

"Fine then. I'll just go get wasted and pick up some weekend company at a bar."

Melanie rubbed her forehead. Why did everything have to be drama with Nikki? Why couldn't she for *once* give Melanie a break?

"Just stay home this weekend, Nik. You know I'll worry about you if you go out by yourself."

"Why should you get to have all the fun?"

"Because I've earned it!" Melanie snapped and marched back

to her bedroom to finish packing. Nikki was a grown woman—though sometimes it was hard to tell based on her behavior—and Melanie couldn't spend all her time worrying over Nikki's poor decisions. She had better things to do. Namely, Gabriel "Force" Banner.

Trying not to picture Nikki lying dead in a gutter, Melanie yanked clothes from hangers and stuffed them into her suitcase in a big tangled ball. She hoped Gabe owned an iron. Did rock stars press their own clothes? She had no idea. She didn't know much about him yet, other than they were insanely hot for each other even when hundreds of miles separated them. She thought about changing out of her work clothes—a simple gray pencil skirt and fitted white blouse—and poking her contact lenses into her eyes, but another glance at the clock had her scrambling for her travel-sized toiletries and make-up kit before rushing for the front door.

Hopping from one foot to the other, she slipped into her pumps and called to Nikki, "Don't do anything stupid, Nikki. Please, for me, just stay home this weekend."

Nikki didn't answer, and Melanie didn't have time to check on her. She was likely just sulking.

"I love you!" Still no response. *"Have a good time, Melanie,"* she answered for the silent Nikki. *"Don't worry about me. I'll behave."*

Maybe if she said it aloud, her wish would come true.

Torn between elation at seeing Gabe and guilt for deserting her needy best friend, Melanie squared her shoulders and left the apartment. She was not going to allow Nikki to dictate her life. Not with the promise of nirvana waiting for her in the Big Easy.

CHAPTER THREE

MELANIE LEFT HER sedan in long-term parking and made surprisingly good time in the airport. As luck would have it, the rear section of the plane was called first to board and she hurried to take her place in line. Things were definitely going her way. She took it as a sign that she'd made the right decision. She was going to have a great time this weekend, and Nikki was going to be just fine at home. By herself. Melanie was worrying over nothing. At least that's what she tried to tell herself. Nikki could be a pain in the ass, but Melanie loved her. Perhaps their relationship was a tad unhealthy, but something about Nikki's dependence appealed to Melanie in a way she didn't understand. Maybe it had something to do with being an only child and never having to look out for anyone but herself. Melanie liked looking after Nikki *most* of the time. And she worried about her *all* of the time.

On the plane, Melanie stuffed her small suitcase in the overhead bin and sat in the window seat, instantly squashed by the broad man who sat in the seat to her left. Squirming for an inch of space, Melanie fastened her seat belt, huddled close to the window, and waited for the rest of the plane to board. Her stomach twisted with a mixture of nerves, excitement, and hunger. She hadn't eaten since lunch. She hoped Gabe was up for a meal, because she doubted the airline would part with so much as a peanut on this short flight.

Gabe.

Had she actually sighed aloud thinking about him, or had it been a mental sigh?

No matter, she couldn't wait to see him again. Only a few more hours and she could lose herself in his arms.

The man beside her gave her a long, hard look, most likely because she was grinning like a simpleton who'd been swimming in a vat of vodka.

"Business trip?" he asked.

"Purely for pleasure," she said. "You?"

"Business. Trying to break in to the UFC. There's an amateur night in New Orleans this weekend."

That would explain his broad shoulders and nicked knuckles. He wasn't a bad-looking man; she just preferred hers a bit on the tall and lean side. Or had ever since she'd laid eyes on Gabe.

"Sounds painful," she said.

"Nah, it's fun."

Getting repeatedly kicked and punched did not sound like fun to Melanie. But perhaps he meant *delivering* the kicks and punches was fun. Her brow furrowed. Nope. Hurting people for sport didn't sound like fun either.

The huge man pushed up the long sleeve of his T-shirt, and her gaze landed on the barbed-wire tattoo that circled his forearm. On cue, her heart rate kicked up. She'd made great strides in her tattoo phobia when Gabe had allowed her to examine his up close—and what a pleasurable experience that had been—but apparently she wasn't completely over her fears. She felt silly for panicking every time she saw certain tattoos, but the fear was still there. She wondered if it always would be. Some people were scared of clowns or spiders or enclosed spaces. She was terrified of certain tattoos. Those rough bikers who had scared the life out of her as a teen had really done a number on her psyche. She just had to avoid tattoos with barbed wire or roses or skulls—so like half of the tattoos in existence— and she could remain perfectly calm.

"Well, good luck with your fight," she said, turning her attention pointedly out the window to stare at the back of the plane wing. If she didn't look at the man's arm, she could sit next to him all the way to New Orleans without having a panic attack. She hoped. She didn't want to send the entire country to high alert because she freaked the fuck out on a domestic flight. She'd just stare out at the wing and make sure the engine stayed fully functional the entire flight. It would keep her attention off Mr. UFC's tattoo. Maybe.

"Melanie," a familiar voice called from the front of the plane. "Melanie Anderson, where are you?"

Melanie's jaw dropped. What in the hell was Nikki doing here?

Melanie assumed there must be some horrible emergency and no one had been able to reach her because she'd turned off her cellphone in preparation for her flight. Melanie shot up out of her seat—or tried to. Her seat belt threatened to break her pelvis. She wrenched the clasp open and jumped to her feet, nearly banging her head on the overhead bin.

"Nikki, what's wrong?" Melanie called, waving her hands. She could feel the heat in her face, and her throat was tight, as if someone were strangling her.

"There you are," Nikki said when she spotted Melanie at the back of the plane.

She was carrying a rather large overnight bag.

Why was she carrying luggage to inform Melanie about whatever emergency had brought her here?

"Hey, big guy, would you mind switching seats with me?" Nikki said to the wannabe cage fighter. "You wouldn't want to come between friends now, would you?"

She turned on her charming pout—the one that made two-hundred-and-fifty-pound walls of muscle climb out of their seats—and then smiled brightly when he took her bag and started to stuff it into the overhead compartment for her.

"You two hotties should definitely sit together," he said. "I'm into feng shui. I like my beautiful decorations in balanced pairs."

Melanie rolled her eyes until they threatened to glimpse her brain.

"You're sweet," Nikki said. "Isn't he sweet, Mel?"

"Like cotton candy. What are you doing here, Nikki?"

"Going to New Orleans."

"Well, duh. The luggage and boarding pass sort of tipped me off to that. Why are you going to New Orleans?"

Nikki held up a finger to put Melanie on hold and turned back to the big guy taking up the entire aisle. "Thanks for switching seats with me."

"Can I get your number?" UFC-guy said in a low, deep voice, his gaze trained on Nikki's push-up-bra-enhanced bust. Her boobs were currently demonstrating the impressive stretch and strength of the cotton fibers in her skintight pink T-shirt.

"I'll bring it to you once we're in the air," Nikki promised.

"I don't think you're supposed to switch seats," Melanie said. "Melanie, Melanie, always afraid to break the rules." Nikki winked at the big guy. "But I'm not. If anyone asks, your name is Nicole. And what will my assumed name be?"

"Richard Bailey," he said. "Or just Dick."

"It's never just dick when I'm around." Nikki laughed and settled into Mr. UFC's vacated seat. She grabbed half of her seat belt and half of Melanie's and tried to figure out how to fasten two female ends together.

Before the guy could deliver his next incredibly lame pick-up line, he was ushered up the aisle to his seat by a harried flight attendant. Melanie jerked the end of her seatbelt from Nikki's fumbling fingers and fastened her buckle again. She counted backwards from a million so she wouldn't strangle the life out of her best friend and greatest liability.

When Melanie was prepared for flight and could talk without breathing fire from her nostrils, she turned to Nikki and repeated, "What are you *doing* here?"

"Following your advice."

Melanie made a face of complete incomprehension. "My advice? I told you that you couldn't come."

"That's not advice, that's an order. Remember just a few days ago you said visualize what you want, gather your courage and go out and get it?" Nikki punctuated her words with opening and closing hands, as if she were putting Melanie's advice up in lights. "I've been visualizing Shade Silverton all week."

In her head, Melanie started counting backwards from a billion. "I was talking about finding a job. You know, those work-type things that bring in money so you can pay your bills and half our rent and buy your own damned gas." Nikki was entirely broke and seemed in no hurry to find employment or to move from Melanie's uncomfortable couch. "How did you even get a plane ticket?"

"I blew the pilot." Nikki suggestively wiped at the corner of her mouth.

Melanie's jaw dropped.

Nikki burst out laughing. "Jeez, Melanie, I'm just kidding. You don't really think I'd do something like that, do you?"

To get what she wanted? Maybe.

"Remember that credit card you gave me for emergencies?" Nikki said, managing to look slightly remorseful. "Well, Shade not calling me for six entire days is an emergency. I'm going to tell him off to his face and then he's going to apologize to my vagina all night long."

"Nikki, isn't it obvious that he doesn't want to see you?"

"Nope."

"And that credit card was for real emergencies. How can I trust you when you go and do something like this?" She felt like such a mom these days. Or a harping wife. What had happened to their friendship? Or had it always been this way between them?

"I just want to spend time with you, Mel." Nikki turned on her best-friend-please-love-me expression, and for once Melanie was too pissed to be affected by it.

"Well, I want to spend time with *Gabe*. Alone. You might as well get off the plane right now and head for home."

Melanie grabbed the armrests as the plane began to back away from the terminal. Too late to fix this situation? Not as far as Melanie was concerned. As pissed as she was, she wasn't against throwing Nikki from a moving plane. She wouldn't even wait for the emergency slide to inflate before shoving her out the exit and onto the tarmac.

"I'm not going to get in the way of your time with lover boy," Nikki assured her. "I just think it would be awesome if we were both dating guys in the same band. Wouldn't that be awesome?"

Awesome? Well, if Shade actually wanted to date Nikki, it might be fun—until disaster struck. And Melanie couldn't fathom the level of drama Nikki would invent in that scenario.

"I don't identify Gabe as the drummer of Sole Regret; I just think of him as Gabe. Your feelings for Shade—if you can even call them feelings—are all about his fame and notoriety. That is the only reason you slept with him."

"Not the only reason," Nikki said.

Melanie blinked at her.

Nikki grinned. "He's also sexy as hell and has a huge cock."

Melanie released a tired breath. "Even if he does like you as more than his current dick wetter, there is no way something like that can last."

"Who said I wanted it to last? I just want to have fun. Keep his dick wet if he wants it wet. You're the one who seems to think sex has to be meaningful and emotional and all lovey-dovey."

And that's what Nikki had been moping about all week. Exactly that. Melanie's head started to swim again. She wished the woman would make up her mind. Did she just want to have sex with Shade again or did she want something more? Did she even know what she wanted? "Don't you want sex to be meaningful?"

Nikki gnawed on her lip reflectively. "Maybe when I'm thirty."

Which was in like two years. Nikki had so much growing up to do before then. But there was a part of Melanie that was a little sad that she herself had grown up too soon. Part of her wished she was capable of Nikki's idea of fun, but most of her was glad that what had started as a night of meaningless sex with a hot drummer had turned into a chance to find something more substantial with a wonderful, deep, somewhat misunderstood man.

"So what if you get all the way to New Orleans and Shade doesn't want to see you?" Melanie asked.

Nikki shrugged. "I'll just join you and Gabe. Every guy wants to have a threesome with two hot chicks, right?"

"Not funny, Nikki."

"I wasn't trying to be funny."

"I'm not sharing him." Nikki had a way of stealing her boyfriends from under her nose, and she was not going to give Nikki an opening with Gabe.

Nikki released a heavy sigh. "Well, you can't blame a girl for trying."

Melanie's head was thrown back against the seat as the plane accelerated down the runway.

"Shit," Nikki said. "I forgot I hate flying."

She grabbed Melanie's hand and squeezed her eyelids shut until they'd left the earth behind. She didn't let go of Melanie's hand until the safety demonstration was long over and the plane leveled out near cruising altitude. Melanie let her hold her hand, stewing over the entire mess. If Nikki ruined Melanie's time with Gabe, she would never forgive her. She would toss Nikki out on the street and let her sucker some rich, older man into taking care of her.

"I'm sorry, Mel," Nikki said.

"For what?" Melanie snapped. The woman owed her a list of apologies a mile long.

"For loving you so much."

Melanie pursed her lips, trying to puzzle through the jigsaw that was Nikki Swanson. "Why are you sorry for that?"

"Because it makes me do stupid things."

"Wow, Nikki, you must love me a hell of a lot."

Nikki pouted the pout that worked on guys, but it didn't make Melanie give her everything she wanted. Much.

"Now you're just being cruel. You know you mean everything to me. Can we take off our seat belts yet?"

On cue, the flight attendant announced that they could move about the cabin. Nikki unfastened her seat belt.

"I'm going to thank Mr. Big, Muscular, and Handsome for letting me have his seat." And she was off to play her field. The damned thing was the size of the entire state of Kansas.

Melanie tried to ignore Nikki's flirtatious laughs from up the aisle as she stared out the window wondering how her mood could have turned sour so quickly. She wouldn't blame Gabe if he left her at the airport with her baggage. Baggage more commonly referred to as Nikki Swanson.

CHAPTER FOUR

GABE SMILED WHEN Melanie's text message popped up on his phone.

We've landed. Should I rent a car or just take a taxi to the stadium?

He texted her back right away. *I thought you'd like to ride in the limo with me. I have a surprise for you. I think you'll like it.*

He glanced at the small package on the seat beside him. Yeah, he was sure she'd enjoy what he had tucked inside. A little something he'd invented a couple years ago.

A moment later his phone displayed her next message. *Limo sounds promising. I have a surprise for you too. Pretty sure you won't like it much.*

Gabe groaned. There was only one thing he could think of that would put a damper on their weekend together. *Are you on your period?* He texted.

O_o You saw my pussy four hours ago. Did it look like I was on my period?

Thank God, he thought.

No, it looked damn hot with your fingers inside it, he typed to her. *I'm sure I'll like any surprise you brought with you.*

We'll see. Are you waiting in the terminal? I'll be off the plane soon.

I'm in the black stretch limousine just outside. I'm pretending to be rich and famous. I sent the driver after you with your name on a sign.

Her response? *K.*

Such a terse reply for Melanie. He should have gone after her, he realized. She was probably expecting the "rush into each other's arms and spin round and round while you lock lips in the terminal" scene. He didn't much like public displays of affection, especially since he'd become somewhat of a celebrity. But he did want to make Melanie happy. And wanted her to know how great he thought she was. And smart. And beautiful. And funny. And sexy. Damned sexy. He just didn't see the point in the entire world knowing how far gone he was over a woman he'd met less than a week ago.

But he didn't mind *her* knowing it, so he started a new message to her.

Actually, I don't trust myself in your company in public.

Send.

Figured you wouldn't want your picture published all over the Internet with Force Banner's tongue in your mouth.

Send.

And his hands all over you.

Send.

He waited eagerly for her next message. He was only half joking. Damn, he needed to be in, on, and around that woman in every capacity.

Her reply came at last. *You overestimate my sense of propriety.*

He laughed aloud as he read her text. Maybe he should have gone to pick her up in the terminal and to hell with what the tabloids published. He would have followed that impulse if he'd been wearing his ball cap and hadn't already dressed for the band's performance that night. His foot-high, red and black mohawk tended to draw attention, and people easily recognized him as someone they should gawk at. He wasn't sure why. Nothing to see, folks. Nothing to see.

His phone sounded its text alert again.

BTW, I'm hungry. I hope you're planning to feed me.

He'd promised to feed her the night they met, and they'd ended up distracted with more pleasurable preoccupations.

I can think of a few things I'd like to put in your mouth.

When she didn't text him back and the minutes ticked by one after another, he decided he had offended her. He really did act like a horny idiot whenever they interacted. She was probably at the ticket counter trying to book the next flight back to Wichita. He decided to curtail his enthusiasm a bit and behave less like a caveman and more like his regular self. It had just been a long time since he'd been this crazy over a woman. So unequivocally *in lust*. He sure as hell didn't want to fuck this up by making her think the only thing he was interested in was sex. He was definitely interested in sex but now that they had an entire weekend to spend together, he was determined to learn everything about her. Everything. So that lust might have a chance to become something more. Or if they found out they were incompatible outside the bedroom, so that he could get the woman out from under his skin. Or try to.

He decided to send another text, even though it did make him seem almost as desperate as he felt. *I'll order something to be sent to the hotel room. What are you in the mood for? Whipped cream or whips and chains?*

Again she didn't respond.

Crap. Had he managed to screw things up already? They always bantered back and forth like this through text messages, but maybe she wasn't as keen to be naughty in real life. If so, the weekend he had planned would have to be entirely reconfigured into something a little less porn script.

The limo door opened, and Melanie peeked in through the door. Gabe's breath stalled in his chest. Had she always been so lovely?

"I'm in the mood for sausage," she said. "Big, thick, and hard."

His breathlessness ended in a chuckle.

"And juicy," a female voice said from behind Melanie.

Melanie closed her eyes and pursed her lips. Gabe got the impression that she was counting in her head.

"Hi, Force!" the same female voice called, and the achingly beautiful face of Melanie's friend Nikki appeared over Melanie's shoulder. "Did you miss us?"

Gabe's gaze darted to meet Melanie's, but she had her eyes squeezed shut. He could tell the enabler in her was losing the battle to the hair-pulling, bitch-slapping she-cat that was about to break loose.

"Is this your surprise?" he asked. His surprise for her seemed to start flashing neon signs—*XXX* and *Live Nude Girls* and *Adults Only*. He grabbed the small package on the seat beside him and shoved it behind his hip as discreetly as possible.

"I told her she couldn't come," Melanie said out of the corner of her mouth, as if that would make it possible for Gabe, but not Nikki, to hear her words.

"But I took some initiative!" Nikki said as if she'd just been accepted into Harvard for Cheerleaders.

"Great," Gabe said flatly. So much for kissing Melanie all the way to the venue while he used his surprise to make her scream his name in ecstasy. "I have to get to the stadium. Are you coming or not?"

"I'm not coming yet," Melanie said with a naughty smile, her eyes popping open. "But I'm sure you can help me with that."

His heart began to thud with excitement as she pinned him with a sultry look that without a doubt meant that she was very keen on being naughty in real life, if only they could manage to ditch her companion.

"Why don't you ride up front with the driver?" Melanie said to Nikki, whom Melanie was very effectively blocking by splaying her body across the open door like an Olympic goalkeeper.

"Why?"

"I'm sure he gets lonely up there all by himself," Melanie said. "And he's really cute. Didn't you notice?"

Gabe scowled. *Melanie* had noticed? He didn't like to hear that.

"He is sort of cute in that tuxedo." Nikki giggled. "Like a handsome penguin."

Melanie rolled her eyes at Gabe. Why did she continue to hang out with that chick? She was obviously annoyed by her.

"Go keep him company."

"Okay!"

Melanie launched herself into the car and slammed the door behind her before Nikki could change her mind about keeping the handsome penguin in the driver's seat company.

"I am so sorry about that," Melanie said, her hazel eyes concealed behind thick lashes and black-framed glasses. "She just showed up on the plane, demanded some big cage fighter give up his seat so she could sit beside me, flirted with him through both flights, and then invited herself to ride in the limo."

"I get the feeling she's hard to deter once she sets her mind on something."

"If only she'd show the same sort of dedication to getting her life back on track."

Gabe had been playing out his reunion with Melanie in his

head all evening, and this was definitely not what he'd had in mind. He'd figured they'd already be locked in an endless kiss—hands roving, bodies pressed together—but Nikki's unexpected appearance made him feel awkward. It was as if Nikki were sitting between him and Melanie, even though the woman was in the front seat. Melanie was obviously affected by Nikki's presence as well. She sat stiffly and glanced repeatedly toward the front of the limo as if waiting for a zombie to launch itself through the glass.

A knock sounded on the window between the driver's seat and the passenger compartment before it slid down with a mechanical whir. Nikki, who was now wearing the chauffer's black cap, faced backwards and leaned over the seat, waving both hands. She had a killer smile affixed to her face, and her blue eyes were wide. She really was a beautiful woman. Stunning. Gabe was sure most men tripped over their dicks trying to get in her pants. He was not one of them. Why would any man settle for superficial beauty when he could have someone like Melanie, who had brains, sensuality, *and* good looks?

"This is so exciting!" Nikki said, and instantly Gabe understood why Melanie put up with her. Why she loved her. Nikki was vividly alive, the kind of woman who would still be young when she was ninety-five. That sort of vigor was addictive to be around, though it could be exhausting. "Why aren't you two humping yet?"

Gabe chuckled. He'd been wondering the same thing himself.

"Because someone keeps interrupting," Melanie said.

"It's okay," Gabe said. "We have three whole days in which to get our hump on. Let's get you some food and cruise down Bourbon Street. We can hump later." He winked at Melanie, and she released a long sigh. Was she relieved or disappointed? He couldn't tell.

"Can we get bourbon on Bourbon Street?" Nikki asked. "I'm thirsty."

"Alcohol makes her lose her pants," Melanie warned.

"I know a great place to get bourbon," the driver said.

Nikki hugged him around the neck. "I knew I liked you, my handsome penguin." She pecked a kiss on his temple.

A strange sound came from Melanie—like a suppressed

snort. Confused, Gabe glanced at her just in time to see her burst into laughter.

"I can't..." She was laughing too hard to breathe, much less speak clearly. "I can't believe..." She gasped for air. "...you called him... ...that to... ...his f-face..."

"Well, I don't know his name. What's your name, handsome?" Nikki asked and brushed a lock of hair from the driver's forehead. He reminded Gabe of a young John Travolta. Dark hair. Blue eyes. Cleft in his strong chin.

The driver pointed to a slender gold name tag on his chest. "Parker."

"Parker the penguin?" Melanie sniggered and then snorted before bursting into delighted laughter again.

"You okay?" Gabe asked her. He was pretty sure she was turning blue from lack of air.

Melanie clutched her stomach and nodded, blinking tears from her eyes as she struggled to get a handle on her case of the giggles.

"She gets like that when she gets wound up too tight," Nikki said. "Eventually she explodes into a fit of laughter. It's best to set her off as early as possible. No telling what kind of fit she'd have if she was allowed to keep winding." Nikki made circles in the air with one fingertip.

"I'm not wound too tight."

"Really?" Nikki said, her eyebrows arched high on her forehead. "I still have about fifty eye-daggers in my back from the plane trip. Care to take them back?"

"You should be glad they don't allow real weapons on flights. I'm still pissed at you, Nicole Evelyn Swanson," Melanie assured her, but the tension she'd drawn into the limo with her had vanished. "Now close the damned window so I can greet my sexy rock star properly."

Nikki grinned. "Better hurry. I'll be interrupting you again when we stop for food. And bourbon." The window slid upward, giving Gabe and Melanie privacy and Gabe a strange case of nerves.

CHAPTER FIVE

GABE WIPED HIS suddenly damp palms on his thighs and stared at his embarrassingly large feet. He wanted so much to pull Melanie into his arms and show her how much he missed her, but he still wasn't sure if she wanted him to. Her signals were mixed and terribly confusing. He hadn't expected these feelings of uncertainty when he'd invited her for the weekend. They always interacted so naturally with each other. What if they spent the entire time sitting in awkward silence? Perhaps this rendezvous was a tad premature.

When Melanie turned to him and rested the fingertips of one hand against his jaw, his nervousness vanished in an instant, replaced with excitement and anticipation. The connection between them wasn't gone. Thank God.

"Are you going to kiss me now, or do I have to make the first move?" she whispered, her gorgeous hazel eyes staring intently at his lips.

He removed her glasses carefully, which caused her to lift her eyes to meet his. He got lost in her gaze and warmth spread throughout his body—in his groin, yes, that was reassuring and familiar, but also in his chest, where his heart began to thud a rapid staccato.

"I was wondering if you were as perfect in person as I'd made you out to be in my memory," he said.

"You see me every day," she reminded him.

"It's not the same," he whispered. "I can't feel your warmth. Smell the sweet scent of your perfume. See little details like those pale freckles on the bridge of your nose and the blue and green flecks in your eyes. I can't touch your smooth skin, your soft hair." He did that now. It felt just as glorious against his fingertips as it looked. Even better than he remembered.

"So you're not disappointed?"

"Disappointed? How could I possibly be disappointed?"

He leaned in close, lost in Melanie's eyes. When his lips brushed hers, a familiar longing stirred deep inside him. He rubbed his lips over hers once, twice, and then angled his head to take the kiss deeper. Melanie opened her mouth to him and wrapped her arms around his neck. Her fingers brushed the row of spiked hair down the center of his head, and she froze. He tugged back to look at her and found her eyebrows drawn together.

"I'm still not used to this," she said, pressing a hand down on his spiked mohawk and watching it spring back up.

"You don't like it?" he asked, hoping it didn't become an issue for her, because it was a trademark of his stage persona, and he was currently on tour. When he wasn't on tour, he let the sides grow and cut off some of the length so he looked halfway tame, but he'd never gone to what most people would consider a normal haircut when he was out on the road. He knew the dragon tattoos on either side of his scalp didn't tame his look any, but those would be there for the rest of his life. If she was going to dump him for his appearance, she should probably do it soon.

"I like it," she said. "I'm just not sure what to cling to when you kiss me. Last time you didn't have it spiked like this, so I had some soft hair to hold on to."

Oh, was that all?

"I'll wash it after the show," he said. "You can run your fingers through it then."

"I didn't mean for you to stop kissing me," she said. "I'll just cling to your shoulders for now so I don't prick my fingers."

He chuckled at her expression. She looked as if she had solved some mystery.

"I shouldn't do that," she said.

"You can cling to my shoulders as much as you want," he assured her.

"I mean I shouldn't analyze everything. The night we met, I was thrown off guard. I tossed caution to the wind, but now that I'm here with you and you're more familiar, I feel sort of…"

"Uptight."

She flushed. "Yeah. Exactly."

"I have just the thing to loosen you up," he said.

He reached behind his hip and pulled the slim package free from where it had been lodged against the seat.

He held it out to her.

"What's this?" she asked, glancing from the paper-wrapped package to his face and then back to the package again.

"A prototype."

Her flush intensified. "Oh," she gasped. "One of your kinky inventions?"

She looked up at him again, and he nodded, a bit nervous about sharing it with her but mostly excited to try it out.

"Is it new?"

"I've been working on this one for a while," he said, "but I do have another project I started on the day we parted in Tulsa. I hope to reveal that later if I can get the kinks out."

"I thought the whole point was to work kinks in," she said.

It took him a second to realize she was joking. He chuckled. "I guess kinks in sex toys are pretty much a given."

She ran her fingers over the piece of tape holding the package closed. "Am I supposed to open this here?"

He grinned sheepishly. "Well, if you're prepared to loosen up."

"I might be," she said. "Kiss me again while I think it over."

She needed to be seduced, he realized. He'd expected them to be past that with all the things they'd showed each other through video chat, but he supposed every woman liked to feel as if a man had to work a little to gain her cooperation and attention. Even women who'd been with the same man for a lot longer than a week needed to feel a little hard to get. So perhaps he should have saved his present until after he had her in that disoriented, I-need-your-body-*now* state. She was always so eager to be open with him on the phone but here in his arms, she seemed almost shy. She turned her head to study the dark glass that separated them from the driver and Nikki. Was that what had her hesitating? Because Nikki was just up front? Perhaps if Nikki had been the sweet, innocent type, Gabe would have understood Melanie's hesitation to engage in lascivious acts in her proximity, but he didn't get that impression about Nikki at all. Heck, of the pair, Melanie was the sweet innocent. Maybe she didn't want Nikki to know she was a whole lot naughtier than she appeared.

"So why did she decide to come with you?" he asked.

"Huh?" Melanie said, turning her attention back to him.

"Nikki."

"Oh, she wants to hook up with Shade again. Or at least talk to him about why he didn't call her this week."

Gabe grunted. "Uh, bad idea. Shade is with someone special now. He's not going to be interested in Nikki. He'll undoubtedly hurt her feelings to get his point across."

"I tried to tell her that. Hell if she'll listen to me."

"Maybe I should drop you and Nikki off at the hotel. You can find her a room," he said, pausing to make sure it was clear that Nikki would not be following them to Austin. Best friend in tow or not, Melanie was *his* this weekend. He wasn't going to bow to the impulses of one of Shade's past lays. "I can meet up with you—*just* you—after the show and we'll head to Austin. Our chartered flight leaves at midnight, so we won't have time to deal with Nikki after the show."

"You don't want me at the concert?" she asked, and he couldn't tell if she was pissed or hurt or just asking a question.

"I do want you there. I want you to be the last person I see before I climb behind my drum kit and the first one I see when I stumble out sweaty and exhausted an hour later. But it's a bad idea for Nikki to be there. I don't mean to be rude, but she wasn't invited, and I doubt that Shade led her to believe she could hope for some sort of relationship with him."

"I know that, Gabe," she said, "but what would you have me do? Desert her at the airport? She needs me to look out for her or she winds up in trouble. She's one of those people who don't even have to go looking for disaster, it finds her. It always finds her."

She placed a hand on his thigh to steady herself as the limo turned a corner and accelerated up an incline. The car stopped and the glass behind the driver slid down.

Nikki turned around in her seat and stared at them. Gabe shoved the package containing his little invention behind his hip again.

"We decided to stop for sandwiches," Nikki said. "Quick and

easy so we can get to the concert on time. Parker still has to go to the hotel and pick up the rest of the band after he drops us off. I figured I could run in and get the sandwiches to go while you two continue to make out." She looked from one of them to the other and offered a disapproving stare to the space between them. "Are you two even copping a feel?"

"We're talking," Melanie said.

"About?"

Melanie glanced at Gabe.

"What's for dinner," he said, not sure if Melanie wanted him to be the one to break the news to Nikki that Shade was currently seeing someone important to him. Gabe had to assume that Melanie didn't want him to make her friend cry, so unless Melanie instructed him otherwise, he was going to keep his mouth shut.

"What do you like?" Nikki asked Gabe.

"I'll eat just about anything, but hold the onions. I have some making out to do." He winked at Nikki and she giggled.

"I'm sure Mel will appreciate that." Nikki glanced at Melanie with an expectant look on her face.

"You know what I like," Melanie said.

"Um, yeah, should I just use the emergency credit card or…" She glanced at Melanie's purse.

Damn, where were his manners? Gabe dug his wallet out of his back pocket and pulled out several twenties. Nikki didn't hesitate to accept the money, not that he wanted her to refuse it. He had just expected her to at least try to turn down his cash since they didn't really know each other.

"You don't have to do that," Melanie said, snatching the bills out of Nikki's hand and trying to stuff them back into his.

"I want to," he said.

"She's always a cheap date," Nikki said, which earned her a scathing look from Melanie. "Has a really hard time taking money from anyone. Miss Financially Independent." She made finger quotes.

"She says that like it's a bad thing," Melanie said.

Nikki took the money again and smiled at Gabe. "Thanks! Maybe I'll buy you lunch sometime when I get back on my feet."

To get back on her feet, she'd have to learn to stay off her back and her knees. Gabe lowered his eyes, feeling guilty for even thinking that way about Nikki. There obviously had to be *something* terrific about her. She was Melanie's closest friend. Nikki opened the front door and slipped out of the car. The driver, Parker, watched her stride to the sub shop with drool practically dripping off his chin.

"She's used to getting whatever her heart desires because she's so pretty," Melanie said. "If I don't give it to her, some guy will. Some guy who expects something in return. At least if it comes from me, I don't have to worry about her repaying their kindness with sexual favors."

Gabe noticed that Parker was eavesdropping. The guy tried to pretend he wasn't taking mental notes on how to get into Nikki's pants, but Gabe was a guy himself. He knew how they thought. Gabe pressed the button that raised the window between them again, glad it was soundproof.

"Maybe she should sit back here with us," Gabe said. "I don't like the way the driver is looking at her."

"Just about everyone looks at her that way."

"Well, I won't," Gabe said. "Not when I have you."

He leaned in to steal a kiss, meaning to offer a chaste brushing of his lips against hers, but something primal sizzled between them and he instantly had her crushed against his chest, his hands buried in her hair and his mouth seeking to devour hers. Her fingers curled into his back, drawing him closer. Her soft breasts felt like heaven pressed against his chest. His tongue brushed her upper lip, and she shuddered before tentatively touching his tongue with hers.

She pulled away slowly and then rested her forehead against his shoulder, breathing heavily. "You were right earlier," she said. "All the sexy video chats are not the same as being here with you. You're a distraction at a distance but in person…" She drew in a deep breath. "In person, you're utterly devastating to a woman's wits."

He grinned and reached for the package he'd hidden behind his hip. "I have something in here to make sure you don't regain your wits anytime soon."

Hands shaking, Melanie opened the package as if she expected something to jump out and bite her. And he had a few items in his arsenal that would have done just that, but not this one. This one was all about pleasure. He liked giving her pleasure. Some women liked a little pain on the side, and he could cater to that need, but he was pretty sure—and actually hoped—that Melanie liked to receive only pleasure. She unrolled the thick brown paper and the three-fingered glove fell out on her lap.

She raised an eyebrow at it and then lifted her gaze to meet his. "What is it?"

He took the device from her skirt and slipped it onto three fingers of his right hand, leaving his pinkie and thumb free. He held his hand out to her so she could fasten the cuff around his wrist. As soon as it was clasped, the circuit was complete and the device whirred to life. Near the tip of his middle finger, a small rubbery rod moved in an elliptical path. At the base of his middle finger, a soft bump vibrated, and metallic plates ran the entire length of both his ring and index fingers; plates that grew warm and tingly as soon as they touched anything wet— Melanie's pussy for example.

"You sit on my hand, and I promise it will show you a good time."

She bent over it for a closer inspection. "I sit on it?"

"This goes just inside the opening of your pussy," he said, indicating the revolving rod near the end of his finger. "It will tease you until you're begging for cock."

"And these?" she asked, tracing the two metallic plates on either side.

"Wet your finger and touch one," he suggested. When she stuck her finger in her mouth to wet it, his cock surged to life. Change of plans—Nikki definitely needed to ride in the front with the driver. He was not even close to being able to function in polite company. He had a powerful need to be alone with Melanie for an extended period, and was painfully aware that didn't have much time to be together before the show started at nine.

Melanie pressed her wet finger to the metal plate on his index finger and her breath caught.

"Tingly."

"And warm," he said. "Those go against your pussy lips. The

wetter you get, the stronger the sensation."

She poked the vibrating nub at the base of his fingers. "For my clit?" She glanced up at him and smiled hopefully.

He grinned. "You didn't think I'd forget that, did you?"

"I hoped you wouldn't," she said, a delightful blush staining her cheeks pink. "You seem to know what feels good for a woman more than I do."

"You can climb on backwards if you'd rather the vibration tease your ass. I want to please you the way you want to be pleased."

She touched her finger to the strong vibrating nub and shuddered. "Lock the doors," she said breathlessly as she reached under her skirt to tug off her panties. "Hurry, before Nikki gets back."

"They're already locked," he assured her.

She slid onto his lap, straddling his thighs, and kissed him hungrily as he slid his gloved hand between her legs.

CHAPTER SIX

MELANIE JUMPED WHEN the vibration at the base of Gabe's fingers pressed against her clit. He carefully slipped the tip of the rotating rubbery rod into her opening, and she groaned into his mouth. She marveled at the man's understanding of female anatomy. He was right; the stretching of her entrance in a wide circle over and over and over again had her craving deep, hard thrusts to quell her building need. The vibration against her clit changed patterns, going from a steady buzz to hard pulses and back to a steady buzz. Her body jerked involuntarily as a quick and dirty orgasm caught her by surprise.

She tore her mouth from Gabe's as her head dropped back and she called out to the moon roof of the car.

"Wait. There's more. Are you wet?" Gabe whispered in her ear.

"Mmm," she moaned.

His index and ring fingers slid against her pussy lips, holding them apart as the speed of the rod rotating in her opening picked up and the vibration against her clit continued to alternate patterns. The warm tingles against both lips made her rock her hips into his hand.

"Oh dear God," she gasped. The pleasure was so intense she couldn't do more than cling to his shoulders.

"You like it?"

"Yes!"

Within seconds she was coming again. This time she grabbed the back of his head and buried his face into her chest. "I need cock," she said and when he didn't immediately fill her, she tugged his head from her breasts and yelled, "I need cock, Gabe! I need it now."

"Here?"

"Yes, yes, anywhere. Fuck me."

He began fumbling with his belt. Fly open, he lifted his hips so he could free his cock. Thank God he was already hard. She took his thick shaft in one hand and gasped when his gloved hand moved away from her throbbing pussy.

"Condom?" he asked breathlessly.

"We don't need one." They'd already discussed not using them, but she was glad he had the sense to ask in the heat of the moment in case she'd changed her mind.

Melanie took him inside, riding him hard. Forcing him deeper and deeper with every downward motion of her hips until she finally felt full. So full. Now she just needed some friction.

"Oh God, Melanie," he said. "You feel so good. So good."

He felt amazing inside her, but she was too worked up to form words. She murmured something and rode him faster and faster, trying to rub the ache away. More, more, more, she thought. Until the pleasure finally exploded and she called out in bliss. He lifted his hips off the seat to pump up into her, once, twice, and then groaned as he joined her in climax.

She went limp against him, trying to catch her breath and regain her senses, but both eluded her.

He rubbed his mouth against her temple. "You made me come way too fast, baby. I'll probably to need to fuck you like that a few more times this weekend," he said, "and then I might be able to keep it together long enough to make love to you slowly and thoroughly."

She smiled against his shoulder. "I don't mind the fucking," she said. "Really, I don't."

There was a knock on the window, and Melanie stiffened. Had she really gotten so wrapped up in this man that she'd forgotten they were in a limo parked outside a sub shop? That would be a yes. A yes, yes, oh God, fuck me, Gabe, *yes*.

Melanie lifted her hips, not quite ready for Gabe to fall free of her body, but she didn't have time to dawdle. Especially not when the locks *thunked* open and she heard the door handle lift upward. She tugged her skirt down her thighs and searched for her panties while Gabe shoved his cock down his pants, removed his glove of delight, and started buttoning his fly. Melanie had her panties in her hand when the back door popped open and Nikki appeared, with some guy holding four drinks for her while she held the sack of sandwiches.

She grinned knowingly at Melanie when her gaze landed on the panties in her hand.

"Oh, did I interrupt something?" she said. "I never thought you'd have her out of her panties that quickly, Gabe. You stud."

Melanie was slightly embarrassed that Nikki had caught her just after the act, but mortified that the good-looking man behind her was biting his full lower lip in appreciation of her sluttiness. Melanie tossed her panties on the seat beside Gabe and sat on them. She found her discarded glasses and fiddled with them, her hands trembling as she tried to get her glasses back on her face.

"It smells like sex in here," Nikki said as she leaned farther into the open door. "You guys already did it, didn't you? Or did I interrupt you mid-coitus?"

"*Nikki!*"

The girl needed to install a filter on that mouth of hers.

"Can't blame you for jumping him," Nikki said, giving Gabe the twice over. "Will you look at the size of those feet? You know what they say about guys with big feet."

Melanie's pussy clenched as her thoughts immediately fixated on that which correlated with Gabe's shoe size. And in his case, he fit the statistics.

"I have a really big, uh, foot," her drink-toting companion said in a deep voice. His brown eyes twinkled as he smiled, and his white teeth flashed bright against his dark-skinned complexion.

"I bet you do. This is Michael," Nikki said, tossing her head in the guy's direction. "He saw me struggling to carry my order and offered to help. Since my *friends* were otherwise occupied."

"We need to get going," Gabe said, tapping his nonexistent wristwatch. He had a reddened ring around his wrist from his glove device. Melanie hoped he hadn't injured himself just to get her off. She stroked his chafed skin, fighting the urge to kiss it all better. She was pretty sure he wouldn't appreciate the gesture in front of Nikki and her latest lackey.

Nikki climbed into the back of the limo and handed Gabe the bag of sandwiches. She then took the drink cups from

Michael one at a time. She passed one to Melanie, another to Gabe, and knocked on the driver's window so that Parker would lower the glass and she could hand one to him.

"Aren't you going to sit up here with me, Nik?" Parker asked.

"She's staying back here with me and Mel," Gabe said.

Gabe pulled sandwiches from the bag and determined which belonged to whom while Nikki gave her phone number to her very nice-looking drink caddy. Unfortunately, fast-food restaurants didn't hand those out through the drive-thru window. If they had, Melanie might be tempted to always order her beverages in fours.

"I gotta get me a limo," Michael said as his gaze flicked from Melanie to Nikki and back to Melanie. "Dude's got two hotties all to himself."

Nikki giggled and took her cup from Michael's hand. "You better call me," she said, and closed the door in his face.

"Did you give him your real number or your fake standby?" Mel asked.

"Real one." Nikki popped a straw into her drink and took a long draw. "He was a gentleman. They're not easy to find these days."

It didn't take much to impress Nikki, but she was right about the difficulty in finding a gentleman. Melanie wasn't sure if it was because men no longer wanted to protect and care for women or if women brought it upon themselves by insisting they were strong and independent. There had to be a middle ground somewhere.

Melanie removed the wrapper from her six-inch turkey club and scarfed down her sandwich. She hadn't realized how truly hungry she was until she started stuffing her face.

"I love a woman with an appetite," Gabe said, winking at her.

"Screw you, Banner," she said with her mouth full.

"Especially one with *that* particular appetite."

Nikki giggled. If she started flirting with Gabe, Melanie was going to throttle her. Nikki didn't require all the masculine attention for herself, did she? Couldn't she just let Melanie have this one without interference?

"Thanks for letting me hang out with you and Melanie back here," Nikki said. "I was starting to feel left out." She sighed happily. "I can't wait to see Shade again."

"About that..." Gabe said before pausing to glance at Melanie.

She had no idea what his questioning look meant, so she shrugged, and he turned back to Nikki.

"He's sort of seeing someone special right now. It's probably best that you keep your distance."

Oh, so that's why he'd been asking for her silent approval. Prepared for a meltdown, Melanie swiveled her attention to Nikki.

Eyes downcast, Nikki took a delicate bite of her veggie sub and shrugged. "You win some, you lose some," she said after a long tense moment.

Okay, who had stolen her best friend and replaced her with this docile facsimile?

"I can still hang out backstage with Melanie while you're onstage, right?" she asked, her blue eyes large and beguiling as she gazed at Gabe.

Oh, there she is. Holding her cards close to her chest.

"I guess so," Gabe said while Melanie tried not to cringe. It wasn't that she didn't want Nikki to be with her while she felt all awkward and alone watching the show from the wings, but she knew how this woman operated. She'd use every card in her hand to get what she wanted and she wanted Shade, whether Shade wanted her or not. Melanie would just have to keep Nikki away from the man if she could. It would be easy enough to keep them separate when Shade was onstage, but what about before the concert? And after?

"So what are we doing after the show?" Melanie asked as nonchalantly as possible. Gabe had already told her, but she wanted Nikki to hear.

"We're heading directly to an airstrip and taking a private plane back to Austin. We won't make it back to my place until really late." He stroked Melanie's back soothingly. "You can nap on the plane if you get tired. I won't be offended. In fact, I'll likely join you."

She took a sip of her drink, trying to form the most tactful version of her next question. "And Nikki..." was the best she came up with.

"Oh," he said, glancing at Nikki's hopeful face. "Well, uh…"

Yeah, awkward. Melanie was sorry she had to put him on the spot like this, but Nikki would figure out a way to weasel herself into all of Melanie's plans if she didn't have Gabe's backing. It wasn't because Melanie was spineless. Nikki was just that skilled at getting what she wanted.

"There's only room on the plane for five passengers," Gabe said.

"So Melanie can't fit on there with the band either," Nikki said.

"Well, Adam and Kellen aren't going back this trip."

Melanie's math brain cringed. It took Nikki a few seconds longer to do her adding and subtracting. "That leaves a spot for me."

"Sorry, but no. Lindsey's flying back with Owen," he said.

"Who's Lindsey?" Melanie asked. "His girlfriend?"

Gabe visibly paled. "Uh, fuck, I hope not."

"Who is she then?" Melanie pressed, wondering why Gabe seemed so flustered.

"Just some chick he's taking home with him."

"So, then, what am I supposed to do?" Nikki asked, that little lost puppy look on her face. Perhaps Melanie should encourage her to go into acting. Lord.

"You can spend the weekend in New Orleans," Gabe suggested. "I have a room at the hotel I won't be using until Sunday night. You're welcome to use it for free until Mel and I return."

Nikki ducked her head and stared at the sandwich in her lap.

"That sounds like fun," Melanie said brightly, hoping Nikki didn't mope for the rest of the night and wishing more than ever that she'd shoved Nikki out onto the tarmac back in Wichita. It would have saved them both some grief.

By the time they got to the venue, Nikki seemed to be okay with their plan to dump her in New Orleans for the weekend. By focusing on the positive (lush, free hotel room in the heart of New Orleans), Gabe was almost as skilled at manipulating Nikki's mood as Nikki was at bending men to her will. Melanie had to admit that she was both impressed and grateful that Gabe had handled Nikki so well.

Melanie did a lot of gawking when they got out of the limo. There were so many people lined up outside the arena's doors that the lines stretched out into the parking lots. There was a loud cheer as Gabe stepped from the vehicle. She guessed his mohawk made him instantly recognizable, even at a distance. He offered the folks waiting in line a friendly wave and instructed the driver to make sure Melanie's bag made it to the plane heading for Austin after the show and that Nikki's luggage was taken to his hotel room. Parker grinned at this. Either he thought that Gabe was banging both women separately, but equally, or he felt privileged to know where Nikki would be staying. Alone. For the entire weekend. Melanie gnawed on her lip, wondering if employing Parker to distribute their luggage had been the best idea. She didn't want the guy hanging around Nikki. She got a bad vibe from him.

Gabe's arm went around Melanie's lower back, and he held her securely against his side as they were ushered through barriers. After the third time Nikki got stopped for not having a backstage pass, Gabe wrapped his free arm around Nikki's waist as well, and he guided them both toward the doors.

Melanie understood why Gabe was touching Nikki in that easy, familiar way of his, but it didn't stop her from seething. He was hers, and she was not in the mood to share him. Not even a little. And especially not with her best friend.

CHAPTER SEVEN

GABE WASN'T SURE why Melanie was walking so stiffly beside him. Was she worried that someone would recognize her with him? Had she spotted a tattoo that freaked her out? Had he done something wrong? He was at a complete loss as to how he could have messed up between the limo and the building. He wracked his brain for things he might have said that she could have taken the wrong way. All he'd done was tell the driver what to do with her luggage. Why would that anger her? Maybe she didn't like him speaking on her behalf.

At the back entrance, a security guard let his small entourage enter the backstage area of the stadium. The guard offered Gabe a wink and Melanie and Nikki an appreciative grin as he checked them both out with interest and envy. Half an hour ago, Gabe would have said the dude was welcome to take Nikki off his hands, but God help him, he was starting to understand Melanie's proclivity for keeping the woman out of trouble. His own protective instinct was starting to show. He wasn't particularly fond of Nikki, but she seemed so, well... *helpless.* Something that Melanie was not, for which he was immensely thankful. Neediness quickly grated on his nerves. He knew some guys loved Nikki's type—Shade for example. His ex-wife was needy, so he must like something about it. But Gabe would rather have an equal at his side than a pretty puppet at his feet.

Melanie grew stiffer with each step. As soon as they could be alone, he'd ask her what was wrong, but this was not the place for a falling out. Strangers watched him very closely backstage. Halfway to the dressing rooms at the end of the hall, Melanie stopped abruptly, sending their trio into an angled trajectory toward a wall. Melanie jerked out of his grasp and stared up at him with sparks of anger snapping in her hazel eyes.

Okay, so he wasn't imagining things. She was pissed. Fuck him if he had any idea why.

"What's the matter?" he asked, deciding they were going to have to have it out after all, whether strangers were watching them or not.

She glared at his left hand, which was draped casually at Nikki's shoulder.

"Are you going to hang all over her for the rest of the evening?" Melanie asked bluntly.

"Hang all over her?" He wasn't hanging all over her. Much.

Nikki shrank from beneath his arm to stand beside Melanie, and he dropped the apparently offensive appendage to his side. He'd only wrapped his arm around her so that she could get through security with less of a hassle. And he told Melanie exactly that.

"I don't see any security here in the corridor," she said.

Nikki clutched at Melanie's sleeve. "I would have told him to stop touching me, Mel, but—"

Melanie slashed out a hand to stifle Nikki's words.

"You're jealous?" Gabe asked as the realization dawned on him. On closer inspection, Melanie was practically green. And he had the lack of sense to laugh at her misguided emotion.

"I'm not jealous," she sputtered, crossing her arms over her chest and turning her head to glare at the nearest wall.

"Good, because you have no reason to be. Next time, I'll leave her to her own methods of getting backstage." He moved a fist back and forth in front of his mouth while poking the inside of his cheek rhythmically with his tongue. Apparently, Melanie did not find his pantomimed blowjob humorous.

Her mouth dropped open and she glared up at him. "You wouldn't."

"Why wouldn't I?" He dropped his hand and shrugged. "I'm not interested in her. I'm interested in you. I only brought her along because you want her here."

The slight flutter of Melanie's eyelashes made it clear that she didn't really want Nikki there either, but she evidently saw reason in his words, and she dropped her crossed arms to her waist and then relaxed them at her sides.

Nikki gasped, drawing Gabe's attention. Her eyes were wide

as she stared at something or some*one* just behind Gabe. She shifted Melanie before her and did her best to hide, her forehead pressed against the back of Melanie's shoulder as she feigned invisibility.

"Did he see me?" Nikki whispered.

"Who?" Melanie said and then a look of recognition spread across her face. "Yeah, he looks pissed. I'd say he saw you."

"Why is she here?" Jacob said to Gabe in greeting.

"If Amanda can come to our shows, then so can Melanie," Gabe said, his ire rising so quickly it surprised him.

"Not Melanie. If you have a thing for her, of course, she's welcome." Jacob reached behind Melanie and yanked Nikki out by one arm. "Her! What is *she* doing here?"

Nikki straightened her spine and started hissing. Gabe wondered where the docile please-protect-me creature had wandered off to.

"What? Did you forget my name already, asshole?" Nikki spat, blue eyes narrowed, her fists clenched.

"No, darling Nikki, I didn't forget your name, but you can't be here. I don't want you here."

She bit her quivering lip, and Gabe was sure she was about to burst into tears.

"I invited her," he lied to Jacob. "I invited both of them, okay? It's none of your concern." He was definitely starting to remember why the band had made that no-women-on-tour pact. With women came drama. Being trapped with the same four dudes for six months was bad enough without the added roller-coaster ride of outside romantic relationships.

"So they'll double up on your dick, but not mine?" Jacob asked.

"You are the biggest pig I've ever met in my life!" Melanie bellowed at Jacob. "I don't know why anyone would do anything with you other than kick you in the nuts."

Gabe snorted. Jacob's faint smile had told Gabe that he was only teasing, but evidently Melanie hadn't gotten the joke.

Until that moment, Gabe had completely forgotten what had so quickly turned him on to Melanie in the first place—her complete disdain for Jacob "Shade" Silverton's typically irresistible sex appeal. Now that was hot.

"Can I talk to you?" Nikki asked Jacob. She seemed for once to be the most reasonable person in the vicinity.

"No," he said simply. "I have nothing to say to you. If I had, I would have called you."

Melanie gnashed her teeth and rounded on Jacob. Gabe would have probably cowered at the look on her face if she'd turned it on him, but Jacob, being Jacob, was used to women berating him. In this particular instance, he deserved it, but that wasn't always the case.

"You have no problem fucking her in a public hallway—"

"Or a sauna," Nikki added helpfully.

"Or a sauna," Melanie echoed several decibels louder than her friend, "but you don't have the common decency to carry on a polite conversation with her?"

"That about sums it up," Jacob said. He turned on his heel and stalked off.

Melanie screeched in fury and started after him—no doubt to have it out on his nuts—but Gabe stopped her with a firm arm around her shoulders. He drew her against his chest, stiffening slightly when her elbow gouged him in the side in her struggle to throw him off.

"Easy," he said. "You'll only hurt your toe."

She jerked out of his embrace and glared up at him, redirecting some of her anger. At him.

"What are you talking about?"

"When you kick Shade in the balls," he said. "You'll just hurt your toe. They're made of steel, you know."

Her jaw dropped. She blinked at him, closing her mouth with a snap, and then snorted before breaking into laughter.

"She got a bit wound up there," Nikki said as Melanie tried to calm herself with deep, gasps for air between laughs. "She always cracks up after an explosion."

Yeah, he'd gotten that from earlier.

"Oh, Gabe," Melanie said, wiping a tear from the corner of her eye. "You do have my best interests at heart, don't you?"

He grinned. "Well, of course. And Nikki's too." His lifted both hands in surrender. "But not because I want to get in her pants or anything."

"Why don't you?" Nikki asked, her head cocked to one side

as she studied him closely. "They're great pants to get into."

Ask anyone, he added silently.

"Because," he said, "I have a thing for your smart, charming, and beautiful friend. The one who *isn't* attracted to Shade Silverton."

"I'd say it's because she has bad taste," Nikki said, her gaze skimming over his body with obvious interest, "but she likes *you*, so she must not be totally lacking in that department."

"Thanks," Gabe said, rubbing Melanie's smooth back, which was still jerking intermittently with her giggles. "I think."

Melanie finally quieted and wrapped her arms around his waist to relax against him. Nikki's presence seemed to take a lot out of her, and he completely understood why. The woman seemed to draw drama the way stink draws flies. Gabe shifted Melanie closer to the wall so that they were out of the flow of intermittent traffic using the hallway to prepare for the concert. She felt perfect tucked against him. He rested his cheek on her soft hair and closed his eyes, giving himself a moment to experience the feel of her in his arms. This is how he'd prefer to spend their time together. Just like this. Close. Not dealing with other people's problems and insecurities. He was sure if Nikki hadn't tagged along, they'd be spending the entire evening just like this. Except maybe they'd be a little more naked. Thinking of Melanie naked had his hands roaming her back, slipping under the hem of her blouse to seek bare flesh. How was he going to make it another several hours without feeling the press of her warm skin against his? Maybe he should call in sick. Would anyone notice if the drummer didn't show up for the concert?

"I'm sorry I got jealous," Melanie said. She drew away and stood on tiptoe to kiss his jaw. She held his gaze, so he knew she was sincere. "But I'm not sorry I want to kick Shade in the balls."

Gabe chuckled. He had a million things to say about why Jacob had acted that way toward Nikki, but because the woman in question was standing right there examining her fingernails with obvious boredom, he decided to keep those thoughts to himself until he and Melanie were alone. And even then he'd have to guard what he said about women with pussies more hot and ready than a Little Caesars' pizza. He didn't want Melanie to get mad at him for inadvertently insulting her friend, so he'd watch what he said about her. He only hoped Melanie could get comfortable after they ditched Nikki. He'd just have to suck it up until then.

When the three of them entered the band's dressing room, Gabe noticed Jacob talking to their tour manager, Sally. Sally was a black-haired bombshell with big breasts that she liked to show off in skintight, low-cut shirts. Talking to her was distracting—you just had to gawk at her boobs. It couldn't be helped. Man, woman, child, or monk, you had to stare at them, wondering if they were real and if your hand was big enough to hold one properly. Jacob was no exception. It didn't matter that he was happily involved with Amanda or that Sally was happily married to one of their road crew—Kris, a giant, weathered biker with a huge heart—it was impossible not to stare at Sally's endowments. Gabe had fallen into the same trap many times himself. So when Nikki saw Jacob paying undo attention to another woman's chest and bristled, Gabe didn't see any reason to correct her false assumption that Shade was not interested in her tonight because he already hooking up with Sally. Nikki would probably understand that arrangement. It might even cause her to keep her distance.

Or it might make her storm across the room, shove Sally in the shoulder, and jerk on Jacob's arm. *Seriously?*

Fuck.

"Control your friend, Mel," Gabe said exasperatedly.

Melanie rubbed the center of her forehead with two fingers. "I think we're going to have to go to the hotel after all," she said. "This isn't a good environment for Nikki in her present state of mind."

Nikki had varying states of mind? Since when?

Gabe watched Melanie cross the room to interfere with the three-person shoving match going on in the corner. He wondered why watching her walk away had his heart panging unpleasantly in his chest. It was obvious who was more important to Melanie. He knew that she had known Nikki for a lot longer than she'd known him, but that didn't make the realization that Nikki was her top priority any easier to take.

Realizing *he* wanted to be Melanie's top priority wasn't easy to take either. He wanted to be the only thing on her mind tonight. The entire weekend. As long as she'd have him. *Seriously?*

"Fuck," he said.

CHAPTER EIGHT

MELANIE WAS DONE. Done running interference. Done preventing catastrophe. Done picking up the pieces. Done.

She grabbed Nikki by the arm and without a word dragged her toward the exit. They were out of the dressing room and halfway down the hall before she stopped and turned to confront her friend. *Friend?* More like soul-sucking leech.

"*You* are going to the hotel right now," Melanie said, providing no opportunity for argument. "*I* am going to the concert by myself and *I* am going to Gabe's house in Austin tonight without you. Do you understand? You are not going to weasel your way into accompanying us."

Nikki opened her mouth to protest, and Melanie lifted a finger of warning at her.

"I'm sorry it has to be this way," she said, "but sometimes I have to think about myself. There is no reason for you to be here. You saw Shade. He doesn't want to see you. You knew he wouldn't, but you came anyway. And right now, I don't want to see you either."

Nikki released a pained gasp and Melanie had to force herself not to look away. She didn't like to hurt people and she'd just shredded Nikki's heart. Melanie could see the devastation in every tense line of Nikki's face.

"If you'd rather go straight home, you do that. Figure out how to solve this problem you created, Nikki. I'm not giving up my shot at happiness because you need someone to take care of you. *You* need to take care of you. Got it?"

Nikki's eyes pooled with tears and Melanie softened her tone—partly because she couldn't stand the look of anguish on Nikki's face and partially because her throat had tightened with emotion to the point of strangulation.

"I can be your friend," Melanie said. "I *want* to be your

friend. But I can't be your knight in shining armor. I have my own ass to rescue."

Tears began to flow freely down Nikki's cheeks and yeah, Melanie's vision blurred as her own tears threatened to overflow. She wasn't good at doling out tough love. It wasn't her thing. Tough love was so much harder than enabling, but she had to do this for Nikki's good as well as for her own sanity. Nikki wouldn't see it as beneficial. She'd see it as Melanie being mean to her. And yelling at Nikki made Melanie *feel* mean. She felt like a horrible person for hurting someone who had been hurt so many times already—broken, used, and abused by those she should have been able to trust—but Melanie couldn't back down on this. Not even if it elevated her to megabitch status.

Heart thudding and eyes stinging with the threat of tears, Melanie pivoted and started back toward the dressing room. *Don't look back. Don't let her see you're about to crumble.* Melanie hadn't taken three steps when a body careened into her and a pair of arms tightened around her waist.

"You can't leave me, Mel," Nikki sobbed against the back of Melanie's shoulder. "You just can't. I have no one in this world but you. I have no one. No one."

This was not another case of Nikki's fabricated drama. Nikki actually believed it, because it happened to be true. Melanie closed her eyes, trying to stop the tears from falling, but a fat droplet crept out from beneath each eyelid and streaked down her face.

"I'm not leaving you, Nikki. I'm leaving this situation you created." And the guilt was already robbing her of breath. She knew Nikki didn't have anyone. Melanie wanted her to be surrounded by caring people. She wanted Nikki to find more friends and a boyfriend who cared about her. She wished Nikki had a family that wasn't completely dysfunctional and abusive. But if Nikki's neediness was trying on their strong friendship, it was devastating to new ones. Nikki tried too hard to make people love her and went about it all wrong. She slept around because for the few hours she was with a man, *beneath* a man, she could pretend that he loved her. But no one could really love her until she loved herself. And Melanie knew how Nikki struggled to see her true self-worth after everything she'd been through.

God, I'm such a selfish cow. How could she have yelled at Nikki when she knew how much her disapproval would hurt her?

She was also a spineless coward, it seemed, because she was totally going to cave again. She could feel her resolve crumbling already. Melanie turned in Nikki's arms and held her while she cried. Tough love was one thing. Leaving your best friend sobbing in a corridor in an unfamiliar city was another.

"Pull yourself together," Melanie said gently. "It's going to be all right. You want me to be happy, don't you?"

Nikki nodded.

"Then give me this weekend with Gabe. Can you do that?"

Nikki hesitated and then nodded slowly, her tears still falling. At least she wasn't sobbing and wailing any longer.

"Do you want to go back to the hotel or do you want to fly home to Wichita tonight?" Melanie realized she was treating Nikki like a toddler again, giving her two solid options and not an open-ended *what do you want to do?*

"I'll stay at the hotel."

"Are you sure?"

Nikki nodded again. "And can we do something together when you get back on Sunday, Mel?"

"Yeah. Of course."

"Just the two of us?"

"After Gabe leaves." She wasn't going to make promises she was unwilling to keep.

Nikki sniffed. "I'll stay here." She took a deep, gasping breath. "Alone."

"I'll get you as far as the hotel and then you're on your own for the weekend. You can handle that, right?"

Enabler, enabler, enabler, a nasty little voice seemed to whisper in her ear.

"I think so," Nikki said, sniffing again.

"I know you can."

Melanie pulled away slightly and waited while Nikki wiped her wet face on the hem of her T-shirt. Several curious men watched them, obviously wanting to comfort poor beautiful Nikki. Poor fragile, broken sex kitten Nikki. But the comfort those men had in mind was the last thing Nikki needed.

"Let's go call you a cab," she said. "Or maybe Gabe will let you ride in the limo."

"Do I have to ride up front with Parker the penguin?"

Melanie laughed. "No, hon." She cupped Nikki's streaked cheek in one palm. "You ride in the back and drink champagne."

"But I don't like champagne."

Melanie smiled and kissed the tip of Nikki's nose. "Drink it anyway. Wait here," she said. "I'm going to go talk to Gabe about the limo. Okay?"

Nikki nodded and the instant that Melanie stepped away, two guys tripped over each other trying to get to Nikki's side, as if the first to touch her could claim her as a prize.

Melanie found Gabe slumped forward in a chair, his elbows resting on his knees and a bottle of beer between his palms. He was staring at the spot between his impressively large feet with a scowl on his handsome face. The high forehead, square jaw, and long straight nose would have looked good on anyone. His lower lip was slightly larger than the upper and just begged to nibbled on. Every visible inch of the man was long, lean, and hard. Masculine. Lord, he was gorgeous. And he was even better looking when he smiled; his perfect grin lit up his mesmerizing grass-green eyes from the inside. Melanie intended to put that smile back on his tasty lips as soon as possible and keep it there. She hated the glum expression he was currently sporting, especially since she knew she was responsible for it. It didn't suit him. Or her.

She squeezed onto his chair, resting on one hip until he scooted over to give her more room. He gaped at her as if stunned to see her. He didn't really think she was going to give up her weekend with him to coddle Nikki, did he?

"I need your help," she said.

"With?"

"Nikki."

"I don't know any hit men, but Adam might. He runs in some rough circles."

"Not to *kill* her," Melanie said. "To get her to the hotel. Can she ride in the limo?"

"The rest of the band should be coming here from the hotel now," he said. "She can ride back after the show."

Melanie crinkled her nose and shook her head. That was not

what she had in mind at all. "She's leaving now."

"And you are…"

"Staying here with you. But that's why I need your help. I can already feel myself slipping up with my intentions to stay strong, just to make her happy. I need you to do my dirty work for me and make sure she gets to the hotel because if I see her looking all depressed and crying, I'm going to cave in to her wishes again and she's going to end up sleeping between us and hogging the covers all weekend."

His brow furrowed with confusion. "You want me to ride with her?"

"No, baby," she said. "I want you to play your rock star card and get someone to do it for you."

"Oh." He grinned, and she melted beneath the warmth of his smile. "Now that, I can do."

"Well, hurry up about it. My lips are lonely."

He gave her a sample of the company his lips could provide hers, climbed from the beige club chair, and handed her his beer. "I'll be right back."

She shifted into a more comfortable spot in the chair and took a swig off his beer. "Maybe there *are* still some knights in shining armor left in the world," she said, and tipped the neck of the bottle toward him in a silent toast to his heroics.

While waiting for Gabe to return—she owed him big time for handling Nikki for her—Melanie scanned the room, feeling as out of place as she had the first time she'd been backstage with the band. She couldn't help but notice people were staring at her with curiosity. Was it because she had just bossed Gabe around or because her attire was unlike anything else in the room? She really liked Gabe, but this scene was a rude reminder that they came from entirely different worlds. She didn't fit in his reality and he didn't fit in hers. So why did she feel that they fit together so well? Maybe she should try a little harder to blend in with his crowd. She lifted the beer bottle to her lips and took another swig. It was going to take a lot more than half a beer to help her with that.

As Shade gave his big-boobed companion a parting hug, his gaze landed on Melanie over the woman's shoulder. He was wearing the sunglasses that had obviously been welded to his face at birth, but Melanie could feel his eyes on her, his gaze was that intense. It took an actual effort to turn her head and not stare at him. She couldn't stand the guy. Or, more specifically, she couldn't stand the way he treated women, Nikki in particular. But she also couldn't deny that there was something mesmerizing about him.

Out of the corner of her eye, she could see him crossing the room in her direction. The man didn't walk, he prowled. And that pissed her off for some reason. Melanie's body stiffened involuntarily and she reminded herself to be civil to him if he approached her. If she wanted to be with Gabe—and she very much wanted to be with Gabe—she was going to have to learn to tolerate this man. She didn't have to like him though.

Shade perched himself on the arm of her chair, and she glanced up, as if surprised to see him.

"I get the feeling that you don't like me much," he said.

"I wouldn't say that," she said, turning toward the door in hopes of spotting a tall, lean drummer with a red and black mohawk headed in her direction.

No such luck.

"Okay, then I get the feeling that you don't like me *at all*," he said.

She stared up at him thinking he was incredibly perceptive, and he did something that completely threw her off guard. He removed his sunglasses and hung them from the neckband of his T-shirt. He had the bluest eyes she'd ever seen. Not a pale blue but a startling cerulean, with dark rims around the irises that made the color appear even more astonishingly bright. Why in the world would anyone hide those gorgeous eyes behind sunglasses?

"I get why you're defensive of your friend," he said, "but I spent a lot of time in her company last weekend and I learned quite a bit about her. She's a manipulator."

Nikki wasn't a manipulator. Melanie opened her mouth to defend her, but then snapped it closed. Okay, she was, but Shade had no right to talk bad about her. He had slept with her—um, *had sex with her*—several times and hadn't even bothered to call her the next day. Assholes had no right to judge anyone. Especially not people Melanie cared about.

Shade lifted a hand to stop her from interrupting, and she could see the concern in his pretty blue eyes. What exactly did he have to be concerned about?

"It probably pisses you off to hear it from me."

"Yeah," she spat.

"But you know it's true."

"She's just misunderstood."

He grinned crookedly. "How did she manipulate you into believing that?"

Melanie glared at him. She didn't care if he had beautiful expressive eyes or that she almost thought of him as a human being when he didn't wear the sunglasses that hid them—she was not going to sit there and let him bad-mouth Nikki when Nikki wasn't present to defend herself.

"I've known Nikki for a long time," Melanie said. "I obviously know her better than you do."

"I don't deny that. That's probably why you don't see what she's doing to you."

"I know exactly what she's doing to me," Melanie admitted, but she sure didn't want Shade to know that she was a slave to Nikki's crazy whims. Unfortunately there was no way around it, because he'd find out as soon as Gabe returned. "That's why I asked *Gabe* to kick her the fuck out of the stadium, because I knew she'd manipulate me into letting her stay."

Shade's eyes widened, and then he burst into raucous laughter.

"What are you laughing about?"

"You surprise the hell out of me, little woman," he said.

She hadn't thought that the man could possibly raise her ire any higher, but apparently she'd underestimated his talent for pissing her off. "*Little* woman?"

"Big woman?"

"*Big woman!*"

"I'll just shut up now. I came to offer a truce, and it seems I set off a couple of loose cannons instead. Maybe one day we'll get off on the right foot."

"I doubt it." She polished off the last swallow of Gabe's beer.

"If you weren't dating the man I respect more than any other, I'd kiss the sass right out of you."

"And it would earn you a fat lip."

He chuckled. "I'm sure it would be worth it."

Her eyes narrowed. "If you really respected Gabe, you wouldn't speak to me with such disrespect."

"I didn't mean to be disrespectful. Usually when a beautiful woman talks to me the way you do, it's to get my attention so I'll fuck her senseless. But I think you genuinely hate my guts. I'm not sure how to handle you."

He was not helping his cause here. "You don't need to handle me. You don't even need to talk to me. What you need to do is apologize to Nikki, but I doubt you have the class."

A commotion at the entrance announced the arrival of the rest of the band and a few women Melanie didn't recognize. She did spot a familiar mohawk above the crowd that was headed in her direction, however. When Gabe appeared at Shade's shoulder, the exasperating vocalist looked glad to see him.

"Does she bust *your* balls like this?" Shade asked.

"She's more likely to lick them than bust them, but I'm not as stupid as you are."

Melanie saw the flash of hurt cross Shade's face before he snatched his sunglasses from his neckband and crammed them back onto his face. "Yeah, well, we can't all be fucking geniuses." He was gone before Gabe could catch his arm.

"I didn't mean it that way," Gabe called after him.

Shade lifted his hand over his head and directed a pronounced middle finger in his direction.

Gabe sighed and took his beer bottle from Melanie's hand, pressing it to his lips and tipping his head back and back until he realized it was empty. He shook the bottle at her, a brow arched in question.

"Sorry," she said. "I was thirsty." She rose from the chair. "I'll get you another."

"Are you tired of me playing my rock star card already?" he asked. "Jordan!"

He extended his arm, holding the empty bottle out and waited and waited and waited some more. Melanie drew her lips further and further into her mouth with each passing moment to prevent herself from laughing. Eventually Gabe turned toward the bar and sighed at the young man talking to a very pretty and very *pregnant* woman.

"Jordan!" Gabe called again.

The young man started and cringed when he looked in Gabe's direction. He was soon on his way across the room with a fresh Corona and an apology.

"Sorry about that. Did you want anything?" he asked Melanie as he took Gabe's empty and handed him a replacement.

"I'll just drink Gabe's," she said.

"Not if I finish it before you get the chance," Gabe said. He caught Jordan by the shirt when he started to hurry off again. "Bit of advice, Jordan."

"Huh?"

"Don't encourage the gold-digger." He nodded slightly toward the pregnant woman who now had the band's bassist by the arm. Owen looked like he was prepared to lop off the appendage just to escape her.

"She's sweet," Jordan assured him. "And pretty."

"And pregnant."

Jordan shrugged. "So?"

"And looking for someone to take care of her."

"Not really. She's just down on her luck. Sorta like me. I don't have any gold for her to dig. So no worries, right?"

Gabe grunted and when the pregnant girl's gaze landed on him, he released Jordan's shirt and immediately grabbed Melanie out of her chair. He gave her an enthusiastic hug, his beer bottle pressing against her lower back. She could feel the cold wetness through her shirt.

The pregnant woman scowled at Gabe, but offered Jordan a bright smile as he returned to his station.

"Not that I mind you hugging me," Melanie said, "but I have to think you have ulterior motives here. Who's the pregnant woman?"

"Lindsey."

"Oh, so that's Owen's girlfriend?"

"No. Owen's gold-digger."

"She doesn't look like a gold-digger," Melanie said.

Lindsey was wearing cheap clothing and no make-up. She did look a bit desperate as she clung to Owen's arm. Jordan chatted with her exuberantly while he mixed her some beverage—

presumably non-alcoholic in nature. His attempts to regain her attention were mostly unsuccessful as Lindsey tried to keep Owen from darting away.

"She showed up a couple of days ago and decided to stay," Gabe said. "Even though no one wants her here."

"Well, I think Jordan likes her," Melanie said. "Is it his baby, then?"

Gabe shook his head. "He's the only guy in the room who couldn't be the father."

Melanie puzzled over that statement for a full minute. "The *only* guy in the room?"

Gabe scanned the room, taking in the four members of his band and even stopping on a guy in a cowboy hat who Melanie thought was the bus driver she'd met briefly in Tulsa. Gabe nodded. "Yep."

But Gabe was in the room. Surely he meant to exclude himself?

"Yourself included?" she asked.

He took a long swallow off his beer. "I should introduce you to Madison and uh, what's her name? Kellen's date, uh... *Dawn.*"

Melanie took note of the two very, very different women, puzzled by why Gabe had ignored her question. She hoped it was because she had nothing to worry about, not because he was avoiding a difficult subject.

The woman with Kellen was tall and elegant, with long and beautiful red hair. An authoritative air of greatness surrounded her as if she were a modern-day equivalent of a powerful queen. She looked more like an Elizabeth or a Victoria or a Cleopatra than a Dawn. Kellen was a couple of inches taller than her and as dark as Dawn was fair. But they fit somehow.

The other woman wore cowboy boots with her jean skirt and was, in a word, adorable. The kind of cute that made Melanie want to hug her for no apparent reason. Madison's long, wavy hair was drawn away from her face in a ponytail, and her gaze darted around the room nervously until she settled on Adam. Then her light-colored eyes went dreamy. It was blatantly obvious that she was head over heels for the band's lead guitarist.

Madison looked wholesome and completely out of place at

Adam Taylor's side. Their looks should have clashed, but the contrast between them actually worked. Adam's spiky, jet black hair, all-black attire, tattoos, and copious chains declared him to be one-hundred-percent-genuine bad-boy-rock-star, while Madison looked like a sweet country girl, far out of her element. One had to wonder how the two of them had ever crossed paths.

Melanie supposed she and Gabe looked a bit mismatched as well. Gabe sported a foot-high red and black mohawk and had dragons tattooed on his frickin' scalp. She'd always stayed far from men with tattoos, and Gabe wasn't the kind of guy she'd normally hang out with in her insular little world. What a huge mistake it had been to limit herself to a certain type of acquaintance. Gabe had shown her how wrong she'd been to judge a person's character according to their looks or lifestyle. He was human, just as she was. It wasn't easy to let go of her old ways, but she was already leading a richer life now that she'd opened herself up to the big wide world outside her tidy little cubicle. She wished she'd have pulled her head of her ass years ago, but she'd been raised to fear a person's differences rather than celebrate them. *Thanks for all the unnecessary anxiety, Mom and Dad.*

"Okay," she said. "I'd love to meet them, but sooner or later you're going to have to tell me what you meant about Lindsey."

"I vote for later," he said. "Or never. Never is good."

"Did you sleep with her?" Melanie asked in a low hiss as he directed her across the room to where Madison and Adam were sitting together in contented silence.

"I don't remember," he said.

"How can you not remember something like that?"

"I was drunk." He then immediately leaned close and said, "So Adam and Madison have been seeing each other for a couple of years, but their relationship just recently turned into something serious. He kind of keeps her to himself, like he's afraid she'll wander off, so it will be good for her to have someone to talk to. She always looks a little lost to me."

Madison did look a little lost. And obviously infatuated with the man who appeared equally smitten with her. They weren't talking, but a current linked them, a bond that went deeper than what was visible on the surface. Melanie got the feeling that they'd been through a lot together. Not that she would pry. As for Gabe's potential drunken sex with Lindsey? She would pry the hell out of that once she got him alone.

"Hey," Adam said when they were close enough to gain his attention. "You're the chick from breakfast," he said to Melanie.

Melanie chuckled. "So good of you to remember."

"You know her?" Madison asked, and there was no question that this news unsettled her.

"She's with Gabe," Adam said, flicking a hand in Gabe's direction.

Madison nodded slightly and shifted closer to Adam, so that their arms touched. Insecurity was shining off the woman like a beacon. "What's her name?" she asked.

"Hell if I remember," Adam said. "I just remember sitting next to her at breakfast."

"Adam was too busy thinking about you to even ask my name," Melanie said. She had no idea if what she said was true, but felt the explanation was something the woman needed to hear. Melanie wasn't insecure about Gabe's affections, but she was definitely the jealous sort, so she understood how hard it was to trust one of these rock star sorts with your heart. Especially when they tried to play down the existence of an unclaimed, unborn child. She slanted a look at Gabe. He didn't really think she was going to let that rest, did he?

"I'm Melanie," she said, introducing herself rather than giving Gabe the third degree in front of the couple.

"Madison," the other woman said and smiled warmly.

"So you've known these guys a lot longer than I have. Any deep dark secrets I should know about?" Melanie asked. Such as who that Lindsey woman was.

Madison chuckled. "I might have a few stories to tell."

"Whoa!" Gabe said, covering Melanie's ears with both hands. "Great to see you again, Madison. Be sure to keep Adam out of trouble."

Melanie caught Gabe's wink at Madison before he turned Melanie in the opposite direction and escorted her toward Dawn. Maybe the svelte redhead knew some secrets about the guys she could share.

It turned out that Dawn knew even less about the band than Melanie did. It was hard to believe that she'd been with Kellen a mere day. They shared a comfort level unusual for two people who'd had such a short acquaintance. Dawn might not have any juicy gossip to share about the guys, but she was fascinating. Melanie was honored to meet the Grammy-award-winning classical composer. She was a bit intimidated, to be honest, but it was cute the way that Kellen bragged about her and then Dawn tried to play down her talents.

"Will you stop?" Dawn said to him, though she was smiling broadly and stood plastered to his side.

"And you should hear the song she composed last night," Kellen added.

"Maybe I'll write another tonight," she said. A look passed between the couple that nearly set Melanie's eyebrows ablaze. Apparently Gabe wasn't the only member of the band who knew his way around the female anatomy.

Gabe cleared his throat. "Would you two like to be alone?"

Kellen started. "Gabe!" he said, smiling widely, and pounded Gabe on the back as if he hadn't seen him in years. "When did you get here?"

"I was here before you arrived."

"Didn't notice," he said.

"With Dawn beside you, I doubt you'd notice if the room was on fire," Gabe teased.

"She does demand attention."

Dawn went pink.

"So you somehow talked Melanie into joining us for the evening," Kellen said, leveling his deep, dark eyes on Melanie. When this man centered his attention on her, she definitely noticed. Her knees wobbled unsteadily. She wasn't sure how Dawn was still standing after being subjected to Kellen's attention all day.

"He didn't have to twist my arm too hard," Melanie said with a laugh.

"I was surprised your friend left in the limo without you," Kellen said. "What was her name?"

"Nikki."

"She didn't seem too happy for someone getting a free ride

in a limo."

Melanie's heart thudded unpleasantly. "Was she crying?"

When three pairs of eyes lowered to gaze at the floor, she wished she hadn't asked.

"She'll get it over it," she said. She hoped sooner rather than later.

"Don't beat yourself up over it, Mel," Gabe said. "She didn't start crying until I told her, rather bluntly, that I would not pressure you into having a threesome with her."

Melanie blinked in disbelief. "She didn't?"

Gabe and Kellen both nodded. So apparently Nikki had been causing a big enough scene that bystanders had caught on to her ploy.

"I honestly don't know what to do about her," Melanie said. She rubbed at her forehead, hoping that would ease the tension gathered there.

"Why do you think she's your responsibility anyway?" Gabe asked.

"Because she doesn't have anyone else."

"Maybe there's a reason for that."

Melanie's jaw dropped. Had that really just come out of Gabe's mouth?

CHAPTER NINE

"THAT'S A REALLY mean thing to say," Melanie said, unable to believe that he could be so cruel.

"You're right," Gabe said, "that was uncalled for. I apologize. I don't want to see her get hurt, but I care about *you,* and the relationship you have with Nikki is obviously stressing you out."

Melanie laughed sardonically. "It's that obvious, is it? She's not so bad when it's just the two of us." That wasn't entirely true. Nikki was always needy, but she wasn't always outlandish. She just needed lots of cuddles. And validation. And cash.

"Good friends are hard to find," Dawn said. "But those who claim to love you shouldn't take advantage of your loyalty, they should cherish it."

Kellen shifted uncomfortably, and Melanie couldn't even begin to guess why Dawn's words of wisdom unsettled him.

A sudden flurry of activity near the dressing room door drew Melanie's attention. The door was propped open and the smell of spice and seafood accompanied several staff members dressed in white aprons. Tables were set up and a buffet was quickly laid out along one wall.

"Dinner?" Melanie asked.

"They do feed us occasionally," Gabe said.

"Why didn't you say something? We wouldn't have had to stop for sandwiches."

He leaned close to her ear. "And you wouldn't have had time to try out my glove."

She bit her lip to hold in a laugh. "Good call."

"Hope you like it hot."

"You should already know that I do."

"I mean Cajun food. Jacob ordered it, and he likes it spicy."

It took Melanie a moment to remember that *Jacob* was Shade's real name. "I've never had authentic Cajun food."

"You're in for a treat then."

When Gabe said hot, he really meant "destroy the lining of your digestive system" spicy. The gumbo and jambalaya were delicious. Well, what she could taste of them. She was certain her tongue, her throat, and her stomach were on fire. She refused to try the crawdads, however. She couldn't bring herself to eat something that still had legs and antennae. And eyestalks.

After dinner the band was escorted out of the room for a meet and greet with a group of VIP fans. Melanie used the time to chat with Madison, who actually had a functioning brain when Adam wasn't plastered to her side. Madison always had one eye on the door, though, eager for her lover's return. Melanie completely understood the desire to be alone with someone she didn't get to see often. Dawn excused herself to call her agent or something. Melanie wasn't sure where Lindsey had gone, but she had to ask someone about her, so she settled for the only person in the room not wearing a "Staff" shirt.

"So what's the story with Lindsey?" she asked.

Madison shrugged. "I don't know. Apparently she got knocked up by Owen, and she didn't have anywhere else to go. They're not a couple or anything."

"So Owen is the father? Gabe sounded unsure."

"As far as I know," Madison said. "She hangs all over him, so I just assumed… Why? Did you hear differently?"

Melanie shook her head, deciding she must have misunderstood what Gabe had meant earlier. She felt bad for Owen, but she felt even worse for Lindsey. She couldn't name a single man whose life had been completely turned upside down by the birth of an illegitimate child, but she knew of dozens of women who had to figure out how to raise a kid on their own while some deadbeat lived it up without a care in the world. She hoped Owen wasn't like that. He seemed like a nice guy, but he obviously wasn't interested in the baby's mother. She supposed the more important question was how did he feel about the child?

When the guys returned—in high spirits after being thoroughly worshipped by the VIPs—it was time to head for the backstage area and start connecting the musicians to their equipment. Gabe's hook-up consisted of being handed a set of drumsticks and having a feed put in one ear. He spent the rest of his time backstage with Melanie in his arms, just holding her against him. He seemed to need the peace of rocking silently with her, and she didn't mind being plastered against his chest one bit. In fact, she groaned in disappointment when he had to release her to take the stage. She supposed she could share him with the 15,000 people in the audience for one hour, just as long as she got him all to herself for the next seventy-two.

"Enjoy the show," he said and pecked her on the lips.

The stage was dark when Gabe climbed behind his drum kit and Owen started the low bass line of the first song.

Melanie had forgotten how loud rock concerts could be. When the rest of the band entered the song, she forced herself not to cover her ears with both hands. Standing in the wings of the stage to watch the concert was a privilege—she didn't want to look like an inconsiderate idiot.

Beside her, Madison was gazing at Adam in worshipful awe. The man could play a guitar, but somehow Melanie doubted that was what had his woman in danger of spontaneous combustion. On her opposite side stood Dawn, who wasn't reacting to the music the way an average spectator would. She seemed to be concentrating on every note, as if dissecting the songs into pieces and mentally reconstructing the arrangement. Melanie couldn't tell if the classical composer was impressed or underwhelmed by the metal band's compositions, but she looked interested. Not only in the music, but also in the stage antics of Kellen and Owen, who fed off each other constantly.

Melanie shifted so she could better see Gabe. It was no wonder she hadn't recognized him as the drummer of the band the first time she'd met him. His drum kit was a behemoth of an instrument. She occasionally glimpsed the blur of his hand or a smidge of crimson red mohawk, but he was mostly invisible from this angle. His sound, however, dominated the stadium. Instead of watching the show as everyone else was doing, Melanie became determined to see more of Gabe. She got a strange thrill of excitement every time an inch of him graced her view.

After the first song ended in a flurry of wailing guitars and rapid drum beats, Gabe shifted to reach for a bottle of water sitting near the edge of his drum set. Excitement raced through Melanie's body. It really was him back there pounding away on the skins. He chugged from the bottle and when he set it back down, he caught her watching him. He grinned and beckoned her closer with two fingers.

Melanie glanced at the main stage uncertainly. The band was waiting for Shade to stop talking to the audience so they could begin the next song. What could Gabe possibly want with her at that particular moment? Her curiosity got the better of her and she carefully made her way around the stage wing, avoiding equipment and wires on her way to the small open area just behind Gabe's left elbow.

"What?" she whispered loudly.

"I just wanted you closer," he said. He pulled something out of his pocket and stretched out his closed fist in her direction. A bit leery, she extended her open palm in his direction and he dropped two small rubbery things in her hand. She stared down at the bright yellow things in wonder.

"Are these for my nipples?" she asked, flushing at the thought of trying out one of his inventions here on stage. It was true that no one would probably see her back here, but she wasn't sure if she was bold enough to give them a try in public.

Gabe snorted with laughter. "They're earplugs, baby. To protect your hearing."

Melanie's face flamed. "Oh."

And before she could thank him, he tapped an upbeat tempo on a cymbal and continued with a rapid progression around his drum kit, both feet stomping the pedals of two bass drums. Melanie crammed the earplugs in her ears and watched him work, astonished by his skill and speed. Though it no longer hurt her ears, she could still hear the music of the entire band, and she could see the audience beyond the stage, but as far as she was concerned, she was privy to an amazing drum solo played just for her.

Gabe was completely entrenched in his music. His face was a mask of deliberation and something that bordered on rapture. She'd seen that look on his face before. He wore it in the moments he was focused on giving her pleasure, just before he lost himself to his own bliss and let go of concentration in favor of instinct. She was pretty sure she was not supposed to get sexually aroused while watching a man thump a punishing rhythm on a set of drums, but apparently her libido had gone into drummer-groupie mode. Her attention focused on the flex of his biceps, the drops of sweat that trickled down his neck, the expansion of his chest as he drew air into his laboring lungs, and the nod of his head as he lost himself in the cadence. For the first time in Melanie's life, she understood why so many women lusted after musicians. She was certainly lusting after hers.

When the song ended, Gabe wiped the sweat from his face with the hem of his T-shirt.

Slightly winded, he smiled at her. She grinned like a fool, only with determination keeping herself from launching onto his lap. He was working, and it would be very bad form to interrupt him in the middle of his job. It was hard to believe he got paid—and paid well—to do something he so obviously loved. She wished she could say the same thing about her accounting job. It paid the bills and she was good at it, but it didn't make her lose herself. She'd never had that absorbed, rapturous look on her face when she was at work. Not unless she was in the bathroom interacting with Gabe on her phone.

Did he realize how lucky he was to do what he did for a living? But then Gabe was the type of guy who would immerse himself in anything he loved. She imagined he had that same look of enraptured concentration on his face when he was tinkering with his inventions. She wondered what other activities inspired that look.

The band played song after song. Melanie was sure everyone was having a great time, but she was too preoccupied with a certain skilled drummer to notice. When Gabe stood and saluted the crowd from behind his drum kit and then hopped down from the riser, Melanie was surprised that the concert was already over. She'd have been content to stand in her little corner of the stage watching him play forever. On his way past her, Gabe gave her a brief, very hot, very sweaty hug, and then trotted to the front of the stage to take his bows and toss his beaten-up drumsticks into the audience.

Realizing her time to fixate on Gabe while he performed was over, Melanie removed her earplugs and edged her way back to where Madison and Dawn were waiting for the band's two guitarists to leave the stage.

"You couldn't see much from back there, could you?" Madison asked.

Melanie grinned. "I saw everything I wanted to see."

"They're quite good," Dawn yelled. "Once the ears become accustomed to the volume." She touched a finger to her ear and winced. "My hearing will never be the same."

"Well, Beethoven was deaf and it didn't stop him from composing," Melanie teased.

Dawn frowned. "I'm not sure I would want to go on living if I lost music. I can't imagine what that was like for such a brilliant composer."

Melanie hadn't meant to make her morose. Luckily Kellen was the first to leave the stage and when he touched her cheek and brushed her lips with his, Dawn lit up from the inside out, all traces of sorrow vanishing in an instant. Melanie still found it hard to believe that the pair had been together for such a short period of time. There was something familiar about the connection between them, as if they were reincarnated lovers who had just rediscovered each other and had a lot of catching up to do.

Gabe jogged off the stage and didn't stop, hooking Melanie's hand to lead her down the steps and along a hall, through a door, and into the dressing room. "I'm going to take a quick shower and then we have to hurry to catch the plane," he said.

"You were amazing tonight."

He grinned. "I'm glad you enjoyed yourself."

"I enjoyed you mostly," she admitted.

Looking pleased by her compliment, he kissed her and grabbed his bag before heading into the bathroom. While she waited, she sent a text to Nikki. *Just making sure you got to the hotel safely. We'll be on the plane in about an hour, so I'll have to turn my phone off. Everything okay?*

Nikki didn't respond, but Melanie wasn't surprised. She was sure Nikki was upset and hurting, but she'd get over it quickly. If there was one thing Nikki was good it, it was bouncing back after a fall. With the fucked-up childhood the girl had had, recovering from devastation was something she'd learned early in life.

Shade entered the dressing room and Melanie stiffened. She really needed to get over her dislike of the man. He was an important part of Gabe's life, and she wanted to be a part as well. Gabe tolerated her friend; it was only fair that she tolerated his.

"Where's Gabe?" he asked.

"In the shower."

"Hurry him along," he said. "Owen and Lindsey are already in the limo. We need to get to the airstrip as soon as possible."

"I'll go see what's keeping him," Melanie said, smiling at the bonus of getting to see Gabe naked.

She knocked on the bathroom door and eased it open. "Gabe, are you almost ready to go?"

She entered the room, making her way through the steam to the running shower. She found Gabe leaning against the tile wall with his hair soapy and his eyes closed.

"You okay?" she asked.

He started and opened his eyes. "Yeah. Shows always sap my strength. I get an incredible high while I'm on stage, and then the adrenaline wanes and I crash hard."

All those lean, wet muscles looked perfectly dynamic from her angle. His slack face looked tired though.

"Do you want me to get you some coffee or something?"

"Naw, I'll catch a nap on the plane. But I would love a Gatorade if you can find one. I think I sweated out half my body weight tonight."

"I'll see what I can find. Shade says you need to hurry. They're waiting for us in the limo."

Gabe rinsed himself, turned off the water and reached for a towel. "I'm on it."

She'd much rather stay and ogle him while he dried himself, but she was concerned for his comfort and so she returned to the dressing room and hunted through a mini-fridge behind the bar. She found mixers, liquor, beer, soda and water, but no sports drinks. She was about to go hunting for a drink machine in the stadium when he came out of the bathroom, fully dressed and looking slightly more alert.

"I looked in the fridge, but all they have in there is alcohol, water, and soda. I was about to go search the stadium."

"Don't trouble yourself," he said. "Water will do."

Melanie felt a strange sense of self-importance as they walked hand in hand toward the exit. Envious female heads turned as they passed, and all she could think was, *Yeah, he's all mine this weekend. Eat your hearts out, bitches.*

CHAPTER TEN

WARM BREATH STIRRED against Melanie's ear and she jerked awake, banging her head on something hard as she was thrown back into consciousness. The something hard grunted in pain. *Gabe!* Her hand shot up to rectify the damage and she caught him in the nose with her palm.

"Jeez, woman, remind me not to wake you by blowing in your ear," Gabe complained. "I'll stand at a distance and poke you with a stick next time."

"I'm sorry," she said, sitting up in the seat. "I didn't mean to become violent. When did I fall asleep?"

"About three seconds after you snuggled up against me."

He'd felt so warm and comforting with his arm around her that she hadn't stood a chance at keeping her eyes open. "I guess I was tired. Are we here?"

"Well, we're in the parking lot where we store our vehicles."

Melanie blinked her eyes to adjust them to the lights that were suddenly glaring inside the shuttle bus. Shade was already halfway down the bus steps. She glanced up at Gabe and smiled. His mohawk was lying flat after his shower, so she reached up and stroked the soft strands.

"I can't wait to see your house," she said. "I have no idea what to expect."

"It's not a mansion or anything," he said. "But I like it. It's a bit outside of town, so we still have an hour of driving before we get there."

She would do her best to keep her eyes open and provide entertaining company while he drove; they could sleep late in the morning. At least she assumed he'd let her get her full eight hours. She couldn't think of anything grander than spending her entire Saturday in his bed. Sleep optional.

"Did you catch a nap while I was sleeping?"

He'd slept some on the plane. She knew, because she'd watched him.

"Nope," he said. "I mostly felt you up to keep you from snoring too loud."

She grinned, knowing he was only teasing. "Enjoy yourself?"

"Until you started moaning some other guy's name," he said. "Who is *Juan*?"

"I did not!" She hooked an arm around his neck and kissed him hungrily. He produced a groan deep in his chest, reawakening the part of her that was addicted to the man on a physical level. She tugged her lips from his and stared up into his heavily lidded green eyes. He looked hot as fuck when he was sleepy. Did she really get to be with him the entire weekend?

"If I'm moaning anyone's name in my sleep," she said, "it's yours."

"I'd rather you moan it while you're awake." His eyebrows wiggled suggestively.

Melanie caught movement out of the corner of her eye and turned her head to the seat across the aisle.

"I'm so tired," Lindsey complained as Owen hefted her to her feet. "Do I really have to check into a hotel tonight? Can't you just let me crash on your couch? I promise I won't sneak into your bed and try to molest you while you're sleeping."

She rubbed her belly with one hand and covered an extended yawn with her other as she shuffled toward the exit.

"I'm tired too," Owen said, sounding more cross than Melanie had ever heard him. "Do you think I want to deal with this right now? I'd much rather be with Caitlyn than trying to figure out what to do with you."

Lindsey's eyes filled with tears and she turned her back to him, struggling not to cry. Melanie was on her feet, prepared to comfort her, when Owen closed his eyes, took a deep breath, and placed a hand on her shoulder. He gave it a slight squeeze.

"Fine," he said, "you can stay at my place tonight, but don't think it's going to become a permanent situation."

"Thank you," she said, and hugged him with one arm. "I wouldn't even ask to stay, but I'm so exhausted. What time will Caitlyn be over in the morning? I'll be sure to be gone before she gets there."

Melanie had a hard time reading the young woman. Lindsey seemed completely sincere, but Melanie couldn't help but wonder if the pregnant woman was really on a mission to turn Owen's head. Melanie didn't know whose side she should champion. She'd never met Caitlyn, though Owen seemed to be smitten with her. But shouldn't a man be a little more concerned about the mother of his child? But was it his child? Melanie still wasn't sure.

She glanced at Gabe and found him looking half-sick as he watched Owen assist Lindsey down the bus steps. "Something wrong?" she asked.

He shook his head. "Everything is right in my world now that you're here," he said.

"Are we going to camp out on this shuttle tonight?" she asked, wondering why he was taking so long to disembark. "I did enjoy my nap on your shoulder, but I can't guarantee your safety when you wake me from that position."

He unfolded his tall frame from the seat and took her hand.

The driver was waiting for them to leave. The woman covered her mouth to stifle a yawn as Melanie and Gabe made their way to the luggage rack.

Within minutes Melanie was scrambling into Gabe's enormous pickup truck and settling into the comfortable leather seat. She smiled at him in the glare of the cabin lights when he climbed in beside her.

"I know you're not compensating for anything," she said, nodding at his crotch, "so what's with the ginormous truck?"

"I need something to pull my boat," he said. "It's badass."

She grinned at him, loving that he could be such a guy.

As it was so late, traffic was light outside of Austin. Away from the city, they scarcely met another car on the desolate road.

She was still a bit sleepy, but did her duty and talked to Gabe about trivial things, such as his boat and the weather, to keep him awake. Though he looked ready to pass out from exhaustion, he perked right up when she got up the nerve to ask what was truly weighing on her mind.

"So what's the deal with Lindsey?" she asked. "Madison seemed to think the baby is Owen's and Lindsey does too, but you don't seem convinced."

"It's probably his," Gabe said, reaching for the stereo knob and turning blaring metal music on.

Melanie turned it back off. "How can it *probably* be his? It either is or it isn't."

Gabe rubbed the back of his neck and became fascinated with the side view mirror.

"Gabe!"

"You're not going to like what I have to say."

Her stomach dropped. "It's yours, isn't it?"

"I'm pretty sure that it's not."

"What the fuck, Gabe? Did the entire band have an orgy with the chick or what?"

He blew at his cheeks, still refusing to look at her. "Yeah, pretty much."

She'd been joking, so his validation of her question made her eyes bug out.

"It was Christmas Eve," he said. "We were far from home and trapped on the bus together in a blizzard with Lindsey and her friend. Things got out of hand. I honestly don't remember much about it. I do know that I never have sex without a condom, but I was completely trashed that night. So like I said, I'm pretty sure it's not mine, but I can't guarantee that it's not."

Melanie was too stunned to form a response. Should she berate him or console him? She couldn't decide.

After a long tense moment, he reached for her hand. "If it is mine, will you turn your back on me?" he asked.

Would she? That was a pretty big question to ask so early in their acquaintance.

"Would you want to be with the mother if it's your baby?" she forced herself to ask, not sure if she could handle his response. She liked him so much. She didn't want anything to come between them.

He lifted her hand to his lips and kissed her knuckles. "No," he said. "I want to be with you, but I can't lie. I would feel an obligation toward the child. Not just financially. Emotionally."

And she wouldn't want him to feel any other way.

"I want to be with you too," she said. "I want this to work even if..." She took a deep breath. "Even if the baby is yours."

He smiled. She saw the flash of his white teeth in the

headlights of a passing car. "But I'm pretty sure it's not."

And secretly she really hoped it wasn't. She wasn't thinking about marriage and having a family just yet, but if she did fall in love with this man and have his children, she selfishly wanted all of his babies to be hers.

"I can't help but wonder why Lindsey's convinced that the baby is Owen's. Maybe she knows he didn't use protection or something."

"She's convinced because she *likes* him and wants it to be his. Owen used protection. He does have his cock pierced though, so if one of us was going to compromise the integrity of a rubber, it would be him. Still, no guarantees that's what happened either."

"So we won't know who the father is until the baby's born?"

"You planning to stick around that long?" He looked at her and squeezed her hand. His hopeful smile was barely illuminated by the dashboard lights.

"I'd like to."

"So we cross that bridge when we come to it."

She paused to reflect on his suggestion and then nodded. "Agreed."

There was nothing they could do about the situation now anyway. Best to not let the slim possibility that Gabe was an expectant father ruin their time together. Her shoulders sagged as the tension drained from them. If they were still together in three months, they would get through this together. She could handle that. She was used to dealing with other people's drama.

They turned off the highway and travelled almost a mile on a bumpy gravel road. When the truck entered a driveway and Gabe's house loomed out of the darkness, Melanie's breath caught. A spectacular A-framed log cabin sat at the end of the long, paved lane. The entire front of the house was an expanse of windows, blocked only by a huge porch and a smaller deck on the second level.

"It's beautiful," she said.

"It's not as big as Jacob's place, but I like it."

If she'd have tried to guess what his house would be like, a log cabin in the country would not have been her first guess or even her twentieth but now that she'd seen it, she knew that it fit him perfectly.

"You're a country boy at heart," she accused.

"What?" he said. "Naw, I'm pure metal, baby."

He turned on the truck stereo and blasted her ears with loud music. He banged his head and roared with the vocalist. She knew he was metal; she'd watched him punish a set of skins before an audience of thousands not five hours ago. It was the country part that she'd completely misidentified.

He turned off the stereo and leaned across the truck cabin to steal a kiss. "Would you prefer if I was all country?"

"I prefer you to be exactly who you are." And she wasn't just saying that. His mix of traits was fascinating. She doubted she'd ever get bored with him. She just hoped she could keep his attention half as well as he kept hers.

"Want to see the inside of the house?" he asked. "Or are you planning on sleeping in the truck?"

"I'm tired enough to do exactly that."

"So I won't be getting any tonight?"

"Is that all you think about?"

"When you're around?" He grinned. "Pretty much."

"I guess we do have something in common," she said.

"We have plenty in common," he said, "and we have all weekend to figure out what."

She was looking forward to spending time with him more than he could possibly realize. They talked on the phone a lot, but those conversations always quickly turned to sex and them spouting their attraction to each other. She was ready to get to know him on a deeper level. He never said much about himself, and she couldn't help but wonder about him. She was naturally nosy.

He opened the truck door and Melanie climbed out her side, practically collapsing from weariness when her feet touched the ground.

"I hope you like to sleep in," she said, stifling a yawn behind her hand.

"My second favorite thing to do."

She had a suspicion as to what his first favorite thing was and that it also involved a bed. *Sometimes.*

She weaved her way toward the front porch, glad she was

responsible for carrying only herself and her purse. She doubted she could have lifted her poorly packed suitcase. She appreciated Gabe being her baggage handler.

When she stepped on the porch, a security light blinded her and a deep, loud woof, accompanied by a second, less terrifying bark, boomed from the house. Heart thudding, she froze. Gabe nudged her in the back with his shoulder.

"I hope you aren't afraid of dogs," he said.

"Are they vicious?"

"Only if you touch me," he said with a grin.

"Then I'm bound to be mauled to death."

He set their luggage by the door and unlocked it. As soon as he turned the knob and pushed the door open, two giant blurs of fur—one blond, one black—knocked Gabe flat on his back and commenced to give his face a thorough cleaning. The two Labradors didn't even notice Melanie standing to the side of the door giggling at their tail-wagging enthusiasm.

"Beau," Gabe said in a tone that didn't sound the least bit authoritative with all the laughing he was doing. "Heel, Beau. Sit."

The larger of the two dogs—the yellow Lab—released one deep, loud bark that made Melanie jump and began to clean Gabe's ears. The smaller of the pair—a sleek black Lab—was bouncing on Gabe's chest and belly as if he were a trampoline.

"Lady," he gasped. "Settle down."

The dog whined loudly and wagged her tail. Only she didn't wag just her tail—she wagged her entire body. And when she could no longer contain her glee at seeing her master, she began to jump up and down on him again.

Breathless, Gabe laughed. "I missed you too, Lady."

"Do you need help?" Melanie asked, wondering if she dared to grab the dog's collar. The animals didn't know her, and she was rather fond of her fingers. They didn't look like mean dogs, but most dogs weren't mean to their owners. Strangers on the other hand…

Gabe struggled to rise to his knees on the large wooden porch. When he finally managed to get his legs under him, his face got another thorough licking by two wide pink tongues, and Melanie couldn't help but laugh at the way he cringed, squeezing his eyes tight and clamping his lips together with comic exaggeration. He wrapped an arm around each dog and forced them to sit on either side of him. Beau licked his nose and sat panting. If dogs could smile, he was smiling. Lady was trembling with her efforts to contain her exuberance, but she managed to keep her haunches mostly on the ground. Her tail thunked loudly against the boards beneath her.

"Melanie," Gabe said from his kneeling position, "I'd like to introduce you to my poorly behaved dogs. The big guy is Beau." He stroked the head of the dog to his right.

Melanie extended her hand towards the yellow lab. He sniffed her fingers and gave her a courteous lick. Melanie petted the sleek fur of his ears. The dog was definitely smiling now.

"Aren't you a sweet boy?" she said. The dog thunked his tail on the ground, seeming to agree with her assessment.

"And the bundle of energy is Lady," Gabe said about the smaller, black lab.

Lady barked happily several times and undoubtedly would have started bounding off the porch planks again if Gabe hadn't had her collar fisted firmly in one hand.

"She's a beautiful dog," Melanie said.

"With very bad manners," Gabe said and laughed. "I'm afraid she's not much of a lady."

"She's just happy to see you," Melanie said. "Aren't you, girl?" She bent closer to Lady and slapped her thighs.

This attention sent Lady into a fit of exuberant barking. Gabe released her collar and shoved her toward the steps. "Go run off some of that energy," he said, and Lady raced off the porch to run circles around the heavily shadowed yard. "Do you need to run too?" he asked Beau.

Beau swiped at his nose with one paw and groaned. Gabe chuckled and rose to his feet.

"I guess I should have warned you that I have dogs," he said to Melanie.

"They are a nice surprise."

"I'm not sure *nice* is the right word." He patted Beau's head affectionately, and the dog looked up at him in adoration, his tongue lolling out to one side.

She wondered why Gabe had never brought up his dogs

before. They obviously meant a lot to him, and he was obviously their god. In fact, he never talked much about his home life at all. Getting him to tell her anything about himself the night they'd met had been nearly impossible.

"Gabe, why don't you ever talk about yourself?" she asked.

"What do you mean?"

"We talk every day, but I don't feel like I know much about your past, your friends and family, your home."

"No one wants to know all that boring stuff," he said, hefting Melanie's suitcase and his duffle bag from the porch.

"I do," she said, following him into the house.

"You don't talk about that stuff either," he said.

"Well, that's because my life is boring."

"Not to me," he said.

She paused just inside the threshold to gape at the interior of his home. It was an open plan. Very open. The two-story living space had Melanie craning her neck to view the exposed wooden beams high above. She could see all the way through the house to the expansive kitchen at the back. A loft above the kitchen looked cozy with its massive fireplace. The home's furnishings were masculine and strong. Tables and shelving were all heavy, dark woods paired with black iron hardware. The fabrics were forest greens and navy blues, beige and browns and plaids. She didn't see any dead animal heads hanging on the walls, but the place definitely had the feel of a hunting lodge.

"Do you hunt?" she asked.

"Do you?"

"Uh, no."

"I'm more of a fisherman. I'll take you out on the boat tomorrow. If I decide to get out of bed."

He whistled for Lady, and the dog scampered into the house, her nails clicking against the dark hardwood floor. Beau flopped down on a thick rug near the door and Lady lay on top of him, much to Beau's obvious annoyance. When no amount of squirming would move Lady from her resting place, the big, yellow dog huffed in acceptance and closed his large chocolate-brown eyes.

"Do you like to fish?" Gabe asked as he shifted both bags to one hand so he could close the front door and lock it.

"I've never been," she admitted.

"You're from Kansas and you've never been fishing?"

She shook her head.

"What in the world have you been doing all your life?"

"Riding tornados to Oz and following yellow brick roads," she teased.

He chuckled. "This way, Dorothy. I'll give you the grand tour tomorrow." He gestured toward the back of the house. "My bed is in here."

She followed him toward a door off to the left of the great room. She bumped into him when he paused on the threshold.

"I guess I shouldn't assume that you want to sleep with me tonight," he said. "I do have a pair of guest rooms upstairs if you'd be more comfortable sleeping alone."

"Don't make me smack you," she said testily. She was too tired to play coy. All she wanted to do was fall into his arms and then fall asleep.

"I was just trying to remember my manners," he said and entered what turned out to be a huge master suite.

Its décor was also very masculine, more heavy furniture with dark woods. More dark colors and not a doily in sight. The king-sized bed in the center of the room was the most beautiful thing Melanie had ever seen. She didn't even have the decency to wait for him to drop her luggage before she kicked off her shoes and began to tug off her clothes in gleeful abandon. She normally wore a cotton nightgown to bed, but she didn't think Gabe would mind if she slept in the buff tonight. She didn't think she could keep her eyes open long enough to find sleepwear, much less don it.

He left their luggage at the door and made a pit stop in the connecting bathroom. By the time he returned, naked and gorgeous, Melanie was already under the covers and blinking drowsily.

He shut off the light, and a moment later she felt the mattress sag beside her. Gabe tugged her against him, pressing his chest against her back and other things against her bottom. She was too tired to be interested in that particular appendage. At least that's what she thought until he whispered, "Good night, sweetheart. I promise to wake you properly in the morning with an orgasm and a smile."

Her eyes popped open, unable to make out more than shadows in the dark room.

"Not if I wake you up *im*properly first," she said.

He didn't counter her statement, but she knew he'd heard her because his cock stirred against her ass.

CHAPTER ELEVEN

MELANIE HAD BEEN woken at dawn by her full bladder and after using the nearest toilet, she had even taken a moment to find her toiletries so she could brush the road-kill taste from her mouth—so not attractive. But what woke her later that morning wasn't the call of nature or even the brilliant sunlight streaming in through the double doors that lead to a back deck. No, what pulled her from a delicious sleep was a pair of strong hands slowly drawing her legs apart, tender, teasing kisses at the tops of her thighs, and a soft, wet tongue flicking sparks of pleasure against her clit. Her eyes remained tightly closed, but her mouth fell open as Gabe licked and sucked and kissed her to earth-shattering orgasm.

Her back arched off the bed, her fingers clinging to the sheet beneath her. She cried out in bliss.

Gabe kissed his way up her belly, pausing at her navel to catch between his teeth the bit of jewelry dangling from her piercing. He gave the decoration a firm tug and then continued his path of gentle kisses upward until they were eye to eye.

"That was your good-morning orgasm," he said. "Here's your smile."

He offered her that perfect knockout smile of his, and she melted into the sheets, her heart throbbing in appreciation of his gorgeousness. How wonderful would it be to wake up to that every morning?

"Where's my smile?" he asked, green eyes twinkling with amusement.

She grinned at him.

"There it is."

She wondered if he was always so chipper in the morning. She was willing to sacrifice all her time and attention to find out.

"You drool in your sleep," he said.

Her mouth dropped open in indignation. "I do not!"

"You do. And you snore like..." He made a series of noises that sounded like a rusty chain saw.

She grabbed a pillow and smacked him in the head with it.

"Oh, she wants to fight this morning," he said.

He grabbed both of her wrists in a vice-like grip and penned them to the bed on either side of her head. Being held down sent her pulse racing. He wouldn't hurt her, would he? Would she mind if he did? Gabe scooted down her body and blew a loud, rude-sounding raspberry on her chest. She giggled at the strange sensation vibrating through her breast.

"Boobies!" he cried gleefully and blew more raspberries on what he obviously considered his morning entertainment.

She squirmed, trying to release her hands from his grip so she could defend her breasts from his tickling assault. He was relentless.

"What have you been eating, woman? Beans and broccoli?" He blew more raspberries. "Dear God, you should warn a fella."

She was soon laughing so hard, her stomach ached.

"Gabe!" she yelled. "I can't breathe."

"If you can talk, you can breathe," he said.

She bucked her hips, trying to throw him off. She couldn't take much more. He caught her nipple in his mouth and she went boneless as pleasure spiked through her breast.

"Mmm, boobies," he murmured in his most sultry voice.

Melanie snorted with laughter.

"Are you laughing at me, woman?" he asked and lifted his head to steal her breath with his smile. Honestly, the man should do toothpaste commercials.

Melanie pursed her lips and shook her head with as much seriousness as she could muster.

"Then I must be doing something wrong," he said and blew a raspberry on her throat.

She squealed and scrunched her neck. "Don't I owe you an orgasm?" she asked, hoping to distract him from his evil plan to make her laugh herself to death.

"Now that you mention it..." He leaped from the bed as if it was on fire. "Stay there."

"I'm not talented enough to make you come at a distance,"

she said.

"You've been making me come from hundreds of miles away all week," he said.

"You've been making yourself come, you mean."

"Trust me; you deserve most of the credit." He continued across the room toward the far corner. "I want to try something on you. Are you game?"

She knew what the guy liked to try—devices he'd invented to make a woman shatter in bliss. "But it's your turn to feel good."

"This one makes us both feel good," he said.

She couldn't deny that she was interested. Dr. Kink E. Inventor had a mind as wicked as his body. "Then I'm game."

Gabe rummaged through an armoire that stood near a pair of doors that led outside. "What kind of lube do you prefer?" he asked.

She was supposed to have a preference? "I've never really tried different types of lube. What do you suggest?"

"I have something I think you'll enjoy."

She giggled, thinking this conversation sounded like they were deciding on the wine to go with their meal. "Is it the house lube?" she said in a snooty accent.

"House lube?" He obviously didn't get her joke.

"Like a house wine."

"No, baby. It's vintage."

"As long as it's not past its expiration date."

"Only the best for my woman's pussy."

"Oh," she said, liking that he'd called her his woman, but confused by where he wanted to put the lube. "I thought lube was for the um…" She flushed despite herself. "Well, um, I mean, for the, uh, *rear* entrance."

He glanced over his shoulder at her and grinned. "Do you want some backdoor action?"

"I liked that thing you used the last time we were together. Remember?" The feel of that large bead popping in and out of her ass with each thrust of his cock into her pussy had driven her insane. In a good way.

"I left that one on the tour bus," he said.

"Oh," she said, trying to hide her disappointment.

"But I have other things."

Of course he did.

He found whatever he was looking for and returned to the side of the bed. She tried to see what he had in his hand but before she could get a good look at it, he flipped her onto her stomach and crawled up on the bed with her. She rolled onto her side and stared at him.

"On your belly," he said.

"But I want to watch what you're doing."

"Nope. On your belly."

Before she could protest again, he pulled her arm out from under her and she found herself face down again.

Gabe's hands spread her legs wide, and he leaned over her to nibble and suck on her ass cheeks while he fiddled with something between her thighs. She gave up trying to figure out what he was going to do and closed her eyes, concentrating on the involuntary tightening of her ass each time he nipped her buttocks. She was starting to feel very needy back there and hoped he put her out of her misery soon.

Unfortunately, he ignored her ass. But fortunately, his slippery fingers massaged her pussy, dipped inside and out again, several times, as he added lube and more lube. She felt wetter inside than she ever had. And definitely warmer.

"Is that the lube making me so hot down there?" she asked.

"You're always hot down here," he teased, sliding long fingers in and out of her body. The more friction he created, the hotter the lube got. He continued to pleasure her with deep thrusts of his fingers and then used his other hand to squirt something on her ass. He rubbed the slippery substance over her back entrance and when the tip of his finger slipped inside, she jerked in surprise. She still wasn't accustomed to being touched there, but she did like it. As he added more lubricant, his finger slipped a bit deeper. The two fingers still thrusting into her pussy felt fiery. The one in her ass was surprisingly cool. She decided he was using two different lubes, and she would have thanked him if she could remember how to produce sounds other than moans.

"Ready?" he asked.

For him to fuck her unconscious? Yes, she was definitely ready. She moaned in the affirmative. He pulled his fingers free and something hard pressed against her ass. It entered her with a sudden pop. She gasped in delight. It was one of those beads she so enjoyed. At least that's what she thought until his fingers massaged more cooling lube around her opening and he pressed forward on the device and another bead popped into her ass. Maybe she was imagining it, but that one felt slightly larger than the first. As he forced a third, a fourth, and a fifth bead into her, she was certain they were getting larger.

"One more," he said, "and then you'll find out why my anal beads aren't like any you've tried."

She didn't want to dampen his enthusiasm by pointing out that *any* anal beads were like ones she hadn't tried because this was a first for her. Due to its size, the pressure caused by the final bead entering her was almost unbearable, but once in place, it felt so delightfully *there*. She cried out in need, lost in the unfamiliar sensation.

"Are you okay?" Gabe asked. He stroked her thighs, drawing her attention to her trembling legs.

"Yes," she said breathlessly. "Love it."

He twisted something at the exposed end of the shaft of beads and it took her a moment to even comprehend what was happening. A small marble—or *something*—was rubbing against the outer surface of her hole in a constant circular trajectory. Each lap of the marble around its track increased her awareness of the pleasure radiating out from and in towards her ass.

"Oh my God, Gabe!" she cried as her pussy and ass clenched rhythmically with the first spasms of release.

"Damn, woman," he said, "don't come yet. I haven't even gotten to the good part yet."

She tried clenching her internal muscles to stop the waves of orgasm and was partially successful. Cutting off an orgasm made her feel miserably needy, however, and she shifted against the sheets. Gabe lifted her hips off the bed until she was on her knees with her face still pressed against the mattress. He could have hung her from the ceiling by her ankles at that point and she wouldn't have protested. She trusted this man to do her right.

"Relax," he said from behind her. His cock slipped inside her pussy.

"God, yes," she groaned into the mattress, and rocked back to try to force him deeper.

"Hold still, baby," he murmured. "Really still. Until I'm all the way inside."

She whimpered and concentrated on remaining still. That little marble rubbing her ass was driving her freaking insane. She needed to come immediately.

It occurred to her that even with the lube, Gabe was having difficulty entering her. And he was so thick. Much thicker than usual. He spread her legs wider, until her hips protested their overextension. Face buried in the mattress, she reached her arms over her head and clung to the sheets.

Gabe used his hands to ease her pussy wider. She was pretty sure he was trying to rip her in half.

"It'll hurt for just a second," he promised. He grabbed her hips and suddenly thrust hard. A large bump on the underside of his cock stretched her beyond her limit.

She whimpered in pain.

"I'm sorry, baby," he whispered. "I need to design a better way to insert it. I promise it will feel amazing once I find your spot."

Gabe, plus whatever sleeve he was wearing over his cock, slipped deeper. When the thickened nub on the underside of the device rubbed against her front wall and found the spot he was referring to, she groaned.

"There it is," he said. "I'm going to turn it on now. Are you ready?"

She didn't know what she was agreeing to, but she nodded. The nub inside her vibrated hard against her G-spot, and pleasure shot through her entire body. Gabe began to move and apparently the sleeve around his cock was doing something for him too because he was groaning and gasping and swearing under his breath with each thrust. The motion of his hips moved the cock sleeve just enough to rub that maddening vibrating nub against Melanie's G-spot over and over and over again. She wasn't sure when she'd started coming, but she was pretty sure she wouldn't ever be able to stop.

"Tell me when you come, baby, so I can pull out the beads," he said.

"I'm already." She gasped.

"Did I miss it? I can't tell when I'm wearing the sleeve. It massages the base of my cock so good, but it prevents me from feeling you squeeze me when you come."

"Still... coming. Oh... God."

"Take a deep breath."

She tried, but she was gasping too hard. Were those tears on her cheeks? Or drool? Was it possible to literally explode from pleasure?

She felt a harsh tug on her ass and the first bead popped free. She cried out, her fingers clinging to the bedclothes beneath her face as she held on for another round of exquisite pleasure. The successive and rapid removal of the beads sent deeper waves of bliss crashing through her body. She couldn't even track what was happening to her any longer. Gabe soothed her raw and quivering ass with his fingertips. She whimpered as he thrust his hips faster and churned deep inside her. She wasn't sure when she started begging for mercy, but she simply couldn't take any more.

"Too much, Gabe. Too much. Too much. Oh God."

"Rub your clit," Gabe murmured. "It will help."

"I don't need to come again," she snapped. "I need to stop coming."

"Well, if you won't do what you're told..."

Still massaging her in the back with one hand, he reached his free hand around her and massaged her clit with the exact same cadence. She cried out as a more familiar orgasm ripped through her pussy, and he was right—it let the one caused by overstimulation of her G-spot to fade from torture to bliss.

Gabe's motions became jerky behind her, and he called out as he joined her in release. He shook and sputtered far longer than was usual, and then he collapsed against her back, his arms falling limp on either side of her body.

"That was fucking amazing," he murmured.

She murmured something unintelligible in agreement. She'd never felt anything like what she'd just experienced. That had been so much more than a typical orgasm. She was going to name it *megagasm*. Or she would once she remembered how to move her tongue.

"I have to pull out before I'm too soft," Gabe said. "It should be easier coming out than going in."

She was boneless, so she didn't have to concentrate on relaxing for him. It was the only condition she could experience at the moment. He tugged the device free of her body and set it aside. She would admire its ingenious design eventually. For now she would just lie face-down on the bed and float on a sea of tranquility.

She must have nodded off. Her next conscious sensation was a wet tickle against the sole of one foot. She lifted her head and found Beau sampling the flavor of her toes.

"Gabe," she mumbled. "I think your dog wants out."

"He's already been out," Gabe said. "There's a doggie door to the back yard."

She flopped her head over in the other direction and found Gabe lying beside her, looking as exhausted as she felt.

"How long have I been unconscious?" she asked.

"I'm not sure. I think it's already Tuesday."

She chuckled. "So four days?"

"At least."

Melanie stretched languorously and snuggled up against Gabe's side. "What?" she said, "No breakfast in bed? What kind of host are you?"

He squeezed her hand. "I'll take you out to a great little diner for breakfast," he said. "As soon as I can move."

"I can't believe you're worn out already." The reason she was giving him such a hard time was because she was pretty sure her quivering legs would be unable to support her. "Is that jetted tub in your bathroom big enough for two?" she asked. Maybe a nice underwater massage would rejuvenate her tired muscles and soothe the ache between her thighs.

"Yeah."

She forced her exhausted body to slide from the bed. She was surprised when her legs supported her weight. "Care to join me?"

"Baby, I couldn't fuck you right now if my life depended on it."

"That's not why I asked," she said. "I'm craving the pleasure of your company, not your cock."

"I'll be there in a minute," he promised and closed his eyes, his face slack.

She smiled, figuring he'd need the better of the part of the morning to recover, not just a minute, but she hobbled toward the bathroom and turned on the faucets to fill the enormous sunken tub with hot water. His bathroom was larger than her entire apartment. And why a single man would need a huge shower with dozens of showerheads was beyond her comprehension.

When the tub was half-full, she collected her shampoo, conditioner, and body wash and climbed into the hot, soothing water. She found an unmarked button on the side of the tub and pushed it, hoping she wasn't about to be violated by one of Gabe's crazy inventions, but the tub sputtered and whirred and began to shoot jets of water over her flesh. She sighed in bliss as the massage worked miracles on her aching muscles. She sank beneath the water, wetting her hair, and then jerked upward with an explosive splash when something brushed against her shoulder.

Gabe chuckled. "Did I startle you?"

"Nope," she said. "That's how I always wash my hair. Whiplash makes it more manageable."

"Can I show you how I'd wash it?"

He sank down behind her in the tub, with her seated between his legs.

"Um, yeah, okay," she said. "But be careful not to get lost in there. My hair's a rats' nest this morning."

"I love your hair," he said. He turned off the water and then reached for the shampoo. He dumped enough on his palm to wash a small mohawk. She didn't bother to correct his folly. He'd soon figure out that it took at least half a travel-sized bottle to clean her thick and unruly locks.

"You have gorgeous hair," he said, burrowing his fingers in the wet mass and snagging on several tangles. "It's one of the million things about you that I can't stop thinking about."

She giggled. "I can't stop thinking about your hair either."

He added more shampoo to his hands and began to work it into a rich lather, massaging her scalp so deeply that she sighed in bliss.

"Yeah, well, my hair is pretty unforgettable," he said.

"It's your smile that's unforgettable," she said and moaned in contentment as he continued to massage frothy, clean-smelling bubbles into her hair.

"If you keep making those sounds, my brain's going to issue a check that my cock can't cash."

"Feels so good," she murmured. "Don't stop."

He washed her hair until her entire body was relaxed, and then he eased her forward so she could lower her head back into the water in the open space between his legs. His fingers worked the shampoo from her hair.

"Beautiful," he whispered, and she opened her eyes to gaze up at him. He appeared upside down to her, but she could tell he was enjoying the view of her wet, naked body almost as she was enjoying the water jets against the soles of her feet.

"Your hair floating all around me," he said. "Your skin shiny wet. Your breasts peeking above the surface of the water. Beautiful."

He cupped her breasts and rubbed his thumbs over her nipples. She shuddered, unable to stop the flood of heat his touch always caused. It didn't matter that her pussy was tender from the pounding he'd given it less than an hour before, she could feel herself swelling with desire once more.

He helped her sit up again and began to work conditioner into her hair.

"Taking a bath was a great idea," he said. "My body has decided it can handle a bit more physical activity if you're game."

"I'm game," she said. "You'll have to take it easy on me though, I'm a little sore." She flushed as soon as she said it. Were they far enough into their relationship that she could share her discomfort with him?

"Then I'll try to curb my enthusiasm for your body until later. You'll just have to dazzle me with your mind."

She laughed. "Not much dazzling in there," she said. Not when compared to someone as smart as Gabe was.

"So what do you do with your time outside of accounting and babysitting Nikki?" he asked. "What's your family like? Did you have pets growing up? Tell me everything."

"Babysitting Nikki is a full-time job in itself," she said with a laugh.

"How did you meet her?"

"I first met her when I was six. We spent an entire summer playing in the park. Then she moved away and I lost track of her. Imagine my surprise when she was assigned as my roommate freshman year of college."

"So you two are the same age?" he asked. "You always seem so much older than her."

"Gee, thanks. Call the retirement home, Melanie's escaped again."

"I didn't mean old, I meant more mature. Like you have your life together. Know what you're doing."

"Does anyone really know what they're doing? Some of us are just better than others at pretending we have a fail-proof plan. Did you plan to be a rock drummer?"

"Well, no, I didn't plan it."

"There you go."

"Did you always plan to be an accountant?"

She laughed. "Nope. I wanted to be an entomologist, but my parents convinced me that collecting butterflies was not a reasonable vocation for a responsible individual."

Thinking about butterflies made her think about Nikki, reminding Melanie that she still hadn't called or texted. Melanie couldn't help the worry that churned in her belly. Or maybe she was just hungry.

"See, now, that's interesting," he said. "I figured you'd be the type to squeal like a girl when confronted by an insect."

"First off, I am a girl. You'd think the breasts would have clued you in." She swept both hands at her fully displayed boobs as if she were a game show hostess showing fabulous prizes. "And second, I'm not fond of *all* insects. Just butterflies. I used to collect them as a child. Dead bugs all over my bedroom walls—pinned to little squares of cotton batting inside wooden shadow boxes, their wings pressed flat against the glass. Kind of morbid, don't you think?"

"Not at all. If you hung cockroaches and dung beetles on your wall, I might be a tad concerned, but butterflies? I'm sure they were pretty. Maybe we'll see some at the lake today. You can tell me their species."

She hadn't focused on butterflies for years. "If I remember them."

"Tell me about your parents. From what little you've mentioned, they sound a bit stuffy."

"Stuffy? That's putting it mildly. They were so overprotective, I'm surprised they allowed me to breathe unpurified air."

"Why were they so overprotective? Because you were so cute?" He tapped her nose.

She shook her head, not because she hadn't been a cute kid, but because their reasons were a bit deeper than that.

"They were in their mid-40s when I was born. I had an older brother, but he drowned in a kiddie pool in the back yard years and years before I came into the world. He was only three, but his loss devastated my parents and they weren't planning on having any more kids. Then surprise! Melanie decides to defy all forms of birth control and make her entrance. They were so afraid of losing me that they smothered me. I can't be too angry with them about it. And at least I never had to wonder if I was loved. What about your family? You never talk about them."

"Not much to say. Eternally married, well-rounded, fairly nonpsychotic parents. Three kids spaced exactly eighteen months apart. Two family dogs. Happy home. Very boring."

"You have siblings?"

"Yeah, two sisters. Both older."

"Are they also musically inclined?" she asked, trying to picture what his sisters would look like, who they were. And she wondered about his parents too. She wished she could meet them all. Maybe someday.

"Nope. I got all the percussion genes in the family."

"Are your sisters married? Do they have kids? Are you an uncle?" She wondered what Gabe was like with kids. Weren't men who were good with animals supposed to be good with kids? His dogs obviously adored him.

"Not yet. My mom is dying for grandkids," he said. "I'm glad she has my sisters to pester about it. Being the youngest and her only son does have its perks."

Under a running tap, Melanie rinsed the conditioner from her hair and turned to face him.

"Can we go fishing now?" she asked.

"Breakfast first," he said.

She'd forgotten she was starving. "Okay, then fishing."

"I thought you didn't want to go fishing."

"I couldn't care less about fishing," she admitted, "but we'll have all day together to talk just like this, right?"

He smiled with thought-shattering perfection. "I suppose we will."

She wrapped her arms around his neck and kissed his lips. "Best plans ever. We don't even have to make love for the rest of the day, and I'll be perfectly content."

Gabe lifted both hands to in an attempt to calm her obvious hysterics. "Whoa! Whoa! Whoa!" he said. "Let's not get hasty here."

Melanie climbed from the tub, and reached for a towel. "I'll also be perfectly content with anything you want to try, Dr. Kink."

CHAPTER TWELVE

THE DINER WAS quaint, the kind of place a person wouldn't likely visit if they were just passing by. The locals held no such qualms regarding the outdated décor and sagging awning outside. Apparently they came for the food, not the ambiance. Melanie tried not to notice the dirty grout between the linoleum tiles or the spots on her fork.

"Well, if it isn't Gabriel Banner," their waitress said.

"Hey, Fiona," Gabe said.

"What brings you to town, sugar?" Fiona nodded toward Melanie. "I'd guess it was the purty lady, but I ain't never seen her before, so she cain't be local."

"We came all the way from New Orleans just for your mama's biscuits and sausage gravy. You know I can't stay away."

She laughed and tapped the bill of Gabe's ball cap with her order pad. Melanie might have been jealous of the woman's obvious flirting, but she had to have been pushing eighty. Melanie couldn't imagine how her *mama* was still capable of running the kitchen of a busy restaurant.

"I don't know why I even bother to take your order. What would your lady friend like?" Fiona stood with her pen hovering over her tablet.

"What's good?" Melanie asked, looking over the single page menu in its yellowed plastic sleeve.

"Uh, the sausage gravy and biscuits are good," Gabe said. "I've never tried anything else."

"He's been coming here since he was knee-high to an armadillo," Fiona said. "And he always gets the same thing. Always. Always."

"I guess I'll have what he's having," Melanie said. "I hope my stomach can handle all that grease."

Gabe cringed, and Melanie wondered what she'd said to

cause such a reaction in him.

He relaxed when Fiona just laughed. "Sugar, if you cain't handle a little grease, you in the wrong restaurant."

Fiona started to sashay away, but Gabe caught the hem of her apron.

"While you're at it, could you put in an order for fried chicken with sides to go?" he asked.

"Headin' to the lake?" she asked.

"That's the plan."

"I gotcha, sugar. You just keep smiling pretty for your lady friend."

Melanie smiled. His lady *friend*. She hoped he thought of her as something a little more serious than a friend.

While they waited for their meal, Melanie asked Gabe about his favorite foods, the restaurants he liked to visit, and even whether he preferred sandwich crusts on or off. He answered her readily enough, but she felt more like she was interviewing him than having a conversation. He never volunteered information willingly. She wondered if he was that way with everyone.

The gravy and biscuits were to die for and she was glad he'd shared a bit of himself by bringing her here. But she was starting to worry that she was trying too hard. Did her endless trivial questions annoy him? Would he rather talk about string theory and existentialism? Or was he just the strong silent type?

After breakfast and after collecting their picnic lunch for later, Gabe drove her back to the house to pick up their fishing gear and a couple of very eager dogs.

He opened the door of the enormous detached garage and strode inside. Melanie followed him. Like the house, the garage had a log cabin façade. Melanie was certain Gabe could fit ten cars in the expansive space, but apparently he wasn't a collector of cars. He was fond of water craft and recreational vehicles, however. Parked inside the garage were four boats on trailers—a row boat, a small speed boat, a large speed boat, and a pontoon. There were also jet skis, a smallish silver camper, several ATVs and a rather beat-up dirt bike. The man was full of surprises.

"I didn't realize you were so outdoorsy," she said as she watched him choose fishing poles from the long rack on one wall.

"I wish I had time to spend more time outside," he said. "There's nothing more relaxing than sitting in the middle of a lake with a line out and nothing to do but think."

She *knew* that he liked to think.

"I get my best ideas out on the lake," he said. "And with you there as inspiration, I'm sure my imagination will run wild."

"It doesn't sound like you get much fishing done."

"The point of fishing isn't to catch fish," he said.

"It's not?"

"Heck no."

"I'll have to take your word for it."

He handed her a fishing pole. "Which boat do you want to take?" he asked. "Or I have the big one docked at the marina."

A marina in the middle of Texas? Weren't marinas supposed to be *marine*, as in *at the ocean*?

"Whatever is easiest," she said.

"Marina it is. Did you bring a swimsuit?"

"I didn't know I'd be going swimming."

"Skinny dipping for you then."

"I hope it's a private lake," she said.

"Not even close."

He grabbed a tackle box from the garage and closed the doors. He convinced her to wear a tank top and shorts and then slathered her with sunscreen. He looked mighty fine in his own shorts and T-shirt but when he replaced his ball cap with a cowboy hat, she laughed. Until he grinned at her from beneath the wide brim and her heart went pitter-pat. Melanie decided there wasn't anything funny about Gabe Banner in a cowboy hat.

Fishing poles, tackle, a picnic of chicken, and two enthusiastic dogs in tow, they headed toward Lake Travis.

Melanie didn't know what she had expected, but the enormous, clear lake surrounded by hills and trees far exceeded her expectations. They bypassed a long line of vehicles at the boat ramp.

"Good call on the marina," Gabe said.

Her very first fishing license in hand, Melanie was soon seated inside Gabe's sleek 37-foot powerboat. She knew it was that long because he had very proudly told her so. There was seating at the front of the boat, which he informed her was the bow, a cockpit in the center, and more seating in the rear. Gabe climbed behind the wheel, and his two dogs scampered toward the bow, standing in the seat with their tongues lolling and ears flapping in the breeze as he directed the boat out of the marina and across the large lake. Melanie chose a safer perch at the back of the boat. At least she thought it was safe. When Gabe increased the boat's speed and cranked the wheel sharply, a spray of water flooded over the side into her lap.

She leaped to her feet and used her hands to sluice the water down her legs. "You did that on purpose," she accused.

He just grinned at her from the shadows of his cowboy hat. "Maybe you should come up here with me," he said. "Do you want to pilot?"

On wobbly legs she slid her feet along the slippery deck on her trek toward the seat beside him. "No, thank you."

"I could teach you to waterski," he said, nodding toward another boat that towed a skier behind it. Water arced away from the skier, who looked to be having a fabulous time racing over the lake at high speed.

For a minute, Melanie thought it looked like fun, but then the skier hit the wake of the boat and face-planted hard on the surface of the water. Melanie decided water skiing looked more hazardous than fun.

"I think I'll pass," she said. "I thought we were going to fish."

"We are. I'm just showing off to impress you. Don't you know how guys are?"

She chuckled. "I was impressed before we arrived."

He pulled back the throttle to slow the boat and directed it toward a quiet cove at the shore. As the lake was a dam reservoir, it was surrounded mostly by cliffs and overhangs, but this hidden cove had a small area of shoreline. When the boat drifted to a stop, both dogs immediately leaped into the water. Beau took a trip around the boat and then climbed up onto a ledge on the stern. He hopped into the boat and shook the water from his fur, showering Melanie with cool droplets. Apparently she needed a swimsuit even if she had no plans to swim. Lady swam all the way to shore and climbed up on the bank.

"Lady, get back here," Gabe said, clapping at her, trying to get her attention. "Come, girl."

She stood on the shore and barked at him, bouncing playfully on her front paws as if to say, *Come and get me if you want me!*

"Pardon my poorly behaved dog," Gabe said to Melanie.

"I think she wants to play."

"I think she wants to drive me nuts."

Beau covered his eyes with one paw, as if embarrassed by the antics of his dark-furred counterpart.

"Get the stick, Lady," Gabe said, flapping his hand toward the shore. "Get the stick, girl."

Lady stopped barking and sniffed the ground. She disappeared into a copse of trees and Melanie gasped, pivoting toward Gabe. How upset would he be if his dog got lost? But he didn't look worried. He was studying the tree line, arms folded across his chest, eyes watching from the shadow of the brim of his cowboy hat. And she needn't have worried either. Less than a minute later the dog appeared back at the shore with a branch in her mouth. She struggled to drag it toward the water, walking backward and tugging when the branch got tangled on some brush.

Gabe laughed her. "That's a mighty big stick you have there."

Lady eventually got it into the lake and after some maneuvering, collected one end of the branch in her mouth and started paddling back toward the boat.

"She's really smart," Melanie said, watching the dog pull the branch through the water.

"She's the most stubborn and independent dog I've ever owned." He chuckled as Lady tried to get the branch onto the boat. "I guess that's why she stole my heart."

Well, Melanie guessed that meant that she would just have to wrestle his heart away from dog, because she wanted it, teeth marks and all.

"That stick is too big, silly," Gabe told Lady as he stretched his body over the back of the boat and grabbed the branch out of the water. He broke off a more reasonably sized length of wood and tossed it toward shore.

"Go get the stick," he said to Lady.

She gave him a look that could only mean *I just brought you a better stick than that little thing, dumbass,* but turned in the water and started swimming toward shore again.

Melanie laughed. "I don't think she's very impressed with your stick, Mr. Banner."

He grinned. "You're the one I'm trying to impress, remember?"

Melanie pinched his ass. "I'm overly impressed with your stick."

"I'll share it with *you* later. It's best to wear Lady out early," he said. "Then I can concentrate all my attention on you."

Melanie looked around for Beau, wondering if he wanted to play too. But he'd already stretched out on one of the seats at the back of the boat for his nap. Melanie decided the yellow lab was more her speed. The black one was already on her way back to the boat, treading water like a pro, her master's puny stick gripped between her teeth.

Gabe took the stick from his dog and handed it to Melanie. "You give it a toss."

Her toss was more like a flop. Lady looked bored as she swam the three feet from the boat to retrieve it.

"Ah, I definitely recognize that you're a girl now," Gabe said.

"So maybe I should leave the hurling to you," Melanie said. "Since you're such an expert at handling a stick."

"But I think you need practice." He grinned at her and lowered his head to kiss the tip of her nose, the brim of his hat beaning her in the forehead.

"And I think you need practice kissing girls while wearing a cowboy hat."

He swept a hand to the side. "The line starts here."

She swatted him. "Oh, really?"

"Yeah, look at all these beauties lining up for a go at me."

She peered to the empty spot to her left. "It seems you have a line of one."

"Luckily, it's the best one."

He leaned in to kiss her again, tilting his head to close in on her lips. Lady's insistent whining shortened his promising kiss as he went to tend to her again. After several additional fetches, Lady scrambled back onto the boat, shook out her drenched coat and climbed on top of Beau for a rest. Beau grunted in protest as Lady wriggled around to find a more comfortable position on his large body—which apparently had to include her forepaw under his chin. Beau didn't move from the spot he'd claimed, though he looked rather annoyed to be considered Lady's personal doggie bed.

"The calm should last at least thirty minutes," Gabe said with a chuckle. "Maybe I should have left the dogs at home."

Melanie shook her head. "They're having a great time."

"Yeah, but are you?"

"Of course I am. I always have a great time when I'm with you."

Fishing pole in hand, Gabe handed her a surprisingly light Styrofoam container that he'd bought at the marina when she'd procured her fishing license.

She gave it a little shake and found it wasn't empty. "What's in here? Coleslaw?"

"I don't think you want to eat that," he said. He pinched his hook between two fingers and held out his other hand in Melanie's direction. "Hand me one," he said.

"One what?"

"Bait."

She shook her head in incomprehension.

"It's in the cup."

"Oh." She hadn't been playing coy when she said she'd never been fishing; she was totally clueless. She pried the lid of the cup and peered into it. Something small and white squirmed in a bed of what appeared to be sawdust. On closer inspection, she saw what appeared to be hundreds of plump maggots writhing about in the cup. She screamed and tossed the cup in the air, scrambling away from the spill.

Gabe stared at her. "What are you so freaked out about?"

"Your bait is infested with maggots."

He chuckled. "My bait *is* maggots."

She covered her mouth with the back of her hand, her stomach heaving. She should have said no to the sausage gravy.

"You are such a girl," Gabe said.

"I thought we'd already established that," she mumbled against her hand.

He stooped down to scoop the escaped maggots back into the cup with his bare hand.

"Oh my God," she said, swallowing hard to keep her breakfast where it belonged. "You are never touching me with that hand again."

"Oh, please," he said, piercing the body of a wriggling maggot with his hook. "You aren't afraid of a baby fly are you?"

"Afraid of? No." She turned her head, unable to watch him add a second creature to his hook. "Disgusted by? Very much so."

"I guess I should have gone with the fish heads," he said. "You have to jab the hook right through the eyes, otherwise you hit bone."

Melanie shuddered at the image his words conjured. "Are you trying to make me throw up?"

"Of course not. What kind of asshole would describe poking a hook into a slimy worm's ass and threading the metal all the way through the center of the squirmy thing's body?"

"*You*, obviously, would never be that kind of asshole," she said.

He chuckled and wiped the sweat from his brow with the back of his wrist. "Ah well, it wouldn't bother you if you weren't such a *girl*."

She glared at him, but couldn't stay perturbed at someone so obviously trying to get a rise out of her.

He cast his line into the water with practiced ease, turned a little crank until something clicked inside the reel, and then placed the handle of the pole into a holder on the edge of the boat.

"Your turn," he said, holding a rod in her direction.

"My turn to what?"

"Bait your hook."

She licked her lips nervously and took a step closer to the container of squirmy things. As soon as they were in view, she averted her gaze and squeezed her eyes shut. "Will you do it for me?" she asked. "Please."

"And I thought you once wanted to be an entomologist. Do baby butterflies freak you out too?

"No, but caterpillars are vegetarians. They don't devour

rotting flesh."

"But these are clean maggots," he tried reasoning with her. There was no way in hell that she was touching a maggot, much less impaling it on a sharp spike of metal.

"I'll just watch you fish," she said.

Gabe sighed and taking pity on her, he baited her hook. He then showed her how to cast and reel in her line. She found she was really bad at casting—her bobbing thingy never landed more than a few feet from the side of the boat—and she didn't have the patience to just let the line sit without reeling. So she cast and reeled and cast and reeled and cast and reeled, lost her bait, and waited for Gabe to resupply it before casting and reeling some more.

Gabe eventually took her pole, cast her line dozens of yards across the lake, and then stuck the handle in a holder rather than giving the pole back to her.

"Now for the most important part of fishing," he said, sitting on a front-facing bench seat and extending his arm across its back. He patted the empty space beside him and she sat.

"What's the most important part?"

"Sitting quietly and letting your mind wander."

He wrapped his arm around her shoulders and gave her upper arm a squeeze. The scenery was breathtaking, but she only lasted about three minutes before she felt compelled to break the silence.

"Have you been fishing a lot?" she asked.

"Mmm hmm, now quiet. You'll scare the fish away."

"They can't possibly hear me all the way underwater," she whispered.

"You'd be surprised."

Determined to be quiet, she stared at her orange and yellow bobber, watching it jerk underwater, rise to the surface, and disappear underwater again.

"Why is it doing that?" She whispered so she wouldn't scare the fish.

"Probably because you have a bite," Gabe said calmly.

She leaped for her pole, jerking it out of the holder and reeling as fast as she could. The tip of the pole bent in arc and the faster she reeled, the harder the fish pulled in the opposite direction. Her heart pounded with excitement, which didn't make a lick of sense to her—she had a fish at the end of a string, not a shark launching itself into their boat.

When the small greenish fish rose from the surface of the water, she turned toward Gabe.

"Nice bass," he said and nodded toward her butt.

"What do I do with it?" Melanie cringed and held one hand in front of her face to prevent the flailing fish from flicking slimy water in her eyes as it struggled for freedom.

A scraping of claws came from the rear of the boat. Before Melanie could comprehend that Lady was after her fish, a pair of paws landed on her chest, sending her staggering backward. The backs of her calves hit something solid. Unbalanced, she toppled over the side of the boat and landed in the lake with a stupendous splash.

CHAPTER THIRTEEN

HEART IN HIS THROAT, Gabe rushed to the bow and was poised to leap into the water to rescue Melanie when she surfaced. She treaded water with one hand and pushed her mass of curls from her face with her other.

"Can you swim?" he yelled, still prepared to jump in after her.

"Yeah, I'm fine." She focused her attention on Lady, who was at Gabe's side barking excitedly and wagging her tail as if trying to kick up a wind storm. "Bad dog," she said and then she laughed.

"Very bad dog," Gabe agreed. "Go lie down."

He pointed to the back of the boat where Beau was still sleeping.

Lady refused to be chastised. She bounced around on the front seat and then leaped over the side to join Melanie's fun.

"I lost your pole," Melanie said as she paddled around to the back of the boat where there was a ledge and a ladder.

"I don't care about the goddamned pole. I just don't want to lose you."

"Don't worry, I'm a good swimmer," she called from the water. "My parents made sure of it."

He remembered that her little brother had drowned, so it made sense that her parents had made sure she could swim. He silently praised them for their overprotectiveness. He felt a bit of it himself. Even though she sucked at fishing, this woman was precious to him. If something happened to her... He shook off the thought, not wanting to even think about the possibility.

Lady swam beside Melanie, obviously thinking they were having some sort of race. Lady showed off her impressive water-dog breeding by swimming laps around the human. Crazy dog. Gabe was going to have to keep her on a leash if she refused to behave.

After Melanie reached the back of the boat and hefted herself onto the diving platform, Gabe grabbed her by her upper arms and hauled her on board. He probably should have teased her about being graceless and a poor fisherman, but all he could do was wrap her in both arms and hold her dripping body securely against his.

He rubbed his lips against her forehead, "You scared me," he murmured. "Don't ever fall off my boat again."

"I think you need to take that up with your dog."

He looked down at the beast in question, now sitting in the seat next to Beau and making a huge puddle. Tongue flopping in and out of her wide mouth as she panted, Lady met his eyes, her head cocked to one side as if to say, *Well, that was fun, what next?* It was really hard to stay mad at the damned dog.

"Do you have a towel?" Melanie asked. She pulled away from him and twisted the hem of her tank top, splattering his bare feet with cool water.

"Yeah."

He released her, begrudgingly, and pulled a towel from a compartment under one of the bench seats.

"I lost one of my shoes," Melanie said, peering down at one bare foot.

He wrapped her in the huge beach towel and then hugged her against him again. He heard his line take off as a fish took his bait, but he ignored it. His need to hold Melanie far outweighed his desire to catch fish. There was another splash, and Gabe sighed when he caught sight of a length of black fur swimming in the water again.

"I think you have a bite," Melanie said.

"Mmm hmm." He drew her closer.

"And Lady is in the water again."

"Yep." He rubbed her back through the towel, wishing they were alone and naked, entwined in each other's arms.

"I'm okay, Gabe," she said. "Honest."

He kissed her deeply just to make sure.

A very wet dog interrupted their kiss by dropping something cold and soggy on Gabe's foot. Startled—because there was no telling what Lady had fished out of the water—he jerked away and looked down at Melanie's lost shoe.

"You found my shoe!" Melanie cried out, dropping to her knees to give Lady an appreciative scratch behind the ears. "Good girl." Lady licked Melanie's face before she could escape the dog's wide tongue. Melanie only laughed and rubbed Lady's head some more.

Lady was so pleased with herself that she picked up the shoe, carried it to the back of the boat, and commenced chewing. In less than half a minute, Melanie's cute canvas shoe was in shreds. Gabe slapped himself in the forehead. "Shit, Mel, I'm sorry. Bad dog!"

Melanie just laughed. "Finders keepers, losers weepers. I'll just have to gnaw on one of her chew toys when we get back to your house."

He was glad his woman was so laid back and, well, *nice*. Not to mention nice to look at. When she lifted the towel to dry her hair, he couldn't stop his eyes from wandering to the wet tank top clinging distractingly to her round breasts.

"You should probably get your fish," she said, apparently oblivious to the turn his thoughts had taken. Or maybe she thought he needed a distraction to keep him from tackling her to the deck and having his way with her.

While she worked at getting herself partially dried, Gabe reeled in his line, glad that the fish had stolen his bait and escaped. He didn't feel much like fishing anymore. He felt like getting lost in Melanie. Maybe it was time to head home.

Something damp smacked him in the back of the head. He peeled Melanie's wet tank top off his neck and spun to look at her. She was wrapped in the towel, but knowing that she was half naked beneath it did tent-like things to the front of his shorts.

She wriggled beneath the towel, squatted down, and then sent her wet shorts sailing in his direction. He caught them in one hand.

"Would you mind spreading those out to dry?" she asked.

He dropped her wet clothes in a small heap on the deck and took two steps in her direction.

"Gabe," she said, one hand extended, "don't look at me like that."

Like what? Like he wanted to devour her whole? Like he was about to shove her down on the deck and fuck her until she screamed his name? How was he looking at her exactly? She couldn't expect him to behave when his emotions were on high and she was in nothing but her bra and panties beneath a towel. Especially when they were in this secluded cove that happened to be void of all humans except for the two of them.

"Take your panties off," he said.

"I was just going to let those dry on my body," she said.

"Take them off." He knocked his cowboy hat off his head as he mindlessly shed his shirt.

"Gabe, I'm not going to take my panties off."

He took another step closer and reached for her, pulling her against him. "Do you want me to rip them off you?"

He reached inside her towel and caught the top of her panties in one hand and gave them a sharp tug. She stared up at him as if in a trance.

"Do you?" He lowered his hand so that his middle finger slid into her cleft.

Her mouth dropped open in shock.

"Where's your daring, Mel?" he asked, fisting his hand in her panties and stopping just short of ripping the fabric. "You'll come for me in the bathroom at work, but not here?"

Her fingertips slid down his belly, bumping over muscles on their way to the elastic at the waist of his shorts.

"I'll show you mine if you show me yours," she whispered.

She tugged the front of his shorts down, scraping the entire length of his cock until it sprang free between them. She slid her hand between his legs to cup his heavy balls in her palm. He gasped as she massaged them gently. The fear of pain—should she get a little too rough with those overly sensitive parts—fueled his excitement.

He tried to lower her panties, but he was immobilized by the feel of her hand fondling him, exciting him. Driving him mad with need.

"You didn't think I'd do this here, did you?" she said in that sultry voice she used when they were being naughty on the phone. "Touch you like this? Want you to touch me in the same way?"

"Thanks for being full of surprises," he said breathlessly.

She grinned at him, tossed the towel over her head to hide her face, and began a slow descent, sucking kisses down the center of his chest, his belly, and lower. She dropped to her knees, her head and upper body still hidden beneath the towel, and grasped his throbbing cock in one hand. When her soft wet tongue began to dance over the head of his cock, he groaned in bliss.

He reached to pull the towel back and tossed it aside, wanting to watch as she suckled and licked his head. And he did watch, watched as she worked him, watched as she stroked and sucked, making him shake and pulse with need. Seeing her kneeling at his feet, the brilliant sunshine kissing her lovely face and her lips stretched wide as she drew his cock deep inside her hot, wet mouth, was finally his undoing.

She squeaked in surprise when he pulled free of her mouth, jerked her to her feet, and shoved her down into the seat that ran around the front hull. He yanked at her panties, his mouth descending on her mound before he even had the garment to her ankles.

"Gabe! Get the towel. Someone will see," she said.

She tried to close her legs on his head, but he held them wide open with his shoulders.

"Keep an eye out," he said. "You'll be able to see anyone's approach long before they see us."

The muscles of her thighs relaxed, and she grasped his scalp with both hands.

"God, why does this make me so hot for you?" she whispered.

He tilted his head to look up at her from between her thighs. She wasn't keeping an eye out at all. She was gazing down at him with glassy eyes. He wished he could watch her face while he ate her out, but a man had to have priorities. He teased her opening with sweeps of his tongue, suckled and nibbled and licked her clit and her swollen lips, and then savored the sweet well between them.

When her body shuddered with release, he wrapped his arms around her waist and pulled her ass off the seat, seeking entry. She reached between her thighs and guided his rigid cock home.

He sank into her, vaguely thinking that she couldn't be very comfortable, hanging halfway off the seat like that, but she felt so good inside that he couldn't fight the instinct to thrust. When her heels dug into his ass to urge him deeper, he didn't give her position another thought. The entire world vanished except for her soft, slick, warm flesh. And her little moans of pleasure. And her gaze locked with his. She was all there was and as he claimed her, grinding his hips to work himself in as deeply as possible, she was all he wanted and everything he needed.

He gasped as his climax neared, catching him by surprise. He shifted one hand to her mound so he could massage her clit with his thumb. He wanted her to join him in ecstasy. *We should always come together*, he thought as she cried out and her pussy squeezed his cock. And then his mind went blank as his body strained against hers and he flowed into her, not just physically—he could have done that with any woman—but spiritually and emotionally. He was all tangled up inside Melanie Anderson, in dozens of ways, and it was a puzzle he never wanted to solve.

After a moment, Melanie struggled upright and Gabe shifted so that his softening cock slipped free of her body. He sat on the deck and pulled her down to his lap, where she sat facing him, her heat nestled against his damp cock. She wrapped her arms around his neck and buried her face in his chest.

"God, that was sexy," she murmured.

It had been—he couldn't deny it—but had she felt any of the emotional or spiritual attachment that he felt? If she had, she didn't say so, and so neither did he. But he held her close and marveled at the beauty of making love to Melanie. It was so different from how he'd experienced sex with other women. Even long-term girlfriends whom he'd once loved hadn't been like this. No one compared to Melanie; he had to find a way to make her his. And not just for a weekend or a month or a year. He wanted her always. There was no way he'd ever be satisfied with anyone else after knowing this feeling of completeness. After having her.

"What's that sound?" Melanie said and lifted her head. She cocked it to one side, listening.

Now that Gabe had been jerked out of his own headspace, he heard it too. It wasn't just one sound, but a mix of rattling, munching, slobbery lapping, and swallowing.

"Lady," he called, "are you in the cooler eating our lunch?"

All the sounds stopped abruptly, replaced by the thumping of a tail against the deck. Gabe twisted and glanced over his shoulder.

Yep, Lady had been in the cooler. There was nothing left of their lunch but crumbs, wrappers, and empty containers. The dog looked proud of her accomplishment, the telltale sign of mayonnaise from the potato salad glistening white on her muzzle.

"Was it good?" Gabe asked.

Lady barked and licked her lips.

Melanie laughed and buried her face in his chest again. "She's a really smart dog."

"Yeah, she waits until I'm completely distracted and then steals my fried chicken."

"I wasn't hungry anyway," Melanie said.

"Let's head back home and I'll take you out for a nice dinner. Without the dogs."

"Okay," she said. "I probably should get out of the sun. I'm not used to it and feel a bit overheated."

"Me too," he said, but the inferno blazing inside him had nothing to do with sun and everything to do with the woman on his lap.

CHAPTER FOURTEEN

WHILE WAITING FOR MELANIE to dress for their evening out, Gabe sat on the porch and tossed a ball across the yard. Lady chased it, ears flying back, muscles bunching, tail wagging as she darted across the wide span of grass toward the gravel road. She tackled the bouncing ball with her front paws, picked it up in her slobbery mouth and trotted back, her sleek black head held high with pride. She dropped the ball at Gabe's feet and gently mauled the back of Beau's neck, trying unsuccessfully to rouse him from his sleepy daze next to Gabe's hip on the top step. When all the excitement Lady got out of her mate was a halfhearted swipe of his paw at the back of one floppy ear, she barked.

"I don't think he wants to play," Gabe told Lady, retrieving the damp, grass-speckled tennis ball from between his feet and tossing it across the yard for her again. She bounded off to fetch it while Gabe gave the more sedate of his two dogs a hearty scratch behind the ears.

The door behind him opened, and he twisted to look back at Melanie. She wore a green sundress the exact same shade as the specks in her hazel eyes. Her hair was piled on her head, the way she wore it to work, with soft tendrils curling against her neck. *Wow.* His heart skipped a beat.

"You look gorgeous," he said, climbing to his feet.

"Thank you," she said, running her hands over her skirt. "It's a bit wrinkly from being shoved in a suitcase."

He honestly hadn't noticed.

"Are you ready to go?" he asked, unable to resist the urge to tuck a stray curl behind her ear.

"Yeah," she said and blew out a breath. "Whew, it's hot out here. Everything I've heard about Texas heat in July is apparently true. Or maybe it's these stockings."

She lifted the hem of her dress to show him the lacy top of her white stocking. He fingered the strap of a garter that ran up the front of her thigh.

"Mercy," he said breathlessly. "Are you sure you want to go out?"

"Oh yes," she said, grinning up at him. "I'm very much looking forward to watching you squirm as you wonder what the matching bra and panties look like."

If the three-inch strappy shoes were a clue, he'd imagine they were completely boner-inducing.

"Just let me get the dogs inside." Unable to take his eyes of Melanie, he yelled, "Lady, get in the house."

When the dog didn't listen—big surprise there—he looked out across the yard and spotted her with her paws on a tree, panting up at a squirrel or a bird or some other wild creature nestled in the branches above. "Get your ball, Lady," he called. "Time to go inside."

The black lab looked at him, wide pink tongue lolling out the side of her wide open mouth, pushed off the tree, and put her nose to the ground, hunting for ball trail, Gabe assumed.

"I think Beau has the right idea," Melanie said, and she sat on the top step on the other side of him. The spoiled dog groaned when she patted his side. He pawed at her knee, seeking more attention, and she laughed, petting him vigorously between the ears, which Gabe knew he enjoyed. Gabe certainly enjoyed when Melanie had her hands on him. And that dress? As if the woman wasn't distracting enough in shorts and a tank top, she had to go and put *that* on. Mercy.

Gabe returned to his seat on the other side of Beau, trying to remember he was a gentleman and that he could get through an evening without jumping Melanie's bones in a fit of uncontrollable lust. *Yeah, right.*

Lady returned, dripping drool on the steps at his feet as she dropped the retrieved ball again. "One more," Gabe said, "and then you need to go inside."

He doubted she'd follow that instruction, but he was very much looking forward to taking Melanie out on the town and showing her off, so Lady's fun would have to come to an end.

Gabe picked up the sopping-wet ball and heaved it across the yard. Lady sped after it joyfully, hitting it with her paws an inch off center. The ball popped forward and bounced out toward the road.

A billow of dust rose up in a long trail as a vehicle sped down the gravel road toward the house.

"Expecting someone?" Melanie asked.

"Nope." He didn't see many vehicles out this way, but it wasn't entirely unusual for the locals to use this road.

Lady chased the ball closer and closer to the road.

The old rattling pickup sped closer and closer to the house.

The ball bounced out into the gravel. Lady bounded after it, oblivious to the approaching truck.

Gabe's heart froze, and he jumped up, scarcely aware that he was racing down the steps and across the yard "Lady! Stop!"

She stopped just short of the road and glanced back at him, tongue lolling, as she gave him one of her speaking glances. This one seemed to say, *What? Do you think I'm an idiot?*

He released a breath of relief and drew to a halt, turning his attention to the truck. It was going far too fast on the gravel road. Fucking idiot. As the rusty vehicle flew past his mailbox at the end of the driveway, Gabe yelled, "Slow down!" even though there was no way the driver would hear him over the rumble of tires on gravel.

The passenger side wheels grazed the grass of Gabe's front yard, sending the truck lurching in the opposite direction as the truck slid in the loose gravel. The driver overcorrected the skid and drifted back into the yard. Gabe didn't have time to process what was happening. There was a thud, a pained yelp, and the crunch and spray of gravel as the vehicle came to a skidding halt.

"Oh my God," he heard Melanie say behind him. "Lady!"

That's when he saw the unmoving mass of black fur lying in the grass several feet from the truck. Gabe knew he was running toward Lady, but he couldn't feel himself move. He couldn't feel anything but an undeniable rage welling up inside him.

He dropped to his knees next to Lady. Blood covered her side and the grass beneath her. Her left foreleg was bent at an unnatural angle. She blurred out of focus as he laid a hand on her head. She wasn't whining, wasn't drawing air, wasn't moving at all.

"Is she okay?" A voice came from the open window of the truck.

Beyond shock and the grief came anger. As it was the only emotion Gabe could handle at the moment, he went with it. He sprang from the ground and stalked toward the truck. He wrenched the passenger door open, reached across the ragged bench seat, grabbed the driver in both hands, and yanked him bodily from the vehicle. Fists clenched in his shirt, Gabe slammed the driver's back into the side of the truck.

"Why in the fuck were you driving so fast?" Gabe yelled.

The kid cowered, and some rational shred of Gabe's senses realized he was just a child. He couldn't beat the ever-loving shit out of a minor, no matter how much he wanted to. "How old are you?" he asked, because if this kid was over eighteen, he was about to get the ass-whooping of his life.

"F-f-fifteen," the kid said, the unmistakable smell of alcohol wafting from his mouth into Gabe's face.

"You've been drinking," Gabe said.

"No, I—"

Gabe cuffed him on the side of the head. "Don't fucking lie to me. You hit my dog, you little shit."

"Is she... is she dead?"

The kid tried to peer around Gabe to see the damage he'd done, but Gabe slammed him against the truck again.

"If you've been drinking, why the *fuck* are you driving?" Gabe yelled, memories of one horrible, drunken night in high school rising up to haunt him. "Bad enough that you killed a dog. What if it had been a little kid? Would you be able to live with yourself? What if you'd hit a fuckin' tree? Is a little drunken fun worth your life?"

"I didn't mean to hit her. I have to get home before my grandpa finds out I took his truck."

"And his whiskey?"

The kid lowered his eyes.

"Gabe," Melanie said, her voice gentle and easy behind him. "We need to get Lady to a vet."

"A vet?"

"She's breathing, but she's losing a lot of blood. I think she's going into shock."

Gabe released the kid's shirt and whirled around. Beau licked Lady's face, trying to get a response out of her. Melanie was holding the gash on Lady's side closed with her hands. With bloody hands. God dammit to hell, here he was hell bent on teaching a fifteen-year-old a lesson, and his dog was bleeding out. Still, he couldn't very well let the kid get behind the wheel again, and he knew that's just what the little shit would do the second they were out of sight.

Gabe leaned into the truck and removed the keys from the ignition.

"What are you doing?" the boy asked as Gabe hurled the keys into the weed-thick field across the road.

"Think about what you did while you're looking for those," he said. "And think about how much worse it could have been. And if after you find those keys, you still think it's a good idea to get behind the wheel drunk, wait for me to return so I can beat some sense into you."

God, he wished he'd taken Joey's keys when he'd had the chance. But he didn't have time to think about Joey at the moment. He needed to get Lady to the vet and try to save her or, if she wasn't going to make it, at least keep her from suffering any more than she had to.

He rushed back to the house and called the emergency number for the vet. Dr. Nelson wasn't in the office on Saturday evenings but after Gabe's breathless explanation, she promised to meet them at the office and do what she could for Lady. Gabe tried to coax Beau into the house, but he refused to budge from Lady's side, so he decided to allow the stubborn dog to ride with them. He wrapped Lady in his shirt, lifted her carefully from the ground, and carried her to his truck. Her eyes blinked open and she whined, her brown-eyed gaze pleading with Gabe as she looked up at him.

"It's all right, girl," he said to her.

"She's scared, Gabe," Melanie said. "You hold her and I'll drive. She'll be calmer that way."

He nodded, glad Melanie was here with him and holding it together. He wasn't sure what he would have done if she hadn't been there.

He maneuvered himself into the truck with Lady cradled on

his lap. Beau sat at his feet, his massive blond head on Gabe's knee as he whined at Lady and offered her an encouraging lick every so often. The drive seemed uncommonly long. He gave Melanie directions to the clinic, but was too choked up to talk. While sitting at a stoplight several blocks from their destination, she squeezed his shoulder, and he looked at her.

"She'll be all right," Melanie said. "Have faith."

He offered a half nod, but the quivering of Lady's flesh, her struggle to draw breath, and the chill in her skin didn't instill much confidence in him. He crooned encouragement to her, probably more for his sake than hers, and ignored the burn at the back of his eyes.

Stupid stubborn dog, she shouldn't have been playing by the road. He squeezed his eyes shut. Stupid fucking dog owner; he shouldn't have let her get that close.

A vet's assistant met them at the door and hurriedly led them to an examination room. The vet arrived moments later and began checking Lady. The dog was calm as Dr. Nelson's skilled hands moved over her blood-matted fur.

At Dr. Nelson's calm, succinct instructions, the assistant placed an oxygen mask over Lady's snout and soon had an IV inserted into her foreleg—the one that wasn't damaged. The doctor looked up at Gabe, who watched them work with a sick ache ripping at his stomach.

"I'll try to save her," Dr. Nelson said. "Her leg is broken and ribs are cracked. I'm not sure how much blood she's lost. She also has internal swelling. I won't know what I'm up against until I take a closer look."

Gabe nodded, feeling numb.

"You should go sit in the waiting room. We'll let you know how she is when we know more about her injuries."

Gabe nodded again, but his feet were rooted to the floor.

A gentle, but firm hand grasped his forearm. He looked down to find Melanie looking up at him, her eyes swimming with tears. She had Beau's collar gripped firmly in her other hand.

"Come on, sweetheart," she said. "Let's go sit down."

Before I fall down, he thought dully.

He allowed Melanie to lead him out of the exam room and

into a gloomy waiting room. Apparently no one had thought to turn on the lights. At Melanie's insistence, he sank into a vinyl chair. Beau immediately jumped onto his lap and made himself as comfortable as an eighty-pound dog could get when crammed into a narrow chair already crowded by a pair of human thighs. Gabe stroked Beau's ears.

"You're worried about her too, aren't you, boy?" he said to the dog.

Beau groaned and snorted, his big brown eyes fixed on the door.

"You okay?" Melanie asked. "Do you want something to drink?"

He nodded. Shook his head. Took Melanie's hand and tugged her into the chair beside him. She sat and held his hand. Both his hands and hers were sticky with blood and her pretty dress was ruined, but she wasn't being a girl about it at all. She was definitely a strong woman, the kind he needed at his side.

"I hate waiting," she said.

"Thanks for driving," he said. "And for realizing she was still alive. I thought... I thought she was dead."

"I thought you were going to beat the shit out of that boy."

"He needs someone to beat the shit out of him. Fifteen years old and already driving drunk. What's he going to be like in his twenties? I should probably call the sheriff and send him after the kid to make sure he doesn't get behind the wheel again. Hopefully, he's still looking for those keys."

Melanie chuckled softly. "I think that will keep him occupied for a couple hours. Do you want to use my phone?" She pulled it from her purse and handed it to Gabe, who struggled to hold the massive dog on his lap and dial for an emergency operator. Within minutes he was assured that someone would head toward his place and check things out. Yet he still didn't feel he'd done enough. He'd done more than he had when he hadn't stopped his friend Joey from driving drunk. One moment of adolescent courage just might have saved Joey's life.

"Is something else bothering you?" Melanie asked. "You know it wasn't your fault that Lady got hit."

He did feel responsible for Lady, but that wasn't all that was bothering him. Gabe's sole regret in life was that he hadn't taken

Joey's keys from him when he'd had the chance. He'd had let his friend get behind the wheel, drunk. Gabe glanced at Melanie, who offered him an encouraging smile. He didn't like to talk about Joey. But Gabe wanted to share things, meaningful things, with Melanie. He trusted her. He liked her as his friend as well as his lover. And after the way she'd supported him this afternoon and continued to support him, he might even be in love with her. Maybe he'd feel better if he talked about the thing with Joey. People he'd grown up with knew the story, but he hadn't shared it with anyone in recent years. It hurt too much.

"I'm torn up about Lady getting hurt," he said. That was no lie. Just saying it made his chest constrict and his eyes burn with unshed tears. It was easier for him to choke down his feelings when he didn't talk. "That kid, though," he said, his voice breathless with emotion. "That stupid fucking kid reminded me of something that happened when I was in high school. Something that ended tragically. Something I might have prevented."

She didn't speak, but looked at him expectantly and squeezed his hand in reassurance.

"We were down by the lake, me and a bunch of the band-kids, having a good time—laughing and talking, listening to music. A few of the guys were drinking. I was... uh... trying to get this girl's attention, but my braces and knobby knees had some strange repelling force on her. Like anti-gravity."

"I'm sure you were adorable," Melanie said with a grin.

"Yeah, right." He snorted. "One of the other drummers in the band, Joey Turner, had about five beers too many and said he wanted to crash the popular kids' party. The one none of us had been invited to. He tried to get me to go with him. He had no business driving, Mel. He was completely wasted. Otherwise he wouldn't have even wanted to crash the popular kids' party. But I was sure if this girl I liked had another wine cooler or two, she'd start to think of me as doable. I was trying so hard to be doable. So instead of taking Joey's keys or driving him, I let him go. Let him get in that fucking car and drive. He hit a tree about two miles down the road." Gabe watched Melanie, searching for her reaction. "He didn't have to die, Mel."

Her eyes glittered with tears that sparkled in the dim waiting room, and she sucked one side of her bottom lip into her mouth, worrying it between her teeth. After a moment, she released a sigh. "I never know what to say at times like these," she said, a hitch to her voice. "In that situation, I'm sure I'd feel guilty too. Even though he made the decision to get behind the wheel, and it's not really your fault, I'm sure it must feel like it is." She took a breath. "I said the wrong thing, didn't I?"

"No. You telling me it wasn't my fault, saying I shouldn't beat myself up about it, wouldn't change the way I feel. I'm glad you understand why it's unbearable for me."

"I do understand. I think that's why I try so hard to keep Nikki out of trouble. For her benefit, yes. But also for mine. So I don't have to feel guilty if something bad happens to her. That's horrible, isn't it? Selfish and…" She glanced at the waiting room door. "I'm sorry. I shouldn't be talking about me at all right now. Not after all you've been through today."

Her hand reached toward his jaw, but she snatched it back and stared at its red-streaked surface in horror. "I'm going to go use the restroom real quick. Will you be okay by yourself for a few minutes?"

He chuckled, touched by her unnecessary concern. "I'll be fine. I'm tougher than I look."

She eyed the tattoos on the side of his head speculatively. "I kind of doubt that."

After she'd gone, he checked out the blood on his hands and clothes too. He went to wash up in the men's room, leaving Beau to rest on the waiting room floor. The shirt he'd wrapped Lady in was completely ruined, so instead of putting it back on, he tossed it in the garbage. He washed his hands and belly in the small porcelain sink, but no amount of blotting his jeans with a wet paper towel lessened the stains.

When he returned to the waiting room, Melanie smiled at him. At least he thought she did. It was hard to see her face around the giant yellow dog on her lap. Gabe leaned over the beast to steal a kiss from his lady friend, and a big slobbery tongue wet the undersides of their chins in a series of enthusiastic licks. Melanie drew away, laughing.

"Save those kisses for Lady, big guy," she said, giving Beau a scratch behind the ears. "She's going to need them."

Gabe wiped dog drool from his chin with the back of his wrist and took the empty seat beside Melanie.

"I can't feel my legs," she said.

"Beau," Gabe said. "Get down."

The dog groaned and then hopped to the floor and lay at Gabe's feet, still as stone. He rested his head on his front paws and turned a watchful gaze to the door.

"Aw, he misses her, doesn't he?" Melanie said. "Did you get both dogs at the same time?"

Gabe shook his head. "Beau is five years older than Lady; she's only two. Still a pup, really. I had another lab before her. A beautiful chocolate female named Sweetie. She was the most docile and loving dog I ever met. Beau still mourns for her, don't you, big guy?"

Beau blew out a breath that made his jowls shudder.

"Did she die?" Melanie asked.

Gabe nodded, his heart constricting in his chest again. "Got tangled up with a wild hog."

"I'm sorry, Gabe. I can tell your dogs mean a lot to you."

"That transparent, am I?"

She smiled. "Maybe a little."

Beau suddenly jumped to his feet and eyed the doorway intently. A moment later, the veterinarian strode into the waiting room. Her reassuring smile did amazing things to reduce Gabe's level of anxiety.

"Lady should pull through," Dr. Nelson said. "Her liver is swollen, so I'm going to keep her here at least overnight. We'll see how she feels tomorrow. Her side needed stitches due to a long laceration, and her foreleg has been set. She'll be in a cast for several weeks. I didn't see any signs of neck or head trauma, but she will definitely be sore for a week or so."

A week during which Gabe had to be on the road with the band, but he nodded. "Can I see her?"

"For a few minutes. She's sedated, so she won't know you're there."

Lady was asleep on the exam table, the fur shaved from her side and dozens of stitches running the length of her dark skin. The assistant was wrapping her leg in gauze for her cast. Gabe stroked Lady's soft ears and told her to be a good dog, though he decided she could chew as many shoes and steal as much fried chicken as she wanted if she made it through her ordeal. He wouldn't even yell at her.

CHAPTER FIFTEEN

ON THE WAY BACK to Gabe's ranch, Melanie checked her phone for messages. She hadn't received a single call, email, or text from Nikki in over twenty-four hours. Melanie would have liked to believe that her friend had finally discovered tact and had allowed Melanie to enjoy her weekend with Gabe undisturbed, but she knew Nikki better than that. Either Nikki was having too much fun to bother checking in—unlikely, because when she was having *that* much fun she liked to brag— or something was wrong. Very wrong. Dread settled in Melanie's stomach, and she couldn't shake it. She sent Nikki a text, asking her to please check in because she was starting to worry. Melanie anxiously waited for the answering smart-ass response, but seconds became minutes and her text was marked *delivered*, but not *read*. Maybe Nikki had forgotten to charge her phone. Though that wasn't likely. Nikki might *forget* to pay her bills or fill up her car with gas, but she never forgot to charge her phone.

"Everything okay?" Gabe asked.

Melanie peered around Beau, who was sharing her seat. Well, sharing wasn't really the dog's forte. He was *hogging* her seat.

"I don't know. I'm really starting to worry about Nikki. It's not like her to not bug me about something for this length of time."

"She's probably just having a good time in New Orleans." He grinned at her reassuringly. "It's easy to lose track of time in the Big Easy."

Melanie prayed he was right. Prayed Nikki was all right.

"We'll be back in New Orleans day after tomorrow," he reminded her. "I'll show you what I mean then."

"What are you going to do with Lady while you're on the road?"

His brow scrunched. "I'll think of something. The guys keep bringing their women on the bus; surely they won't protest if I bring along my own Lady."

"But I have to work on Monday." Unfortunately. She'd love to spend more time with Gabe. Hell, she'd love to spend all of her time with Gabe. But she had a life in Kansas. And she wasn't missing it at all.

"I meant the dog."

Oh. So that was where his loyalties lay. She scowled.

"I wish you could travel with me too," he said hastily. "Do you have any vacation time saved up?"

She felt marginally better. Very marginally. "A little."

"Could I interest you in wasting it all on me?"

She craned her neck to try to see around the eighty-pound hairball panting and drooling all over the dashboard. Didn't dogs like to sit by the window? Apparently this one preferred a front and center view with the air conditioning vent blowing cold air at his throat.

"You might," she said.

"You could join the tour for a couple days, which isn't very pleasant once the novelty wears off."

She couldn't tell if he was trying to dissuade her from joining the tour or sincerely thought she wouldn't enjoy riding on the bus with him.

"Or you can visit me at my place again. It's usually calm and peaceful. Today has just been a day from Hell."

Despite the emergency with Lady, Melanie had to admit she liked being a part of his day-to-day life. She loved his home. Loved his dogs. Loved... Well, she didn't want to get ahead of herself with thoughts like that.

"Or," he said, "we can take off somewhere, just the two of us, and have a real vacation."

"Like where?" she asked. She so rarely got out of Kansas. She'd always wanted to travel, but had never found the time or a likeminded individual who wanted to travel with her.

"Anywhere. You pick. Our last option would be hanging out at your place for a few days."

She cringed. Now that didn't sound like fun. "I think it would be fun to go someplace unique."

"Are you talking The Bahamas-unique or Antarctica-unique?"

She instantly knew where she wanted to go. The place she'd been dreaming of visiting since she'd seen the movie *The Gladiator.*

"How about Rome-unique."

He made a sound of interest—a short *mmm.* "I've never been to Rome," he said. "Rome it is."

Really? Was she really going to live her dream of seeing the coliseum at Gabe's side? If a wall of beige fur hadn't separated them, she would have hugged him.

"But that'll have to wait until the tour is over," he said. "I don't have enough time off between gigs to do a proper vacation."

"When is the tour over?" she asked.

"November."

"November?" She scowled. "I won't get to see you until November?" This dating a touring rock star thing was a challenge she hoped she'd live through. Just being away from him for five days had been torture. What would it be like to not be able to see him for weeks or months? She'd go mad.

"We'll see each other," he said. "Just in small bites. You might discover that's all of me you can handle in one setting."

"Gabriel Banner, I want to eat you whole. Trust me, I can handle being with you for extended periods of time."

He chuckled and turned off the highway onto the gravel road that led to his home.

When they pulled into the driveway, the first thing Melanie noticed was that the beat-up pickup was no longer parked along the side of the road.

"I hope to God that little fucker didn't find those keys and drive," Gabe said. "I should have pocketed them instead."

Melanie opened the door and shooed the massive form of Beau out of the truck so she could actually interact with the man who was so obviously in turmoil.

"Don't beat yourself up, sweetheart. You had to take care of Lady first. There was no time to make sure that kid did the responsible thing. You did what you could under the circumstances. You even called the police."

Gabe didn't look at her. Instead he dropped his face into his hands and scrubbed at his eyes.

"I love my dog and all, she means the world to me, but..." He huffed out a heavy breath and dropped his hands to reach for the door handle.

She caught his arm before he could escape. "You can talk to me, Gabe. I want you talk to me. Whatever it is, you can tell me, okay?"

"Can I tell you that you really need a shower? You smell like dog."

She let him off the hook—for now—by rolling her eyes and offering him a half grin. He'd tell her when he was ready. She hoped. She really wanted to build a relationship with him and that couldn't happen if he didn't trust her with his baggage. Hell, she had *Nikki* for a best friend. If she couldn't handle Gabe's baggage, no one could.

"I might be tempted into taking a shower," she said, suddenly self-conscious about the dried blood on her dress. The legs of Gabe's jeans were covered with it as well. "If you'll join me."

"Melanie Anderson, I'm starting to think you only have one thing on your mind."

"If you think it's seeing you naked," she said hotly and then grinned, "guilty as charged."

She honestly didn't want to shower with him just to see him naked; she wanted his defenses down. She wanted to get tangled up in more than his arms. Soul bared, heart exposed, she wanted all of him. He opened up when he made love; that's what had sealed the deal for her. That's what kept her coming back for more, those brief glimpses of what he usually tried to hide behind tattoos and a foot-high mohawk.

She hoped that one day she wouldn't have to seduce him to lay his heart open to her, but she'd stick with what worked for now.

He leaned across the seat and claimed her mouth in a soft, loving kiss that set her heart aflutter. "Thanks for being wonderful you," he said, lifting a hand to brush a stray curl behind her ear. She turned her face to kiss his palm and caught a strong whiff of dog on his hand. She crinkled her nose.

"About that shower" she said.

He laughed, climbed out of the truck, and grabbed her around the waist, hauling her out through the driver-side door.

He slammed the door and carried her toward the house, getting an eyeful of her stockings and thighs as her skirt slid to her waist. She didn't bother to make herself presentable.

"Looking good, Miss Melanie."

She wrapped her arms around his neck and buried her nose in his throat. His neck didn't smell like dog at all. It smelled like Gabe. She nuzzled closer and breathed him in.

"Beau!" Gabe called when they reached the porch.

She lifted her head to search for the dog and saw him nosing around the spot where Lady had lay in the grass after she'd been hit.

"Come on, boy. Let's go inside where it's cool."

The dog gave Gabe a morose look and flopped down in the grass, his chin resting on his large paws.

"We'll bring her home as soon as she's better, buddy. Come on."

Beau ignored his master. Gabe sighed, walked to the porch, and set Melanie on her feet. "I'll have to get him. You can get that shower going," he suggested.

Melanie nodded, but made no move to go into the house. She watched Gabe cross the yard and drop down next to his dog. She couldn't hear what he was saying as he stroked Beau's velvety ears, but after a moment, the dog rose to his feet and collected Lady's discarded ball from the ditch. Gabe stood and waited for Beau to return to him and they walked side by side to the house.

Melanie didn't know why she found the two of them so touching. She'd never had a dog, so she found the obvious connection between man and beast hard to comprehend. Obviously Beau didn't know what was being said to him, but the tone of Gabe's voice and his soothing hand had somehow reached the animal. She'd probably have just grabbed the dog by the collar hand hauled him into the house. Or scolded him for disobeying. Gabe's way was better. Lots better.

What a truly remarkable man.

His face brightened and his lips stretched into a smile when he noticed her watching him, but his eyes were hidden under the shadow of his baseball cap. She felt those eyes on hers, though. Felt some connection between them that she couldn't explain. She was in over her head with this guy and found that realization wonderful, amazing, and scary as hell.

CHAPTER SIXTEEN

MELANIE LOOKED DAMNED BEAUTIFUL standing on his porch with the light of the setting sun making her skin glow. He doubted she realized how happy he was to have her here with him—just the two of them at home—or how much he appreciated her help with Lady. If Melanie hadn't been there, he probably would have been too busy losing his head over the teenaged drunk driver to realize his dog needed medical attention and not a hole in the ground.

He felt bad for Beau too. The dog had never been as close to Lady as he'd been to Sweetie. It was as if Beau was afraid to get too attached to another mate. Could a dog have a broken heart? Gabe knew one could. Beau still had one. The dog cared about Lady and had sired her first batch of pups, but he had loved Sweetie. Gabe had always believed that there was one true love for everyone—even his damned dog—and that a man could love many women in his lifetime, but not the way he loved his one. As Melanie waited for him to join her on the porch, he wondered if she was his. His one. Did a man know that kind of thing right away, or did it take a while for the feeling to develop? Did a man choose his one and only or was it written in the stars? He'd never pondered those kinds of things before and wondered why this particular woman put these strange thoughts in his head. Time to get her naked, so he could think about something a less terrifyingly life-altering than Melanie as a permanent fixture in his life.

"I thought you'd be naked by now," he said.

"Just admiring the view," she said.

He glanced over his shoulder at the spectacular sunset behind him. A red-orange globe hovered just above the horizon and shot veins of pink, violet, and green through the clouds. The brilliant blue sky above the clouds had begun to darken to cobalt.

"That is a beautiful sunset," he agreed.

"What sunset?" she said with a laugh. "I was ogling you."

He took his cap off, smoothed the strip of long hair down the center of his scalp with one hand, and plopped the hat back on his head. His face felt uncharacteristically hot. Was he blushing? Dear lord, what was the world coming to? "Wouldn't you rather ogle me naked and wet?"

She reached for his hand, grabbed it securely in hers, and tugged him toward the front door. "Good call."

Beau followed them into the house and took his regular spot on the rug near the threshold. He gnawed on Lady's ball and completely ignored the humans who were already pawing at each other like a couple of animals.

Gabe drew Melanie against him, pressing her soft breasts tightly to his bare chest. His emotions were a blend of joy and turmoil, hope and despair, and he couldn't get a firm handle on any of them. Which is why he needed a distraction. He smiled when her hands found his ass and gave both cheeks a playful squeeze. She tilted her face up and trailed sweet tickling kisses under his jaw. Apparently she was ready for a distraction as well.

He lowered the zipper at the back of her dress, so sorry that it was ruined but glad that it was easy to remove so he could expose her beauty and touch the warm smooth flesh of his little Melanie. Yes, his. She had to be his.

She shrugged her dress straps off her shoulders, dropping the dress on the floor and lifting her arms to rub her hands over his bare chest.

She looked devastatingly sexy in her garters, thigh-high stockings, lacy white bra, and panties, but nothing material could match the beauty of what was hidden underneath. When she lifted her arms to remove the clip from her hair and let the glorious mass tumble down around her shoulders, Gabe groaned in approval.

He reached behind her and pinched the bra clasp at her back before brushing the straps from her shoulders to free her beautiful breasts to his eager eyes. She lowered her arms and let her bra join her dress on the floor. Her fingertips glided up his quivering belly, bumping over the hard contours of his body.

She paused to rub the barbell in his nipple with one thumb, staring up into his eyes and working his sensitive flesh until it was hard and achy beneath her touch. When he groaned, she leaned forward to kiss his chest, her lips brushing over the wolf tattoo on one side and the cougar on the other. Her breath was warm and moist against the skin over his heart as she kissed between her splayed hands. She paused unexpectedly and gave her hand a hesitant sniff. She pulled a face and stepped away abruptly.

"Oh gross, I do smell like dog," she said. "Let's continue this in the shower."

She slipped her garters, lacy thong, and stockings down her legs, leaving the remainder of her clothes and her shoes in a tangle on the living room floor. Struck dumb by the sight of her glorious nude form streaking through his house toward the bedroom, Gabe didn't blink until she was completely out of sight.

He stripped off his clothes where he stood—from ball cap to tennis shoes—and followed Melanie into his bedroom.

He heard the spray of water and Melanie's, "What in the world?" echoing off the bathroom tiles.

He supposed she'd just discovered he didn't have an average, everyday shower. His was a shower designed for a thorough cleaning. And if one was so inclined to utilize the showerheads advantageously, an added kick of pleasure.

He watched her sidestep out of the jet of water spraying her in the ass in favor of the overhead flow that she used to wet her skin as she lathered on the soap. Most of the showerheads were currently off. How would she respond to getting sprayed from all directions?

He smiled, knowing how adventurous she could be with the slightest encouragement, and opened the glass shower door to join her.

She immediately went after him with the soap. "You smell like dog too," she said and then nodded at one of the walls of showerheads. "What's with all the plumbing? It's like a carwash in here."

"Would you like a demonstration?" he asked.

She eyed the brushed silver fixtures warily. "I'm not sure."

He took her by the shoulders and judging the best location, shifted her back a few paces. "Stand right there," he said, giving her a kiss of encouragement on one cheek. "Spread your feet apart."

"For balance?"

He chuckled. "If that's what you want to believe."

She took a deep breath and spread her feet apart.

"A little more."

She obeyed without question. He loved how she trusted him so thoroughly with her body. He began to turn the showerheads on and adjusted the heads to spray water over her erogenous zones from multiple directions. He focused on her breasts first—directing a few showerheads so that each nipple was stimulated from the side, above, and below. She sighed in pleasure, shimmying slightly to move her stiff nipples in and out of the warm spray. He set several showerheads to massage her shoulders and lower back with strong, pulsating bursts. He had additional jets tickling the backs of her knees and then finally turned one particularly vigorous spray to hit her in the ass. She gasped and bent forward, opening herself up to the pleasure. It also gave him a spectacular view of the slick, swollen pussy between her thighs. One he very much wanted to investigate on a more personal level. But first...

He removed a handheld sprayer from the wall, turned it on, and handed it to her.

"What's this for?" she asked.

He twisted the showerhead and it began to pulsate. "I think you'll figure it out," he said.

He stepped back to stand near the shower door—the only surface not covered with fixtures—and just looked at her. Her skin was slick with water and rosy from stimulation. Her long hair was almost black when wet and hung in limp waves, sticking to her shoulders, her back, and breasts like the brush strokes of an admiring artist. When she directed the handheld's spray between her thighs and began to moan in pleasure, he would have loved to simply continue watching, but he honestly didn't have the willpower to keep his hands off her for another moment.

He stepped up behind her, the gush of water that had been

spraying up her backside hitting him in the thigh. It was times like this that he wished he was several inches shorter. He cupped her breasts in his hands and massaged them so that her nipples entered and left the spray in cycles that made her groan in delight.

The spray she was directing between her legs hit the tip of his cock, and he shuddered. Fuck, he was hard. He couldn't stop himself from rubbing his dick against the sweet, slick heat beckoning him inside.

She bent forward and gyrated her hips, rubbing against him, encouraging him to take her, claim her, make her his.

He bent his knees and slipped the head of his cock inside her, surging forward, taking what he wanted.

"Yes, Gabe," she said, using the handheld sprayer against her clit, where their bodies were joined, and against his heavy balls. He smiled to himself, glad she was sexually brilliant. His perfect match.

Unfortunately, the tiles of the shower floor were a bit too slippery to get the leverage he needed to thrust properly.

He turned her toward the wall, his well-placed water flow no longer hitting her in all the places he'd aimed them at. She still had the handheld massager, though, and used it to quickly bring herself to orgasm while Gabe filled her from behind and squeezed her nipples between his fingers. Her cries of ecstasy echoed off the tiles as her pussy convulsed around his driving cock. In her excitement, she dropped the sprayer that had been doing maddeningly delightful things to his balls.

Shuddering intermittently, Melanie went limp and almost sent Gabe slipping to his death on the hard tile floor as he tried to keep her on her feet. His cock sprang free of her body, still hard as granite and far from finished.

"I think we should take this to the bedroom," he said.

Leaning hard against the wall, Melanie nodded, her eyes closed, her body still shaking from her orgasm.

He shut off the water and stepped from the shower. She followed him on shaky legs and reached for a towel, but he caught her hand.

"No time for that," he said, lifting her into his arms to carry her to his bed.

CHAPTER SEVENTEEN

FOR A MAN so intent on getting her into his bed, Gabe was sure taking his sweet time in getting down to business.

Now that the sun had set, the bedroom was dark except for a single lamp glowing on a side table across the room, near to where Gabe stood with his back to her. He was sorting through gadgets inside his large armoire. Melanie watched, admiring the phoenix tattooed on his back. Admiring his firm ass. Admiring his long, well-muscled legs and his huge feet that correlated in size with what he had going on between his legs. But even gazing appreciatively at his backside lost its appeal after ten minutes of waiting.

"Gabe," she said when she couldn't bare another moment lying there without him. "It's awfully lonely over here."

From the armoire came a strange series of clicks and then what sounded like a jackhammer pounding against a tin can. A belt screeched, gears grinded, and Gabe pounded on something in the armoire out of her line of sight. The sounds died with a clunk.

She sincerely hoped he wasn't thinking of trying that, whatever *that* was, out on her. It sounded like a machine dying a thousand painful deaths.

"Fuck," he said. He scrubbed his face with both hands and turned slightly to glance at her. "I don't think it's quite ready."

She checked out his nearly flaccid cock and had to agree. "Perhaps it's because you've been standing all the way over there, while I've been way over here, for far too long."

He scowled and then followed her gaze to his cock. "Not that. That works just fine, thanks," he said. "The new invention I've been working on. I don't think I should use it on someone I care about. I fear it just might fuck you to death."

Melanie was not ready to die, even by fucking. "Your

inventions are spectacular, baby, but maybe I could give Gabe, *sans* equipment, a go."

She wiggled her eyebrows at him, hope blossoming in her chest. That's what she really wanted. Not the rock star. Not the kinky inventor. She wanted him, just him, open and exposed. The way she doubted many women had seen him.

He turned away from her and slammed the door of the armoire, clearly frustrated. "This weekend has been one disaster after another," he grumbled and smashed his hands to his hips as he tried to glare a hole through the wall.

"It's been life, babe," Melanie said. "That's all."

"I wanted everything to be perfect for you."

"This weekend has been perfect."

He grunted. "Hardly."

"It has been," she insisted and sat up on the bed, "because I was able to spend it with you."

He turned to look at her then. And not a cursory glance. He stared openly, as if trying to commit every inch of her to memory.

"Are you going to stare at me all night or are you going to join me in this bed?" she asked, patting the mattress beside her.

He turned back to the armoire and opened the door again.

"I think I have something in here…"

She growled and then sprang from the mattress, crossed the room, and plucked some device out of his hand. She tossed it into the cabinet and slammed the doors shut, leaning her back against them to prevent him from tinkering with anything else.

"Gabe," she said.

"Fine," he said, "if that's what you want."

"That's *who* I want," she corrected.

"But you won't come near as hard as you would if we used—"

She reached up and covered his lips with a finger. "I think I should be the judge of the strength of my orgasms," she said.

Besides, when he used one of his devices, he concentrated on making her come as quickly as possible, over and over again until she couldn't move. Which was admittedly good, but she never got to appreciate the more tender part of making love. The part where she felt him—him, the man—deeper inside her than his very impressive cock, even with attachments, could ever reach.

She took his hand and led him to the bed. She could feel his resistance, almost reluctance. Didn't he want her?

"Are my inventions weirding you out?" he asked. "I understand if they are."

So he was still fixated on the gadgets? Or maybe just her acceptance of them.

"Nope. Not weirded out at all," she said. "In fact, tomorrow I want you to show me everything in that cabinet—"

"And in the basement?"

"Yeah, and in the basement."

"And the garage?"

She hoped her trepidation didn't show. She feared her pussy would never be the same if she gave him free rein to use all his gadgets. "Yeah, the garage too, but tonight—"

"What about the shed? And the barn?"

She swallowed hard and nodded.

"And the attic?"

"Dear God, Gabe, how many fucking inventions have you designed?"

He laughed. "All the good ones are in there," he said and pointed to the armoire with his thumb.

"Sometimes I think you're trying to scare me away," she said.

His killer smile faded, and he lowered his eyes, looking guilty.

"You are," she said in disbelief. "Why?"

He shrugged. "I don't really want you to go. I just... I've never had someone accept everything I am the way you do. The women I've been with in the past have mostly known me as Force, the drummer of Sole Regret, but you... You insist on getting to know Gabe, the geek who couldn't get a date in high school. And I guess..." He shrugged. "I guess I'm just looking for your deal breaker to see if I can overcome it and win you for real."

"My deal breaker?" Her heart did a strange fluttering thing as she looked him up and down. "You've known my deal breaker since the night we met."

He looked halfway sick with nerves and she felt halfway guilty for teasing him.

"My *deal* breaker, Mr. Banner, was all of those crazy tattoos. What *were* you thinking, young man? Don't you know those things are permanent?"

He laughed and grabbed her, hauling her body against his. Fucking finally. His fingers dug into her sides, and she laughed along with him, trying to free herself from his vigorous tickling. After a moment, he stopped and just held her against him while she caught her breath.

"Being rejected for what you are on the outside is easy," he said. "It's when you're rejected for what you are on the inside that really hurts."

She snuggled closer to him. "Then you have nothing to worry about."

He leaned back and tucked a finger under her chin to lift her head. Her gaze settled on his gorgeous green eyes. Got lost in them. Practically melted under their attention.

Damn.

"How did I ever luck into finding you, Melanie Anderson?" he asked.

"You can thank Nikki's libido for that, Mr. Rock Star," she said. "She forced me backstage against my will, you know. So she could rock Shade Silverton's world." A brief stab of concern stole Melanie's breath. She still hadn't heard from Nikki. Melanie didn't know whether to be worried or pissed.

"I'll send her vag some flowers," he said.

Melanie's worry vanished when he lifted her by the waist and set her on the edge of his king-sized bed.

In fact everything on earth but him vanished as he peppered her skin with soft kisses until he'd claimed every inch of her as his. She claimed every inch of him as well, with fingertips and lips and tongue, until at last he covered her body with his and, staring unwavering into her eyes, claimed her deeply. His strokes were agonizingly slow, giving her plenty of time to cherish each one. He entwined his fingers with hers, holding her hands above her head as he slowly, slowly pushed her body towards release. When she finally shattered, he kissed her sputtering lips and followed her into bliss. He'd been completely wrong about that orgasm not being as strong as her others. She'd felt that one in her clenching pussy for sure, but she'd felt it deeper. She'd felt it inside her heart, in her soul. In all the places she felt Gabe.

Damn.

She closed her eyes and swallowed hard to fight back the emotion clogging her throat. Was she seriously about to cry after sex? Who did that?

Gabe went limp on top of her, and she freed her hands from his so she could hug him close. She inhaled him deep into her lungs and held on to that breath for as long as she could, wanting more of him inside her. Wanting all of him inside her.

I'm so far gone, she thought as the breath she'd been holding burst from her lungs and she breathed him in again.

"Okay," he whispered. "I'm going to roll over and go to sleep now."

Typical man, she thought with a grin.

"And pretend I didn't just give you my heart."

Or not so typical. What was she supposed to say to that?

He slid from her body and rolled beside her. Instead of closing his eyes and commencing to snore, he lifted a hand and traced the lines of her face with one finger.

"You'll probably need a replacement for that heart you just gave me," she said.

He lifted a questioning eyebrow.

"Will mine do?" she said huskily.

He covered her pounding heart with one hand and smiled that wide gorgeous grin that made her toes curl in pleasure. "It seems to be in good working condition. I'll take it."

CHAPTER EIGHTEEN

A STRANGE SOUND pulled Melanie from sleep. Heart thudding, she blinked her eyes open. It took her a moment to recognize the dimly lit room and massive, walnut furniture as Gabe's. A heavy weight lay across the center of her back. That also belonged to Gabe. She smiled in contentment and closed her eyes once again, only for them to spring back open when Gabe groaned in his sleep.

He thrashed in the tangled covers, kicking Melanie hard in the shin.

She cringed and tried to move out of his reach.

"No," he moaned. "No, please."

She barely avoided a fist to the ribs. If she was going to survive the night unscathed, she'd have to wake him from his nightmare.

"Gabe," she said calmly, laying a hand on his shoulder. She gave him a gentle shake. "Sweetheart, wake up. You're having a bad dream."

"No!" he shouted and sat bolt upright, nearly knocking Melanie clean off the mattress. His eyes searched the room wildly, finally settling on her. He let out a heavy sigh and swung his long legs over the edge of the bed. He sat taking deep breaths and then scrubbed his eyes with both hands. He rested his elbows on his thighs and buried his face in his palms, his breathing slowly returning to normal.

"Is everything okay?" Melanie asked. He'd looked terrified when he'd first opened his eyes. She wasn't sure she wanted to know what was haunting him so profoundly, but she asked anyway, because she wanted to be there for him if he needed her. "Do you want to talk about it?"

He shook his head almost imperceptibly.

"You'll feel better."

"I haven't had that nightmare in years," he said. "Stupid kid. Stupid fucking kid. Brought it all back. Fucking all of it."

Melanie puzzled over his words for a moment. "The kid who hit your dog?"

He nodded slightly.

"He didn't mean to," Melanie said, not knowing what else to say.

"Did he mean to get drunk? Did he mean to get behind the wheel?"

"I-I guess so."

"Then stop making excuses for the little shit."

"I'm not. I guess I don't understand why you're more upset about him being drunk than him hitting Lady."

She crept across the mattress and knelt behind him. When her hand touched his shoulder, he jumped as if she'd slapped him.

"What were you dreaming about?"

"You don't want to know."

"I do. Tell me."

"He wasn't dead, Melanie."

She crinkled her brow. "Of course he's not dead, sweetheart. I'm sure he made it home safely. You worry too much." As if she could talk.

"Not the kid from this afternoon," he said. "Joey. They told his parents that he died instantly when he slammed into the tree. Told them that he didn't suffer. It was a lie, Mel. A merciful lie, maybe, but still a lie."

She slid her hand over his smooth back and rested her head on his shoulder, waiting for him to continue.

"I heard the crash. I knew it was Joey, and I ran to see what had happened. I didn't have any problem locating the car. I just followed a strange orange glow in the distance. The car was on fire. I could hear him screaming, Melanie. He wasn't dead." Gabe ran one hand around his neck. "I never heard anyone scream like that before. When I got to the car, I stood there in shock. I couldn't move. I didn't help him. His legs were pinned, and the car was too damaged to get him out, but I didn't know that at the time. I didn't even fucking try to help him. It was like the whole thing was happening to someone else, like I wasn't really there. Just watching a movie or something. Not watching a friend burn alive."

Her heart ached for Gabe and for Joey, a boy she didn't even know. A boy long gone.

"No one expected you to pull him out of a burning car, Gabe."

"Someone did," Gabe said. "Joey did." He dropped his head. "He must have seen me standing there because what he was screaming and screaming and screaming was my name." He covered his ears with both hands. "Standing there, I wished I was deaf. Wished I was deaf so I didn't have to hear him scream. Why didn't I wish for him to be saved, Melanie? Isn't that what I should have been wishing for? I didn't. I just wished I was deaf."

She covered her mouth with the back of her hand, feeling sick. She forced herself not to fall apart, wrapped her arms around him and hugged, hoping to give him strength. He was shaking so hard, he couldn't even hug her back.

"There's nothing you could have done," she whispered.

He made a sound—half laugh, half moan of misery. "I could have taken his fucking keys away. I could have called his parents to come pick him up. I could have stopped him from driving. That would have been easy. Hearing him screaming for help? Not easy. Hearing it in my nightmares over ten years later? *Still* not easy." He gripped his knees until his knuckles turned white. "Fuck. I should have done more to stop that kid this afternoon. What if he overturned the truck? What if he's out in some desolate field, trapped inside, dying right now? No one would even know where to look for him."

"He's not, sweetheart. I'm sure he's fine."

"But how do you know?"

"I don't," she admitted. She ran her fingers through the soft strip of hair down the center of his head, trying to comfort both of them. She tried to catch his eye, but he was too busy staring into the horror in his own mind to see her. "Why don't you call the police station and see if they picked him up? You'll feel better knowing that he's safe."

Gabe tensed and then turned his head. His eyes focused on hers at last, and she breathed a sigh of relief.

"Why didn't I think of that?" He kissed her and pushed up

from the bed. "My woman is a genius," he said. Before she could track his movement, he was already out of the room.

She prayed that the cops had come to pick the kid up after Gabe had called them. If they hadn't, she'd pack Gabe into the truck and go looking for the teen and his rusted old pickup truck. Gabe wouldn't be able to rest until he was sure the kid was safe.

She pushed her hair off her face and rubbed her eyes. Lord, she could only imagine the guilt he felt over Joey's death. She didn't even want to think about what it had been like for him to hear his name screamed in agony. And to keep hearing it in his dreams? She shuddered.

She was glad they'd lied to Joey's parents and told them that their son had died instantly. No one needed the burden of the details. Certainly not her hunky, nerdy, sweetheart of a rock star. She wished she could erase that memory from his mind and his heart. She couldn't even fool herself into believing that she'd made any sort of a difference in listening to him tell the story. And now it would haunt her too.

Wide awake, she climbed from the bed, stretching her arms over her head and taking note of the time. It was just after ten p.m. Her stomach reminded her that they'd skipped dinner. Again.

She was going to write a book on the Gabriel Banner Diet Plan: how to lose weight by being too distracted to remember to eat. The accompanying exercise book would be X-rated for sure. Equipment not included. Readers would have to find their own distracting hunk and accessories—Gabriel Banner was her workout partner and hers alone.

She headed toward the kitchen for something to eat and hoped he didn't mind her making herself at home.

She was bent at the waist searching for food in the fridge—and she was pretty sure that three olives did not make a meal—when she heard an intake of breath behind her.

"Now that is definitely the most delicious thing that's ever been in my kitchen," Gabe said.

"Food?" she asked, backing out of the refrigerator and looking for whatever Gabe had discovered as delicious. "Where?"

He chuckled. "I was referring to you," he said.

She flushed. "Oh. Thanks. But I could really use something that *I* would find delicious."

"How about a protein shot?"

"Eww, Gabe!" She cringed and he laughed.

"I keep the fridge empty when I'm on the road, but there are probably some nonperishable goods in the pantry."

"I was starting to think you don't ever eat. It would explain why you're so lean." And why he looked so damned good naked.

"I think that's from all the energy I expend drumming."

"Oh."

"And when you're near, fucking."

All part of the Gabriel Banner diet plan, she thought, but she didn't want to sound stupid, so she refrained from voicing her thoughts.

He went to a narrow door off the kitchen and disappeared.

"Let's see," he called out to her. "We have beans, peaches, and spaghetti sauce. What sounds good?"

"Protein shots."

He popped his head out of the pantry to look at her in surprise, and then he laughed. "That can be dessert. I don't think you should swallow that stuff on an empty stomach."

"I don't think I should swallow it at all. Do you have any pasta to go with that spaghetti sauce?"

He brought out a mostly empty box of penne, a bit of elbow macaroni in a cellophane bag and half a serving of fettuccini. "This should be interesting," he said.

She followed him into the kitchen and leaned against the counter to watch him as he set a pot of water to boil.

"Did you get in touch with the police about that kid?" she asked, thinking he must have because his mood had improved significantly.

"Yeah, the truck was impounded and his grandfather came to pick the kid up from the station," he said. "I bet he'll think twice before getting wasted and stealing his grandfather's truck in the future."

"I'm glad he's safe."

"Me too," Gabe said and rummaged through the freezer until he found some frozen meatballs, frozen garlic bread, and frozen vegetables.

"So that's where you hide all the food," she said.

"I guess I should have gone shopping this afternoon instead of making you go swimming against your will."

"I had fun at the lake," she said.

"I'm glad you're easy to satisfy." He tossed the frozen meatballs into the microwave.

"I wouldn't say that. I'd say it's the company I've been keeping that made today perfect."

She caught his pleased smile as he wrested a cookie sheet out of a cabinet with a loud clatter. She knew people complimented him all the time about his musical talent, but she got the feeling that few truly appreciated him for who he was off tour.

The doorbell rang, and Melanie stiffened, acutely aware that she was naked and that the entire front of Gabe's house was glass.

"Who would be visiting at this hour?" she said, hurrying toward the bedroom for clothes.

Gabe was right on her heels. "It can only be one person," he said.

A female voice called from the foyer. "I saw your lights on. Are you fit for company?"

"Who is it?" Melanie said, thinking it awfully rude for someone to barge into someone else's house without an invitation at almost eleven o'clock at night. She shimmied into a clean pair of panties and hunted through her suitcase for an outfit that sort of matched.

"That would be my mother," Gabe said, tossing a long-sleeved T-shirt over his head. He was fully dressed and rushing out the bedroom door before Melanie could get her arm in a single sleeve.

"His mother?" she said under her breath. She eyed his bed, not because she wanted to roll around in the sheets with him, but because it looked like a decent place to hide.

CHAPTER NINETEEN

GABE FOUND HIS MOTHER in the living room, holding up Melanie's discarded bra with one finger.

"I see you've been busy," she said, her tone disapproving.

Gabe scooped up the clothes scattered all over the room and hurried to hide them in the half-bath.

"Is she still here?"

"Don't embarrass her," Gabe said. He was used to the constant condemnation of being a disappointment to his mother, but Melanie wouldn't know what hit her when Katherine Banner let loose her better-than-thou routine.

"Well," his mother said. "Where is she? In your bedroom, I suppose."

"If I'd known you'd stop by unannounced, I'd have hidden her in the barn."

"Will you cover up those horrible tattoos?" she said. "You know I can't stand to look at them."

She was referring to the ones on his head. He'd already covered the ones on his body with long sleeves. He didn't bother to argue since they'd been over this a thousand times in the past. She treated him almost normal as long as she wasn't confronted by his body modifications. He slipped a baseball cap onto his head and heard the hiss of water hitting the hot burner in the kitchen.

"I have something boiling over on the stove," he said and jogged to the kitchen.

He was glad to see Melanie taking care of his forgotten meal, but not glad that his mother had followed him.

"And you would be...?" his mom said in a tone dripping with disapproval.

"I'm Melanie." She extended her hand toward his mother and they exchanged a terse handshake. "It's a pleasure to meet you, Mrs. Banner."

"Kathy," she said.

Gabe was a bit surprised that she'd offered up her name so readily. She smiled warmly at Melanie.

"You look positively normal," she said, her body going limp. "The last girl he brought home had pink hair and her nose pierced."

Melanie looked to Gabe for guidance. He shrugged slightly. His mother had never taken a shine to any woman he dated.

"Well, I must warn you," Melanie said. "I do have my navel pierced."

His mom patted Melanie's arm as if a pierced navel was the least of her concerns. "That's nothing. My son has tattoos on his head." She pointed to her own mass of short light brown curls. "On. His. *Head.*"

Melanie chuckled. "Yeah, I noticed that."

"It doesn't bother you?"

"I was a bit startled by them at first," Melanie admitted, "but I'd already seen what he was like on the inside and the outer package was just gravy."

Gabe smiled to himself, loving that Melanie was unashamed to speak of her attraction to him. Could she tell how much his mother abhorred his tattoos? If Melanie truly wanted to gain his mother's favor all she had to do was agree that the only thing worse than Gabe dropping out of college to become a drummer-of-all-things was having his scalp tattooed. Apparently, Melanie declaring that she liked who he was on the inside was a good strategy as well.

Gabe watched dumbfounded as his mom looped an arm through Melanie's and sat with her at the breakfast bar, leaving him to finish cooking.

"He had such a promising future before he joined that rock band," his mother said, as if she were trying to talk Melanie out of doing something foolish, like fall in love with her rock star son. "We all thought he was going to follow in his father's footsteps, though Gabe was always more interested in the application of physics than in the theory behind it."

Melanie choked, no doubt thinking about how he applied physics. The tips of his ears burned with embarrassment. He in no way wanted his *mother* to know about his little hobby.

"I think he's doing all right for himself," Melanie said, and offered Gabe a wink. "Are you a nurse, then?" Melanie asked, examining his mother's dark blue scrubs.

Gabe cringed. Melanie's honeymoon period with his mother was about to come to a crashing end.

His mom clicked her tongue against her teeth in disapproval. "And you were doing so well, Melanie. If I was a man in scrubs, you'd have thought I was..."

"A dentist?" Melanie guessed.

"A doctor."

"My mother is a surgeon," Gabe said, to let Melanie off the hook. His mother always played these little games with people. It drove him nuts.

"Oh," Melanie said, looking impressed, "what kind of surgeon?"

"Heart surgeon. I was on my way home from the hospital after an emergency procedure when I saw Gabe's lights on and thought I'd stop in to say hello. Doesn't my son talk about his family?"

"A bit," Melanie lied kindly.

"Where are you from?" his mom asked. "You don't sound local."

"Kansas."

In the ten minutes it took Gabe to finish cooking their meal, his mother questioned Melanie about her education, her career, her family, her health, her parents' health, her grandparents' health, and her future prospects. Gabe's head was spinning just from hearing the interview. He assumed Melanie would be exhausted after the extensive third degree.

Gabe mixed the hodgepodge of pasta with spaghetti sauce, microwaved meatballs, and parmesan cheese and set the pan on the granite countertop of the breakfast bar with a clunk.

"Are you staying for supper, mama?" he asked, praying silently that she would see her way out the door.

"What in the world are you feeding our pretty little Melanie?" she asked, eyeing the pan of pasta speculatively.

"Smells wonderful." Melanie tossed him a bone.

"Spaghetti-less spaghetti," Gabe said and removed the

toasted garlic bread from the oven. He tossed it on the counter with a clatter and turned back to the stove to collect the pan of mixed vegetables that had boiled dry and were slightly scorched. "Um," his mom said, sliding from the stool. "I should probably head home. Your father will be worried."

At this time of night, his father would be obliviously asleep in his recliner, but Gabe wasn't going to argue her out of leaving. He loved his mother dearly, but at times he had a hard time dealing with her unending scrutiny. He simply could not relax in her company.

His mom slipped from her bar stool, gave Melanie an enthusiastic hug, and crooked a finger at Gabe to beckon him to the door.

"Go ahead and start without me," he said to Melanie. "I know you're hungry."

"She must be if she's willing to eat your cooking," his mom teased.

Melanie made a show of heaping her plate with spaghetti-less spaghetti and scorched vegetables. It warmed his heart to have her so firmly in his corner. His mother was not a person easily crossed.

At the door, his mother gave him a quick hug. "She's wonderful," she said approvingly. "Don't let her get away."

"If you didn't manage to scare her off, I don't think she's going anywhere."

Beau stood up from his place on the rug by the door and nudged his mom's hand to receive his customary scratch behind the ears. She obliged enthusiastically. "Where's Lady?"

"She's at the animal clinic," he said. "She got hit by a truck this afternoon."

"Oh my God," she said. "Why didn't you tell me? Was she seriously hurt?"

He nodded. "Yeah, but the vet thinks she'll pull through."

Kathy patted his cheek. "You should have called, Boo. We could have helped you with her."

His mother hadn't called him Boo in over ten years. What was up with her tonight?

"Melanie helped me out."

She smiled. "She'll make a great mother for my

grandchildren."

Gabe's stomach sank, and his balls tried to hide in his belly. *Grandchildren?* What the fuck? His mother had known Melanie for less than half an hour and already had her popping out Banner offspring? Wasn't that a tad premature?

He opened the door. "Love you, mom."

She beamed and shrugged her shoulders up to her ears in a very girlish gesture he had never witnessed out of her in his entire life. "Love you too, Boo."

She practically skipped across the porch, and Gabe gaped at her, wondering when pod people had invaded the earth. Who was that woman? She looked like his mother, but she sure wasn't acting like her.

When she was safely inside her Cadillac, he closed the door, made sure to lock it this time, and returned to the kitchen. Beau followed at Gabe's heels, looking for a bite to eat, no doubt.

"I think my mom has a girl crush on you," Gabe said to Melanie as he scooped food onto two plates—one for himself and another with extra, extra meatballs for his dog.

"She was certainly interested in getting to know me," Melanie said. "But she seemed really nice."

"That"—he pointed at Mel with his fork and shook his head—"is what worries me."

CHAPTER TWENTY

THE NEXT MORNING, Gabe left Melanie and Beau to sleep and climbed in his truck to go visit Lady.

Lady was so happy to see him, the vet assistant threatened to make him leave the room so the dog didn't pull out her stitches with her overenthusiastic tail wagging. Lady tried to get up to greet him, but didn't make it to her feet. He didn't know if it was weakness or the awkwardness of her cast, but he figured she shouldn't be standing anyway. He entered her temporary kennel and sat on the concrete floor beside where she lay on a thick pallet. He petted her face, head, and shoulders, careful to avoid the large white bandage on her side and the cast on her foreleg. He bent to kiss her whiskery nose and said, "What am I going to do with you while I'm on the road for the next two weeks? Do you think you can stand it in here for that long?"

She whined piteously and swatted at him with her good leg.

"I know it's not ideal, but I can't imagine taking care of you on the tour bus. Your regular dog sitter can only come out once a day, but maybe I can hire someone else to stay with you fulltime."

The vet assistant was working at a counter at the end of the cavernous room, but she apparently had good hearing.

"Why don't you take her to your parents' house?" she suggested. "They're good people. I'm sure they wouldn't mind taking care of Lady while you're gone."

One problem with living in a small community was that everyone knew who your parents were and everyone knew all your business.

"They're busy," Gabe said.

"Lady can stay here while you're gone, but she's sure to get really lonesome. Some dogs get so depressed when they're injured and abandoned that they fail to thrive and…" She shrugged.

He didn't want to think about what she meant by that shrug. Lady was the type of dog that craved constant attention. And his parents liked his dogs. Maybe they wouldn't mind keeping her at their place for a couple weeks. Well, the entire summer if he was being truthful about the matter. But maybe in a few weeks Lady would be able to stay at her own home without constant care and supervision.

"If they're too busy," Gabe said, "would you be interested in keeping her for a couple weeks? I could pay you."

She chuckled. "I don't think my cats would appreciate that. And Lady is a high-strung dog. She'd be much calmer around people she knows. Besides, your mom is a people doctor, so I think she could handle the limited care for an injured dog. And doesn't your dad have the summer off?"

How did the woman know so much about him? He couldn't place where he knew her from, but he must know her fairly well. Of course, her back was to him, so he couldn't see her face clearly.

"He works on his research over the summer," Gabe said. But compared to his school-year schedule, summers were a lot less busy for his physics-professor father.

Gabe guessed he could try persuading his parents to help out and if that didn't work, he'd see if any of his local friends would watch over Lady. If all else failed, he'd pack her up on the tour bus and try to keep her as calm as possible. He didn't really see that as a reasonable option. Maybe Melanie would be willing to take her back to her apartment in Kansas. But how would they transport her there? He doubted Lady was in good enough condition to fly. And Melanie had work and other life responsibilities, so he couldn't expect her to stay at his place to take care of his dog.

He sighed. Yep, parents, it was.

Even though it made the most sense to ask them for assistance, he hated to ask them for any help. It must remind them of what a disappointment he was to them.

"So how are your sisters?" the vet tech asked, as if to shred his pride a little more. Neither of them were disappointments to their parents. "I haven't heard from Leslie in years."

Gabe suddenly recalled that the tech and Leslie had been in the same graduating class in high school. She'd been one of popular-cheerleader-Leslie's many, many friends.

"She's in Boston finishing up her second residency," Gabe said.

"I always knew she'd be a doctor. Smart as a whip." Following in her mother's footsteps.

"And Jennifer?" the tech asked.

"Associate Professor of Mathematics at MIT."

Another doctor in the family. Gabe was the only one without any letters behind his name. Hell, he hadn't even finished his bachelor's degree. He was surprised his family hadn't disowned him already. Even his grandparents on both sides were either medical doctors or had their PhDs.

"And then there's the black sheep of the family—their little brother, the famous rock star," the tech teased, turning from her work at the counter to grin at him. "How did that happen in a family of brainiacs?"

Gabe shrugged. "Debauchery by proximity."

"Ah yes, so how is Jacob Silverton, Mr. Debauchery himself?"

Jacob would have graduated with Leslie and the tech-whose-name-escaped-him if he'd actually finished school. Even Gabe's tutoring hadn't kept Jacob in school long enough to earn his high school diploma.

"He's fine," Gabe said, not wanting to revisit old times.

"And Adam? I heard he's had a few episodes of overdosing and is lucky to be alive."

One of many reasons why Adam never wanted to come home. People talked, a lot, and for some reason it made them feel better about their own pathetic lives to focus on the worst part of a successful person's plight.

"He's doing well." Thanks to Madison, he added silently. No way was Gabe going to feed the small town gossip.

"I always figured Jake and Adam would be famous rock stars one day, but I wouldn't have put my money on *you* becoming one."

Gabe shrugged. That would have made two of them.

"You were the geekiest thing in high school," she added with a nostalgic laugh.

Okay, ouch. Enough already.

"So can I take Lady home today?" he asked, hoping to deter the woman from further prying and from delivering additional kicks to his pride.

"I doubt Dr. Nelson will release her just yet, but I'll go ask her."

Gabe stroked Lady's soft fur absently as he waited for the tech to return. He wondered how different his life would have been if Jacob hadn't recruited him as the drummer of Sole Regret. Would he have been happier as a geeky physicist? He doubted it. His current life rocked. But he supposed he'd never know. Even though he wondered about what he could have made of himself had he chosen differently, he didn't regret leaving college. He didn't even regret being the odd man out in his family of doctors. He would probably always wonder what he could have been if he'd taken a different path, but didn't everyone?

The tech returned and leaned over the kennel door.

"Dr. Nelson thinks Lady should stay at least one more night. Can you pick her up tomorrow?"

"It'll have to be early. I have to catch a flight back to New Orleans in the morning."

"You could always ask one of your parents to come get her."

And after all his mental back and forth, he *still* didn't want to ask them for assistance. But he would. For Lady's sake.

"I'll make it work," he said. He bent low to kiss Lady on the head and closed the door to the large kennel behind him as he let himself out. "Be a good dog," he said in parting. She didn't open her eyes, so he doubted that she'd heard him. She didn't know how to be a good dog anyway, but it didn't stop him from loving her.

On his way back home, he thought about driving past his house and to the stately colonial a mile down the road, but he was missing Melanie already, so he turned in to his drive instead of going directly to his parents. He found her sitting on the front porch steps, Beau at her hip, while she stared at her phone with a scowl on her face.

Beau wagged a greeting, but Melanie only offered Gabe a

slight nod when he dropped down beside her on the step. He'd been hoping to find her still in bed so he could wake her with an orgasm and a smile.

"Something wrong?" he asked.

"I still haven't heard from Nikki. It's been two nights, Gabe. I'm really worried about her. Do you think I should call the hotel?"

"Will it make you feel better?"

"Only if she answers."

He cupped the back of her head and slid his hand down to give her neck an encouraging squeeze. "I'm sure she's fine, but go ahead and call her so you can stop worrying."

She stared at her phone for a solid minute. "She's probably still asleep at this hour. Maybe she's learned to be responsible and doesn't need me, so that's why she hasn't returned my calls or texts."

"If she'd learn to be responsible, she would have returned them so you didn't worry about her."

Melanie sighed and nodded. "If she hasn't called by noon, I'll call the hotel."

"Sounds like a plan."

She shoved her phone into the pocket of her shorts and smiled at him. "I missed you this morning. How is Lady doing?"

He'd left Melanie a note by a freshly brewed pot of coffee explaining where he'd gone. Apparently, she'd found it and had been able to read his illegible scrawl.

"She was awake for a while and she knew who I was. She looks pretty beat up, though. I have to find someone to take care of her while I'm on the road."

"I wish I could help, Gabe, but there's just no way."

He took her hand and held it. "I know, baby. Don't look so guilty. I was thinking of asking my parents to watch her, I just..." *Need you there to support me.* "...uh, thought maybe you'd like to go with me so my mother can fawn over you some more."

"Will I get to meet your dad?"

"He should be home. He occasionally takes a Sunday off."

"Let me get my shoes."

She let Beau into the house with her. Gabe closed his eyes,

basking in the Texas heat, listening to the serenity around him. Except for the hum of insects, the occasional chirp of a bird, and a persistent toad croaking in the distance, his ears were blessed with silence. His home life was so different from his life on the road. And he was ready to share it with someone special. But was someone special ready to share it with him? He'd wait a while before asking her. He didn't need to rush. The last thing he wanted to do was scare her away by moving too quickly.

The screen door bumped closed, and he glanced over his shoulder at Melanie, who had her shoes on now. She also had all of her hair stuffed under the cowboy hat she wore.

"Nice hat," he said.

"I wouldn't want to offend your parents with my bed hair," she said.

He almost said that if his hair didn't offend them, nothing would, but his hair did offend them. "You look cute," he said, "but you know I love that hair of yours, even when birds are eyeing it as nesting material."

She laughed. "Not birds," she said. "Raccoons."

Since it was only a mile to his parents' house, he convinced Melanie to ride with him on one of his ATVs and take the scenic route. He made her trade her cowboy hat for a helmet and zoomed across a pasture, weaved through trees in a bumpy wooded area, and splashed through a creek at the bottom of a heart-stoppingly steep hill before skidding to a stop behind his childhood home. While Gabe's log house blended with the woods and the scenery, his parents' stately colonial looked like it belonged in a Louisiana bayou. It was impressive, to say the least.

"That was fun!" Melanie said breathlessly.

"Better than fishing?"

"Well, *dryer* than fishing," she said.

He wiped a few splatters of mud from her bare leg. "Potentially," he said.

"Gabriel!" his father called from the back porch. He pulled himself out of his favorite rocking chair, using a heavy wooden cane for assistance, and hobbled down the steps on his stiff left leg to meet them in the yard. Melanie took off her helmet and attempted to smooth her untamed hair. It was a losing cause;

raccoons were already closing in.

"Is this the young lady that has your mama mooning about grandbabies again?"

"Nice, Dad. Let's terrify her before you've even been introduced," Gabe said. "This is my old man, Luke. And this is my new girlfriend, Melanie."

Melanie's gaze darted to Gabe's as he tried out the *girlfriend* word for the first time, but she didn't make him retract the statement, so he was feeling pretty good about his prospects of making it a reality.

His dad extended his tanned and weathered left hand because his right was tightly gripping his cane. Melanie naturally extended her right hand so instead of shaking hands, they ended up awkwardly holding hands, but her charming giggle melted the old man on the spot. Gabe was feeling pretty good about that too.

"Come up on the porch in the shade," his dad said. "You'll bake your brain in this heat."

By the time they made it to the porch, his mother had brought out a pitcher of iced tea and four glasses.

"So glad you stopped by," she said. "Even though my Gabriel only lives a mile down the road, I hardly ever see him."

"You saw me yesterday," Gabe reminded her.

"How's Lady?" his dad asked. "Mom told me she was hit by a car."

"I visited her this morning. She's going to be fine." It was a perfect opening to ask if they'd be willing to take care of her while he was on tour, but he reached for a glass of tea instead.

"That's great," his dad said. "Kathy made it sound like your dog was pretty banged up."

"I thought she was," his mom said. "Will she be okay by herself while you're gone?"

Opening number two, gaping wide. Gabe took a sip of his tea and glanced at Melanie, who gave him an odd look.

"I wish I could stay and keep an eye on her," Melanie said, "but I have to work."

Opening number three slipped right by.

"Do you need someone to watch her?" his dad asked.

"Well..."

Melanie squeezed his leg beneath the table.

"I could probably use a hand with her," Gabe said, "but I know how busy you both are."

"Yeah, watching this grass grow all summer keeps me overextended," his dad said and then laughed.

"Aren't you doing research this summer?" Gabe asked.

"Didn't we tell you?" his mom asked.

"Tell me what?"

"Your dad is starting to hand off his unfinished projects to the junior scientists in the department so he can retire next spring."

"Dad's retiring?" Gabe sputtered. But only old people retired. Sure, his dad was in his sixties, but he was far from old.

"I know we told you," his mom said, patting his father's hand. "We told him, Luke. Didn't we?"

"No one told me anything," Gabe said.

"We told you on the phone months ago," his mom said.

Gabe shook his head. He would have remembered that his father was retiring. It was sort of a big deal.

"Maybe we told Leslie and Jennifer and forgot to tell him," his dad said, looking reflective.

"All anyone in this family ever tells me is what a huge disappointment I am," Gabe blurted.

"What are you talking about, Gabriel?" his mother said sternly. "No one ever—"

"*He had such a promising future before he joined that rock band,*" he mimicked her exact words from the night before. "*Leslie is our MD and Jennifer our PhD and Gabe, well, let's just say he turned out a little different from what we expected.*" He'd heard her tell some stranger that a couple of months before.

"We aren't disappointed in you, son," his dad said, "but you *are* a little different." He chuckled at Gabe's expense

"I'm glad he's different," Melanie blurted. "It makes him that much more wonderful."

Stunned, Gabe glanced at Melanie, who covered her mouth with trembling fingertips and looked from one of his parents to the other, a horrified expression on her face. He couldn't tell if she was about to cry or punch someone in the nose, but he could tell that she was upset. And once again standing firmly in his corner.

"I can't believe you think we're disappointed in you, Gabe," his mother said. "I never thought you'd take my bragging the wrong way."

"You have a right to brag about Leslie and Jennifer," Gabe said, "they're both everything you expected them to be."

His mom reached over and patted his face, rather harder than necessary. "You, hush. I was bragging about *you*. Every family has a doctor. Hell, ours has twelve, but not everyone can say they have a rock star for a son. But I still hate those damned tattoos. On. Your. Head. Gabe. Why did you have to get them on your head?"

Melanie giggled.

"The young lady seems okay with them," his dad said.

The young lady seemed okay with everything about him. And for the first time in a very long time, he found he could relax in the company of his parents. He still didn't quite believe that his mother actually *bragged* about him, but he almost believed that they weren't entirely disappointed in him and hadn't written him out of their will.

"So about that dog of yours…" His father prompted, giving him opening number five or number six. Gabe had lost track.

"Would you mind going to pick her up from the vet's office tomorrow and nursing her back to health?" Gabe asked.

"On one condition." His father lifted a finger at him, and he half expected him to require he get the dragon tattoos removed from his scalp.

"What's that?" he asked.

"That Beau stays here with her so she doesn't drive me nuts with her constant need for attention."

Gabe smiled, his love for the man squeezing his throat. "You have a deal."

"Good," he said. "Now I insist on Melanie telling me everything about herself since I already know all about you." His dad winked at him and then turned his attention to Melanie. She soon discovered that she was the most popular rock star at this particular table.

CHAPTER TWENTY-ONE

FINDING HERSELF SPRAWLED NAKED across Gabe's bed once again, Melanie touched the back of his head, her eyes closed in bliss. Sparks of pleasure danced along her nerve endings as he sucked at her nipple, apparently intent on making it as hard as a diamond.

"Do you think they like me?" she asked, still thinking about their visit with his parents. She and Gabe had returned to his house less than ten minutes ago and before she could ask him if he thought things had gone well, he'd had her naked and moaning in his bed. His parents had made her feel welcome during their short visit, but maybe they were that nice to everyone.

"My lips definitely like you," Gabe murmured.

"I mean your parents. Do you think *they* like me?"

His head popped up, and he stared at her, his long nose crinkled in displeasure. "Please tell me you are *not* thinking about my parents right now."

She couldn't help it. Meeting them had been a big deal to her. "I just didn't expect them to be so friendly."

Gabe dropped his forehead against her chest. "I can't believe you're actually thinking about my parents right now."

"I'm sorry," she said. "Please continue."

She grabbed his head and directed his mouth back to her nipple. His warm, wet tongue traced the sensitive tip and she shuddered.

After she enjoyed another moment of his tender assault on her breast, the thoughts racing through her busy brain still refused to quiet, so she asked, "Why are you always so tightlipped about your home life? Whenever I ask you questions about yourself or your family, you change the subject."

He bit her nipple, *hard*, and she sucked a breath through her teeth.

"Is it because you'd always had your family's approval and now you think you don't?"

"Maybe," he said.

"That really bothers you, doesn't it?"

Gabe sighed loudly. "This calls for some assistance," he said and rolled off the bed.

She lifted her head and watched his sexy ass flex with each step he took toward his armoire. He was after his toys again.

"I'll be quiet," she promised. But she really wanted to talk about his reluctance to share his personal life. Maybe he'd be more open to conversation after he took care of the raging hard-on he was currently sporting. There were times to be nosy and times to shut up. She'd completely missed the mark on this one.

"Too late," he said. He scooped armloads of gadgets against his chest, carried them to the bed, and dropped them on the mattress beside her. "Maybe, I have a gag in here somewhere."

"I'll be *quiet*," she said again.

"I don't want you to be quiet. I want you screaming. But not about my parents."

He lifted an oddly shaped phallus from his collection of implements, inspected it, and then set it aside. She wondered what it was for and whether he'd just placed it in his use-it or his reject pile. He held several gadgets up to her breast, added them all to the pile that included the intriguing phallus and then he lifted a very long, slender rod. He tested its flexibility against his palm before setting it aside. As he reached for the next tool in his arsenal, Melanie slid the discarded slender rod into the growing assembly of inventions she assumed he planned to use.

Her pussy tingled and throbbed as she anticipated the variety of pleasures Gabe was undoubtedly about to bestow upon her.

He finished fiddling with what looked like a small saddle with two holes in it and again studied his piles of toys. He frowned at the relocated rod. His head jerked up and his gaze settled on hers.

She smiled timidly. "I thought I might like that one." Even though she had no idea what it was for.

"I guess I'll just have try out everything," he said, "since I can't decide what will make you scream my name the loudest."

"I don't mind experimenting," she said.

He grinned, and her heart stumbled around in her chest like a lame antelope.

"All in the name of science," he said.

"I have a feeling this is going to be a Nobel Prize-worthy discovery," she said, fingering a wide, flat piece of red latex and wondering what the hell it was for.

"I don't think they have a Nobel Prize for production of the greatest female orgasm."

"Only because they're afraid you'll win every year."

He touched a finger to her lip. Must be time to stop talking and start screaming.

"Today we'll start our experiment with your lovely nipples."

He tried clamps that squeezed, nubs that vibrated, and pinchers that released mild shocks. She enjoyed all of the sensations, but Gabe seemed unsatisfied with her soft gasps and moans of pleasure. He next chose a harmless-looking cup that covered more than half her breast. Something inside the cup rubbed, massaged and pulled at her nipple until she had to squeeze her legs together to keep from coming.

"Oh God, Gabe," she cried.

"I think we have a winner," Gabe said. He located the device's twin and placed it over her exposed breast.

"Wait!" Melanie gasped, knowing she wouldn't be able to stand having both nipples stimulated by his ingenious invention. "Something else on that one. Something that *hurts* a little."

One corner of his mouth quirked upward. "You are just full of surprises, Miss Melanie."

He clipped a metal clamp to her free nipple and turned up the voltage. She couldn't decide if the shocks hurt or felt good, but there was no doubt that they turned her on.

"Ah fuck," she groaned and rocked her hips to ease the building need between her thighs. Every pulse of energy at her breast travelled down her belly and to her pussy, making it clench with need.

Her hand moved between her legs. She dipped her fingers into heated wetness and then rubbed herself to release using rapid strokes against her clit. She shattered, pleasure coursing through her body as her thighs clamped shut over her hand and she quaked with bliss.

"Fuck, you're sexy, Mel," Gabe said.

She forced her thighs apart, still rubbing her clit slowly to ease herself gently back to earth.

"Mmm," she murmured, but her relief was short lived. The stimulation to her breasts was already moving her toward the point of painful arousal once again.

Gabe used both hands to push her trembling thighs farther apart. He was kneeling between her legs on the bed. She'd been too lost in sensation to know when he'd joined her, but her pussy throbbed with excitement as she stared at the thick cock standing rigid between her open thighs.

"I want you," she said, her voice thick and low.

Gabe's belly visibly quivered. "I love the tone of your voice when you're turned on. Tell me what you want, Mel."

"You," she said.

"How do you want me?"

"Inside me. Slow. Deep. Your thumb rubbing me here," she said, massaging her clit in gentle circles.

He grabbed a pink object off the bed and inserted his thumb into it. He moved her hand aside and stroked her the way she'd asked, except his rubbery thumb attachment added stimulating pulses of vibration to an already pleasurable experience.

"I was going to use this on your sweet pussy," he said, lifting the oddly shaped phallus she'd seen earlier. He lowered it and rubbed the tip against her opening. "I was going to shove it inside you and fuck you with it until you begged me to stop."

She whimpered, suddenly aware of the emptiness she felt deep inside.

"But I'm feeling a bit selfish at the moment." He tossed the tool aside and crept forward. "I need to feel that hot pussy around me."

She groaned in admiration of his so-called selfishness.

"Lift your hips for me, baby," he said.

Her butt rose off the bed, and he shoved a pillow under her lower back to help her maintain the angle. He stared down at where his thumb massaged her clit and watched his cock penetrate her one agonizingly slow inch at a time. His mouth dropped open a little more with each inch he claimed and his green eyes glazed over with pleasure. Melanie's fingers dug into the mattress beneath her as her inner walls clenched rhythmically around his thick cock, drawing his fullness deeper. Deeper. *Good God, Gabe, fill me. Fuck me.*

"Stretched around me like that, your pussy looks fantastic," he murmured. His eyes drifted closed and the muscles of his face twitched. "And it feels even better."

He began to move inside her, maintaining the slow rhythm she'd claimed to desire. But the pleasure and pain rippling through her nipples and the vibrating pulses coming from the thumb massaging her clit soon had her pleading for more.

"Faster, Gabe. Please."

He massaged her clit faster, but his deep, slow thrusts never lost their unhurried cadence.

"I think I'm coming," she gasped, surprised by the intensity of her pleasure. There were no accompanying waves of release, just a building of ecstasy.

"You're not there yet," he said, changing the direction of his massaging thumb. The motion sent even more waves of pleasure spiraling through her core.

By the time she finally let loose, she was screaming his name.

He pulled out unexpectedly and straightened his body to rise above her. "Watch," he said.

Her eyes sought out his slick cock. He gave it two sharp tugs that sent cum shooting across her lower belly. She'd watched him come for her during their video chats, but feeling his load splatter across her skin added a level of eroticism she had not expected. She reached up to pull him against her, squashing his hand and cock between them.

"God, you make me hot, Gabriel Banner."

He chuckled. "The feeling is mutual, baby," he said in her ear. After a moment, he shifted away slightly. "So what do you want to try out next? We have all day to continue with our experiments."

She blindly groped the mattress beside her and picked up another of his unidentifiable toys. "This thing," she said. She wasn't sure what it did or even where it went, but if Gabe had designed it, she had no doubt she was going to love it.

~ ~ ~

Melanie had relished her morning of being Gabe's sexual test subject, but there was something soul-satisfying about just hanging out with him in his cozy kitchen. When they'd found the strength to join the living world—ravenous hunger had driven them from Gabe's bedroom—they'd made a trip to the store and purchased enough perishables to make a large lunch. They worked well in the kitchen together. Well, he spent most of his time on the deck grilling their steaks and ears of corn while she tossed a salad and baked potatoes, but even though they weren't in the same room, she felt like part of his life when she was in this house.

"Medium rare," he said, placing a rather bloody plate on the counter. "And well done for the lady." He deposited her steak next to his.

"Smells delicious," she said.

"I'm a much better cook when my mother isn't breathing down my neck." He kissed the tip of her nose. "It's been a great day, hasn't it?"

It had. There was only one small dark spot on all her joy. She still hadn't heard from Nikki. On their way to the store, Melanie had called the hotel in New Orleans and they'd patched her through to Gabe's room. Nikki was supposed to be staying there, but she hadn't answered. Recognizing Melanie's distress, Gabe had taken pity on her and had sent Adam, who was staying in the same hotel, to knock on Nikki's door. She hadn't responded his summons either. Maybe she'd decided to go back to Wichita after all. It would have been nice of her to let Melanie know that.

The steaks were delicious. The company was delicious. But Melanie's sense of dread was unsavory at best.

When a familiar ringtone began to blare from her purse in the living room, Melanie paused mid-bite.

"That's Nikki," she said and scrambled from her chair, her heart racing.

She pulled out the phone and answered just before it went to voicemail.

"Nikki?" she said. "Where the hell have you been? I've been worried sick."

The only sound Melanie heard was a sniffle on the other end

of the line.

"Nikki?"

"Can you come get me?" Nikki said, her voice strained.

"Where are you? Are you still in New Orleans?"

"Y-yeah."

"I'm in Austin, hon. I can't come get you until tomorrow."

"He hurt me, Mel."

"Who hurt you? What happened? Are you safe?"

"Please. Please, just... just... come get me." Nikki's broken gasps tore Melanie's heart in two.

"Do you need me to call an ambulance? The cops? Nikki, what happened? Tell me."

"I need you," she said brokenly. "Please, Mel."

"I'm on my way."

CHAPTER TWENTY-TWO

GABE'S ROCK STAR CARD came in handy for getting them to New Orleans quickly. Melanie had tried to get Nikki to tell her what had happened, to get her help from someone who wasn't 500 miles away, but she was adamant that she just needed Melanie.

Gabe held Melanie's hand in support and got her on the chartered flight, but she was too consumed with anxiety to even thank him properly.

"I knew I shouldn't have left her in New Orleans by herself," she muttered under her breath. "It was only a matter of time before something bad happened to her."

"It can't be that bad," Gabe said. "She won't even tell you what's wrong."

But she could still hear those three words echoing through her head. *He hurt me.* No amount of cajoling had gotten Nikki to give her any details and when Melanie had threatened to call for emergency services, Nikki had gone completely hysterical and refused to even tell Melanie where she was.

"I'll tell you where I am when you get to New Orleans," she'd said.

Melanie knew that Nikki depended on her, but it was more than a little scary to realize how much. If she'd been on a larger plane, Melanie would have started pacing the aisle. As it was, she was feeling incredibly claustrophobic in the tiny, incredibly noisy aircraft, and she'd snapped at Gabe more than once.

"Maybe she's exaggerating," Gabe said. "Or making stuff up just to get you to come back a night early."

Melanie glared at him. "How can you say that?" she spat." How can you even *think* that?"

She was glad he was smart enough not to press his theory further. Melanie was still too distraught to want to consider that he might be right.

"She'll be okay," he said, running a hand over her hair and pressing a kiss to her temple. "We'll get her taken care of. I promise."

Melanie buried her face in her hands and took several deep breaths. Her stomach was seizing with nerves. "I feel like I'm going to throw up," she said miserably.

"That's probably my cooking."

She chuckled half-heartedly, knowing he was trying to cheer her up, but until she could see Nikki and know that her friend was truly all right, cheerfulness just wasn't a possibility.

As soon as the plane landed, Melanie called Nikki. When she didn't answer, she really started to panic.

"Isn't there a way to track the location of cellphones?" Melanie asked Gabe. She was ready to go full-out detective if she didn't get Nikki on the line soon.

On her second attempt, Nikki answered. Melanie breathed a sigh of relief. "Why didn't you answer?"

"I was in the shower."

"So where are you? I'm in New Orleans now."

"At the hotel."

"In Gabe's suite?"

"Yeah."

"Have you been there the entire time?"

"No." Her voice sounded hollow. The single word, the distance in her voice, was worse than listening to her cry. Melanie swayed and Gabe was right there to grab her before she collapsed on the sidewalk where they stood waiting for a cab.

"We'll be there as soon as we can."

"We?"

"Gabe is with me."

"Of course."

Nikki was quiet for a moment and Melanie didn't know what to say to break the silence. "Will you tell me what happened?"

"I'm going to take another shower," Nikki said.

She disconnected, and Melanie told Gabe what she'd said and where she was. He didn't press her for more information, just helped her into the nearest cab and told the driver to hurry.

When their knock on the door of the hotel suite went

unanswered, Gabe used his spare key card and unlocked it. Melanie heard the water running in the bathroom. Was Nikki still in the shower?

"I should probably talk to her alone," Melanie said to Gabe.

He nodded and stood back while Melanie let herself into the steamy bathroom and closed the door behind her. There were wrappers and empty containers all over the floor—soaps and shampoos, disposable douches, toothbrushes and mouthwash. She recognized Nikki's need to get clean inside and out. She didn't need a degree in psychology to know what it meant.

"Nikki, honey," she said, her heart in her throat. "I'm here."

"Can you wash my back for me?" she said in a small voice. "I can't reach. I tried. I tried, but I can't reach."

Melanie was almost afraid to open the shower curtain. She had no idea what to expect. Would Nikki be beaten black and blue? Was Melanie strong enough to see someone she cared about like that? Eyes closed, Melanie drew back the curtain slowly. She steeled herself for the worst and opened her eyes. She let out a sigh of relief. Nikki wasn't completely unscathed. Her lip was scabbed over where it had been split and she had several bruises, mostly on her wrists, hips, and thighs, but she mostly looked like herself. A very subdued, dead-eyed facsimile of Nikki Swanson, but at least she was recognizable. Her skin was red from being scrubbed in unbearably hot water and her eyes were swollen from the fall of countless tears, but were now dry. Maybe Nikki didn't have another tear to shed, but Melanie did. Knowing she'd completely breakdown if she spoke, Melanie took the soapy wash cloth out of Nikki's trembling hands and scrubbed her back over and over again while hot tears dripped down her own cheeks.

"Harder," Nikki whispered. "I can still feel him."

Melanie didn't have the know-how to deal with this. She needed to get Nikki some help.

"You're clean now," Melanie said, burning with rage at the fingertip-shaped bruises on Nikki's shoulders. Whoever had done this was going to pay. Melanie would make sure of it.

"I still feel him. Please."

Melanie washed her back again, more gently this time, afraid to add to her pain.

Nikki started to shake uncontrollably. "I'm so cold."

How could she possibly be cold? The water was almost scalding.

"Let's get you dried off and put some warm clothes on," Melanie suggested. "Do you want some soup, maybe?"

"I don't know. I don't... know."

Melanie turned off the water and wrapped Nikki in every towel in the hotel bathroom.

She opened the door and Gabe jerked away from the wall he'd been leaning against. He met Melanie's eyes, a question in his gaze. She shook her head slightly. He then looked at Nikki, and both hands clenched into hard fists.

"Why is he here?" Nikki asked dully.

"He's going to help me take care of you," Melanie said. "Gabe, Nikki is cold. Can you go down to the restaurant and order her some hot soup and some cocoa." She rubbed Nikki's back. "Does that sound good?"

Nikki nodded.

"I'll just call room service," Gabe said.

Melanie gave him a stern look. There was no way she was going to help Nikki dress in front of a man. Not even Gabe. "Go down to the restaurant—"

"Right," he said, and after one last heart-sick glance at Nikki, he left the two of them alone.

Melanie dried Nikki's hair with a towel, and then dug through her huge overnight bag for warm, comfortable clothes. She ended up dressing Nikki in her workout clothes because most of Nikki's wardrobe was far from comfortable. She then swaddled her in blankets and sat on the bed beside her, easing Nikki down until she was lying on her side with her head in Melanie's lap. They'd sat the same way many times before. It broke Melanie's heart that this was such a familiar scene between them.

Melanie stroked Nikki's long damp hair gently and said, "Tell me."

Without embellishment Nikki told her about being alone and bored in the hotel room. About calling that UFC fighter she'd met on the plane. How he showed her a good time on the town. And not such a good time in his hotel room. She left out a lot of details, claiming that she couldn't remember everything. She had a lot of holes in her childhood memories as well. Her psychiatrist's prognosis stated that Nikki's mind had learned to blot out the most disturbing occurrences in her life, past and present. Occasionally her greatest horrors plagued her in nightmares, but she'd been doing well since Melanie had taken *her* under her wing. And now this.

Melanie was still broken hearted for Nikki, but her rage toward Dick Bailey was nearly choking her.

"Did he rape you, Nikki?" Melanie asked.

Nikki nodded, her lower lip trembling.

"When did it happen?"

"Friday night."

"What have you been doing since then?" Melanie asked.

"Praying for you to come get me." Nikki sobbed and turned her face into Melanie's lap.

Melanie cradled her head, stroking her hair to soothe her. "I'm here now," she said. "I'm here."

When Nikki settled down again, Melanie asked, "Why didn't you answer your phone, hon? I tried calling and texting, but you never answered."

"I left my phone here because I was mad at you and then after he finished with me…"

Her shaking intensified, and Melanie squeezed her shoulder. "It's okay. Just breathe. Take deep breaths."

After a moment she quieted. "I got lost, Mel. I couldn't remember the name of this place, so I used your credit card and stayed in some scary hotel near where he dropped me off. I just couldn't stand feeling so filthy inside. I had to get clean." Nikki glanced up at her, her brows crumpled with remorse. "I'm sorry I used your credit card again."

"It's fine." She tried smoothing Nikki's troubled brow with her fingertips. "Don't worry about it."

"From that other hotel, I tried to call you, but couldn't remember your number. I kept dialing some Chinese take-out place in Wichita." She actually chuckled. "*Stop cawing us, wady,*" she said in a very bad attempt at a Chinese accent. "*I awedy tell you dey no Mewanie here.* I didn't know what to do. I was freaking out. And then I got really tired. I must have slept for an entire day in the grossest bed in New Orleans."

"Isn't the hotel name on your key card?" Melanie asked.

She shook her head. "No. Just a logo. I looked in the phone book, but none of the names sounded familiar. And I asked the hotel maid, but she didn't speak English and refused to look at me. I think because of the bruises. So I called a cab and described the place to the driver as best I could remember. I told him I was willing look at every hotel in the city until we found it. He knew the place I was talking about right away and brought me here."

"You must have been scared. I know what it feels like to be lost. I hate that feeling."

Nikki snuggled deeper into Melanie's lap.

"Have you gone to the police and reported what happened?"

Nikki shook her head.

"The hospital?"

She shook her head again. "I don't want to. Please don't make me."

"Nikki, I know you're distraught right now, but you can't let him get away with this. You need to go to the police."

"But Dick Bailey is above the law," she whispered. "That's what he said while he was hurting me. *You're just a little slut and deserve to be fucked like one.*" Her voice turned deeper and Melanie knew Nikki was repeating words she could hear in her head. "*You better shut up and take it or I'm really going to hurt you. That's it. Say please. I love when you beg. Beg for it, cunt. Beg.*" Nikki winced as if someone were striking her. She cried out and covered her head with her arm.

Melanie drew her closer and rocked her. She needed just a minute to crumble, just a second to let the tears fall. Just one moment to be weak so afterward she could be the champion Nikki needed her to be.

"Don't cry, Mel," Nikki pleaded, her hand clenched in Melanie's shirt. "Please don't cry. Anything but that."

Melanie wiped at her tears and she plastered a wavering smile on her face. She held Nikki's sad blue gaze with her own.

"He's not going to hurt you or anyone else again," Melanie said as evenly as she could, hoping to convey strength. "Put your shoes on, Nikki. We're going to the police station."

She shook her head and buried her face in Melanie's lap

again. "I don't want anyone else to know what happened," she said, her words muffled.

Melanie rubbed her back reassuringly, but she wouldn't make Nikki do anything against her will. She'd been forced enough, and Melanie refused to be one more tyrant in her life.

"I know you're scared, hon," Melanie said, "but I'm here with you now, okay? You can count on me. I've got you."

Nikki lay across Melanie's lap, staring unblinking into space. She was considering her options, Melanie guessed, and Melanie let her take the time she needed to gather her strength. No matter how strong Melanie was, she couldn't do this for Nikki. Nikki had to do it herself. When Gabe returned with several kinds of soup and a carafe of cocoa, Nikki rose from Melanie's lap and without another word put on her shoes.

CHAPTER TWENTY-THREE

"THERE'S NO PHYSICAL EVIDENCE," the officer said to Melanie. "No witnesses. We questioned him and he denies everything. Said it was all consensual. So it boils down to her word against his. She can press charges and we can arrest him, but he'll be out in days. I have to be honest here—even if he did do it, unless he confesses, he won't be convicted. There's no evidence anywhere on her body."

What he meant was that they hadn't been able to get a semen sample. There was plenty of evidence as far as Melanie was concerned.

"What about her bruises? And the trauma to her vagina?"

"A night of rough *consensual* sex could explain all of it."

"Can't you *beat* a confession out of him?" Melanie said, completely exasperated. Where was the justice in the world?

"Then it would be coercion and he'd definitely walk away a free man."

"At least he'd be limping," Melanie said.

The officer chuckled, but Melanie wasn't joking.

"I'd love to go vigilante on this prick," he said, "but I have to be on the side of law and the law says—"

"I don't want to hear what the *law* says. It's wrong. I was hoping you could guarantee a conviction. Nikki doesn't even want to press charges. She just wants to forget the whole thing ever happened."

"That's not uncommon for a rape victim."

Melanie understood Nikki's reluctance to relive her ordeal for a judge or a jury or even a police officer, but she couldn't stomach the thought of this guy getting away with hurting her.

"What if he does this to someone else?" Melanie said, still trying to appeal to the officer's sense of justice. "Wouldn't it be better to put him away now?"

"Of course, but—"

Melanie lifted a hand. She'd already heard all the *buts* she could take for one night.

"It's good you're sticking up for her," the officer said. "She has a good friend in you."

Melanie didn't feel like a good friend. She'd deserted Nikki to go off for a weekend of fun with a man. She should have trusted her gut and never have left Nikki to fend for herself in an unfamiliar city. If she couldn't protect Nikki, who could?

"I'm going to take her home," Melanie said. "Is she free to go?"

"She can go; we have her statement," he said.

"Yeah, just not her rapist," Melanie said acidly and stormed out of the office.

She found Nikki sitting on a bench near the exit, staring at the industrial-grade tile at her feet. Gabe sat beside her, looking as comfortable as a bed of nails. He lifted a brow, and Melanie shook her head. He glanced at Nikki and clenched his jaw. Melanie sat beside Nikki and took her hand in hers.

"What did they say?" Nikki asked.

Melanie was tempted to lie, but she couldn't bring herself to do it. "Unless they can find some evidence or he confesses to what he did of his own free will, he's gonna walk."

Nikki nodded. "I probably shouldn't have cleaned up so well," she said. "I just couldn't stand the feel of him all over me. Inside me."

Melanie touched Nikki's cheek so that she'd meet her eyes. "It's okay. I would have done the same."

There was a loud crack from the opposite side of Nikki, and Melanie leaned around her to find Gabe holding the broken and splintered bench arm in one hand.

"Cheap furniture," he said, his voice raw with emotion. "I have to go." He left the broken arm on the bench seat and strode out of the station without another word.

Melanie couldn't believe he would desert her at a time like this. Didn't he know that she needed him to be strong for her so that she could hold it together for Nikki?

"Men," Nikki said under her breath as the slightest semblance of a smile graced her split lip.

Melanie hugged her against her shoulder and rubbed her back. "Are you ready to go back to the hotel and get some sleep?"

"Can I sleep with you?" Nikki said in that small voice that tugged at Melanie's heart.

"Of course," Melanie said.

"Then I'm ready."

CHAPTER TWENTY-FOUR

THERE WERE TIMES when having a backstage pass was very convenient. This would be one of those times. No one seemed to care that Gabe's pass was for a different event or that he was a drummer, not a cage fighter. He had free run over the backstage area and with unbridled fury coursing through his veins, he was searching for one man.

The lowlife could not get off without punishment; Gabe wouldn't allow it. He was about to inflict some Texas-sized justice on his ass, if only he could find the prick.

After asking around, he found Dick Bailey sitting on a bench, taping his knuckles. He was already dressed for his fight, and Gabe wasn't sure what he'd expected, but this huge hulk of a man was more than he had bargained for. That, however, didn't stop him from sucker-punching the fighter in the mouth and knocking him from the bench.

Dick climbed from the floor, pressing the back of his hand to his bleeding lip.

"What the hell?" he said in an impossibly deep voice. "Who the fuck are you?"

Gabe was several inches over six feet, but this guy towered over him and outweighed him by a good fifty pounds of solid muscle. Gabe supposed if he'd retained a shred of intelligence, he'd have been terrified of such a massive dude, but he was too pissed off to think clearly. And the idea that this beast had used all that muscle to rape a woman, and not just any woman, but someone who Melanie loved dearly, caused Gabe to lose his mind entirely.

He advanced on the massive fighter, just wanting to hit him and hit him and never stop hitting him. A sense of satisfaction suffused Gabe as his fist connected with Dick Bailey's gut.

For some stupid reason, Gabe wasn't expecting the guy to hit back. Or for the force behind the blow to knock the wind out of him.

"I don't know who the fuck you are—"

"The cops might have let you go, but I'm a whole 'nother story," Gabe said.

"The cops? Of course they let me go. I didn't do anything."

Gabe managed to hit him in the face this time. The return blow felt as if it dislocated Gabe's jaw, but damned if he cared.

"You don't think raping a defenseless woman is wrong?" Gabe yelled.

"Is she your sister or something?" He sidestepped Gabe's next punch. "Look, dude, I don't know what she told you, but I did not rape her. We got a little rough maybe, but she said she wanted it that way."

Gabe might have believed him—God knew Nikki was a master of manipulation—but he'd seen how emotionally torn up she was. That wasn't an act. Even if this jackass didn't think what he'd done to Nikki was rape, she'd been violated body *and* soul. She was a victim. Gabe believed that from the depths of his soul and he was done talking. He'd come here to kick some ass, and he wasn't leaving until he was satisfied that he'd done the job properly.

After he'd been pounded on a couple times himself, however, he decided that perhaps a job mediocrely done was sufficient. He got in his licks, but the retaliating blows soon had his head swimming and his body protesting its punishment.

Perhaps he should have challenged this guy to a match of wits instead of fists.

"Had enough?" Bailey asked after several minutes of bruising give and take.

Gabe was happy to see that the big guy was breathing hard. He personally felt as if his lungs had collapsed, but he was not giving up. He refused to give Dick Bailey the satisfaction of rendering him unconscious or defeated.

Gabe was somewhat relieved when security came to break up the fight. He wished he'd been able to beat the guy down, but at least he himself was still standing. Someone grabbed him by the back of the shirt and hauled him toward the exit. By the time he found himself face down in the parking lot, his shirt had been ripped clean off.

"Get out of here, punk. Before we call the cops."

He knew they wouldn't let him back inside to finish the job. He climbed to his feet and spat gravel out of his mouth. Or maybe it was teeth. Gabe tipped his head back to send the flow of blood down the back of his throat as he considered his options. He wouldn't mind getting arrested. What he did mind was that Dick Bailey was only going to have one black eye while he was pretty sure he'd be sporting two.

CHAPTER TWENTY-FIVE

MELANIE HAD JUST SHIFTED Nikki's head from her shoulder onto a pillow when her phone rang. Gabe's ringtone. She considered not answering it. She still couldn't believe that he'd abandoned her at the police station with no idea why he'd left or where he'd gone. He'd better have a good explanation. Wanting to hear what excuse came out of his mouth was the only reason she answered.

Or so she told herself.

"Where are you?" he asked. "I came back to our room and you're not here."

"I got my own room."

"What? Why?"

"Because Nikki needs me and you apparently don't."

"What are you talking about? I don't need you? Where did you get that idea?"

"You just fucking left us there at the police station, Gabe. You didn't even bother to say goodbye. Don't you think I have enough to worry about with Nikki without you acting like a complete asshole?"

"I didn't think. I just..." He took a deep breath. "Fuck, Melanie. What did you expect me to do for her?"

"Not a damned thing, Gabe. I didn't need you there for *her*. I needed you there for me!"

Nikki stirred beside her, and Melanie took a deep breath to calm her frayed nerves. "I have to go. Nikki's sleeping. I don't want to wake her."

"Are you in this hotel?" he asked. "I need to see you, Mel. I need to touch you. I need to know that we're fucking okay. Are we okay?"

Irked as she was, she wanted to see him too. She wanted him to hold her while she fell apart, but she couldn't leave Nikki alone again. She just couldn't.

"I just… I just need to be with her right now."

He was silent for a moment. Even listening to him breathe was making her chest ache. Making her miss him.

"She's sleeping, isn't she?" he asked.

Melanie stroked Nikki's silky brown hair from her face. Nikki smiled peacefully in her sleep and snuggled into her pillow.

"Yeah. She's sleeping."

"Can we talk in the hallway or something? Where are you? Wherever you are, I'll come to you."

She hesitated, considering. What harm would it do to talk to him as long as she was in earshot of Nikki?

"Melanie, please," he said.

"We're in Shade's room. Adam gave us Shade's spare key because you left us and Nikki forgot her key in the room."

"Oh," he said. "So you didn't leave me because you were mad."

"I would have if I'd thought of it," she snapped.

He chuckled and there was a soft knock at the door. "I think someone at your door wants to see you," he whispered. "But I don't think you realize how much."

She disconnected the call, climbed from the bed—careful not to disturb Nikki—and hurried to the door. She blinked in the bright glare of the hallway and gasped when she saw Gabe's face. Both eyes were well on the way to being black, and he had a cut on the bridge of his nose, a horrible bruise creeping up the strong line of his jaw, and blood on his upper lip.

"Oh my God, Gabe" she said. "What happened to your face?"

He shrugged, still holding his phone to his ear. "I got in a little fight."

"A fight with who?"

"A certain cage fighter we both despise."

He'd gotten into a fight with Dick Bailey? Was he insane?

"What in the world happened?"

"I figured since the cops weren't going to do anything to him, I'd kick his ass." He ran a hand gingerly over his face. "You didn't tell me he was so fucking huge."

"Are you crazy? You went after him? Gabe! He's a

professional fighter."

"Semi-professional," he corrected. "And yeah, well, he doesn't look as bad as I do, but I got in a few good licks before they threw me out."

"Is that why you left us at the station? So you could go beat up someone?"

He winced. "You make it sound like a crime. I was beyond pissed at the time, and it seemed like a good idea to release my anger on the responsible party's face."

She wrapped her arms around him and squeezed. He gasped, and she immediately let go. Apparently his face wasn't the only thing that had taken a pummeling.

"Don't let go," he said, drawing her against him again.

"I don't want to hurt you."

"Then don't ever again make me think you've left me."

She pressed her face into his bare chest, but kept her hold loose. "I'm sorry if I hurt you."

"You did," he said. "Far more than getting punched in the face by a cage fighter." He rubbed his lips against her hair. "I thought you'd gone back to Wichita without saying goodbye."

She tilted her head back so she could look at him. He smoothed her hair with both hands and then lowered his head to claim her trembling lips. She couldn't believe he'd risked himself for Nikki. If Melanie hadn't already been completely enamored with the man, that reckless act of selfless heroism would have done the trick.

His kiss was too short. She'd have liked it to go on forever.

"Melanie?" Nikki mumbled from the bed. She sat bolt upright. "Melanie!"

"I'm right here," Melanie said. "I'm just saying goodnight to Gabe."

"You're going to make me leave, aren't you?" Gabe said.

Knowing she had to send him away made her sick with longing. She'd much rather snuggle against him all night than fight Nikki for covers, but sometimes sacrifices had to be made. Melanie knew Nikki wouldn't sleep if she left her alone. And Nikki needed sleep. And to feel safe and loved. Nikki needed cuddles even more than Melanie did. So she brushed a kiss against Gabe's lips, pushed him into the hall, and shut the door.

CHAPTER TWENTY-SIX

GABE HAD SPENT half the night missing Melanie, half the night being jealous of Nikki, and half the night feeling guilty about that jealousy. Yes, his nights were now fifty percent longer. At least they felt that way when he attempted to sleep alone and ended up feeling sorry for himself.

Jacob called near noon.

"Can you vacate my room now? Adam said he gave my spare key to your girlfriend. Why are you guys in my room anyway? Did you break another set of box springs?"

Gabe knew Jacob was joking, but he was in no mood for banter.

"I'm not with her," he said. "She's in your room, and I'm in my room."

"Oh," he said flatly. "What's going on?"

"Shit," Gabe grumbled. "Lots of fucked-up shit." He rubbed at his tired eyes and was served a painful reminder that he'd gotten his ass whipped the night before. Well, most of the whipping had occurred to his face, but he felt it in every inch of his body.

"Sounds like the morning I'm having," Jacob said. "So what should I do? I don't want to just barge in on her."

Gabe climbed out of bed and reached for his jeans, holding his phone between his head and his shoulder while he slipped them on. "I'll go with you."

"Aren't you two fighting?"

"No. She just has better things to do than me." He knew that kind of thinking wasn't fair to her, but after eight hours of tossing and turning—*aching* for her, body and soul—his attitude was more than a little skewed.

He entered the corridor and cringed as the bright lighting stabbed through both eyes and into his brain. Next on his agenda: pain relievers.

"What the hell happened to your face?" Jacob asked.

"I bounced it off some guy's knuckles a couple dozen times," Gabe said. "Good times."

Gabe noticed a bruise on Jacob's forehead and pointed at it. "And what happened to you?"

"Ex-wife," Jacob said.

"Bitch."

"Ball-buster."

Gabe poked at Jacob's bruise. "Head-buster."

Gabe attempted a grin. Jacob grinned back. And the pair of them ended up in a back-slapping bro hug because they couldn't dissolve into a sobbing embrace like a couple of little girls.

Jacob handed Gabe his key card. "Are you going to bust in there without knocking?"

"Yep," Gabe said, because he really hoped Melanie had nothing to hide. Strange thoughts had begun to enter his head after several hours of sleep deprivation and the splitting headache from Hell. Thoughts that gave him a real reason to be jealous of Nikki.

The women were still asleep, entwined in each other's arms like sated lovers. Nikki's hand rested on Melanie's breast, and her face was pressed into Melanie's neck. But they weren't naked, so Gabe breathed a sigh of relief.

"Well, what do we have here?" Jacob said.

Melanie's eyes flipped open, and she glared when she recognized who had interrupted her sleep. "What are you doing in here? Get out!"

"Melanie?" Nikki murmured in her sleep.

"This is my room," Jacob said. "You get out."

Gabe pressed his fingertips to the center of his forehead. "Not the time to start an argument," he said. "Mel, why don't you take Nikki back to my room? I'll hang here with Jacob if you still need to be alone with her."

Melanie eased Nikki's hand from her breast and her head from her shoulder. She slipped from the bed and wrapped her arms around Gabe's neck. "You can't possibly know how hard it was to spend the night without you, knowing you were so close yet so far away."

He did know how hard that was actually, but he wasn't going to say so in front of Jacob. He did manage a whispered, "I missed you too." But he wasn't quite ready to hand her his bro card.

Nikki sat up and stretched her arms over her head. "I guess I got to spend the night in Shade's bed after all," she said, her typical flirty smile lighting up the room.

Gabe blinked at her in disbelief.

"Feeling better this morning?" Melanie asked her.

"Yep. All better." Nikki climbed from the bed. "Is it too late for breakfast? I'm starving."

"If you want breakfast, we'll find you some breakfast," Melanie said. "Why don't you go get dressed? Gabe and I will be there in a minute."

Nikki patted Gabe on the ass as she passed. "Give me your key card," she said.

Jaw on the floor, he handed her his key card and she was gone.

"What just happened?" Gabe asked.

"That's Nikki," Melanie said. "Tragedy strikes, she falls apart, I put her back together, and she's back to normal the next day. Well, for the most part. She springs back quickly, but only if I'm there to help her."

"That's not normal," Gabe said.

"Not in the least."

"So what the hell happened?" Jacob asked.

They gave him a much condensed story about what had happened to Nikki while she was alone in New Orleans and Gabe's ordeal with the cage fighter.

"So that dickhead is just gonna walk?" Jacob said.

"With a slight limp, thanks to Gabe," Melanie said. She traced his bruised jaw gently.

"A *very* slight limp," Gabe said.

"I'll try to get Nikki to press charges," Melanie said. "Even if he doesn't go to jail, maybe it will damage his reputation."

"Is she strong enough to go through that?" Gabe asked.

"Probably not," Melanie said. "But I'll work with her. She listens to me." Melanie laughed. "Okay, that's a lie. But she wants to please me, so maybe she'll listen this time."

"I think she needs professional help. A good psychiatrist."

"She has one," Melanie said, "but she insists she likes my therapy better. Nevertheless, I'll make her an appointment when we get back to Wichita."

Gabe stroked her tangled hair, and she gazed up at him with weary hazel eyes. This woman was every sort of wonderful, and he had a chance to make her his. He wouldn't mess it up.

"Do you want to accompany me and Nikki on our girls' day out?" she asked.

"Wouldn't miss it."

Perhaps he'd been a bit hasty. He did get to spend the entire day with Melanie, checking out the local flavor and stealing kisses, touches, and glances from the woman who had stolen his heart. He had to steal moments with Melanie because Nikki never left the woman's side. Melanie offered him apologetic smiles, but he understood why she indulged Nikki's every whim that day. Even if it did put a damper on their limited time together. By the time the trio headed to the arena so Gabe could prepare for the concert that evening, he was exhausted. Exhausted from lack of sleep and exhausted from keeping up with two women with a credit card. He left them on the tour bus, eyeing his bunk with weary longing, but went to do his sound check. Maybe he could catch a nap afterwards. And maybe, just maybe, Melanie would join him. Without Nikki.

"Hey, man." An employee of the arena stopped him as he walked down one of the echoing hallways. "You're that guy from last night."

"Huh?"

"Aren't you the one who tried to beat up Dick Bailey for hurting your sister?"

Sometimes he wished he was less recognizable. Now everyone would know he got his ass kicked by a douche bag. "She wasn't my sister," Gabe said. "Just a friend."

"Some of the other fighters heard what you accused him of and beat the ever-loving shit out of that guy."

"They did?"

"Yeah."

"I would have liked to have seen that." Since he'd mostly been seeing stars.

"You taking him on like that was pretty badass," the guy said.

"Badass or stupid?"

"Badass," the guy assured him. "Everyone is talking about it."

Gabe didn't feel badass, but he'd take his accolades when he could get them. "Thanks."

A slight smile on his face, Gabe headed to the stage to beat on something that never hit back.

After sound check, Gabe paused at the top of the tour bus steps, smiling at the obvious closeness between the two friends. Nikki sat on the kitchen counter with Melanie standing between her legs. Melanie's arms were wrapped loosely around Nikki's waist, and Nikki's arms were resting on Melanie's shoulders, her hands linked together behind Melanie's head.

"We had fun today, didn't we?" Nikki said, looking positively giddy with happiness.

"Yeah." Melanie chuckled. "I think we melted my credit card with all that swiping, but it was fun."

"Mel?"

"Yeah, hon?"

"I love you," Nikki gushed. "I don't think you'll ever realize how much."

"I love you too."

"Always?"

"Always."

"No matter what?"

"No matter what."

Eyes closed, Nikki leaned forward and kissed Melanie. Not a peck on the cheek. Not a friendly brush of her lips on Melanie's. A deep, open-mouthed, let-me-introduce-your-tonsils-to-my-tongue, sexually charged kiss.

Suddenly light-headed, Gabe stumbled backwards down the stairs, catching the handrail at the last minute. It was the only thing that saved his ass from meeting the pavement.

Regaining his footing, he stood outside the bus, thinking he should be angry, that he should be livid that Melanie had been hiding her romantic entanglement with Nikki from him. But he mostly felt a hollow ache in his chest and unbelievably stupid for not believing the signs. He'd recognized them—and they'd haunted him while he'd lain awake the night before—but he hadn't *believed* them.

Apparently he should have trusted his gut.

Friends didn't have the kind of dependent relationship that Nikki and Melanie shared. No simple friend would put up with Nikki's drama for as long as Melanie had, not unless she had deep, romantic feelings for her. Roommates didn't sleep in the same bed, cuddled together like lovers. People with platonic relationships didn't kiss the way he'd just seen the two of them kiss.

Jesus, no wonder Nikki had kept trying to talk Gabe into a threesome. The two women probably picked up guys and did it all the time. He was just the latest dupe.

Melanie had played him for a complete fool.

And she had actually made him fall in love with her. The fucking bitch.

CHAPTER TWENTY-SEVEN

MELANIE PULLED AWAY from Nikki's kiss and stared at her in astonishment.

"What the hell are you doing?"

"I told you," Nikki said, her big blue eyes suddenly flooded with tears. "I love you, Mel. I love you. You said you love me too."

"Nikki," Melanie said. "Honey, you're confused. You're not attracted to me. We're just friends."

Nikki dropped her chin to her chest and whimpered like a wounded animal. "But you must love me, Mel. You're the only one I care about who has never hurt me. The only one."

Melanie swallowed the lump in her throat, knowing she was going to have to hurt Nikki now, when she was at her most vulnerable. Melanie was *not* interested in a romantic relationship with Nikki, and she didn't know if there was a way to salvage their friendship with this on the table. She should have recognized the signs. She'd honestly thought that when Nikki made sexual advances toward her—and she'd been making them more and more frequently—that she'd just been playing around. It had never occurred to her that her best friend—a *woman*—could be sexually attracted to her. She was having a hard time processing that reality.

"Do you remember why we became friends?" Melanie asked her.

Nikki sniffed. "You mean when we were little?" she said in a tiny voice.

"Yeah. We met in the park. You were sitting under a bush, sobbing. Remember?"

Nikki swallowed and nodded. Melanie lifted a hand to brush Nikki's hair back, but thought better of it. She clenched her hand into a loose fist and dropped it to her side. Melanie *did* love Nikki as more than a friend. She loved her like the little sister she'd never had. Someone to take care of. To defend. To cherish.

"I went over to see what was wrong and you had this huge bruise on your face," Melanie said.

"My stepfather was an abusive son of a bitch."

"But that wasn't why you were crying. Do you remember why you were crying?"

Nikki nodded again. "I had found a beautiful blue butterfly. I held it so gently and stroked its velvety wings. And it died right there in my hand."

"We spent the rest of that summer chasing live butterflies in the park."

Nikki smiled. A slightly watery smile, but a genuine one. "And every time you caught one, you'd put it in my hair and say I was beautiful. No one had ever told me that before. Or made me feel beautiful."

"You are beautiful, Nikki. Not just on the outside, on the inside. I knew it from the moment I saw you crying over a dead bug."

"Butterfly," Nikki corrected. "I wouldn't cry over a beetle. Well, maybe if it was a lady bug."

Melanie laughed. She so wanted to give Nikki a hearty squeeze, but a line had been crossed, and Melanie knew she had to be careful not to give Nikki the wrong message.

"I was sad when you moved away," Melanie said.

"Yeah, well, sometimes abusive sons-of-bitches beat your mother to death and you're sent to live with your alcoholic father."

The alcoholic father who had sexually molested her for six years, but Nikki didn't have to say it. Melanie was very aware of Nikki's past. She just wished she could have been there for Nikki at the time, to help put her back together.

"I thank God that we ended up going to the same college," Melanie said. "It must have been fate."

Nikki dropped her head. "Not fate so much as me stalking your social media pages."

"So you went to Wichita State—"

"To be with you. I never forgot you. Mel, the little girl with the kind eyes and the uplifting words who put butterflies in my hair." She touched her hair as if she could feel wings flapping against her. "Memoires of those butterflies got me through a lot of very dark nights, Mel, even when you weren't there."

Nothing could have stopped Melanie from hugging Nikki then. She crushed her against her chest, squeezing until her arms began to tremble.

"Do you hate me for loving you?" Nikki said dully.

Melanie drew away and cupped Nikki's face in her hands. She tried not to look at the scab on her lip, because it was a harsh reminder of even more pain that Nikki had suffered, and Melanie couldn't allow herself to be wishy-washy about this.

"I don't hate you—at all—I'm just not attracted to you. I don't love you that way. Do you understand?"

Nikki lowered her gaze.

"I do love you unconditionally," Melanie said. "I *do*. Nothing you do will change that. So stop testing it, okay? I'm not going anywhere. You're my baby sister for life."

"Are you sure?"

"If I haven't given up on you by now, it's not going to happen."

Nikki laughed. "I'll try to behave."

"Just keep yourself safe," Melanie said. "And if you kiss me again, I'm going to tell my boyfriend to kick your ass."

"Okay. I don't want an ass-kicking from a guy with a bad haircut." She was laughing when she said it.

Melanie glanced around the empty interior of the bus. "Speaking of Gabe, shouldn't he be back by now? He said sound check wouldn't take long."

"You should go look for him. I've been hogging your attention all day. I'm sure you two would like to be alone for a while."

"Ain't that the truth?" she said. This weekend hadn't quite been the endless love-making session she'd envisioned. "You okay now?" she asked Nikki.

"I'll get over you," she said. "Eventually."

Knowing Nikki the way she did, Melanie figured it would take her no more than twenty minutes or so to move on. "Stay out of trouble."

"Yes, ma'am."

Backstage, Melanie asked several people if they'd seen Gabe. The rest of the band was in the dressing room, bull-shitting. Gabe was not among them, and no one had seen him since sound check. They all said he'd been headed to the tour bus with instructions not to disturb him. Melanie knew that he'd never made it to the bus. At least, she hadn't seen him. Maybe they'd crossed paths somewhere.

When she saw Jordan in a hallway and asked if he'd seen Gabe, he pointed toward the stage. "I think he's rehearsing."

Rehearsing? Rehearsing what? When she concentrated, she could hear him playing, sticks hitting skins with such powerful, rapid percussion that it couldn't have been anyone but Gabe.

She hurried to the stage and climbed the steps to watch him. She stumbled over a cord not yet taped down and then stood to the side of Gabe's drum kit. His instrument was tucked away behind the equipment for the opening bands, far to the back of the stage where the overhead lights didn't quite reach. His eyes were closed as he punished the drums; there was no other way to describe how he was playing. His face held none of the rapture, none of the fervent concentration she'd witnessed at the concert three nights before. There was only anger and retaliation.

She was afraid to interrupt him and would probably have stood gaping all day if the skin on his snare hadn't ruptured.

"Fuck," he said. He flung his ragged sticks between two of the drums and dropped his elbows to his knees. He pressed the heels of his hands into his eyes, his fingertips digging into the wicked-looking dragons on his scalp. Gabe looked anything but wicked at that moment. He looked... broken.

"Fuck, fuck, fuck, fuck!" he yelled. And then he kicked one of his bass drums clean off the riser, taking a set of crashing cymbals with it.

Melanie was stunned and half-tempted to back away and pretend she hadn't seen him. "Gabe?" she said quietly.

He tensed and turned, searching for her in the shadows.

"Is something wrong?"

"Yeah," he said in a harsh, raspy tone. "Everything is wrong. Get the fuck out of here. I don't want to talk to you."

She sucked in a breath, certain she was hallucinating. Who was this guy? Definitely not the Gabe she'd come to know over the weekend.

"What?" she said breathlessly.

He glared at her. "You heard me. Go back home to Kansas! And take your fucking girlfriend with you."

"Well, yes, I'll be taking Nikki when I go home," Melanie said, still more confused than insulted, hurt or angry. Though she could feel those emotions quickly taking hold of her. "What's wrong with you?"

"What's wrong with *me*? What's wrong with you, Melanie? How many guys have you done this to? Did they think it was sexy to be caught up in your kinky little triangle? Well, I don't want any part of it. Take your loser friend and fuck off. We're through."

She obviously wasn't registering words correctly, because his made absolutely no sense.

"Gabe, I don't know what you're talking about. You don't want to be with me? Where is this coming from?"

"You can't have us both, Melanie. It's me or her."

She gaped at him, unable to believe her ears. She knew some people were naturally jealous—hell, she happened to be one of them—but what kind of asshole slapped down that kind of ultimatum out of the blue? He knew what Nikki had been through. He couldn't possibly expect Melanie to desert her.

"Are you asking me to choose between you and Nikki?"

He crossed his arms over his chest, his jaw set in a harsh line. "Yeah, I am."

"Asking that of me makes it very easy to pick," she said, struggling to get the words out around the lump in her throat. "How can you even *ask* me to choose between the man I love and my best friend? *Why* would you ask me to?"

He threw out a hand, pointing toward the parking lot. "Your best friend? Don't you mean your *lover*? I'm sure there are plenty of guys who would love to be the spare dick in your bed, but I'm not one of them. If you're going to be *my* one and only, then I have to be yours as well."

Melanie's head started spinning. She wasn't sure what to

focus on: the fact that he thought Nikki was her lover or that he thought she would actually cheat on him or that he considered her his one and only.

"She's not my lover," she said finally, needing more time to process the rest of what he said. "Never has been. Never will be."

"Bullshit, Melanie. I saw her kiss you."

Melanie touched the back of her hand to her lips, feeling suddenly queasy. "You saw that?"

"Yeah, I saw it. I also heard you say that you love her."

"And I suppose you didn't stick around long enough to hear my reaction to Nikki's misguided confession of love?"

Some of the tension went out of his long, lean frame. "I'd already seen all I needed to see," he said quietly.

"So you didn't hear me tell her I considered her my *sister*? Did you hear me tell her I am not attracted to her? Maybe I went easy on her, but for fuck's sake Gabe, hasn't she been hurt enough? I'm not fucking my best friend!"

He didn't say anything. But his eyes narrowed, as if he were considering her words.

"What do you mean that I'm your *one and only*?" she blurted without thought.

"Don't change the subject," he said. He hopped down from the riser and took several steps toward her, but stopped short of touching her. "Did you mean to say that I'm the man you love?"

She laughed hysterically, light-headed from the see-sawing emotions surging through her. "Oh, you heard that little slip up, did you?"

"Did you mean it?" he pressed.

He reached out and cupped her shoulder, and she forced herself not to pull away. And not collapse into his arms.

"I don't know if I can love a man who believes what he sees with his *own* eyes over my word," she said, hoping to break some of the tension between them before it broke her.

"Maybe I need glasses," he said, one side of his mouth lifting in a grin.

"Gabriel Banner in glasses?" she said, touching her fingertips to her chest. "Be still my quivering loins."

His arms went around her hesitantly, and the tension immediately dropped away. She pressed her ear to his thudding heart.

"I'm sorry I didn't trust you," he said.

She shook her head slightly. "I guess if I saw you macking with Shade, I'd have probably jumped to the same conclusion."

"Ugh, that's disgusting," he said, shuddering dramatically. "Do you have any idea where that man's mouth has been? Have you met his ex-wife?"

Melanie chuckled and pulled away so she could look into his grass-green eyes. "I do love you," she said. "I meant that. I just figured it was much too soon to tell you."

He smiled. "The time feels right to me."

She laughed a little, embarrassed, and then she snuggled into his chest, hoping he'd say the words in return, but not wanting to pressure him.

"I have this strange idea about love," he said against her hair. "I think a man can love many women in his life, *until* he finds his one and only. Then it's game over. He's stuck loving her, and no one else, for the rest of his life."

"Is that a bad thing?" she asked.

"I don't know. I haven't known my one and only long enough to know what fifty or sixty years with the same person feels like, but the first week has been pretty fucking spectacular. Well, except for the part where I thought she was in love with someone else. That pretty much sucked."

"She isn't," she whispered. "She's only in love with you."

"That's a relief."

Melanie lifted her face to look at him, and he claimed her lips in a deep, passionate kiss. He drew away much too soon.

"Will you tell me one thing?" he asked.

"I'll tell you anything."

"Is she a better kisser than I am?"

Melanie swatted him on the butt. "What kind of a question is that?"

"A competitive one."

She pursed her lips, considering. "I'm not sure. I think you'd better show me your best game so I can decide."

She grabbed the back of his neck and surged up on her

tiptoes so she could kiss him more thoroughly.

"Mel?" he whispered against her lips.

"Gabe?"

"Would you consider becoming my personal traveling accountant for the summer?"

Her heart skipped a beat as a world of possibilities opened wide before her. "I don't know if you can afford me," she teased.

"The job has a great benefits package," he said. "I promise to wake you every morning with an orgasm and a smile."

"Hmm," she murmured, snuggling closer to his chest again. She could never seem get close enough to the man. She doubted she would ever feel he was close enough unless they were naked—skin on skin—and he was buried deep inside her. And if she spent the summer on the road with him, being woken each morning with his promised orgasm and smile, there would be plenty of opportunity to experience the closeness she craved. "Not bad perks." She slid her hand down his belly and cupped his cock. It jerked against her palm, and her pussy clenched in response. "Is *this* package included as a benefit?"

He laughed. "That's up for negotiation."

She grinned up at him, her heart near bursting with the love she felt for this man. "I'll put in my two weeks' notice tomorrow."

"I promise you won't regret it," he murmured before claiming her mouth in a deep, toe-curling kiss.

Melanie couldn't regret anything that kept her in Gabe's arms.

When he drew away, she stared up into his eyes—rimmed with dark bruises that made her heart ache—and whispered, "Tell me."

"Tell you, what?"

She toyed with his shirt, too embarrassed to flatly request the words she wanted to hear. "You know."

He touched her cheek and her hair, searching her eyes for clues. "I love you. Is that what you want me to tell you?"

She smiled brightly and nodded, happiness giving her heart buoyancy.

"Then I'll tell you again. I'll tell you as often as you need to hear it. I love you, Melanie."

"I love you too," she gushed.

"Now let's go find a nice private location so I can *show* you."

"Oh yes," she said. "Let's." She did adore the way the man's mind worked.

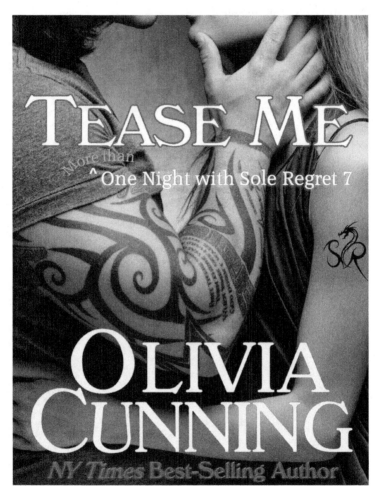

TEASE ME

More than
^ One Night with Sole Regret 7

OLIVIA
CUNNING

NY Times Best-Selling Author

Tease Me
One Night with Sole Regret #7

CHAPTER ONE

HER LIFE WAS OVER.

Madison couldn't believe this was happening. Not to her. She was good at her job. Maybe she'd misunderstood her boss's words.

"What do you mean, I'm being let go?" Madison said in a raw voice.

Joanna stared at her hands for a moment and then lifted her gaze. "I have to fire you, Miss Fairbanks."

Fire her? Somehow that sounded much worse than being let go.

"Why?" she asked. She was so utterly shocked that her face tingled. Her heart raced out of control. She doubted her knees would support her if she stood up from the scratchy, wool-upholstered chair beneath her. "I'm good at my job. I'm a good employee. Why would you fi—let me go?"

Joanna's dark eyes shifted to her desk calendar, and she rubbed a finger along its smudged edge. "It's been brought to my attention that you've been sleeping with a client."

Madison's breath came out in a whoosh. She couldn't deny it—it happened to be true. But how did Joanna know about her relationship with Sole Regret's lead guitarist? She'd been careful to keep their involvement hidden from everyone at work. Hell, her parents didn't even know she was seeing him.

"*In* your office," Joanna added.

Madison couldn't deny that either. Who had found out? Who had tattled on her? Had they been overheard? She'd been really careful about that too, keeping her cries of pleasure locked inside.

"Do you deny it?" Joanna pressed.

Madison was a bad liar, but if lying meant keeping her job . . . She loved her job.

But she loved Adam more.

"Do you have proof?" Madison asked, her stomach twisted in a knot.

"Enough."

Madison lowered her eyes to stare at the photograph on Joanna's desk. The woman's pet collies seemed to be smiling at her. She fixed her gaze on the dogs as she struggled to find her rational mind.

"This is my first offense," she said calmly. "And Adam no longer comes here for therapy. Perhaps an unpaid leave of absence would be more reasonable."

"I'd rather dismiss you now. Before your habit causes irreparable damage to our reputation."

Her habit? She didn't have sexual relationships with clients—Adam being the exception.

"I made the mistake of falling in love with a client," she said. "I admit it."

"And what should you have done about it?"

Madison closed her eyes. She knew what she should have done. She'd even started the process, before deciding it wasn't right for Adam the addict, even if it would have protected Adam her lover.

"I should have referred him to a different counselor," she said. "But he was finally making real progress in his treatment, and I knew that dropping him on someone else would have sent him back to square one. He isn't someone who opens up easily. It took me months to get him to even talk to me."

"Yes, you should have referred him to another counselor." Joanna reached for a pen and tapped the end of it repeatedly on her desk. Madison fought the urge to yank it out of her hand and toss it across the room. "Your other option would have been keeping your legs closed."

Madison stiffened and her jaw hardened. *What?* She could not believe Joanna would say something so insulting to an employee. Ex-employee, Madison reminded herself.

"Unless you're willing to give up seeing this man—"

"I'm not," she blurted out.

"Then I really have no other alternative. You're a nice girl, Miss Fairbanks. It's just too bad that you fell prey to the wrong sort of man."

Madison scowled. Why did everyone always assume that she was a victim and Adam was some bad guy? "He's a good person. Just—"

"Misunderstood?" Joanna raised an eyebrow at her.

"Exactly!"

"Well, everyone makes mistakes," Joanna said. "Too bad this one had such disastrous consequences for your career. I wish you well, Miss Fairbanks. Dionne will help you clear out your office."

Madison sprang from the chair, unable to listen to another word this woman had to say about her or about Adam. Her knees no longer wobbly, she stormed out of Joanna's office and burst into her own much smaller workspace. She was too angry to beg to keep her job now. How dare anyone make assumptions about Adam? He was not a mistake. He was the best thing in her life. She would never choose a job over him.

Dionne entered her office carrying several empty boxes and wearing an unreadable expression. Had she been the one who'd told Joanna? As the common receptionist, Dionne knew the comings and goings of the counselors and clients more than anyone in the office. Maybe she knew far more about Madison's comings than she'd let on.

"I'm completely baffled by this one," Dionne said.

"By what?"

"I'm not going to ask why you were fired, because it's none of my business, but if I had to rank everyone in this office on the likelihood of being fired, you would have been at the bottom of that list, baby girl. Everybody loves you."

Madison's bottom lip trembled. She was not going to fall apart right now. She was going to pack up her office, store her belongings in her car, and head directly to the airport. More than anything, she wanted to get lost in Adam's arms. To be reminded why she was willing to risk everything just to be with him.

Dionne yanked a tissue from the box on the desk and pressed it into Madison's hand. "Don't do that. If you start crying, then I'll start crying, and that's a downright ugly sight to behold."

Madison dabbed at her eyes with the tissue. It was only slightly soggy when she tossed it in the wastebasket. "I'm not crying," she said. "Just a little shaken."

"You aren't going to tell me why you were fired, are you?" Dionne asked.

Madison released a shaky breath. Why shouldn't she tell Dionne? She wasn't ashamed. "I fell in love with the right man at the wrong time."

Dionne lifted a questioning eyebrow at her.

Madison shook her head. "I don't want to talk about it. Let's get this over with," she said and began placing pictures in one of the empty boxes. Pictures of her and her twin sister, Kennedy, on their first day of kindergarten and at their high school graduation. Pictures of her parents. Her favorite pets. Her horses. There was even one of her beloved grandmother who'd passed away years ago. But not a single picture of Adam was on display. So there was at least one good thing about getting caught and losing her job: she didn't have to hide her relationship with Adam Taylor from anyone. Not from her boss. Nor her co-workers. Not from her parents or even the general public. There was something freeing about finally being able to let the world know that he was her man.

She was already coming to terms with being unemployed, and in a few hours she'd be back in Adam's arms. So maybe her life wasn't over. Maybe it was just beginning.

Or maybe she was too optimistic for her own good.

CHAPTER TWO

ADAM'S JAW HARDENED, and he jerked the sketch pad from Jacob's hands. He couldn't have anything to himself on this fucking tour bus.

"Is that your lyrics notebook?" Jacob asked.

Adam shoved the sketch pad under his bunk mattress, not sure why he was hiding it. It wasn't as if anyone respected his privacy. "Yeah. So?"

"It's almost empty." Jacob lifted his eyebrows. "Except for sketches of boobs and eagles."

Adam shook his head and tried to stifle a grin. Jacob never coddled him—which was good—but he also never cut him a break, which frequently pissed Adam off.

"Yeah, well, there's nothing inspiring about being on a tour bus with a bunch of dicks." He didn't really think his bandmates were dicks. But on this particular occasion, Jacob was definitely being a dick.

Jacob tilted his head, his brow knitted with confusion. "So what have you been doing when you lock yourself in the back of the bus? Jacking off? I thought you were writing. You usually find all your inspiration while on tour."

But not this tour. Adam didn't know what the problem was. He wanted to write songs. He tried to write songs. He did lock himself in the back bedroom with his guitar and his sketch pad. But he ended up staring at the blank page for hours, nothing coming to him. His mind was as blank as the page that mocked him. When they were on tour he usually wrote page after page of lyrics, so many that when the band sat down after a tour to write songs for a new album, they had to reel in his superfluous output. He'd never had a creative dry spell while on tour. Of course, he'd spent their last three tours high out of his mind. He couldn't help but wonder if that was the problem.

Maybe his drug abuse had fueled his creativity, and the outpouring of lyrics had nothing to do with the excitement of the tour.

"We still have months on the road," Adam said. "I'm sure I'll have plenty of material by the end of the tour."

But he wasn't sure. Not even a little sure. In fact, he was starting to panic that he wouldn't be able to come up with anything usable and that Sole Regret would be over. Or worse, that they'd replace him with someone who wouldn't let them down.

"Maybe we should collaborate on this album," Jacob said. "I know you like to see your name as head composer of all our music—"

"He just likes to collect all the royalties!" Owen called from the front of the bus.

Adam gave him the finger. Jacob ignored him.

"Maybe if we put our heads together we can come up with something."

"Something on par with my usual stuff?" Adam challenged.

Jacob shrugged. "We won't know until we try."

"Just give me the rest of the tour. If something doesn't click by the end, we'll try something different."

"Maybe Kellen's chick has some ideas on getting past your writer's block. The woman is a composer, you know."

Yeah, he knew. Of course he knew. Kellen had shared that tidbit of information several times over the past few hours. He was currently listening to her various compositions and making the attractive redhead blush as he pronounced her brilliant over and over again. But Dawn composed classical music, so Adam wasn't sure how she was supposed to help him write the dark and disturbing lyrics he usually wrote.

Adam pulled his sketch pad from beneath the mattress and headed toward the bedroom at the back of the bus. "Actually, I think I have an idea."

Jacob smiled. "Good. You know we all depend on you for our livelihood." He winked at Adam to let him know he was only joking, but the pressure that weighed on Adam was beginning to crush him into the dirt.

"So keep it down out here," he said, glancing around the

bus at his bandmates who were all rather subdued this morning.

He closed the door, settled himself comfortably on the bed in a nest of pillows and stared at a blank page in his notebook, wishing he was high, but glad that he wasn't.

"I'm fucked," he said hours later when the bus pulled to a halt behind the venue in New Orleans. Besides the doodle of a spider on one corner, the page was still completely blank. "Completely fucked."

Rubbing his face with both hands, he wondered if Madison had ever heard of a junkie losing his talent when he got clean. He would have to ask her about it this evening. Maybe she had some advice for him. She was good at helping him fix his problems. Everyone knew he sucked at fixing them on his own.

Unable to stand being stuck on the bus with his blank sketch pad mocking him, Adam shoved his trademark hair under a ball cap and headed outside. He wandered the streets of New Orleans alone, his mind clouded with doubt. He had no idea where he was but when a display in a store window caught his eye, he stopped short.

Madison needs that, he thought.

Adam pulled his baseball cap low over his forehead, tugged the collar of his leather jacket close to the back of his neck, and took a steadying breath. He checked over his shoulder to make sure no one was looking before he pushed open the swinging door of the shop. A bell jangled a greeting, sending his heart racing and making his palms damp. Was he really going to do this? He must be out of his mind.

He took another deep breath and eyed the nearest display case full of precious metals, colorful gems, and glittering diamonds.

Before he could take a step toward the sparkly wares, a timid voice from behind a counter asked, "Can I help you, sir?"

Adam lifted his head and found a petite brunette smiling weakly at him. Her hand was wrapped around the edge of the counter. Adam didn't doubt that her finger was perched over the panic button in case he was there to rob the place. He wondered if it was his everyday thug look or his obvious nervousness that had the clerk on edge. Likely a combination of the two.

"I'm not sure," he said. "I think I'll just browse a bit."

"Looking for anything in particular?"

"Nope," he said. "Just looking."

He gravitated toward a case of simple gold chains. Maybe he'd just buy another chain for his collection and pretend that was why he'd entered the jewelry store. He wasn't sure if following through on his original impulse was a good idea or not. When he'd seen the engagement ring in the window, he'd thought immediately of Madison and had had a crazy notion to put it on her finger, but as the initial urge waned, he started to wonder if she'd even accept it. They'd been seeing each other for over a year, but the *I love you*s and the commitment were both brand new to their relationship. Perhaps he was rushing.

Perhaps he *should* rush. Only days ago, his father had insisted Madison would soon realize Adam wasn't good enough for her. Nice girls didn't end up with guys like him. Eventually they came to their senses and realized nothing would fix what was broken. And he was all sorts of broken. With Madison's help, he'd only just begun to put himself back together.

Adam ran a hand over his face. Shit. Maybe the old man was right. Maybe Adam would never live up to Madison's expectations. Maybe he'd never be her ideal man. But Adam wanted to be. Wanted to be good enough for her. An ideal man. Not the fuck-up he'd always been and would probably always be.

He covered his mouth with one hand and squeezed his face, his thumb pressing his inner cheek against the sharp edge of his teeth. Why the fuck was he letting his old man's drug-withdrawal-induced ravings get to him anyway? It wasn't as if the guy was a paradigm of sage fatherly advice. He'd never even met Madison. So how could he know that she was too good for his son?

Probably because he and his father were too much alike for comfort.

"Are you interested in gold chains?" the clerk asked.

Adam started and lifted his gaze to focus on her uneasy but still smiling face.

She had released her grip on the panic button and had come to stand on the opposite side of the case from him. She lifted a hand toward his chest and inclined her head. He glanced down at the collection of chains hanging around his neck and grinned.

"Actually, no," he said. "I have a friend who thinks I'm hard to buy for, so he gets me a new chain every year for Christmas. I was . . ." He glanced at the display window. " . . . thinking of . . ." He tore his gaze from the direction of the ring to meet the woman's brown eyes. "You see, there's this woman. And maybe I'm moving too fast, I don't know, but I saw the ring in the window and . . ." He shrugged, mildly embarrassed by his flustered rambling.

"Oh!" the clerk said, suddenly coming alive with eagerness. "I thought—"

"That I was going to rob the place?"

"No! Of course not," she said, much too quickly. "You just seemed more nervous than most guys who come in the store, and we aren't supposed to open display cases unless another employee is watching. But I can tell you about the ring. Which one are you interested in?"

"The one in the window." He jabbed a thumb toward the window display that had caught his eye.

She headed in that direction, and Adam followed. He had to crane his neck to look into the display case from behind and figure out which of the pieces was the one he wanted.

"The gold one second from the right end. The one with the huge square rock." He pointed at it as if she could tell what he was pointing at.

The clerk's head jerked around, and she gaped at him with wide eyes. "Are you sure? That's probably out of your price range. We have less expensive rings in the case over there." She nodded to the far side of the room.

Adam bit his tongue so he didn't unleash upon Little Miss Bigot. Had he arrived in an Armani suit, she wouldn't have been fingering the alarm button or assuming that he couldn't afford something outlandishly expensive for Madison.

"Can I speak to another person who works here?" he asked.

"Margaret went to the bathroom, but she should be back any minute. *I* can show you whatever ever you want to look at."

"No, you can't."

Her brow furrowed. "Why not?"

"Because I don't want you to earn the commission on this sale."

And because of the clerk's rudeness, there was no way in hell he was leaving without that ring, even if it did nothing more than sit in his pocket for the next thirty years waiting for him to find the courage to offer it to one special lady from Dallas, Texas.

CHAPTER THREE

MADISON CLUNG TO THE ARMRESTS as the plane touched down with a harsh thud followed by several bounces. She was not a fan of flying and if not for the promise of seeing Adam, she wouldn't have gotten on the plane in the first place. The man was a strong motivating force in her life. She couldn't deny it.

Deceleration pressed the back of her head against the seat, but as soon as they were taxiing slowly toward their gate, she peered out the window, half expecting Adam to be waiting for her on the tarmac. Which was silly. She couldn't imagine his desire to see her was half as strong as her need to be with him. The past week had been a true exercise in restraint. The man hadn't been far from her thoughts for more than a minute at a time. When she wasn't wondering what he was doing, she was thinking of all the things she wanted to say to him—and *do* to him—this weekend.

And after the terrible morning she'd had, she couldn't imagine anything better than getting lost in him forever.

When the plane drew to a halt, Madison was the first on her feet. She yanked her purse out from beneath the seat and slung it over one shoulder. The college-aged man seated to her left looked up at her in surprise. He hadn't even unfastened his seat belt yet.

"Got a hot date or something?" he asked, tugging open the clasp of the belt and fishing under the seat in front of him for his backpack.

Madison flushed and licked her lips self-consciously. Was she that obvious? "Yeah, actually, I do."

The guy chuckled. "I wish I had a pretty girl that eager to see me. Any advice for a dateless guy?"

"Um," she said, racking her brain for foolproof ways to

land a date. "Learn to play guitar?"

Sole Regret's music wasn't the reason she'd fallen for Adam, but his talent hadn't hindered her attraction, and she knew the thousands of women who lusted after the man were completely seduced by his skill on the guitar. Madison was looking forward to seeing him play live that night. Couldn't wait. Of course, given a choice, she'd rather spend every moment alone with him, but she had to admit watching him play live was a potent aphrodisiac.

"I tried that," the guy said. "It didn't work out so well for me. What about trumpet? Any babe-magnet qualities in that instrument?"

She chuckled. "In New Orleans? Yeah, there just might be. Do you play jazz?"

"The Star-Spangled Banner mostly."

"Maybe some extraordinarily patriotic woman will find that irresistible," she said with a laugh.

The guy gave her the twice-over. "And would you consider yourself extraordinarily patriotic?"

Madison realized that the guy was flirting. She really could be clueless about those things. Sometimes she wondered if she'd have ever figured out that Adam was attracted to her if he hadn't spelled it out so clearly by stealing that first kiss as she was showing him out of her office one evening. After months of counseling sessions, she'd still had no idea that his teasing was actually flirting. She'd wanted him, even though she'd known it was inappropriate to fantasize about a client, but she'd never thought for a fraction of a second that he reciprocated her desire until he'd pushed her up against the back of her office door and showed her otherwise.

"Not especially patriotic, no." She focused her gaze on the aisle, wishing the hopeful trumpeter would take a hint and let her out. She didn't want to flirt with the guy and was pretty sure he'd gotten the wrong idea just because she'd talked to him. For the duration of the flight, she'd been engrossed in a mystery novel. Okay, that was a lie. She'd reread every sentence dozens of times because she couldn't stop thinking about Adam. When she'd managed to draw her thoughts from the man, they immediately shifted to the bombshell her boss had dropped on her hours ago. But pretending to read had kept the stranger next to her from engaging her in conversation. It hadn't kept him from staring though. She'd caught him watching her every time she glanced his way.

When her row mate didn't budge despite her intense staring at the line of passengers shuffling past, she said, "Can you let me out, please?"

"If you tell me your name."

She sighed, figuring she'd get what she wanted more quickly if she just played along. "It's Madison."

"That's cute," he said, stepping into the aisle at last. "Just like you."

She scrambled in front of him, and he trailed after her.

"I'm Chris. Are you from here? I could really use someone to help me find my way around."

"No, I've never been to New Orleans before. I'm meeting someone. My boyfriend," she clarified, smiling as she used the word. He really was her boyfriend now, though it sounded so seventh grade to call him that. Yet significant other sounded so cold and lover too risqué. So boyfriend would have to do.

"So that hot date comment wasn't in jest?"

"I'm afraid not."

As she exited the plane, Madison smiled at the friendly flight attendant and then hurried down the ramp toward the terminal.

"So what hotel are you staying in?" Chris asked, rushing forward to fall into step beside her.

"Not sure," she said, hoping she didn't have to get rude with the guy, but he couldn't seem to take a string of very large hints that she had no interest in talking to him. She didn't want to be mean, but he was starting to make her uncomfortable. "My boyfriend arranged everything. He said he wants to surprise me."

She was sure all of Adam's surprises would be exceptional. They always were. They were also guaranteed to take her mind off her troubles. All of them. Even the big one she was pretending to ignore. How could she have been fired? Her parents would be so disappointed in her. And she'd never live down the *I told you so* from her sister.

"I came to NOLA to unwind," Chris said. "I just graduated with my bachelor's degree and landed my first job. I figured I should blow off some steam before I have to play at being a real adult."

Job. Madison's stomach plummeted. No, she wouldn't think about that now. She'd worry about it on Tuesday when her time with Adam was over and she returned to her stark, stark reality.

"That's nice," she said in a strained voice. She paused at the end of the ramp to scan the unfamiliar airport for directional signs to baggage claim. Chris stopped beside her. She glanced at him; the poor guy looked almost as lost as she felt. So maybe he really was just looking for someone to help him navigate a new city, but he'd latched on to the wrong person. She had an agenda and it involved only Adam.

"Congratulations on earning your degree and landing a job," she added. "It's not easy to do in this economy."

She cringed at that reality too. Shoot! She might never find another job. Especially if Joanna gave her a crappy reference. Maybe she should try to fight Joanna's decision to fire her. But then Madison's affair would become very public knowledge and she might never find another job. Shit, shit, shit! What was she going to do?

Think about Adam, only Adam. He'd make all the crap fade into the background. At least for the weekend.

Madison took a deep breath and hurried off in the direction of baggage claim, following signs while avoiding collisions with other passengers who were also trying to find their way.

"I actually had two job offers," Chris continued, still trailing her.

Madison stifled an annoyed sigh. Surely she could lose this guy in baggage claim. Adam would rescue her.

"That's nice." For him.

"So which college do you attend, Madison?"

She laughed, her ego stroked despite herself. "I graduated years ago."

"I don't believe it. What, were you a prodigy or something?"

She lifted her eyebrows and shook her head. "No such

thing. I've been playing at being a real adult for quite a while now." And sometimes it sucked. But most of the time she loved her life.

"So you're from Dallas?"

"Yeah. Well, a ranch outside of Dallas." What was with the third degree?

"Oh, you're a cowgirl." He wiggled his eyebrows at her as if his every fantasy had just come to life.

"No, I'm a counselor." *Had been* a counselor. She bit her lip and ducked her head so he wouldn't see the absolute panic in her eyes.

Oh God, what was she going to do? How was she going to support herself? She didn't think her sister would kick her out of the house, but she would feel terrible if she couldn't contribute financially to their joint living situation.

"Like a marriage counselor?" Chris pressed.

Why wouldn't this guy go away and leave her alone? "Addiction."

Chris whistled. "I bet you meet some interesting people."

There was no deterring this guy, but the last thing she wanted to talk about was her job—or lack thereof. She spotted a sign marking the nearest restroom and found her out. "Yes, I do. Good luck with your new career," she said and ducked into the ladies room. She took her time relieving her bladder, washing her hands, checking her face and hair, applying lip gloss, and sending a text to Kennedy, telling her twin she'd made it safely to New Orleans. She didn't tell her about her meeting with her boss—her *ex*-boss. Kennedy already disliked Adam. She'd really rip him a new one when she found out that he was the reason Madison had been fired.

Fired.

Oh God, what was she going to do?

Think only of Adam. He was worth barreling through any obstacle life tossed at her, no matter how hard she fell on her ass when a particular challenge blindsided her. She could get through this. She *would* get through this. She didn't have a choice.

As soon as she sent the text to Kennedy, a message from Adam buzzed her phone. She hugged her phone to her chest and took a deep breath before reading it.

Meet you outside in passenger pickup. I have a surprise for you.

A surprise? Her heart thundered, and the flesh between her thighs began to swell with need. No telling what the man had in store. She was sure it was exactly what she needed at the moment.

Can't wait, she texted. *Be there shortly. Just getting my bag.*

She hurried out of the bathroom and stopped dead in her tracks when Chris—who was standing just outside the women's restroom—offered her a welcoming smile. The guy had just gone from annoying to stalkerish. She suddenly wished Adam was in the airport holding her hand—looking all hard and tough and completely unapproachable. Just because Madison knew better than to fear Adam, that didn't mean Chris would. Fighting the urge to run, she turned on her heel and stalked purposefully toward baggage claim—avoiding Chris's gaze and definitely not returning his smile.

"I get the feeling you don't want to talk to me," he said, nudging several people out of the way as he fell into step with her again.

"I don't know you," she said.

"I'm an okay guy, honest."

"I'm sure you are," she said, "but you're making me uncomfortable. Please stop following me."

She found the baggage carousel and prayed her suitcase was already off the plane. Surely her delayed—but apparently not delayed enough—sojourn in the restroom had given the crew time to unload the baggage.

"So where's this boyfriend of yours?" Chris asked as he moved to stand beside her while she watched unfamiliar bags circle the conveyor.

"Waiting outside," she said.

"Likely story," he said. "You aren't the first woman to blow me off, and I'm sure you won't be the last. Have a nice life."

Out of the corner of her eye she watched him leave, noting that he didn't pick up any luggage before he left the baggage claim area. Madison blew out a calming breath. She didn't like to be mean to people, but surely Chris understood that a woman traveling alone felt more than a little threatened when a guy followed her around an airport for no reason other than to follow her.

She tucked several stray curls behind her ears and smiled with relief when her pink suitcase plopped out on the conveyor and slid against the rail. Now she could see Adam and forget she had a care in the world. He freed her from all constraints, and that feeling was far more addictive than any substance she'd ever treated. At least it was for her.

Madison wheeled her suitcase to the passenger pickup area outside the terminal. She couldn't help but sneak a glance at the hot biker parked on the sidewalk in front of the exit doors. Nothing hotter than a hot guy dressed in denim and leather straddling a Harley. The broad-shouldered man's skin was decorated with tattoos, his dark hair had been cut in a shaggy, shoulder-length style that beckoned her fingertips, and his jeans drew attention to a pair of slim hips and a tight ass that begged to be squeezed. His head was turned away from her as he spoke to a cab driver parked beside the bike, but Madison would have known him anywhere. That wasn't just any hot biker. He was hers. But how in the world had Adam gotten his motorcycle from Austin to New Orleans?

Plagued with a strange case of nervous excitement, Madison clutched her suitcase handle tightly and forced herself not to run toward him. She was sure Adam was much too cool to appreciate being tackled off his motorcycle or having every inch of his face kissed in front of a cab driver. The driver noticed her standing behind Adam and smiled at her.

Adam turned his head and before she could even form a greeting, his arm wrapped around her waist and she found herself sideways on his bike seat, wrapped in his strong arms. His lips moved against hers as he claimed a deep kiss. He pulled away slowly, the smile on his lips shining equally bright from his dark gray eyes.

And as expected and appreciated, all her troubles vanished under his attention.

"Well, hello," she said breathlessly, wrapping her arms around his broad back, her fingers rubbing against the worn leather of his jacket.

"I missed you," he said, his voice low in her ear.

"Me too." She kissed him again and then, finding herself too worked up for the public eye, she buried her face in his neck and inhaled the heady mix of his cologne, his skin, and leather. "Mmm," she murmured, "that kiss was a fantastic surprise."

"That's not the surprise," he said with a low chuckle.

She leaned back to look him in the eye, and her heart rate kicked up just because he was near. God, what this man did to her. "Then what is it?"

"You're sitting on it."

"Your lap?" she asked with a wicked grin. "You know that's my favorite surprise."

"That surprise is for later. I meant the bike. I rented it so we could go for a ride. Since we got in trouble last time we took off with the band's limo, I figured I'd try to be a little more courteous and find us our own mode of transportation."

He was notorious for taking whatever he wanted without consideration for consequences. Frankly, it turned her on, but thinking of others was a good sign that his recovery from addiction was going well. He touched her hair as he searched her eyes.

"But you're wearing a skirt, so you'll have to ride in the taxi with your suitcase until we can get you outfitted properly."

Her joy at the thought of riding behind him, plastered to his back with her hands wandering over his hard chest and flat belly, turned to bitter disappointment.

"What?" she said. "Why?"

"I need you to be safe."

"I don't date you because you're safe, Adam Taylor," she blurted.

"Then why do you date me?"

Because he was the opposite of safe. That wasn't the only reason, but if she were honest with herself, it was the main one.

"Because I love you," she said.

The corners of his mouth turned up. "That's not a reason."

"Let me ride with you," she said, kissing just beneath his ear in an attempt to win him over. "I trust you to get us to our destination in one piece."

"But do you trust every driver on the road between here and the hotel? I sure as hell don't."

"Please."

His expression softened. "Woman, you know I can't say no to you; why do you tempt me so?"

"Is that a yes?" she asked hopefully.

"Yes," he said. "But you're wearing a helmet. I don't care if it messes up your hair." He smoothed a curl between two fingers.

She grinned and threw her arms around his neck to squeeze him enthusiastically.

"So that means our first stop will be an outfitter," he said.

"Outfitter? I can pick up a pair of jeans anywhere."

"Jeans? You're wearing leather, baby. I'm not relenting on that, so don't bother trying to change my mind with those pretty blue eyes. I will see your fantastic ass encased in leather by the end of the hour."

Leather pants? There was no way she could pull off a pair of leather pants. She opened her mouth to protest, and he covered her lips with a fingertip.

"No arguments," he said, pinning her with a sultry look that made her tremble, "or you're riding in the cab."

She nodded. She supposed she could wear a pair of leather pants if it made him happy. He always did force her out of her comfort zone, and she had loved every minute of it. She was sure this little adventure would not be an exception.

Adam instructed the cab driver to take her suitcase to the hotel and have someone deliver it to their suite. He gave the man two hundred dollars and told him to keep the change. After the driver had loaded up the suitcase and took off, Madison asked, "Do you really trust him to take my suitcase to the hotel? He could easily just keep the money *and* all my belongings."

"I would have trusted him to get *you* safely to the hotel, and you're far more precious than any belonging."

Well, when he put it that way, Madison didn't care if the cab driver jumped on eBay and sold everything she owned.

"I really do love you," she said.

"Me too. Now get on the back and hold on tight." When

she scrambled off his lap and was standing next to the bike, he handed her a helmet. "And put this on."

She crammed the black helmet on her head, and he fastened her chin strap before lending her an arm so she could climb on the bike behind him. He put on his own helmet before starting the bike. The engine roared to life, vibrating through Madison's entire body. She gasped in surprise as her panties became instantly saturated with sexual excitement. She was so going to learn how to operate one of these and get one to ride on the long, lonely nights she couldn't see Adam. She arranged her loose denim skirt into makeshift pants by tucking the fabric between and around her legs. Her cowboy boots were a bit slippery on the footholds, but the heels caught the bars and made her feel more stable. Until Adam cranked the accelerator and they took off.

Her thighs clamped down on Adam's hips, and she clung to his chest like a cat avoiding a bath, squashing her breasts into his back so hard they ached. Maybe she should have accepted that cab ride after all.

Adam stopped at a red light and covered her hand with his. "You okay back there?" he shouted over the engine noise. "You aren't afraid, are you?"

Afraid? Of course she wasn't afraid. She loosened her death grip on his body and tried to relax her thighs, but they refused to cooperate.

"I'm fine!" she yelled.

When the light turned green, the pokey car in front of them forced Adam to accelerate slowly. He switched lanes, sped past the car, and whipped back into the lane in front of it.

Okay, so she was a little afraid and felt completely powerless clinging to his body. She trusted Adam and he seemed to know what he was doing, but she wished he'd take it a little easy on her. This was her first time on a motorcycle. She needed a few moments to get used to the idea of whipping around with nothing between her and the street except for air. The experience reminded her of the first time Adam had fucked her—he hadn't taken it easy on her then either. He'd pounded her pussy so hard, she'd felt him for days afterward. And she'd found herself utterly sexually fulfilled for the first time in her life. She'd never expected to *like* being fucked so ruthlessly, but he'd obviously known what he was doing then too.

Madison's leg lock loosened on his hips as she concentrated on breathing slowly. Once she relaxed, she started having fun. That was what the man did for her, tossed her straight out of her comfort zone and directly into a good time. She just needed to remember that whenever they ventured into territory new to her. This kind of adventure was part of his everyday life, so it couldn't be that big a deal. She knew she had to let go of her sheltered existence and live a little, but being as uninhibited as he demanded her to be was still hard. Well, it was difficult at first. Once she found the courage to embrace her wild side, it was just a whole lot of fun.

She snuggled against Adam's back and slid a hand up his chest until the steady beat of his heart pounded beneath her palm. As long as she was with him, she had nothing to fear.

They pulled into a parking lot. The bump over the curb jostled Madison into tightening her grip on Adam again.

He found a parking place near the door, set the kickstand, and shut off the bike. He removed his helmet, set it between his legs, and ran his hands through his thick black hair.

"You no longer have to cling to me like you're going to die," he said, his voice deep and slightly amused. "We've stopped now."

She released him immediately and scrambled gracelessly from the bike. If he hadn't caught her arm to steady her, she would have no doubt gotten good use out of her helmet when her forehead met the asphalt.

"So I guess motorcycles aren't your thing," he said, popping the snap on her helmet and tugging it off her head. Their eyes met, and she felt as if she'd been caught in some horrible lie.

"That was my first ride," she said. "I liked it once I relaxed a little."

He chuckled. "Is that why your legs finally unclamped from my hips? I thought muscle fatigue had set in."

Her cheeks went hot. "I just had to remind myself that you knew what you were doing. That I trust you not to hurt me."

She grinned. "Unless I ask you to."

He stroked her hair from her face. She was sure the helmet had flattened the curls, except for the long ends that had been whipped into a tangled bush by the breeze.

"No one has ever accused me of knowing what I'm doing," he said, staring at her lips.

"That's because they don't take the time to really see you."

Not that he gave anyone the chance to see him. She was pretty sure the only reason she ever got to see who he was on the inside was because she was his counselor and she'd been infinitely patient with him as she'd slowly gained his trust. It had gone against everything she'd ever been taught as a professional when she fell for the angry rock star who'd spent the first month of their counseling sessions glaring a hole through her desk and not saying a word and the second month telling her things that no one else knew about him. Even though her brain had tried to keep her from falling for him, her heart had been right—the man was worth understanding. Worth knowing. Worth loving. No job in the world was worth giving him up. She would be okay, and her situation would work out. As long as she had Adam.

"I have something to tell you," she said, dropping her gaze to the wide zipper on his leather jacket.

"Is it good news? I'm not sure I'm up for any bad news this weekend."

She lifted her gaze to his. It would bother him that she'd gotten fired over their relationship. He would blame himself. And it wasn't his fault. She was the one who should have kept up the boundaries. She was the one who should have requested he see a different counselor when she started having feelings for him. She was the one who should have given him up for his own good. She was the one who should have kept her knees locked together no matter how wobbly he made them. But she'd been weak. And that wasn't his fault at all.

"Of course it's good news," she said. "I have some extra time off, so I thought maybe I could tag along to the next city on the band's tour. I mean, if that's okay with you."

He stared at her for what seemed like a solid minute. "Baby, I'm not sure that's the best idea," he said finally.

Her heart plummeted. "Oh."

Did he have another woman in the next city? He'd told her that he'd given up all those other women, but maybe—No, she couldn't let herself think like that. She had to trust him. Have faith in him.

"The band . . ." He rubbed the back of his neck and stared over her head. "I'd like you near, but they . . ."

"It's okay," she said, wincing at her dejected tone. She'd just sprung the idea on the guy out of the blue—because the single positive thing about losing her job (time off) had only just occurred to her. How had she expected him to react?

She'd expected him to be as excited by the idea as she had been.

"We'll figure something out," he said and climbed off the motorcycle. "You and I both know that a weekend isn't enough time together."

She smiled, her happiness returning. He hadn't completely rejected the idea. But she would treat these three days and two nights as if they needed to treasure every moment. He headed for the store's entrance and held the door open for her as he ushered her inside.

The scent of leather permeated the shop. Madison inhaled deeply. The smell of leather always reminded her of Adam. Leather jackets, pants and chaps filled long racks. Leather boots were displayed on one wall, black T-shirts on another. Bandanas and leather jewelry took up all other available space.

"Back so soon?" a rather attractive female employee asked Adam. "Not that I'm complaining." The heavily tattooed woman smiled at Adam, and Madison—feeling inadequate and all unworldly country girl—slid her hand into his.

"I need to hook up my woman with some riding gear," Adam explained, tugging Madison into view. "Something leather and skintight."

"Better hook her up with a few tattoos while you're at it," the woman said with a smirk. "She's too clean for the likes of you, Adam Taylor."

"Actually, I think I'm too dirty for her."

Madison shook her head vigorously, and the woman chuckled. "It's a lot easier to add dirt than to clean it off," she said. She aimed for a rack of black leather pants and started looking through them. She pulled out a pair and handed them to Madison.

Madison checked the tag, surprised they were the correct size. She held them up to her waist, trying to imagine what they'd look like on. Definitely skintight.

"Go try them on," Adam said in her ear, his tone low and seductive. It played on her nerve endings and sent them sparking with anticipation.

"The dressing room is in the back," the clerk said. "I'll find you some boots."

"I already have boots," Madison said, peering down at her scuffed brown cowboy boots.

"I meant decent boots," she said. "Riding boots."

"I've been riding in these boots for years." Of course her rides were on four-legged beasts, not two-wheeled machines.

"She keeps the cowboy boots," Adam said with a grin. "She wouldn't be my Madison without them."

"Then we'd better go with a different leather," the clerk said. She took the shiny black pants from Madison's hands and replaced them with a pair of creamy white ones in a matte finish. Feathers and curvy designs had been embroidered around the top of the seat and down the hips and outer thighs with beige and black threads.

"Nice," Adam said in that same seductive tone. He was obviously imagining her wearing them.

Madison made a beeline for the dressing room.

"There's a matching jacket with angel wings embroidered on the back," the clerk said to Adam. "Seems appropriate for your sweet little thing."

Madison got the feeling the woman was mocking her, but when she peeked over her shoulder to find Adam trailing her to the dressing room, she didn't much care. The clerk was obviously jealous, and Madison couldn't blame her for that.

"Yeah, that," Adam said calmly as his long strides quickly brought him closer to Madison. "And a black T-shirt."

Madison hurried into the dressing room and closed the door. Her pulse was in a frenzy. Her nipples were erect. Her pussy swollen and achy. All because he'd followed her to the dressing room and spoken in that commanding, seductive voice of his. An entirely different reaction than she'd had when that creeper had followed her to the bathroom in the airport. She didn't mind being stalked as long as it was Adam hunting her.

Madison unfastened her skirt and let it flutter to the floor. She kicked off her boots and pulled the leather pants on. She presented her backside to the mirror and ran her hands over her ass. She was pretty sure Adam would like the way the leather hugged her curves since the embroidery just under the waistband drew attention to her ass. Not bad.

"Well?" Adam said just outside the dressing room.

She unlatched the lock and eased the door open, looking up at him with her heart thudding hard. Would he like them on her? Or was she too clean to look good in leather? Even off-white leather.

"How do they look?" she asked quietly.

"Turn," he said, his expression completely unreadable.

She turned to show him the back, and his hand hit the dressing room door, sending it crashing into the wall.

His arm circled her waist, pulling her backward to collide with his chest. She could feel his cock—already hard as granite—against her ass. He took two steps, drawing her into the dressing room and slammed the door behind them, fiddling with the lock at his back while he looked her over in the mirror. The sound of the lock engaging made her entire body throb. He yanked open the snaps along the front of her plaid shirt and filled his hands with her breasts. His open mouth caressed the side of her neck as he squeezed her tits through the hindrance of her pink lace bra.

"You drive me insane, woman," he said into her ear.

She could only answer with a moan of torment. Oh God, was he going to fuck her here? With that really cool clerk out there knowing what they had to be doing? She sincerely hoped so, and would do anything in her power to convince him to take her body. Hard. Madison wanted that woman to know that she wasn't as clean as she looked. And that she had every reason to be jealous.

Madison reached behind her to unfasten Adam's fly. His

hand slid down her bare belly and into the front of the leather that had him so turned on. The tightness of the pants didn't let his hand get far, so he cupped her pussy over the thick material and squeezed.

When she freed his cock and held its thick, smooth length in her hand, he gasped.

"I didn't mean for this to go this far," he said.

"Why not?"

He groaned in torment as she stroked his length slowly. Gently. Knowing that teasing him made him crazy.

"For your sake, honey," he said, in a hoarse whisper, "not mine."

He yanked open the button at her waist and pulled down the zipper. Next thing she knew, her pants and panties were on the floor, she was bent forward at the waist, and his talented fingers were exploring the slick folds between her thighs. He slipped those fingers inside her, and she shuddered.

Adam groaned as she gave his fingers a coaxing squeeze. God, she wanted him.

"I always think that one day I'll touch you like this and you won't be ready for me."

She grinned and met his eyes in the mirror. "Today isn't that day."

She shifted her hips backward and rubbed his cockhead against her where his fingers were buried deep. He twisted his wrist, fingertips pressing down into the spot inside that made her moan in ecstasy. His thumb massaged her throbbing clit. She tugged at his cock impatiently, until he pushed her hand aside, taking himself in his free hand.

He pulled away unexpectedly, spun her around, and pressed her back to the wall, his forearm across her chest. Making her feel trapped. Her heart thundered with excitement and a hint of fear.

"What do you want, Madison?" he said, his face so close, she felt the breath of his words against her lips.

"You," she said without hesitation.

"My fingers?"

"Yes," she admitted.

"My cock?"

"Yes."

"Which is it?"

"Both," she said, her brain so addled with need that she'd have taken anything he wanted to give her.

"Both?"

He slid a finger up inside her, and her pussy tightened around it. He massaged her inner wall until she sputtered. His thumb brushed her swollen clit, and she cried out.

"Then you'll have both," he said.

Her mouth fell open in surprise when he pressed the tip of his cock inside her. He still had a finger in there and with a few slow and gentle thrusts to wet himself with her juices, his cock was in there was well.

"How does that feel?" he asked, slowly withdrawing his finger as his cock slid deep, and then pressing his finger deep as he slowly pulled out.

She answered with a moan of bliss.

"Good?" he asked. "Does it feel good, Madison?"

"Y-yes. And—and my clit too," she said, sounding as desperate for stimulation as she felt. "Touch me."

She cried out when he did what she'd hoped he would and rubbed her clit with his thumb. Her pussy clamped tight over his cock and his finger, trying to tug him deeper.

"Your pussy is always greedy for cock," he said to her. "You know that?"

"Yes!" she agreed. "Fuck it."

"Fuck what, baby?" He continued to thrust into her slowly, the added stimulation of his finger driving her mad.

"Inside," she panted.

"Inside where?"

God, he was such a tease. "My pussy. Fuck it hard, Adam. I can't stand it anymore."

"You know I love it when you get so worked up you forget to be proper."

"Please. I need to be fucked." She fisted a hand in his thick jet-black hair. "Now."

"I can't take you hard when we're like this," he said, his hips moving oh so slowly as he forced his cock and his finger deeper.

"Then how? I need it. Please."

He pulled out, and she sucked in a sob of torment. "I'll have to turn you around to fuck you hard when we're in such a small space."

She didn't resist when he forced her to face the wall. She opened her legs eagerly, delighted when he didn't waste any time and claimed her pussy with a hard, deep thrust. His long, calloused fingers—guitarist fingers—dug into her hips as he pounded into her, rubbing that itch deep inside that was never satisfied with gentle lovemaking. She needed to feel him. Hard. Deep. Until it almost hurt, but not quite. Only Adam knew how to give her exactly what she needed. His thumbs massaged her always eager back entrance until she thought she might die if he didn't fuck her ass next. He knew how much she liked being taken in her forbidden place. He always did right by her there as well.

He didn't give her the extra she wanted, though. His fingers shifted to her clit, rubbing her most sensitive spot rapidly until she came with a cry of release. He then shuddered behind her as he let go, grabbing her tits to pull her upright and tight against him as he spent himself inside her with several gasping jerks. He massaged her breasts as he slowly thrust into her for several moments after he finished.

"You wanted more, didn't you?" he asked, watching her in the mirror.

"That was perfect," she said.

"You didn't want me to fuck your ass?" He kissed her ear, grinning knowingly. "The only thing greedier for cock than your pussy is your tight little hole."

He slapped her flank, and her ass tightened with need. Yes, she wanted him inside her there. Even now.

"Well," she said, her cheeks pink. "Maybe a little. You know I love it."

"I have set up a little something for you to enjoy at the sex club tomorrow night. But until then, no anal."

She didn't know whether to be excited about the upcoming experience at the club or disappointed that she had to wait for butt sex.

"None?" she asked. "Not even a finger? A plug? Nothing?"

He laughed, obviously finding her desperation amusing. "Not until tomorrow night."

"Did anyone ever tell you that it's not nice to tease?" she asked, reaching between her legs to rake her fingernails over his balls and then caress him where his body was still joined with hers.

He tensed and released a huff of breath against her neck.

"I don't think you'll feel that way after tomorrow night," he said, churning his hips to burrow deeper. He was slowly growing soft inside her, but seemed content to stay buried within. "You're in for a surprise."

"Another one?" she asked.

The devious grin she caught in the mirror made her belly quiver.

"The best one."

God, she couldn't wait to see what he had in store for her.

When Madison and Adam exited the dressing room moments later, the clerk produced a slow clap, shaking her head at them as if she'd caught a pair of naughty children playing doctor in her closet. Madison buried her face in Adam's upper arm, her cheeks so hot that his leather felt icy against them.

"You do turn good girls bad, Adam Taylor," the woman commented with a throaty chuckle. "I should have never doubted your skill."

Adam wrapped an arm around Madison's lower back. "She's just a little bad, Phaedra," he said. "She's been working hard at turning me good."

Phaedra laughed hysterically. "She definitely has her work cut out for her there," she said. "Personally, I don't think she stands a chance. You're better off finding someone who likes you for who you are, not the person she thinks you should be."

Madison stiffened and lifted her head to stare the woman down. "I love him for who he is on the inside. That tender part of him that he doesn't let most people see."

Phaedra shook her head at her. "He really has you fooled, doesn't he?" Her brown-eyed gaze shifted to Adam. "Let me know when you get bored with her Pollyanna bullshit, baby. You know it will never be enough for you."

Adam kissed Madison's temple and whispered close to her ear, "Go wait for me outside."

"What?" Narrowing her eyes, she looked up at him. Her hurt for being insulted by Phaedra was rapidly replaced by utter confusion. And a touch of suspicion. "Why?"

"I need to speak to Phaedra in private." He didn't look at Madison. His cold gaze was fixed on the woman who was suddenly clutching to her chest the cream-colored jacket that matched Madison's leather pants.

"But—"

"Go."

"Adam?"

His gaze softened when he looked at her. He lifted a hand to touch her cheek and stroked her skin lightly with his fingertips. "It's okay, baby. Just do what I ask, please."

She still didn't want to leave him alone with this woman who seemed to know him and was obviously interested in him as something more than a regular customer, but she did as Adam asked and went outside. She did not, however, take her eyes off him as she stood outside the store, staring in through the windows. She couldn't hear what he was saying, but he was obviously very angry as he yelled at Phaedra, gesticulating aggressively—one arm swinging out toward the door Madison had just exited, the other curled inward as he patted his chest and then pointed at Phaedra, who winced as if he'd slapped her.

Madison strained her ears, but couldn't hear over the traffic sounds behind her. So she tried to read his lips. It appeared that Adam's every other word was *fuck*, but she couldn't be sure. Why had he sent her outside to wait? She would have liked to hear him cuss out Phaedra. Madison reached for the door handle and pulled it open, catching the tail end of Adam's tirade.

"—better if no one besides her gives me a fucking chance!"

A ringer behind the counter *bonged* to announce someone had entered the store, and Adam turned his head to look at Madison.

"I told you to wait outside," he said, his tone still harsh from anger.

"I'm not waiting outside," she said and stubbornly crossed her arms over her chest. "You should trust me enough to hear what you have to say."

"She's right," Phaedra said. "Has she ever even seen this side of you?"

Madison had seen it plenty in the early days of his treatment, but he'd let go of his anger once he'd opened up to her and trusted her with his real feelings. Or maybe all this time he'd been burying his anger for her benefit.

"This isn't me anymore," Adam said to Phaedra.

"It looks like you and it sounds like you and it acts like you, so who exactly is it supposed to be, Adam?" Phaedra asked.

"Fuck off, Phaedra," Adam said. He shoved past Madison on his way out of the store.

Madison started to go after him, but Phaedra's warning stopped her.

"You can't leave with those pants unless you pay for them."

She could have jerked off the pants and gone outside in her underwear, but instead she dug a credit card out of her small purse and extended it toward the woman.

"Charge them for me."

Phaedra took the card from her hand. "And the jacket?"

"Yeah, whatever."

"And a black T-shirt." It wasn't a question.

Madison hurried out of the store and searched for Adam. She spotted him near the end of the building. His back to the road, he had his forearm pressed against the bricks and was staring down at the cracked asphalt between his boots. His right hand was clenched into a fist, and every line of his body was hard with tension. Madison took a steadying breath and strode in his direction. When she touched his shoulder, his body jolted as if she'd stabbed him.

"Give me a minute," he said. "I need to cool down."

"Why are you so upset? Talk to me."

He shook his head slightly. "I don't want a counseling session right now, Miss Fairbanks."

"Talking to me doesn't mean we're having a session, Adam. Besides . . ." she said, her chest suddenly tight and achy. She took a deep breath and forced the words out. "I'm not a counselor anymore."

His head jerked around, and he stared at her with wide gray eyes. "What do you mean?"

"I got fired this morning."

"What?" He shifted and took her shoulders in his palms. "What happened? Why didn't you tell me sooner?"

She shrugged. "I don't think I've fully digested it yet," she said. "It was a shock. And I didn't want my problem to ruin our weekend together."

"Madison, baby, you can tell me anything. Anything."

"The way you tell *me* anything? Or the way you send me outside when you have something to say that you don't want me to hear?"

His gaze shifted to her forehead, and a muscle in his jaw twitched. "I was pissed. I don't like you to see me like that."

"Adam, I *need* to see you like that. I need to see all of you. I love you."

"I try so hard not to be that guy anymore, but sometimes . . ." He shook his head. "Tell me what happened with your job."

There was no use in hiding the details from him. "Someone reported me for having an affair with a client. And my boss, well, she seemed to think I'd form a habit of it."

"So it's my fault you got fired." He scowled, his fingers curling into her shoulders.

She shook her head. "Of course it isn't. I could say I should have been more careful—not let you get close, kept my legs shut—but I don't regret sleeping with you, and I don't regret falling in love with you."

"But someday you might."

Madison shook her head. "No chance."

His arms slid around her back, and he hugged her. "I'm so sorry, baby. Will you be able to find another job? I know how much you love your work and how much all the fuck-ups in the world need you. I know I'm not the only one you've saved."

"I didn't save you. Just helped you save yourself. And I'm sure everything will work out," she said, more to soothe his fears than to state her true feelings. She'd probably never be able to get another job working with addicts. But Adam was worth any adversity. It was just a job—a job she'd worked hard to obtain, an important job, a fulfilling job, but still just a job. There were countless other jobs she could try, but he was the man she loved, and there was only one of him. "I love you."

"I love you," he said against her hair. "Do you want me to contact your boss? Maybe I can set things right."

Madison was pretty sure Adam's idea of setting things right would include a lot of yelling and swearing.

"No, it'll be fine," she said. "And I don't want you to blame yourself for this."

"How could I? It's your fault."

She jerked away and glared up at him in disbelief. He had to take at least a little credit for her ending up without a job.

"Maybe if you weren't so damned sexy," he said, "I could have kept my hands to myself."

He slid those hands over the curve of her ass and crushed their lower bodies together.

"Maybe if you weren't so damned sweet," he said, "I could have kept my lips off you."

He kissed her jaw. Her lips. The tip of her nose.

"Maybe if your heart wasn't so big, I wouldn't have been so tempted to win it for myself."

He cradled the back of her head in one hand and pressed her face to the crook of his neck. She wrapped her arms around his waist and snuggled closer. He felt so good. So solid. So strong against her. She knew everything would be okay. There was a reason they'd met. She was sure it was so they could spend their lives together.

"So it *is* all your fault, Miss Fairbanks," he murmured. "It's your fault I fell in love with you."

She smiled against his chest. "Well, when you put it that way . . . I'm happy to take the blame."

CHAPTER FOUR

TORN WITH INDECISION, Adam fingered the ring in his pocket and stared in through the glass of the shop where Madison had gone to collect her purchases. He didn't think the time was right to ask her to marry him. Not when she'd just dropped that bombshell on him. Even though she'd played down losing her job as if it wasn't a big deal, he knew it was a big deal. Once her jobless situation had time to sink in, she was going to be devastated. And he wanted to be the one to hold her and kiss her tears away when she shattered.

Fuck.

When had he started having tender thoughts like those? Sometimes he couldn't believe the syrupy bullshit that filtered through his mind and came out of his mouth.

This woman had him all sorts of out of his head. And though he'd responded to Phaedra's words with anger, what she'd said about Madison not liking him for who he was had bothered him. The man Phaedra had once known was all sorts of wrong for the sweet counselor who owned his heart and he knew that, but he was a new man now. A good man.

Oh, who the fuck did he think he was kidding? Maybe only himself. Everyone around him still saw him the way he'd always been, and maybe they were the ones who were right about him. Maybe it was only a matter of time before he embraced his darkness again. And if that happened, he knew he couldn't stay with Madison. He didn't want to hurt her feelings, but he couldn't drag her down into the darkness, into his pit of shit and misery. He wouldn't be able to stand it if she started to hate him. He'd rather die than earn her hatred.

When Madison stepped out of the store wearing her sexy as sin leather pants, any thoughts of darkness were completely obliterated by her light. Maybe there was a place between his shadows and her radiance where they could exist together in harmony. He had to believe in her, in them. If he didn't, he wouldn't care where life took him. All paths led to death eventually, and he'd glimpsed his mortality more than once, so dying didn't scare him. It never had. But losing her did. He couldn't lose her. She was his light. His everything.

"So how do you know that woman, anyway?" Madison asked, trying to appear nonchalant, but looking like she was about to explode.

Adam tugged her closer and began to unsnap the mother-of-pearl fastenings of her cutesy pink and blue plaid shirt one by one. Her eyes widened, and she slapped a hand over her chest to halt his progress.

"*What* are you doing?" she asked.

Avoiding your question. "Helping you change," he said.

"Here?"

"You can't wear this shirt with those pants. It's bad enough that you're keeping the boots." He moved his hands to the hem of her blouse and unsnapped it from the bottom up until the only snap holding it shut was the one under her dainty hand.

"Adam!"

"What?" He took her chin between his thumb and forefinger and kissed her. "I'm just trying to help."

"Sure you are. I'll be right back." Clutching the front of her shirt closed with one hand, she raced back inside the store.

He chuckled and shook his head. She was still a good girl. And maybe that was what he found so appealing about her. No matter how hard he pushed her into his darkness, her core was intrinsically light. He doubted he'd ever truly corrupt her, but the prospect of failure didn't stop him from trying. Just like she never stopped pushing him to be a better man. He wondered if either of them would ever really change the other for better or for worse.

Madison strutted out of the store a moment later, shoving her plaid shirt into her sack of purchases and wearing a tight black T-shirt that made Adam's jeans snug in the crotch. Damn, the woman made his blood run hot. He'd just had a taste of her and already he wanted more. His latest addiction,

Madison Fairbanks. No one would ever convince him to give this one up.

She shrugged into her new leather jacket—the creamy leather hugging her gorgeous figure—and met his eyes.

"Better?" she asked.

"Better for riding," he said, "but I prefer you naked."

"Hey, this ride was your idea." She planted a fist on one hip. "I thought we'd be naked most of the afternoon."

"Well, shit, why didn't you say so? Get on the bike so we can head to the hotel and ditch these clothes."

"Oh no you don't, Adam Taylor," she said. "I didn't buy this outfit so you could immediately strip it off me. You promised me a ride."

"I was planning on taking you for a ride in the hotel bed."

Her sack of clothes smacked him in the chest.

"I'll take *that* ride later. The only way you'll be between my thighs now is with me on the back of that motorcycle."

Well, if that didn't conjure up all sorts of erotic images . . .

"Are you sure you're not too scared to ride?"

He was teasing, but she looked grievously offended.

"Of course I'm not scared. I'm wearing leather." She tossed her mass of curly hair behind her shoulders and straightened her spine. Which made her tits jut forward in a most distracting way. "You can't be scared when you're wearing leather. It's not possible."

He laughed and hugged her tightly. She always lightened his mood. Made him smile. Made him laugh. Made him crazy with lust. He never imagined he'd end up as one of those guys who would love a woman more than anything else in his life, one of those guys who'd go down on one knee and ask a woman to spend the rest of her life with him. He released her abruptly—not sure why his heart was thudding so hard—and busied his hands by handing her a helmet. Not the ring. He wasn't quite ready to do that.

"So are you going to tell me about Phaedra now?" she asked as she pulled the helmet on over her curls and fastened the chin strap.

"I'm not wearing enough leather to be brave enough to tell you that," he assured her.

"I won't get upset. I just want to know. You can tell me anything. Remember?"

Defenses instantly high, he stiffened. "We used to get high on coke and fuck for days. Is that what you want me to say?"

"Is it the truth?" She held his gaze and no matter how much he wanted to, he couldn't turn away. And for some reason, though he was an expert at hiding secrets, he couldn't lie to her.

"Yes."

"Then that's what I want you to say. When was the last time you fucked her?"

"A couple years ago."

She smiled. "Right answer."

She grabbed his arm and used it to lift herself on the bike behind him. When her arms went around him and she pressed securely against his back, the tension drained out of his body. That was it? She wasn't going to go ballistic about his past with Phaedra? Maybe he really could tell her anything. He'd already told her more than anyone else in his life, but he'd become so accustomed to hiding his reality from those he cared about, that it had become a habit. A bad one that he needed to break.

"You aren't mad?" he asked.

"Why would I be mad? She was your past; I'm your now. And I will continue to be yours in the future."

She was his. For now and always. He lifted a hand to squeeze her hand into his chest.

"I gotta say, I do think she's an incredible bitch." Madison gave him a squeeze and added, "If I were a violent person, I would have slapped her."

Grinning, Adam started the bike, and they entered traffic. He had no destination in mind, he just wanted to ride. They headed out of the city, off the interstate and onto a lonelier highway. From the way Madison's body molded against his and her hands explored his chest and belly and eventually the thickening length of his cock, she was obviously more relaxed on the bike now than when they'd left the airport. Maybe the leather actually had fortified her bravery. She was always hesitant to try new things, but once she let go of her natural reserve, she enjoyed their adventures together. But if she kept teasing him through his pants like that, there was no way they'd make it to the hotel before he had to get her naked and add "fucking on a motorcycle" to their list of adventures.

Adam's cellphone buzzed in his pocket. Seeing that the only person he cared to talk to at the moment had her hand in a most compromising position, Adam ignored the text. Besides, he was driving. He couldn't very well check his messages. A minute later the phone buzzed again. And again a few seconds later. He decided it must be an emergency if someone was so insistent. He pulled off the main road onto a side street and eased to a halt beneath an enormous oak tree. The shade might offer a bit of relief from the relentless heat and humidity, since they no longer had the cooling breeze of their ride to make wearing leather in June bearable. Madison unzipped her jacket almost at once and began fanning her throat with one hand. Her other remained in his lap.

"Why did we stop?" she asked. "Need a rest?"

"You know what I need," he said. "Or your hand does."

Said hand gave the bulge in his pants an appreciative squeeze.

"But someone keeps buzzing my phone."

Adam pulled his phone out of his pocket, hoping it wasn't who he thought it might be: his father. He did not want to deal with the old man this weekend.

Adam was surprised to see several messages from the band's lead singer. And for once Jacob wasn't ripping him a new one for being late or some bullshit. Adam smiled and chuckled as a photo of Owen mooning a rather offended-looking cow loaded on his screen.

A cow? Did they even have cows in New Orleans? He could only guess why Owen had his pants around his knees.

Where the hell are you guys? Adam texted.

Owen said he heard of some in-the-sticks Cajun restaurant I had to try. We stopped for some entertainment in a pasture.

Dude, that's just wrong.

Not THAT kind of entertainment.

Is Kellen with you?

He's with that redheaded chick. Owen and I thought we'd blow off some steam. And avoid Lindsey for a couple of hours.

Heat rose up Adam's face, and he peeked at Madison. He should probably tell her that he might have gotten some chick pregnant, but that news was sure to put a damper on their good time this weekend.

His phone buzzed again.

Do you want to join us for an early supper? You're not too far from us.

How did Jacob know that? Adam started to type the question when he remembered he'd been convinced to add an app to his phone that let his circle of friends locate him whether he wanted to be found or not.

I thought you were mooning cows.

Another picture came through of Owen climbing a split-rail fence with an incredibly offended-looking bull racing up behind him.

Adam laughed, and Madison's fingers dug into his shoulder when she lifted up to look at his screen.

"What in the world?" she asked.

"Owen and Jacob's idea of an entertaining afternoon."

He flicked backward to the picture of Owen mooning the cow, and she laughed. She laughed harder when he showed her the second picture of the angry bull chasing the band's bassist.

"I don't think that bull appreciated Owen making a m*oooo*ve on his woman," Madison said.

Adam snorted and shook his head. So his woman told lame jokes, so what?

I think Owen is tired of insulting bovines. Jacob's next text came through quickly. He always used a voice-to-text app, as if he couldn't be bothered with typing. *Join us. You can bring your girl. We won't embarrass you.*

There was a pause, and then Adam's phone received a single word text.

Much.

Adam was sure they'd embarrass the hell out of him, but he wouldn't mind it too bad. He missed the camaraderie of the band's early days. Back before his troubles with addiction tried to destroy his friendships. He was grateful those bonds hadn't been completely severed and was more than ready to strengthen them again.

"Do you like Cajun food?" Adam asked Madison.

"Sure do. The spicier the better."

"Do you want to join Jacob and Owen for a late lunch? They say the restaurant isn't far from here."

"I guess so."

At Adam's request, Jacob sent him directions and by not far, Jacob meant twenty miles away on a completely different highway, so Adam had a bit more time to enjoy the feel of Madison at his back, the breeze against his neck, and the bike rumbling between his thighs. Life was good. He couldn't stop grinning.

It turned out the Cajun restaurant was an old camper that had been converted into a portable kitchen. The picnic tables surrounding the little eatery were mostly full. Considering that there were only eight tables, the crowd wasn't excessive. But the pile of crawdads in front of Jacob bordered on obscene.

"Are you going to share any of those?" Owen was asking as Adam directed Madison to the table with a protective hand on her lower back.

Jacob slapped Owen's hand and, as his mouth was full, responded with a grunt of denial.

"No one comes between Jacob and his crawdads," Adam said.

Jacob paused in his feasting long enough to nod at Madison and smile at Adam, but he wasn't distracted enough to miss Owen's attempt to sneak another crawdad from his plate.

"We're supposed to share those," Owen complained. "That's why we got a double order."

"Let's go get some for ourselves," Madison suggested.

"Order me another mess," Jacob said as he snapped another crustacean's shell to get at the presumably delicious meat inside.

"Get your own," Owen said and climbed over the picnic table bench to get to his feet. He seemed to notice Madison for the first time. "Hey," he said, "when did you become hot?"

"She was always hot," Adam said, wrapping an arm around her waist to hold her close at his side.

"No," Owen said. "She was always *cute*. Now she's hot."

"Must be Louisiana's sweltering heat," Madison said, piling

on the Southern accent and fanning herself dramatically.

"I do believe it's the leather," Owen said.

"It is rather stifling in this humidity, unless we're riding. That's a bit cooler. And fun. I love it. It's a lot like riding horses, only faster and a bit more predictable."

She tipped her face up at Adam to offer him a proud smile, and he couldn't resist kissing her lips softly.

They followed Owen to the order window and talked about Owen's adventure with disgruntled cattle while they waited for their food.

"Why were you bothering the cows in the first place?" Adam asked.

"They looked bored," Owen said.

"Cows always look bored," Madison said and laughed.

"They just need someone to show them how to party," Owen insisted, drawing his basket—crawdads and Cajun fries, with sides of red beans and rice—across the counter toward him.

"And I'm sure you're up for the task," Adam said. He shook his head at his friend and collected his and Madison's baskets. She carried their drinks and plastic forks.

"I'm a perpetual party, baby," Owen said as he skirted the table and settled on the bench next to Jacob.

"Your perpetual party is in your pants," Jacob said, eyeing the line at the counter. His pile of crawdads had dwindled to unacceptable levels, and not one of them was keen on sharing with him when he'd refused to do likewise. He'd even tried to stare Madison down, but she merely raised a brow, pulled her basket closer, and started eating.

"Better be careful with that kind of party," Madison said with a chuckle, "or you'll end up knocking up some groupie."

Adam's stomach dropped. Jacob produced a full body shudder. Owen turned an unsettling shade of green.

"Yeah," Owen said quietly. "We wouldn't want *that* to happen."

Jacob shoved his few remaining crawdads to the center of the table. He'd apparently lost his appetite. Owen tackled his fries and carb-rich sides as if he hadn't eaten in months. Adam picked over his food, wondering if he should warn Madison about the situation with Lindsey now or wait until the obviously pregnant woman was staring her in the face. More than likely the two women would meet before the concert. How awkward could it be? Girlfriend meet baby mama. Baby mama meet . . . *Ugh*. He didn't even want to think of Lindsey that way. Adam was almost positive that her baby wasn't his. And he hoped to God it wasn't. He'd make a terrible father, and he knew it. The last thing he needed in his life was a baby. Thinking about babies made him queasy. Unlike Jacob . . . Jacob actually liked kids. Adam glanced at his friend, who was staring down at his clenched fists on the weathered table. He was a good father to Julie, but Adam hoped it wasn't Jacob's unborn child either. The guy had a hard enough time dealing with one crazy baby mama. He sure as hell didn't need two. And Owen . . . Well, he seemed willing to take the fall, so he was more than welcome to. More power to him.

"What's wrong?" Madison asked, looking from one man to the other.

She must have sensed how the atmosphere had completely changed after her offhanded remark about knocking up a groupie. She was good at picking up on that kind of thing, which was a trait that made her an excellent counselor. And because he couldn't keep his dick in his pants, she'd lost her job. And because he couldn't keep his dick in his pants, soon there *might* be a kid in the world cursed with half of its genetic material coming from Adam. Perhaps he should invest in a cock cage to keep his troublemaking dick locked safely in his pants.

"You haven't told her?" Jacob asked.

"Told me what?" Madison slurped from her soda as if she'd been crawling through a desert for days.

"Nothing," Adam said. "Do you want another drink?"

"You'd better tell her," Jacob said. "It might be yours. No sense in making this worse than it already is."

Frowning, Madison released her straw and looked from Adam to Jacob and back again.

"What might be yours?"

"It's probably mine," Owen said glumly. "Damn party in my pants was bound to get me into trouble sooner or later."

Madison's eyes shifted from Adam to Owen and then to Jacob. "Will someone please tell me what you guys are talking about?"

"Some knocked-up groupie showed up a couple of days ago," Jacob said. "She's like six months pregnant and claims one of us is the father of her baby."

"Which one of you?"

Jacob shrugged. "Don't know."

Madison shook her head as if trying to rid it of the stupid words rattling around between her ears. "How can you not know? Whichever one of you had sex with her is the father."

"Therein lies the problem," Jacob said.

"We all had sex with her," Adam said, rubbing a hand over his face.

Madison's hand smashed into his chest. "You promised me," she shouted.

No, he hadn't. He hadn't promised her he wouldn't sleep around until recently. Six months ago wasn't recently as far as he was concerned.

"I did not," Adam said. "Don't overreact."

"Overreact? How can anything short of murdering you with my fork be an overreaction?" She shoved her white fork in his face and looked mad enough to gouge his eyes out with it. "How could you do this to me, Adam?"

"Shh," Jacob said when all eyes turned their way. "This is not the place for an argument."

Adam agreed, but apparently Madison had more to say. She did lower her voice to an angry whisper, but did not lower her plastic weapon.

"You promised me that you always wore protection with other women. *Always*. You promised me that. I never would have allowed . . ." She broke off with an angry growl.

Oh, that was what she'd meant.

"I did wear protection," he said. And he wasn't just saying that to appease her.

"Then how could you potentially be the father of this baby, Adam?" She poked him in the collarbone with her fork, fire sparking in her blue eyes. "How?"

"We all wore protection," Jacob said.

"Then *how* is she pregnant?" Madison yelled.

"Wish I had the answer to that," Owen said.

Madison's stiff spine relaxed slightly as she scowled at her food and finally lowered her fork. Adam could practically see her mind trying to piece together the information that had been thrown at her.

After a moment, she said, "If you all wore protection, what's to say she got pregnant by any of you? Maybe she's a goddamned liar."

Adam had already decided that was probably the case. Lindsey had gotten pregnant by some loser back home and not, as she claimed, by any of the losers in his band. She was just looking for a quick and easy bankroll. He really hoped Madison's suspicions proved to be true.

"She's got her sights set on me," Owen said, "so unless the kid comes out with wild black hair, a permanent scowl on his face, and a Stratocaster in his little hands, then you don't have anything to worry about, Madi."

She actually smiled at this. Oh no, thinking about a miniature Adam should not make her smile. Or maybe she was smiling about something else. Adam hoped so. He wanted no babies in his life. Not even hers. But especially not Lindsey's.

"All you have to do is make her get a paternity test," Madison said. "Prove it isn't any of yours. Get rid of her once and for all."

"We'll have one done as soon as the baby is born," Jacob said. "Until then, we're just playing a waiting game."

"Fuck that," Madison said, and the three men stared at her in stunned disbelief. She wasn't the kind of woman who said *fuck* in polite company. Sure, she screamed it in the bedroom, but she'd never cursed in front of Adam's bandmates. "They can do the test during pregnancy now. You don't have to wait until she delivers."

"They can?" Owen turned another shade greener.

Adam wondered why. Maybe there was a reason Lindsey was so insistent that the baby was Owen's. Maybe he was hiding something about what had happened between himself and Lindsey and causing the rest of them undo anxiety for nothing. The bastard.

Madison nodded. "One of my clients got a girl in trouble—or so she said. The baby turned out not to be his. They did the test before she gave birth."

"I'm not sure I want to know," Owen said.

"It's yours, isn't it?" Adam accused Owen. "It's yours and you know it, no *maybe* about it. You nutted inside her, didn't you?" Adam made a grab across the table for Owen's T-shirt, but Owen jerked back and threw up an arm to block him.

Owen shook his head. "Not that I know of. I honestly don't know for sure if it's mine. I just have this sick feeling in the pit of my stomach that it is. Probably because she keeps saying it is. I guess if you hear something enough times, you start to believe it's true."

"That's why I made him leave the bus with me today," Jacob said. "The chick will not leave him alone. She's psycho."

And Jacob knew what psycho chicks were like firsthand, so Adam didn't even question the guy's claim.

Madison reached across the table and patted Owen's hand. "Everything will turn out how it's supposed to."

Adam highly doubted that. Someone in his band was fucked. And not in a good a way.

"As long as it isn't mine everything will be fine," Adam said. "I knew I should have gotten that vasectomy last year. Had the appointment set and everything, but had to cancel."

Madison's head turned slowly, and her mouth dropped open. "A vasectomy?"

"Here we go again," Jacob muttered.

"Were you even going to consult me before having it done?" Madison sputtered.

Adam lifted an eyebrow at her. "Why should I consult you? They're my balls."

"But *our* future children," she said.

Adam stared at her, completely stunned that she was imagining children in their future. "Children? We aren't having children."

"When did we decide that?"

"We didn't decide." He pointed to his chest. "I decided."

Her mouth opened and closed several times, as if she couldn't find words scathing enough to spew at him.

"Don't you think we should discuss this?" she finally asked.

"Nope." There was nothing to discuss. He didn't want kids. End of discussion.

She glanced at Jacob and Owen, who were both staring at her as if their spat was a spectator sport and the ball was in her court.

"We'll talk about it later," she said.

Not if he could help it.

"You done eating?" Jacob asked Owen. "I'm ready to head back to the bus."

"Why don't you go order some dinner for the rest of the band and the road crew while I finish?" Owen said.

"Sounds like a plan," Jacob said.

Jacob stood from the table and every chick in the vicinity watched him walk to the counter. Even Adam's chick.

"What are you looking at?" he asked. He was used to everyone staring at Jacob and not in the same way they stared at him, so he wasn't jealous. He just liked fucking with her.

Madison's heat-flushed cheeks reddened a shade brighter. "Um . . ." She cleared her throat and tore her gaze from Jacob's broad back. Or maybe she'd been checking out his ass. "How's your dad doing?" she asked, her eyes now focused intently on Adam. "Is he still in the hospital?"

Adam lifted a brow at her. "Are you trying to change the subject?"

Owen laughed at her obvious discomfort, and she threw a french fry at him, which he stuffed into his mouth before adding a few more of his own.

"I'm genuinely interested," she said and fixed her best *I'm an excellent listener* look on her pretty face. He wanted to talk about his father almost as much as he wanted to discuss having kids.

Jacob returned to the table and started picking at his last few crawdads. Adam focused on his meal as well. Until Madison put a hand on his thigh and leaned into his arm.

"Adam?"

He sighed. Prying-assed woman, there was no deterring her. "He's out of the hospital and going to stay with a friend in El Paso."

"So he's not at your place anymore?"

"Nope. I kicked him out."

"And how did that make you feel?" she asked.

Adam lifted an eyebrow at her. She wanted to engage him in therapy? Right here in front of the guys? Not happening.

"We'll talk about this later," he said.

She glanced at Jacob and Owen, who were watching them closely, and offered Adam an understanding smile.

"Have you ever met Adam's old man?" Jacob asked, tossing the last of his crawdad shells into the discard pile and helping himself to a large one from Adam's plate.

Madison shook her head.

"He's not all bad," he said.

"Just ninety-nine percent of him," Owen added with a laugh.

"I don't want her to meet him," Adam said.

"Why not?" Jacob asked.

Adam shrugged, but he knew why. He didn't want her to look at the train wreck that was his father and realize Adam hadn't fallen far from the tree.

By the time they finished their meal and collected a to-go order that cleaned out the food shack's entire inventory of crawdads, it was too late to relax in the hotel before the show. Adam and Madison followed Jacob and Owen back to the venue. As far as Adam was concerned, he could ride his bike for eternity and ignore all the weights that dragged him down, but he had to learn to cope with real life. Had to cope even if his first instinct was to use drugs to make his problems go away—Madison had showed him that drugs only made his problems worse, he'd just been too high to recognize the truth of that—and his second instinct was to run from them by avoiding them. He was still working on how to get over the tendency toward avoidance.

He left the bike behind the bus and helped Madison climb off.

"My luggage is at the hotel, isn't it?"

"Did you need something out of it? I don't have time to go with you, but we can send you over in a cab. Unless you want to take the bike out on your own."

She appraised the motorcycle as if she were actually contemplating climbing back on, but ultimately she shook her head. "I don't think that's a good idea. I'll just change back into the clothes I wore on the plane. I'm sweltering in this leather."

That was unfortunate, because she looked fantastic in her new outfit. But Adam wanted her to be comfortable, so he patted her butt and sent her up the bus steps with her sack of old clothes.

Owen headed toward the venue with the food. The guy loved doing nice things for people and really loved taking all the credit for his random acts. Jacob headed onto the bus with Adam behind him. Jacob pulled a beer from the fridge and twisted off the cap.

"So how did the song writing go this afternoon?" Jacob asked, drawing on his beer.

Adam's stomach dropped, and he immediately bristled. "Fine," he said. Which was an outright lie. He hadn't written a thing all afternoon. Hell, he hadn't written a thing since he'd gotten clean. He tried, but nothing gelled. He could sit there with his guitar in his hands for an hour and produce nothing but a scale. Stare at a blank sheet of paper for twice as long and write a single word. *The.* All of his lyrics started with "the" these days, and every song went nowhere from there. Maybe he should try starting with "a" or "when."

"So you wrote something?" Jacob pressed.

"Yeah." *No, no I didn't write a damn thing.* Shit. Why did he always lie to cover his weaknesses? But if he could come up with some new lyrics quickly, Jacob would never know he hadn't written them earlier that day.

"Is it good?"

"Of course it's good."

"I'd like to hear it," Jacob said.

So would I. "I'd rather surprise you," Adam said.

"Is it in your notebook under your mattress?" Jacob straightened from the counter he was leaning against and headed toward Adam's bunk. "Let's see it."

Adam charged between the man and his bunk. "You'll see it when I'm ready for you to see it."

"Just be straight with me, Adam. You're not as good a liar as you think you are."

Adam's jaw hardened. He didn't like to be called a liar, even when it was true. He knew he had to get out of the habit of trying to cover for himself, but it had become a pattern when he'd been trashed all the time, and he couldn't seem to break it.

"I didn't write much," he amended. "Or anything," he added, when Jacob continued to stare at him eagerly.

Jacob nodded. "I kind of figured that," he said. "So what's the problem?"

"I dunno." Adam shook his head. He kind of did know. Maybe. "I think . . . I think maybe I'm too happy."

Jacob gave him a strange look. "Huh?"

"The music always came from the darkest part of me. It was a balm to my miserable soul, and now that I'm not miserable . . ." Adam held his palms in front of himself, lifted his shoulders and shook his head.

"Do you want me to make you miserable? I'm probably up for the task." Jacob chuckled.

"I don't know. If it would help. I don't want to let you down. Or the band. The fans. If I have to be miserable to make music, then do your worst."

Jacob lifted a fist. Adam stiffened, preparing for the blow that was sure to rattle his teeth.

Jacob pounded Adam's shoulder cordially. "It will come, just give it time. I still think you should talk to Kellen's chick. She composes. She might have some pointers for you."

Adam scowled at Jacob. "She composes classical music. Entirely different."

"Not entirely different," Jacob said. "It's music. She has to have an ear for various instruments to come up with harmonies and crescendos and all that stuff."

"But I start with lyrics. I always have. The words are a story I add music too. No story, no music. You know that."

"Maybe it's time for a change."

Adam hated to admit that Jacob might be right, so he didn't respond with anything more than a shrug.

"And maybe it's time to let the rest of us write some music," Jacob added. "You aren't the only one in this band with talent, you know." He winked.

If he lost his tenuous hold on being the primary songwriter for Sole Regret, Adam really would feel replaceable. The reason the guys put up with him through his struggles with addiction was because he was the main creative engine for the band. He had to show them all that their patience had been worth the trouble.

"I'll work on some stuff this weekend," he said.

Jacob opened his mouth but then shut it again. He nodded instead. "Can't wait to see what you come up with."

Adam kind of wished Jacob would give him a little grief. Give him something to be pissed about or depressed about. Adam drew on emotion for his work and if his life continued to be sunshiny and easy, he'd soon be writing songs about kittens and pixies with glitter shooting out of their asses.

Madison came out of the bathroom in her loose denim skirt and plaid shirt. She'd carefully folded her leather and had it cradled into her chest.

"That's better," she said. "I thought I was going to sweat myself into a coma."

"Adding that to my list of things I don't need to know," Jacob said and tugged his sunglasses out of the neckband of his shirt. Before he left the bus, he said, "I still think you should talk to what's her face."

"Dawn?" Adam said. Her name was easy to remember because she had hair that reminded him of a sunrise.

Ugh. There he went with the happy thoughts again.

"Yeah, her."

Once he and Madison were alone, she turned to him. "Dawn?"

"Some girl Kellen met and is currently mooning over."

"Oh. Is she pretty?"

Was that a hint of jealousy in her tone? He smiled. Madison had nothing to worry about in that regard. She was the only woman he wanted.

"Yeah. So?"

"Why does Jacob think you should talk to her?"

"She's a composer. He thinks she might be able to help me with my writer's block."

"You have writer's block? You never told me that."

He shrugged. "I didn't think it would interest you."

She set her clothes on the table and wrapped her arms around his neck. She stared up into his eyes and said, "Of course it interests me. Everything you do interests me. I love you. I'm here to support you whenever you need me."

He stroked her hair from her upturned face and searched her eyes. He had never had anyone available for him in the capacity she offered. Her devotion delighted him and at the same time terrified him. She was too good for him. He didn't deserve her. But his heart didn't care. It gladly accepted all she gave him and was greedy for more.

When he kissed her, he didn't mean for his passion to escalate, but as always, the heat between them burned intensely. She pressed more firmly against his body, and he instantly ignited, his kiss deepening, his hands sliding down her back to draw her closer.

He pulled his mouth from hers and turned her to face the opposite direction. His fingers dug into her hips to pull her succulent ass against his hardening cock. She groaned and rubbed up against him. He couldn't lose himself now. He had a plan to tease her incessantly until the next night when they went to the sex club to play. Otherwise, he wasn't sure if she'd be open to what he and club owner Tony had devised for Adam's sweet little lover. But he wanted her to know he was hard for her. Wanted her to crave his cock inside her. Wanted her to beg him to fill her. Wanted to leave her wanting, even if he was left wanting too. Even if denying them meant the death of him.

He cupped one breast in his palm and tugged at its hardened peak through her clothes until she gasped. He bent his knees to rub himself against her ass and so he could draw his hand up her bare thigh beneath her loose skirt. His fingers sought the slick, warm flesh between her thighs, sliding beneath the elastic of her panties and finding her wet already. He smiled at her willingness and used his face to brush her hair aside so he could suckle on the pulse point beneath her ear as his fingers massaged her clit, then dipped into her pussy, and then teased her clit again.

She rubbed her ass against his stiff cock, making it difficult for him to remember that he couldn't have her. Not yet. And when she began to whisper his name between her moans of pleasure, it took every shred of his willpower not to yank his cock out and fill the silken passage his fingers repeatedly explored. Her body shuddered as her pleasure intensified, and her pussy tightened around his fingers as she struggled to find release. He slid his hand from beneath her skirt and took her jaw between his thumb and ring finger. He touched his index and middle finger to her parted lips. They were slick with her juices.

"Lick them," he growled in her ear. "Suck them clean."

She didn't hesitate to obey. His cock pulsed with excitement as she licked and sucked his fingertips.

"Good," he murmured. "You keep doing as I ask and you'll eventually get what you want."

He gave her breast a squeeze and then stepped away. His stomach was in knots, his balls felt full and heavy, his cock ached with need. But the discomfort of waiting would be worth it later. He knew she wouldn't disappoint him.

"What the hell, Adam?" she said as he headed for the exit.

"I'm going to go talk to Dawn now," he said. "Before the show starts."

"You're just going to leave me all hot and bothered?"

He grinned. "Yep."

"It isn't nice to tease," she said with a pout.

His grin widened. "I think you'll be screaming a different tune tomorrow night."

He winked at her and trotted down the bus steps in search of Kellen's new flame.

He found her seated beside the band's ever-shirtless rhythm guitarist on a sofa in the dressing room backstage. Kellen had a hand on her knee and was whispering something in her ear that made her grin.

Adam sat beside her on the sofa and ignored Kellen's affronted stare. It wasn't like Adam had come to steal her away. He just wanted to pick her brain for a few minutes.

"How did you get past your writer's block?" Adam asked. He didn't have time for small talk. He wanted to play with

Madison some more before the show. He would have waited to talk to the slender composer—who he just noticed had a lot of adorable freckles—but knowing the staying power of his bandmates' romantic flings, he doubted he'd have another chance to talk to the woman before Kellen scared her away.

Dawn's face flushed bright red. "Um, well, I uh . . ."

Adam didn't take her for a woman who had a difficult time expressing herself, so her stammering baffled him. Adam's gaze shifted to Kellen, who was grinning so wide, his face was liable to split in half.

"She was inspired," Kellen said.

Was Kellen bragging? Adam snorted at his friend's obvious immodest pride.

"By your dick?" Adam guessed.

"Uh," Dawn gasped. "No, his dick came later."

Kellen laughed and wrapped an arm around her shoulders. "Not that much later."

"Stop," she said, slapping Kellen's thigh. "You make it sound so tawdry, and it was beautiful."

She turned her head to look at Adam. "I was inspired by his passion."

Adam peered around her to appraise Kellen closely. "Whelp," he said, pushing off his thighs as he rose from the sofa. "That's out."

Dawn grabbed Adam's wrist and tugged him back down beside her. "Your inspiration doesn't have to be a gorgeous, soaking wet warrior of a man rising from the sea in a storm."

"Say what?" Owen said from near the bar where he appeared to be trying to forget Lindsey was clinging to his arm by using his free hand to down copious amounts of liquor.

Jacob, who was apparently eavesdropping as well, burst out laughing.

"I think inspiration can be found in anything that shakes you up." Dawn took a deep shuddering breath and pressed her fingertips to her rosy cheeks. "I don't know, maybe it *was* his dick that I found so inspiring."

"Care for a bit more inspiration?" Kellen whispered.

"You don't have enough time before the show to give me the care and attention I deserve," Dawn said and kissed his nose.

Adam chuckled. He liked this woman already, but Madison entered the room at that moment, and his entire universe shifted to revolve around her.

"Uh, later," he said and rose from the sofa.

He approached Madison slowly, watching her out of the corner of his eye as he made his way across the room and paused at the bar for a drink just to see how she would react to his delay. He knew Madison felt uncomfortable backstage—especially when left to her own devices—but she needed to get over her skittishness if they were going to be together. He was pleasantly surprised that she'd showed up in the dressing room on her own so quickly. He figured he'd eventually have to go back to the bus and coax her out. Perhaps she was finally getting used to the idea of being a rock star's girlfriend. He wondered if she was ready to be a rock star's wife.

Adam claimed a beer for himself and got a bottle of water for Madison. She didn't drink alcohol. Ever. When he'd asked her why, she'd told him that her grandfather had been killed by a drunk driver, leaving her beloved grandmother to face the rest of her years a widow. It was strange to Adam how something that had happened before she'd been born had had such an impact on her life. Hell, he'd personally experienced numerous negative consequences at the hands of drugs and alcohol and it had never stopped him from going back for more.

Madison's searching gaze landed on Adam, and she smiled. Good. She wasn't mad at him for his deserting her on the bus.

He headed toward her and handed her the bottle of water. She thanked him, but scarcely looked at him. Her gaze was now plastered to the pretty, pregnant blonde attached to Owen's side.

"Is that her?" Madison asked in a hushed tone.

"Nope," Adam said. "Owen has pregnant chicks coming out of his ears."

Madison rolled her eyes at him, but at least it took her attention away from Lindsey and put it where it belonged. On him. "Why did you leave me alone on the bus?"

So maybe she was a tad miffed, after all.

"So you'd have time to think about how I made your body feel."

"I don't need time to think about that," she said. "We both know how your teasing makes me feel."

"How's that?"

"Horny."

He forced himself not to grin in triumph and moved closer so that his chest brushed her shoulder and his thigh touched her hand. "Did you think of a way I can do something about that feeling?"

Not that he planned to do anything about it just yet. He wanted her in an aroused state all night and all day tomorrow, because he was pretty sure she would have to be delirious to agree to the arrangements he'd made at the sex club. He'd almost been too chicken to agree to the scenario himself, but Tony had a way of making a guy agree to just about anything. And in all of Adam's experiences at Tony's clubs, the man had never steered him wrong.

"I was mostly thinking about you doing that thing you do with your tongue," she said, her gaze shifting to his mouth.

"This thing?" He tilted his head and gently sucked on the flesh just under her ear. His tongue flicked repeatedly over the pulse point in her throat exactly the way he moved it when he pleasured her clit with his mouth.

She released an excited gasp, her body going taut beside him. "Just like that," she whispered. "Only lower."

He dragged his lips several inches down her throat and repeated the motion.

"Oh," she gasped breathlessly.

Adam lifted his head and nipped her earlobe. Her entire body quaked.

He was seconds from forgetting his plan to tease her all night and instead head into the nearby bathroom to give her the release she craved. He eased her to the sofa instead, hoping to calm himself down enough to perform later by keeping a few inches between them. Unfortunately, the distance between them didn't lessen his awareness of her one bit.

"Adam?" she whispered, a beguiling blush on her cheeks.

"Yeah?"

"I left my panties on the bus."

Fucking A!

Adam caught movement out of the corner of his eye and groaned inwardly when Gabe stopped in front of him with some woman on his arm. Adam recognized the pretty brunette, but hell if he could remember her name. He'd always been bad with names. Especially when he was fixated on the fact that Madison was sitting beside him without any panties on under her sweet little denim skirt.

"Hey," Adam said to Gabe's companion. "You're the chick from breakfast."

Madison stiffened at his side. Probably wondering why he was having breakfast with some attractive brunette.

The woman chuckled. "So good of you to remember."

"You know her?" Madison asked, glaring a hole into Adam's forehead.

"She's with Gabe," Adam said.

Madison nodded slightly and shifted closer so that her arm touched his. He liked the *back off, bitch, he's mine* vibe coming off of her. "What's her name?" Madison asked.

"Hell if I remember," Adam said. "I just remember sitting next to her at breakfast."

"Adam was too busy thinking about you to even ask my name," the woman said.

Adam wanted to kiss her in gratitude. But not really. He'd rather kiss parts of Madison that were hidden beneath her skirt.

The woman glanced at Gabe, who'd gone entirely mute and said, "I'm Melanie."

That's right. Melanie. Adam remembered now. She was friends with that incredibly gorgeous woman who'd banged Shade in the sauna the same morning they'd had breakfast together. And hell if he could remember that woman's name either.

"Madison," Madison introduced herself and smiled at Gabe's acquaintance.

"So you've known these guys a lot longer than I have," Melanie asked. "Any deep dark secrets I should know about?"

The fact that Madison's gaze shifted to Lindsey was not lost on Adam. He stiffened, hoping Gabe had prepared Melanie, because if he hadn't, she was sure to get an earful in the next five seconds.

Madison chuckled. "I might have a few stories to tell."

"Whoa!" Gabe said, covering Melanie's ears with his hands. "Great to see you again, Madison. Be sure to keep Adam out of trouble."

Gabe winked at Madison before he turned Melanie in the opposite direction and escorted her toward Kellen and Dawn. Strange how he could remember *her* name. He was actually glad the pair hadn't stuck around long. It wasn't that Adam didn't like Melanie or that he didn't think it was important for Madison to get to know the other women associated with his band, he just had a distracting situation going on in his pants and didn't really feel up to small talk. Especially not when Madison had been stroking his thigh beneath the cover of her skirt the entire time. And she wasn't wearing any goddamned underwear.

"She seems nice," Madison said.

"I don't know much about—" Adam sucked in a breath when Madison's hand found a particularly sensitive spot just inside his hipbone.

"Does she know about Lindsey?" she asked, her eyes scanning the room, presumably for the pregnant blonde.

"Not sure," he said. "It's probably best if she hears it from Gabe."

She lifted an eyebrow at him. "The way I heard it from you?"

His gaze shifted to his hand, which was resting—none too restfully—on his knee. "I told you about the situation."

"Only because someone else mentioned it."

He so did not want to argue with her. "Do you really want to talk about this now?"

"Would you rather talk about wanting a vasectomy?"

"No."

"Adam, I know it's hard for you to open up, but if we're going to make a life together—"

He silenced her with a kiss, his lips lingering on hers until she melted against him. His hand slid up her thigh, stopping just short of touching her pussy. He was a bit afraid of what he'd do once he proved her claim of exposure with his questing fingertips. She groaned in his mouth, and he tugged his lips free of hers.

"If you really want to talk right now..." he murmured, rubbing his nose down the side of her neck.

Madison shook her head and whispered, "No, I really want to drag you back to the tour bus."

"And do what?" he asked.

Her breath tickled his ear when she said, "Worship every inch of your cock."

"With your hands?"

"Yes."

He could practically feel the gentle touch of her fingertips against his sensitive flesh, and his dick jumped with excitement.

"And my lips," she said, brushing a feather-light kiss against his neck.

He remembered well what those full lips felt like on his cockhead, kissing and sucking and teasing him to the point of madness.

"And your tongue?" he pressed, lost in fantasy land despite the crowd in the room.

"Of course," she whispered. "But I mostly want to bury you deep in my—"

The delicious promise of her words was cut off by the arrival of warmed over Cajun food. It was actually a blessing in disguise. Maybe he could get his lust under control if he stuffed his mouth with something other than her tongue and kept his hands occupied somewhere other than beneath her skirt.

Adam practically leapt from the couch before he lost every shred of his willpower, dragged Madison to the nearest corner, and fucked her brains out. He offered her a hand to help her to her feet, but she wasn't looking at him. Her gaze was trained on the bathroom door.

"Aren't you hungry?" he asked.

"A little," she said, still watching the door. "I need to use the restroom. I'll join you in a moment."

Adam watched her purposefully cross the room. She'd better not be going in there to work out her sexual frustration on her own, because if she did, he'd make her regret that decision all night long.

CHAPTER FIVE

MADISON EASED the bathroom door open and peered inside. Her gaze landed on the pretty blonde with the enormous belly who was using the mirror to apply lip gloss—probably so she could lure Owen into kissing her. Though Madison had intentionally come to the restroom to corner the woman and get her side of the story, she tried not to gawk at her distended abdomen. It was an exercise in futility. What if the baby belonged to Adam? What if this bitch got to have his child and Madison was never afforded the same opportunity? She couldn't believe Adam had never mentioned his aversion to kids before. They never really talked about the important things in life. Everything between them was all frivolous and fun. And she was perfectly okay with that for now. But in a couple years she might want to settle down, have a few kids, and then what? She couldn't picture Adam in domesticated bliss. At all. What would a future with him look like?

Madison stepped up to the second sink and washed her hands, watching Lindsey in the mirror. She didn't know what she expected the pregnant woman to look like—a giant, walking vagina capable of engulfing six cocks in a single bound? a filthy dumpster with a CUM logo painted boldly on the front?—but she looked deceptively innocent and *normal*, with wide blue eyes and an angelic face. She couldn't be much over twenty years old. Madison wanted to hate her, but she couldn't quite bring herself to do so. She didn't exactly pity her either. Lindsey had spread her legs willingly—Madison assumed—and repeatedly. The woman had to know that pregnancy was always a possibility even if the sex was merely recreational.

Lindsey noticed Madison trying to glare a hole through her reflected tummy and she lowered her arm, rubbing her lips together to spread the gloss evenly. She no longer had Owen to cling to, since she'd had to release his arm long enough to enter the women's restroom. Even Jordan had restrained himself from following her in here. Alone for the first time since Madison had laid eyes on her, Lindsey looked particularly vulnerable as she fumbled to get her lip gloss in her bag so she could get out of the bathroom as quickly as possible.

Lindsey's lip gloss missed her bag and bounced off the tile floor before scuttling into a stall. She didn't bend to retrieve it. Wary eyes on Madison, Lindsey headed for the door. She pressed her back against the wall and slid toward the exit, keeping as much distance between herself and Madison as possible. She acted as if she thought Madison had an incurable infectious disease or was going to beat her to death or something.

Madison couldn't let the opportunity to talk to the woman in private pass her by. She hurried to block her exit. Standing in front of the door, Madison turned to face her and lifted both hands in front of her chest to get Lindsey to stop.

The woman flinched and shied away. Weird.

"Hey, it's okay," Madison said and lowered her hands. "I just want to talk to you."

"Punch me in the face, you mean?" she said.

"No, just talk. Has someone punched you?" Madison asked. Lindsey's behavior was setting off all kinds of warning bells. Madison might no longer have a job as a counselor, but she couldn't shut off the instincts.

"No one here," Lindsey said, "but I keep expecting someone to."

"So someone did hit you? Who was it?"

Lindsey bit her lip and lowered her eyes. "I don't want to talk about it. Did you need something from me?"

Madison wondered if Lindsey realized she was slowly backing away. She obviously felt threatened.

"I just want to talk."

Lindsey gazed longingly at the blocked door. "I'm not sure that's such a good idea."

"Adam and I—"

"I don't think it's his," she said hastily, her arms tightening around her belly.

"You don't think it's his or you don't want it to be his?"

She cringed. "Both. I don't think he'd make a very good daddy. He's kind of . . . harsh."

"But Owen would make a good father?"

Lindsey smiled and stroked her stomach with both hands. "I think so. Don't you? Owen's so sweet. The best of the bunch."

Madison scowled, wholeheartedly disagreeing with Lindsey's opinion. Of course she *was* a tad partial to Adam. And even though he didn't seem keen on having kids, she knew he'd be a great father if he opened himself up to the love a child offered. And how could he not?

Lindsey gave the door one last look of longing and then took several steps backward to lean against the wall beside the paper towel dispenser.

Madison took a few steps forward, but kept some distance. She didn't want to spook the woman into silence. "I happen to think Adam would make a fine father," she said. "If he'd just trust himself. Lots of people have trust issues. They don't trust other people. But Adam doesn't trust himself. Once he gets past that . . ." Madison realized she was prattling on, as if trying to convince Lindsey that Adam would be the best father for her baby, and that was the opposite of how she felt. "So you've latched on to Owen because he's the most sympathetic to your cause. Does that about sum it up?"

"He was the first."

Madison's jaw dropped. "You were a virgin?"

Lindsey snorted on a laugh. "Uh, no. He was the first that night. With Kellen. And then Shade. And after that it really got out of hand. But Owen was nice to me. Even afterwards. And he doesn't have to love me to be a good father. I'm not pursuing him for myself. I just want our baby to grow up knowing his daddy, that's all."

Our baby. Lindsey really was convinced that Owen was the father. And Madison didn't buy that Lindsey wasn't interested in Owen for herself. It was obvious that she had a crush. Whenever Owen was in the room, she lit up like a laser show and made sure she was close to him at all times. Heck, she was surprised Lindsey hadn't dragged him into the bathroom with her. How devastated would Lindsey be if she found out Owen wasn't the father of her child? Madison was certain she'd be crushed. But wanting something—no matter how strongly— didn't make it a reality.

"What are you going to do if the paternity test shows that Owen is not the father?" Madison played devil's advocate.

"I'll worry about that after the baby is born. But I know this baby is his. I can sense it."

More like she was fixated on the idea. And Madison wasn't sure that even a paternity test would change her mind about the parentage of her child. Madison wondered if Owen had it in him to be mean to the woman, because he was going to have to take the initiative to break Lindsey's unhealthy attachment. There was no way Lindsey was going to give up on him if he kept being so nice to her.

"Has he talked to you about having a paternity test before the baby is born?"

Lindsey's face went ashen. "Before?"

Madison nodded. "He hasn't mentioned it?"

"No. We haven't had much time to talk. I never realized how busy he would be on tour. I'm already exhausted just trying to keep up with him."

He was probably being difficult to keep up with on purpose. Madison didn't know who she should feel sorrier for—Owen or Lindsey.

"Have you been talking to Owen a lot since . . . the night it happened?" Madison asked. If they'd been corresponding secretly, Lindsey's infatuation might make a little more sense.

"Only in my dreams."

Obsession could turn ugly quickly. Madison needed to warn Owen. Surely if he knew what he was dealing with here, he'd stop encouraging Lindsey to think he was the moon and stars. Or maybe they were meant to be together. As disturbing as Madison found that thought, such a solution would make things easier for everyone. If Owen actually loved this girl and wanted to be her baby's daddy, then she wasn't going to be a buttinsky. Madison just got the feeling from what Owen had said earlier that this was entirely a one-sided love affair. Which meant someone would get hurt. She hoped it wouldn't be the child.

"Is there really a paternity test that can be taken before the baby is born?" Lindsey asked, staring down at her knotted hands.

"Yeah. Two types, actually."

"I'll have to look into it." Lindsey released her grip on her own fingers and wrapped both arms around her belly.

"I wish you well and hope your baby is loved by both of his or her parents," Madison said.

Lindsey lifted her head, locking gazes with Madison, and then smiled.

"But if that's not possible for whatever reason, you can do this alone, Lindsey. Lots of women do."

Lindsey's eyes narrowed, and her careful smile vanished. "But they shouldn't have to raise a child alone. *I* shouldn't have to."

She had Madison there.

"I know everyone thinks this pregnancy is all my fault and I somehow deserve what happened because I not only had sex for fun, I enjoyed every minute of it with every last member of the band. But every man on that bus was having sex for fun. And if they say they didn't enjoy it, they're liars. So how is it any different when I do it? Because I'm a woman? Because I'm supposed to be the responsible one? Why doesn't any of the responsibility fall on any of these men? Because they're rock stars and it's expected that they sleep around? Or is it because people have it in their heads that I'm a gold digger?"

Madison forced herself not to nod and to just listen to the woman's tirade. Lindsey shook her head at her as if she could read Madison's thoughts.

"I don't give a fuck about money," Lindsey said. "I just want what's best for my baby. I tried to do it by myself and I failed, okay? I can't even afford a place to live. No one will hire me in my condition. Would you rather I go on public assistance instead of making one of these men own up to their responsibility? Is that what you want? The taxpayers to be punished for what we did? Yes, *we*. It takes two to make a baby."

Or in this case *five*. Or was it *six?* Madison opened her mouth to speak, but Lindsey still wasn't finished with her tirade.

"Sheezus, why do these guys get to play the victim because *I'm* pregnant? No one forced any one of them to put his dick in me."

Madison couldn't argue with her logic. It happened to be true. There was a gross double standard in the world when it came to sex. And it wasn't fair.

"Besides," Lindsey continued, throwing her hands out for emphasis. "I was safe! I was on fucking birth control pills, and I took them every day like I was supposed to. Despite what people are saying about me, I did *not* try to get pregnant. I did not *want* to get pregnant. But I *am* pregnant, and I'm sick and tired of trying to be nice to all these dickheads and their jealous girlfriends while I take all the blame and responsibility for the entire situation!"

Madison wasn't sure if she should admire or be leery of Lindsey's sudden backbone. She'd been hiding it all evening— Madison wasn't sure why—and this woman wasn't all she seemed. "Lindsey . . ."

"Screw you." Lindsey shoved off the wall and strode toward the exit, apparently too angry to waddle. "And if you really think Adam would make a good father, you need to have your head surgically removed from your ass."

Lindsey shoved Madison aside, wrenched the door open, and slammed it behind her, leaving Madison to gawk. Did she really come across as having her head up her ass? Madison wondered if the reason she so enjoyed anal sex was because she was so used to the feel of her head up there and she got off on it.

Madison used the restroom, taking a moment alone to get her thoughts in order. Perhaps confronting Lindsey had been a bad idea, but at least she knew where the woman stood.

By the time she joined the band, crew and guests for dinner, all of the food had been claimed. She noticed that Owen had saved a plate for Lindsey though. Bizarre. Madison was sure he was just looking out for the baby, but she'd never encountered a man as thoughtful as he was. Especially toward someone he claimed not to be interested in. It was no wonder Lindsey clung to him.

Adam beckoned Madison to sit beside him and share what little was left on his plate. "I didn't know you would be so long," he said. "I would have stopped Jacob from getting thirds."

"You might have tried," Jacob said to his plate of empty crawdad shells. "But you would have failed."

"Crawdad populations dwindle drastically when Jacob's in the region," Owen said from beside her.

"And your point would be?" Jacob asked, reaching across the table to steal a crawdad off Lindsey's plate.

Madison wrinkled her nose. She wasn't sure how he could stomach more spicy food. Just thinking about eating more crawdads made her want to hurl. "I'm not that hungry anyway."

"I'm sure Adam could offer you a protein shake to tide you over—" Owen's words were silenced by Adam's hand in his face.

Lindsey was concentrating so hard on her plate—and not looking at Madison—that it was a miracle the piece of plastic didn't melt beneath the heat of her gaze. Madison would never say anything about their private conversation in front of all these people. She could only imagine how hard it was for Lindsey to sit among them knowing what everyone must be thinking of her.

Madison stiffened when Adam's hand slid up her leg, pushing her skirt up until she felt a cool breeze against the heated flesh between her thighs. If anyone's head had been under the table, she had no doubt they could have seen parts of her normally concealed by her panties. The panties she'd left on the bus.

His thumb rubbed circles over her aching labia, causing her to swell and grow wet with anticipation. She opened her legs beneath the table, surprised by her own brazenness and even more surprised when her action was rewarded with the tip of Adam's finger sliding down her seam and dipping into her slick opening.

Her mouth fell open and a small gasp escaped her. She

snapped her jaw shut and glanced around, seeing if anyone had noticed her reaction and guessed its cause. She stiffened when she noticed Jacob's knowing smirk. Did he suspect she was getting fingered right there at the dinner table?

"Okay, guys," the band's impossibly sexy tour manager, Sally, said from the doorway. "It's time for your meet and greet."

"We'll finish this later," Adam promised, sliding his finger an inch deeper before withdrawing it. He dropped a kiss on her cheek and left her sitting there all flushed and aroused.

Damn, how she wanted him.

Madison squeezed her thighs together and tried to collect her thoughts. One thing was clear: Adam was attempting to kill her via lack of sexual fulfillment. She'd never have believed it was possible to actually die from horniness, but the man was determined to prove her wrong. As she glanced around the room, trying to think about anything besides the incessant throb between her thighs, she spotted Lindsey whispering something into Jordan's ear. He nodded and tripped over his feet as he hurried after the band. Lindsey followed him out of the room a scant moment later.

Well, that did the trick. Madison's excitement fizzled out like a soggy firecracker. What was Lindsey up to? She better keep her meat hooks out of Adam or heads were going to roll. Or maybe Madison would do something slightly less violent to her.

Madison glanced up when Melanie sat beside her in the seat Adam had recently vacated.

"So what's the story with Lindsey?" she asked, without warning.

Gabe hadn't told her anything yet? Madison didn't want to spread rumors and divulge secrets, so she shrugged. "I don't know. Apparently she got knocked up by Owen, and she didn't have anywhere else to go. They're not a couple or anything."

Melanie stared at her. Could she tell that Madison was withholding information? She was such a bad liar. Her belly was quivering as she waited for Melanie's next words.

"So Owen is the father?" Melanie asked. "Gabe sounded unsure."

"As far as I know," Madison said. "She hangs all over him, so I just assumed... Why? Did you hear differently?"

If Melanie already knew the shocking truth about Lindsey's pregnancy, Madison was more than ready to talk shit about her, but if Melanie didn't know anything, then Madison didn't want to get Gabe into trouble. She really liked Gabe. There had to be a reason he hadn't explained things to Melanie yet.

Melanie shook her head. Well, damn. Madison had no one to gossip with then. She wondered how Melanie would react when she found out that Gabe might be the father of Lindsey's baby. Or that it might be Adam's . . .

Madison couldn't imagine Adam trying to fit raising a baby into his already full life. Something would have to give. And she couldn't deny she worried that the thing that would have to take a backseat was herself.

"So where are you from?" Melanie asked.

Madison was glad that Melanie had switched the direction of their conversation to small talk. She'd wanted her weekend with Adam to help her forget about her problems, not add more of them. And as far as problems went, Lindsey's condition was a whopper. With cheese.

And extra bacon.

CHAPTER SIX

ADAM CLOSED HIS EYES briefly as the full brightness of the stage lights hit him in the face. The crowd roared as his fingers raced along steel guitar strings. There were only two places he knew he belonged—on stage with his four faithful friends and in Madison's arms.

When the intricate guitar work of the intro segued into the more repetitive riff of the first verse, Adam glanced to where Madison stood in the wings. Even though she was watching the performance, he couldn't help but notice her preoccupation. He knew she had a lot on her mind, but he hoped she'd let it go for a while and enjoy herself. He had every intention of having a blast tonight—both during the concert and afterward. If he couldn't capture her attention with his guitar playing, he was sure he could find a way to keep her distracted from real life when they were alone in his hotel room. But until then, he'd do his damnedest to put a smile on her face.

When the first song ended and while Jacob waited for the crowd to quiet enough so he could start his typical banal greetings, Adam dashed offstage, took Madison's hand, twirled her around until she giggled, patted her on the butt, and then raced back to stand next to Jacob.

"It's a little known fact that Adam started as a blues guitarist," Jacob said into his mic, his eyes concealed by his trademark shades.

Actually, Adam's beginnings in blues had *once* been a little-known fact. But seeing as Jacob shared the same fact every time they toured the South, it was now a rather well-known fact. Especially in New Orleans.

"It's true," Adam said, playing a string of notes that sounded more metal than blues. The entire reason he'd given up and switched to metal was because every genre he attempted sounded metal under his fingers. "I was never very good at it, though."

"He even tried country for a while," Owen said.

"Well, I am from Texas," Adam reminded him, playing a country riff that also sounded very metal. He laughed at his lack of skill. "Apparently from the metal part of Texas."

The crowd really got behind this idea, cheering for their preferred genre of music.

"Cuff's better at country than I am," Adam teased Kellen, who promptly played the intro to a well-known banjo tune.

Adam mimicked the notes and, as expected, the backwoods banjo music sounded like incredibly distorted, loud and heavy guitar when he played it. "I'm sorry," Adam said with a grin. "No matter how hard I try, I can't seem to play anything but metal."

The audience cheered, not minding his lack of range.

"Then you've come to the right stage," Jacob said, and he lifted his hand to signal Gabe to start the opening drum progression of the next song.

Adam entered the song with a rapid string of notes, carrying the final in the series with a loud wail. Jacob caught on to Adam's enthusiasm, hamming it up for the crowd with even more gusto than usual. Kellen seemed more concerned with playing every note perfectly—probably because he was trying to impress his composer guest—but it was Owen who was behaving completely out of character. Usually the life of the party, he kept to the back of the stage and played his bass lines with an air of glumness. It wasn't as if bass riffs were ever particularly cheerful, but if Owen kept playing them like that, they'd all be suicidal by the end of the evening.

Adam snuck up behind him and did his best impression of twerking to rub the strings of his guitar against Owen's wireless receiver and produce a hideous cacophony. From the front, Adam was sure it looked like he was dry humping his bassist's ass, but it was worth the hilarity that ensued as Owen stumbled forward several steps in absolute shock and then burst out laughing when he saw who was assaulting him.

"Are you high?" he asked, and then his face fell when he

seemed to think he'd discovered the truth.

"On life!" Adam shouted and climbed up on the platform supporting Gabe's drum kit so he could clang a symbol with his guitar stock.

"I don't know what's in the water down here," Jacob said at the end of the song, "but it apparently makes Adam feel real good."

Adam pointed at Madison, who was gaping at him from her position at the side of the stage, and then hopped off the drum platform to join Jacob.

"I do feel good," Adam said. "How do you all feel tonight?" he asked the audience.

They cheered enthusiastically.

"Well, I for one," Jacob said, "am feeling a little twisted."

Which was Adam's cue to start the intro to one of their most popular songs. He briefly wondered if he'd ever write anything as good as "Twisted" in the future or if he'd peaked early and his career was all downhill from here. He shoved the thought aside as he gave his all to the fret board. He'd worry about the future later. Or never. Never sounded like a better plan.

When the stadium lights went up after the encore, Adam tossed his guitar to a waiting roadie and headed directly for Madison. After stealing a lingering kiss, he scooped her off her feet and tossed her over his shoulder, one hand under her skirt and resting securely on her bare thigh. He spun on his heel and trotted down the steps.

"You're crazy!" she accused with a laugh as he carried her down a corridor toward the exit.

"Oh no, gust of wind," he said, flipping her skirt up. Not high enough for anyone to see she wasn't wearing panties, but still she slapped a hand over her butt, laughing and squirming on his shoulder.

"Stop it! Have you lost your mind?" she asked.

Quite possibly. He had an entire weekend free to enjoy Madison's company, and he wasn't going to allow stupid crap like responsibility and worry and reality put a damper on his enthusiasm.

As the rest of the band were heading out of town for the

weekend, Adam was doubly glad he'd rented the motorcycle for personal use. That way he didn't have to wait for the rest of the guys to get their shit together. He was more than eager to get Madison back to the hotel and spend time together. He had plenty of teasing in store, but he also just liked to be around her. She made him happy to be alive. He couldn't say that about any other person on the planet.

He dropped her off at the bottom of the tour bus steps. "Put your leather back on," he murmured into her ear. Just thinking about her in those tight leather pants had him all hot and bothered and the effect had little to do with the sultry night air.

"I think—"

"Unless you'd rather wait half an hour for a cab." He didn't want her to argue. And he wasn't going to allow her to ride on a motorcycle in a skirt. He'd seen what the road could do to bare flesh, and he refused to risk damaging her perfect skin— no matter how unlikely they were to meet the pavement in the few miles between the venue and their hotel.

"I wasn't refusing," she said. "I was going to say I think I'll need your help."

She took his hand and led him up the bus steps.

"You seemed to be having fun on stage tonight," she said as she walked backward toward the empty bedroom, her eyes never leaving his.

"I was," he said. "You put me in a good mood."

"I do?"

He nodded. "I usually try to hide the way you make me feel from the guys, but—" He shrugged. "I'm to the point where I don't care what they think about us." After all, the next time they saw her, he planned to have put a huge fucking diamond on her finger, and then they'd know for sure that he was pretty serious about Madison.

"Are you ready to put *me* in a good mood?" she asked, the suggestiveness in her tone making his cock twitch with interest.

"You aren't already?"

"I'm feeling pretty good, but I could be feeling a whole lot better."

He kicked the bedroom door closed behind him, bathing

them in darkness. Her hand pushing down on his shoulder was the only cue he needed. He dropped to his knees before her and pushed her skirt up. He found her swollen mound by feel, working her heated flesh with his mouth.

"Oh, Adam," she moaned. "I need you so bad."

He grinned to himself, pressing his tongue into her cleft. If she thought she needed him now, he couldn't even guess how much she'd need him by the next night. He unfastened her skirt as she clung to his hair with both hands and ground her pussy into his face.

If he could kick his drug habit with the might of his willpower, teasing this woman incessantly while not giving in to his own needs should be as easy as strumming an A chord.

Yeah, right.

He tipped her back onto the bed and pulled her boots off. He had planned to dress her in her leather pants immediately, but he had to have a little taste of her first. She was already so worked up that he'd have to take great care to not let her come. Madison opened her legs wide as he settled his knees on the floor at the end of the bed. When he gripped her ass in both hands and pulled her pussy to his mouth, she cried out and her back arched off the mattress.

He twirled his tongue in her opening, collecting the musky taste of her sex in his mouth. His cock pulsed with excitement at the promise of being enveloped in her slick heat.

He pulled away and took a deep breath. Fuck, how was he supposed to keep her teetering on the edge if he wanted to fly beyond it with so little prompting? Her heel dug into his back and pulled him into her. He groaned, his fingers digging into her ass cheeks as he found her clit with his mouth and flicked it with his tongue until she was writhing with pleasure.

He pulled away again, panting hard through his nose as he tried to regain his will to refrain from what he really wanted to do—fuck her as hard as she liked it.

"Adam," she moaned as she sat up to grab the back of his head. When he resisted her pull, she released her grip on him and reached between her thighs, rubbing her clit with rapid strokes that would quickly give her the release she craved. He captured her wrists and trapped her hands on either side of her hips.

"If you come tonight, I'm not taking you to the sex club tomorrow," he said.

"What?" Her voice was breathy with excitement, and the sound of it took hold of his balls and tugged.

He lowered his head and lapped at her drenched pussy. "No coming," he said, turning his attention back to her clit.

"Oh God," she moaned, her hips rocking in time with the motion of his tongue. "I have to."

"Not if you want to see what I have in store for you tomorrow."

"That doesn't make sense," she complained.

He chuckled. "It does to me." He knew what a challenge it could be to push her out of her comfort zone. She would have to be at her tipping point before they arrived at the club the next night, or she'd never agree to what he proposed.

"Put your pants on," he said, rising to his feet and backing toward the door, because he knew if he stayed to help her, his so-called willpower would last about twenty seconds and then his own pants would be on the floor.

"And if I refuse?" she asked, exasperation strong in her voice.

"I'll go to the hotel without you and text you pictures of me jacking off."

He turned on the ceiling light, and his breath caught at the sight of her looking all disheveled and aroused in her cutsie plaid shirt and nothing else.

"You wouldn't!"

"Are you sure about that?" 'Cause he was about to start jacking off any moment. Lord, the things he put himself through to take this woman on creative sexual adventures and offer her new heights of excitement.

While staring at him, she slid one hand down her belly and used two fingers to part her folds. "You shouldn't turn me on if you don't plan to get me off."

"I do plan to get you off," he assured her and leaned over to gently tug her hand from her pussy. He drew it over her head and pinned it to the mattress before kissing her deep and long. His hips seemed to have a mind of their own as they gyrated, rubbing the aching length of his erection against her. Even through his clothes, he could feel her heat beckoning him, promising him nirvana.

He tugged his mouth from hers slowly and stepped away before he lost complete control.

"Get dressed," he said, his voice gruff.

She nibbled on the tip of a finger, watching him closely. He was as turned on as she was, and she damned well knew it. "I think I need a spanking first," she said. "I'm having all sorts of naughty thoughts."

"You aren't the only one."

He grabbed her leather pants off the dresser and tossed them at her. Her pink lace panties tumbled through the air as well. She must have hidden them so no one would see them when she'd so boldly left them behind earlier.

"Put those on," he demanded gruffly.

Instead of obeying, she slid a finger into her cleft. "But I want to play some more first. Don't you want to play with me?"

Fuck *yes*, he wanted to play with her, but he said, "Not until tomorrow."

She sighed—loud and long—and reached for her panties. "You are going to give me a complex."

He watched her slip her shapely legs into her panties and pull them up, lifting her butt off the bed to draw them over her hips. She put those goddamned leather pants on next. He'd have thought her covering some skin would cool his ardor, but if anything, those sexy-as-fuck leather pants made his cock even harder. He wasn't sure how that was physically possible, but God, he wanted her. She caught him watching and yanked her top open, the snaps popping free all at once to expose her lacy pink bra. She tossed the shirt aside and he expected her to put on the black T-shirt she'd purchased, but instead she reached behind her back and unfastened the clasp of her bra, tossing it aside to bare her breasts.

"Madison," he said. He'd meant it to be chastisement for making him delirious with lust, but the word came out as a tormented groan. "What are you doing?"

"Wearing my leather," she said and shrugged into her new

jacket. Not bothering to zip the garment, she reached for a discarded cowboy boot and began to tug it on.

He couldn't help but stare open-mouthed at the inner curves of her breasts, exposed for his delight between the open edges of the jacket. She stomped into her second boot and stood, sweeping both hands beneath her mass of golden-brown curls to pull her hair free of her jacket. The movement gave him a glimpse of her rosy nipples and sent his tenuous grasp on self-control into a tailspin.

In an instant he had her pressed up against the back of the door, his mouth on hers, hands filled with her soft breasts, thigh lodged firmly between her legs and his painfully hard cock ground against her hip. He was far too aroused to stop her when her fingers began to unfasten his fly. Too excited to protest when her soft, gentle hands tugged his cock free of his pants. Too close to exploding to do anything but groan as she slid down the door to her knees and brought the head of his cock to her lips. She held the shaft in both hands as she kissed and sucked and licked the over-sensitized head. He burrowed his hands in her hair, concentrating hard on not moving, on not ramming his cock down her throat and fucking her face. His fingers dug into her scalp, and he cried out as she took him into the warm recesses of her mouth. She pulled him deep, then deeper still, until his cockhead was lodge in the back of her throat. She sucked hard as she pulled slowly away.

He groaned, his balls full to bursting. He wouldn't last long, and he was too excited to care. When his cock popped free of her mouth, she grasped it in her hand, her thumb massaging the tip gently. He looked down at her, on her knees at his feet with his cock inches from her sweet lips, and his balls tightened in expectation.

She grinned deviously and tucked his cock back into his pants before rapidly closing his fly.

"You aren't the only one who knows how to tease," she said.

She climbed to her feet and zipped her jacket, stopping just below her breasts so that the soft globes were pressed up and together with their tips barely covered, presenting him with the most mind-boggling, cock-teasing cleavage he'd ever encountered.

Oh fuck, he was in trouble.

CHAPTER SEVEN

A WARM, WET SOMETHING tugged at Madison's nipple and pulled her from a fretful sleep. Her fingers tangled in Adam's hair and held his mouth to her eager breast. He stroked her quivering belly, fingers trailing lower until all she could think about was how cruel he was for keeping her in this perpetual state of arousal all night and not giving her the release she so desperately needed. She held in her sighs of pleasure, tensed her muscles so her writhing didn't give her away. She'd never been turned on enough to come simply by having her nipple sucked and her tummy stroked, but she was almost there. Just a little more stimulation and she could finally let go of all the sexual tension driving her crazy.

Her body betrayed her by shuddering involuntarily, and Adam lifted his head. He smiled at her, stroking her hair from her face. They'd made a pact not to give themselves release and though she couldn't deny she wanted to lock herself in the bathroom and take matters into her own hands, she knew he was setting her up for something spectacular and she didn't want to ruin his surprise. Besides, she knew he was hurting for fulfillment as much as she was. He wasn't withholding her peak to be cruel; he was doing it to make what came later all the more exciting. It had taken her hours of pleading and coaxing the night before for her to arrive at this conclusion, and the man had maintained his agenda without succumbing to his own desire. But if he slipped up this morning and finally gave her the release she craved, she wouldn't complain. Hell, she'd probably cry in relief.

"Did you sleep well?" he asked. A devious glint sparked in his steel-gray eyes.

"Not especially," she said. "Some guy kept disturbing my rest."

"That wasn't very nice," he said. "How did he disturb your rest?"

"His favorite tactic was to kiss my pink flesh."

"Such as your lips?" he murmured before brushing a gentle kiss against her lips.

"Sometimes," she admitted. "But he seemed more interested in my southerly parts."

He rose to straddle her thighs, leaning forward to take her breasts in either hand. He massaged her nipples until they pebbled beneath his thumbs, straining for further attention. "Are you talking about this pink flesh?" he asked, pinching her nipples and drawing a gasp from her.

"Yes, those, but he went into the Deep South," she said breathlessly, "and set up camp."

Perhaps he'd reconsidered his intention to tease her mercilessly and was finally ready to take her. She lifted her head to gaze down between her breasts, and her heart thudded wildly in appreciation of the sight of his stone-hard cock. He released one breast to take his length in his hand and rubbed its tip into the cleft between her swollen lips. She squirmed, trying to spread her legs, but they were immobilized beneath his thighs.

"He kissed you here?" he asked, a fabricated look of concern on his handsome face. "While you were trying to sleep?"

"He did," she said, clinging to the bedclothes so her hands didn't get too grabby. She wanted to toss him on his back and ride that long, thick cock of his for hours. "But that wasn't the worst of it."

"I honestly don't know how it could get any worse."

"He put some tingly lube on my butt and rubbed me there until I thought surely he was going to take me in the ass, and then he rolled over and fell asleep."

Adam looked highly affronted. "That bastard!"

She snorted on a laugh.

"Did you disobey him and clean it off?"

She shook her head. "No, but it stopped tingling after a while."

"So it didn't keep you awake all night thinking about being

taken from behind?"

"Not all night," she admitted. "But it's still slippery and wet back there, which is pretty distracting."

"Ah, poor thing," he said with a wicked grin. "I'm surprised you got any sleep at all."

So was she, to be honest. "How did *you* sleep?" she asked.

"Quite well between dreaming about eating pussy and sucking on tits all night."

"You sure you were dreaming?"

"I must have been, because I woke up horny."

"I think we should do something about that," she said, releasing the sheet she was gripping and reaching for the cock resting against her shaved mound.

He caught her wrist. "I think we should head out and explore the city. New Orleans is one of my favorite places. I'd like to share it with you."

"We should probably stay in bed all day," she said. "I'm sure to embarrass you by dry humping your leg in public at some point today."

He laughed. "That wouldn't embarrass me in the least. But if we stay in bed all day, I won't make it until tonight. I'll have to have you."

"Now I really don't want to get out of this bed," she said.

"Suit yourself," he said and leaned over to kiss her lips. He then climbed from the bed and tossed open the light-blocking curtains.

Silhouetted by the morning sunshine, he stretched his arms over his head, lengthening his back and drawing her eyes to his firm ass, trim waist, and broad shoulders. He truly was a beautiful man. She groaned in torment, her hand sneaking between her thighs, because she couldn't take the lack of fulfillment for another moment.

He glanced at her over his shoulder and caught her doing exactly what she'd promised she wouldn't.

He turned, and her mouth watered at the sight of his stiff cock. That was what she really wanted. Not her own hand. It wasn't a satisfactory substitute by any stretch of the imagination.

"Adam," she whispered.

He crossed his arms over his well-cut chest, his toned abs tight, as if he'd just been doing crunches. "I guess I'll watch you get yourself off before I head out for the day," he said. "Carry on."

"But I want you," she insisted, massaging her clit in slow circles, which made her dripping wet but wouldn't get her off. She really did want him to take her to nirvana. It wasn't half so spectacular when she took herself there.

"Are you finished?" he asked. "I'll call Tony and tell him you don't want to be the guest of honor at the club tonight after all."

Her hand went still. "Guest of honor?"

"Yeah. Why do you think I've been working so hard to prepare you for this? But he'll understand. I warned him in advance that you're not very adventurous. And he said he had confidence in my ability engage in acts neither of us thought we were capable of. I guess his faith was misplaced."

She knew he was manipulating her to get her to behave a certain way, but as a horny-as-fuck and intensely curious woman, she didn't care.

"I can be adventurous."

"Prove it."

"How?"

"Don't wear any panties under your skirt today."

Her pussy twitched at the very idea. "Why? Are you going to fuck me up against the wall in some secluded alley?" She certainly hoped so.

"Not today," he said. "But I am going to keep that pussy needy and wet all day."

"Then I'd better put in a tampon."

He scowled. "You aren't supposed to start your period, are you?"

She shook her head. "As wet as you make my pussy, I'll have cum dripping down the insides of my thighs if I don't have on panties to stop it."

She was trying to get a rise out of him—and admittedly his cock was still fully risen—but he only nodded. "Good. I like it that way."

He turned and headed for the bathroom. Either he trusted

her not to break her promise or he'd left his phone in there and would call Tony immediately and cancel their appearance in the club. Then she eyed his phone on the nightstand and smiled. He trusted her. That was a big deal for him.

She wasn't sure if she'd be able to take his teasing all day, but she did want to see what had him so willing to delay their gratification. She heard the shower kick on and an instant later Adam's loud yelp. She leapt from the bed and stumbled into the bathroom to find him shivering under a stream of water.

"Are you okay? Why did you yell?"

"I wasn't prepared for a cold shower to be so fucking cold," he said, his crooked grin doing fluttery things to her heart.

"I should probably join you in there."

He yanked the shower curtain closed. "Oh no you don't. If you join me, I'll never get my dick soft enough to fit into my pants."

She grinned. Now there was a challenge she was up for.

Her attempts to get him worked up were successful, but only furthered her own delicious misery. By the time they made it out of the hotel room, it was well after ten and they'd both decided it was best if she wore panties. A chastity belt would have served them even better.

"We're doing the tourist thing in the French Quarter," Adam informed her.

She couldn't help but be disappointed when they climbed into a taxi.

"We aren't taking the bike today?" she asked. The powerful machine had already grown on her, and she'd been looking forward to pressing herself up against Adam's firm backside while they explored the city. And all that vibration between her thighs . . . She squirmed uncomfortably in her seat.

"Not with you in a skirt."

"I could change into my leather."

He released a breathy half laugh. "I have zero chance of success if you put those leather pants back on."

"Success at what?"

"Keeping my dick in my pants."

"Strange thing to aspire to," she said and slid her hand

across his thigh to rest between his legs. She didn't touch any of his private parts, but by the way he tensed and squirmed, anyone would think she was giving him one hell of a blowjob in the back of the cab.

The driver dropped them off near Jackson Square and while she gravitated toward the stark white cathedral with towers that were tipped with spired black roofs that looked like something out of a Disney-princess movie, Adam tugged her toward a crowded café with a green and white awning.

"You can't visit the French Quarter without getting an order of beignets and a café au lait from Café du Monde," Adam said.

"A *ben* what?"

"They're good. Trust me."

"I do trust you."

He smiled and kissed her. She couldn't help but notice a few heads turning. She told herself it was because Adam was undeniably sexy, not because as a couple they appeared to be mismatched. She wondered if they would have gotten the same stares if she'd donned her new leather.

As they walked past the outdoor seating area, a couple rose from their table near the railing. Without hesitation, Adam wrapped his hands around Madison's waist and lifted her over the wrought-iron fencing to stand next to the vacant table.

"Hold our seats. I'll go order from the counter."

He kissed her and then hurried toward the entrance, which had a line. People waiting for tables, she presumed. She glanced around to see if anyone had seen Adam's disregard for protocol. Yep, more staring. Blushing, she scooped her skirt beneath her thighs and sat at the prime table he'd snagged, absorbing the ambience of the locale. The sweet scent of fried confections teased her nostrils and made her belly growl. It reminded her of funnel cakes at the fair, and she smiled nostalgically. She'd spent a lot of time at fairs and rodeos in her teens, and she always splurged on funnel cakes—sometimes sharing them with her sister, sometimes eating one all by herself. She doubted that ben-gays, or whatever Adam had called them, were anything like her favorite county fair treats. They were French, after all.